HALLOWEEN BEDTIME STORIES

Boyd D. Spiker

Published by

Magic Thoughts Photography

881 E Arrow St

Tooele, UT 84074-9156

MagicThoughtsPhotography@gmail.com

Copyright © Magic Thoughts
Photography, 2013

Boyd D. Spiker

Born in Madisonville, Kentucky and raised in the Shenandoah Valley in Virginia. He now lives with his wife, Judi, in Tooele, Utah.

FOREWORD

Loyd & Nancy

Dear Reader, Thank you for looking into my book. The stories inside are fiction and do not represent any real person living or DEAD. I believe in the pages you will find out much about the place I grew up in the northernmost portion of the Shenandoah Valley.

The Valley is a place rich in history and, perhaps, even more rich in folklore. Many great battles of the American Civil War were fought in the fields, woods and streams that wind through the rich farmland. Most of the residents know that stories abound of unfortunate spirits who roam the darkness of country roads or frequent the many cemeteries that dot the entire valley.

This area was settled by mostly Dutch and German immigrants in the late 1600's. The residents of the valley have a great respect for the Indian battles, Revolutionary War skirmishes and raging Civil War battles fought in the area, and their stories are full of descriptions of the many departed spirits who lost their lives. I am sure that as a child some of my respect for and love of ghost, goblin and witchcraft stories was shaped by the very place itself. Many of the old houses in the district served as hospitals during the Civil War where wounded and bleeding soldiers were carried to be hacked on by Army

I hope you both enjoy the Stories - Great seeing you Neighbor

FOREWORD

doctors or to die in peace away from the raging battles. Stories abound of the departed spirits dwelling in or near the places they departed from their earthly bodies.

With this type of background, I was bound to develop a great respect for and belief in the supernatural spirits who live alongside us and share the space we inhabit. I realize many do not believe in spirits or ghosts, and I feel sorry for them. As for me, I believe, and I think after you read my stories, you will come to believe as well.

There are stories set in many other locations in the book as well, to help make the plots work. You will find yourself transported to a farmyard in Indiana, a dimly lit bar in New York City, a plantation in Louisiana and other locales. Of course you will always have company.

So, Dear Reader, get a nice warm cup of tea, and a cookie if you like. Place yourself comfortably in a darkened room with a reading light. Open the book, and let yourself *feel* the spirits guide you through the pages. Their stories could happen to anyone.

ILLUSTRATION CREDITS

- Author Photograph, by Judi Spiker

- Brick House, by Boyd Spiker………….....Pg 1

- Mausoleum, by Boyd Spiker………...…..Pg 39

- Tree, by Boyd Spiker……………………..Pg 117

- Strasburg Hotel, by Boyd Spiker………....Pg 269

- Beeler Tombstone, by Boyd Spiker…....…..Pg 280

- Civil War Buttons, by Boyd Spiker………Pg 308

- Plantation House, by Judi Spiker………....Pg 315

- Front and back cover photos and design by Judi Spiker

- All photographs by Magic Thoughts Photography

INDEX

Spirits... 1

Princess of Summer...........................…........ 41

Halloween Cruise................................…........ 79

Tall Trees..…........ 103

Flight..…..…… 129

Dreams of Halloween..........................…........ 159

The Crowning of a Queen.....................…… 182

The Collectors...................................…..… 233

Crissy Beeler...................................…..… 264

The Buttons..................................…........… 281

PREFACE

Halloween Bedtime Stories...... is a collection of short stories about spirits, ghosts, death and dying and other pleasing thoughts to fall asleep by. These stories are a form of truth in that the facts are well researched and many of the settings, incidents and props in the story are very real and well documented.

As you progress through the pages and read the information, I invite you to look into, for example, who made the sports car James Dean was killed in or what are the names of Willies first cousins? Did Patsy Cline perform at a bank opening in Strasburg in the 1950's? As you find the truth about these things, the stories will take on the feasibility and possibility of being real. You will realize that these things really may have happened, or at least could have happened.

These fast moving stories will cause you to turn the page and to get to the conclusions so quickly that you will want to go back and re-read the early parts to see where things started to go off track and lead to the ending.

I will tell you now in the privacy of these pages that while the facts are true and the props are researched to the very details of time and place, all of the stories are fiction (I say this to protect myself and my family). I made all of this stuff up..... Yeah..... sure I did.... Just read on and enjoy, and when you awake screaming in the middle of the night, think fondly of me........

SPIRITS

Strasburg, Virginia 1959

Bill Wilson stepped outside the back door of his house, ran his hands through his thick brown hair and took a deep bracing breath. It was almost like taking in a refreshing drink of cool water. He could smell the beginnings of autumn and feel the lighter, cooler air. He looked through the trees in the lawn toward the mountains and saw a variety of colors that could not help but raise his spirits. He had often heard his mom and dad talk about the mountainsides in the autumn and how they looked like a bouquet of brightly colored flowers. As a younger child, he had never been able to see the comparison, but now that he was older, he could see how well the description fit the view from the back porch of his large old Virginia home.

"One good frost is all it takes to turn the mountains into a blaze of color", his Uncle Ken used to say. "A good

Halloween Bedtime Stories

frost that gets rid of the clinging heat and humidity of summer, and replaces it with coolness and color. That is what we need, some weather that causes the fish to start eating from the top of the water again and the squirrels to get busy stocking up for winter."

Bill's Uncle Ken was the most vocal of his five uncles but usually summed up what they all were thinking.

Autumn always brought a flurry of activity in the small Northern Virginia community for lots of reasons. It was a season of harvest for farmers and gardeners, which made up well over three-fourths of the population. In a few weeks people would be butchering the hogs and cattle they had raised to provide meat for their families. It was a season of preparation for hunters who liked to shoot squirrels, rabbits, quail, deer and bears. It was a time for getting back into the routine of school, looking forward to the football games under the lights, and feeling the cool night air. But, most of all, it was getting close to the season of Halloween when the spirits that made the special setting of this little town on the Shenandoah River take on a festive, though eerie, nature.

The little community of Strasburg endured several name changes during its long history, and along with several other Northern Virginia communities, had been said to change forms of government numerous times. Part of the change was due to being a village prior to the Revolutionary War when hostile Indians still roamed the valleys rich with game. Some people still had old record books showing when the money system changed from English to American. Most of the reasons for the changes were during the American Civil War. Strasburg, it was claimed locally, had changed hands

Spirits

eighteen or nineteen times from North to South.

Uncle Ken often said people lost track of who to salute and which flag to show respect toward. Naturally, the changes occurred after major battles or skirmishes in which many people were killed. Some famous general, a Yankee the locals reckoned (many believed it was Sherman) said the floor of the valley would be soaked with rebel blood, the river would run red, and a crow flying over the valley would have to bring his own provisions, because no crops would be left standing...or something like that.

One reason Halloween was more than a little scary in this region, was that someone had died in nearly every field or wooded area in the valley. In fact, most of the houses were pretty old and there was a good chance someone had died in nearly every house in town as well. Spirits of the departed were often seen and reported by many of the German-Dutch descendants of the original settlers. It is no wonder then, that many of the natives of the northern Shenandoah Valley were excellent tellers of stories about the spirits and apparitions that were seen and/or heard.

Once the leaves turned and the weather became crisp, it was only a matter of time until the first big fall storm rolled in, a day when the weather was too cool and rainy to work in the fields or garden. On this first stormy day when no one wanted to be outside longer than it took to do necessary chores like feeding the animals; when a little wood in the fireplace created the perfect smells, sights and feeling for a long sit in a chair and a story. It was on these fall days when mother nature got serious about removing the remnants of summer from the area

Halloween Bedtime Stories

and inviting winter to show its face, that Bill sat by the fire and learned stories of the many spirits that haunted not only the house he lived in but the fields near the river, the overlook rocks at Fisher's Hill and the cemetery near the edge of town. He heard these stories from his grandfather, his grandmother, his aunts and uncles, but his favorite teller of ghost stories was his old great aunt. She could conjure up a story that always made the hair on the back of his neck stand on end and gave him a slight-but-certain chill right down his spine.

Aunt Dorothy could scare the hell out of little kids, and would often create enough doubt in adults that they would turn on too many lights in the house or watch over their shoulder as they walked past the site of her latest tale. She was considered the best ghost story teller in the area by far, and she always denied any credit. She only told "what the spirits wanted her to say and added nothing what was not the truth, so help her God".

She was a woman of average height but very heavy.

"It was the sugar," she said. She had sugar in the blood, and it caused her to be *on the heavy side*. Dorothy was homely as well and had no teeth. She had some dentures that she kept in a cup near her bed. She found them to be uncomfortable and chose not to wear them most times; "lessen I wanta eat an apple or sumthing needs bitin' real hard," she would comment regarding her teeth. She had steely blue eyes that seemed old and watery behind her thick glasses that were often splattered by whatever she had been cooking most recently. Her glasses were small and rested well on her large, porous nose which had more than a hint of a mole on the left

Spirits

side. She could have passed for a witch in appearance, but did not dress like one at all. She always wore house dresses and most times an apron over the front of the dress to catch the splatters from cooking, which was her main job and the reason she lived in the small two-room guest house just across the lawn from Bill's family.

She had never stopped calling him Billy, even though he clearly saw himself as far too adult to be called that by anyone but her. Bill would tolerate the fact that she ignored his obvious age and insisted on calling him by his childhood name because she did it with everyone.
She still called his oldest uncle "Booty"; a name he had not been called by anyone else for over 30 years.

Even though Bill came to believe some of Dorothy's stories were exaggerations or not true, and, even though he was nearly seventeen, he still loved to hear one
of "Aint Dot's" typical introductions.

"The other evening along about dark when I was walking back home from the Safeway store, I heard someone calling my name. Or, the other night I woke from a good sleep to hear a woman's voice screaming as though she was in pain. Or, it was the strangest sound like something trying to scratch on my door." She had at least twenty or thirty introductions, but the beginning always created a question to be asked, that begged for more information. She only told her stories on days when the weather was bad enough so that everyone had time to sit and listen to the whole tale. She would toss the beginning of the story out like bait. She was

5

Halloween Bedtime Stories

patient and always waited for the question, a question that indicated interest:

"Where was the voice coming from?"

Once she got the question and knew that someone was listening and interested to know more, she would put down her large spoon or other cooking implement, draw up a chair and sit down and begin.

Most of her stories were of witchcraft, haunts, murders or grisly sightings of soldiers killed in one of the many battles that had taken place within sight of the house. But the best tales and the stories that everyone loved to hear the most were her stories of times when she had to walk past the cemetery "long bout dark it was". She always called them spirits, but anyone who heard even one of her stories knew they were more than simply spirits.

So it was with great anticipation that Bill stood on the back porch enjoying the beautiful colors and crisp air. He knew it was autumn, the fifth football game of the season would be tomorrow, and the harvest was well along. He knew the forecast, and it was going to get stormy in a day or two. He picked up his books and walked down the back steps.

"Morning, Billy," the old voice crackled in the crisp autumn air. "Looks like a storm's on the way, and the chickens are actin' restless, and the squirrels across the street are real busy burying nuts this morning. I bet it may even snow a little on the mountain and ruin all our purty colors".

"Morning Aint Dot, "he replied. " I gotta run so I'm not late for school. Me an Butch are going to cut through the cemetery to look at some of our Halloween

6

Spirits

plans. We are gonna do something that really scares the girls this year".

"Well, Billy, you better be careful around that place. You don't want to get the spirits up there stirred up. They don't like people coming into the cemetery and disturbing them, especially a bunch of disrespectful kids. There have been times when…"

"Gotta run Aint Dot. Will talk to you after school. I hope you are baking some hot rolls for tonight."

"Too hot for baking today honey, but when the storm comes in tomorrow or tomorrow night it will cool right down, and we'll have them hot rolls for you then."

"See ya after school then," Bill shouted over his shoulder. He walked quickly the half block to Butch's house and did not have to even walk up to the house. Butch had seen him coming up the street and was halfway down the walkway pulling on his light jacket.

"We better hurry, Bill, if we are going to cut through the cemetery this morning."

The two boys walked about as quickly as they could without breaking into a run. They talked about the fall decorations that were placed in front lawns or on the porches of houses along the way. Both were more excited than they wanted to admit about Halloween, and both were feeling the child-like enjoyment of seeing fall and Halloween decorations appear on the houses. They remembered how, when they were smaller, it was the houses that decorated for Halloween that gave out the best treats and were the most welcoming to the trick-or-treat traditions. They talked excitedly about stories they

Halloween Bedtime Stories

had heard about the older boys who had taken gates from gardens and hung them on telephone poles. They heard stories from their fathers about tipping over outhouses on Halloween and they longed to join the ranks of teenage boys past and present who did something worthy of becoming a story to be repeated.

Bill repeated the story that his Uncle Ken told about when several boys who were in the same class at high school took a teacher's garden gate, tied it to a rope, then tied the rope to the clasp that held the flag at school, and hoisted the gate on the flagpole. That little trick earned a couple of the boys a visit to the principal's office and an introduction to the principal's paddle board, a special tool created by the school shop teacher for use on difficult boys.

Bill and Butch were tempted, but failed to join a group of boys who had pulled a Halloween stunt the year before. They remembered feeling left out as the offending boys were punished, then became school heroes as the story grew. They dressed a duck in a Superman costume, then released it on the porch of a teacher who was known around school as "Super Duck".

The teacher's nickname had been developed when the boys were much younger, and the teacher in question served as the local Boy Scout advisor and Scoutmaster. He looked very much like George Reeves, the actor who portrayed Superman on TV. He wore glasses and could have been Clark Kent (the guy who everyone in the world, except the other actors in the story, knew turned into Superman). The only flaw to the Scoutmaster's portrayal of Superman would be that he walked very much like a duck. To the young boys in the

Spirits

Troop 59, it was an easy jump to call him "Super Duck".

When those boys got old enough to be in high school, the prank of the Halloween season that year was to capture a large, white duck, have the girls in home economics class create a small cape and some small shorts, then paint a large S on the duck's chest with spray paint and release the animal on the teacher's porch. After trying to release the poor, confused duck and having it run away before the teacher even noticed it, they considered tying the duck to a railing on the porch and securing it so it could not get away, but found the duck was very hard to restrain. Once excited, it tended to flap the costume off and still escape. The plan changed to having someone ring the doorbell and simply toss the duck through the open door into the house when the door was answered. The obvious problems with this plan were too numerous to list, but when high school boys fall in love with a prank, problems and logic do not get the consideration they deserve. Leonard, being the smallest of the boys and most timid, got the job of dressing in a costume and delivering the duck. Leonard was dressed in a full mask and costume draped over his clothing, which would have made him hard to recognize if the duck had not flapped his mask off just as the door opened as the door opened. The other boys, who had taken up observation posts across the street, were spotted by Mr. Gibson as his unfortunate wife chased the flapping duck around the living room causing it to become even more excited and to start pooping and squawking. The duck, now being chased by Mrs. Gibson and both of the Gibson children, escaped through the open door while the old Scoutmaster made careful

9

Halloween Bedtime Stories

notes of the names of the boys in the area.

Those boys could have been in real trouble, but good ole Mr. Gibson was a good guy after all and only made them apologize to his family, replace a few broken items from the duck's escape efforts, and pay to have the carpet cleaned. He even started taking pride in the fact that he bore a striking resemblance to the actor who portrayed Superman on television.

The tales of "Super Duck" became part of the local lore of Halloween tricks played by exuberant high school boys. Butch and Bill were determined that they were going to come up with a plan for a prank that would top the "Super Duck" story and become a local legend.

As Bill and Butch approached the cemetery, they started talking about how they would plan carefully and keep participants to as few as possible. Hopefully, not more than just them or, perhaps, one more accomplice would be brought into the plan.

"The Plan", as they had begun to call it, was going to revolve around a tradition that had been taking place in Strasburg for at least 20 years involving a girls' sorority that was always composed of a very small group of the most affluent girls in the school. The girls were in a sorority that had been formed in the distant past and was still very much *THE* group to belong to if you were a teenage girl in Strasburg of the 1950's or 1960's. Part of the initiation for the girls coming into the club took place in the cemetery on Halloween night. The older girls in the sorority would take an initiate to the leader's home on Halloween during the daylight hours. They would then tell the initiate that the group was going to

Spirits

meet in a secret place and that the initiate must be blindfolded and taken to the meeting sight. The sorority sisters would then administer the oath of secrecy to the initiate and would prepare her for what would certainly be a "frightening, but rewarding experience". The member of the sorority would then place a blindfold over the eyes of the initiate, then a hood made of black or dark material so that the initiate really could not see anything at all. They would then drive (if they were old enough), or have their parents drive them to the school where they met with all of the members of the sorority and the initiate. It would be a ten minute or more walk from the school to the cemetery where the initiate's hood would be removed at the appropriate time.

Butch and Bill had been gathering all the information they could about this obscure initiation, as they planned to have their Halloween prank take place during the most scary and significant part of the ceremony. They began to share what they had learned; Butch, from his older sister Shelly, and Bill, from Susan, a girl he liked who only two years ago had been an initiate.

Bill was certain he knew exactly where the ceremony took place and even some of the details about the scare tactics. Butch had learned some details that seemed to confirm and fit well with facts that each had garnered separately and pieced together. They were going to give all the sorority girls a scare to remember, but had to be very careful not to tip their hand to anyone. They spent about ten minutes walking around the strangely shaped, small building, considering the approach the girls would take and how to best position

Halloween Bedtime Stories

themselves to pull a surprise.

"Well Butch, we had better get on to school. I don't much like being late for home room, especially since I've been sitting right across from Nancy. I really like talking to her. She is really smart."

"Yeah, really smart and kinda purty too, huh"? Butch responded. "I wonder if she is part of that sorority too? I mean, she is smart and in the Latin Club and all, so I bet she is."

"Well, we will know that on Halloween won't we?" Bill said.

"Yeah," Butch said, and we will know a lot of other stuff on Halloween, if we do this right".

The two boys headed across the steep hill to school and made it just ahead of the first bell, calling students to their home room. They would not see each other again until after school or maybe even the next day, because Bill would stay for football practice and Butch would be in band practice, then head home.

By the time the sixth period bell rang, the wind had started to blow, which made football practice even harder than normal. 'Seems like Aint Dorothy was right about the storm. It will probably come in tomorrow or by tomorrow night at the latest', Bill thought as he tried to practice a punt into the wind. 'I'll bet that storm really changes the weather, and it will start getting a lot cooler, but I sure hope it don't get too cold for Halloween. Most years we have pretty good weather until about a week or two after Halloween, then early winter seems to set in. I sure hope it is a mild night this year, because if it is cold and nasty, it will make the surprise all that much harder to pull off'. Practice was pretty boring on this day, and

12

Spirits

the weather had the boys all unsettled. It just wasn't as much fun to try to play football in the wind. Coach Jim knew the boys were feeling restless, and, to be honest, he was not enjoying the wind that much either. He called the team together and explained that they were doing real well so far this season and thought with the wind and the coming storm it would be good to knock off early.

"Looks like we will be playing in the rain tomorrow anyway, so no need to stay out in this wind. I have a feeling we may get our first rainy game tomorrow boys, so let's say a quick prayer for strength and safety and knock off early. Tomorrow we have a game. It may just be our first big test of the season, Stonewall Jackson, and they are out to stop us. Let's remember the new option play we put in just for them and think about how to win. Thanks boys; see you all tomorrow."

Bill rushed through the shower and changed into his street clothes and started walking home. He watched clouds forming above the mountains and wondered what Aint Dorothy had fixed for dinner. Although, at this point, it did not matter much. He was hungry, and could eat his weight in just about anything after a day at school and football practice.

When the family gathered around this evening, Aunt Dorothy served a nice cured Virginia Ham dinner with peas and mashed potatoes. All cooked on top of the gas stove "to keep the heat down". She had not baked rolls, but announced that she had got some yeast and was thinking about doing some baking tomorrow if that storm comes in. She smiled at the kids and added, "Maybe we will even build a little fire and have some

Halloween Bedtime Stories

hot rolls and honey with some warm cider."

The family all said they hoped the storm would come soon, because they were hungry for some of Aunt Dorothy's rolls. Bill felt a little cheated knowing he would miss out on the rolls and honey because he would be getting knocked around on the football field…probably in the rain. He knew that he could catch up on Saturday when the smaller kids would be doing little kid things. He would hang around the kitchen with Aunt Dorothy and help her by lifting heavy pots and pans, then be rewarded with some rolls and honey she had set aside just for him.

Amazingly, the next day dawned cloudy and cooler, but the storm seemed to be hanging just on the other side of the mountains. It was no longer windy, but the damp coolness of being near a storm was unmistakable. It only started to rain and get cold about half an hour before game time. It rained steadily, not a harsh rain, just a steady soaking rain, causing the temperature to drop a couple of degrees about every half hour. The Strasburg boys played well and were met by a team that was every bit as good as they were. The game came down to the last with Strasburg leading by a touchdown. Stonewall scored with less than one minute left and the rain and slippery conditions caused the Stonewall kick holder to miss spotting the extra point attempt. Strasburg held on to a one point win. Coach Jim was bubbly and enjoying the good fortune of winning a game that easily could have gone the other way, and the ride home in dry clothes and with a victory under their belts felt good. Bill was happy that they won the game, but he knew that his team had been lucky, and,

Spirits

if the kick had gone through, Stonewall would probably have won the game in overtime. It was late when Bill finally arrived home. He was happy, tired and loved to drift off to sleep while listening to the rain falling on the metal roof just outside his bedroom window.

Cold!....? He awoke slowly but was definitely feeling cold. He reached for the blanket at the lower part of the bed and pulled it up around his shoulders. Better, he thought. Then he remembered the rain as he drifted off to sleep. It was Saturday, and he did not have to get up yet so he took a look toward the window. The clouds were dark and low, and there was a constant drizzle. The house felt cold for the first time since about March. He glanced at his watch lying across his shoes and suddenly felt more awake…it was after 8 o'clock, but the dim light in the bedroom made it seem more like 6 o'clock. He reached for his tee shirt and pulled it on while still covered, then sprang from the bed grabbing his blue jeans and pulling them on quickly. He then pulled on his first sock, realizing it was still wet from being out in the rain last night on the way home. He dashed to the dresser drawer and grabbed a dry pair, pulled them on, and made a dash for the kitchen where he knew there would be warmth and most likely his mom and aunt planning dinner. At the top of the stairs he paused to look out the hall window one more time to confirm that it was still raining, then dashed down the stairs. He burst into the kitchen in the way only a teenager looking to get warm can.

"Are ye cold Billy?" Aunt Dorothy crackled.

"Yeah, I guess I am a little," he answered.

"Well, it's no wonder, it's almost freezing out

Halloween Bedtime Stories

there. It's thirty-three degrees and drizzling. Bet it's snowin' on the mountains. Weatherman says it is gonna stay in the thirty's fer two days before it warms back up. I reckon it's a good time to bake those hot rolls you was askin' about yesterday. I fixed you some bacon. Would you like a piece of bread and an egg with it?"

"Boy, I sure would", he answered.

"Did yer team win the game last night at Mount Jackson?"

"Just barely. We really didn't do very well and probably should have lost. They were a very good team and did not want to lose on their home field."

"Oh," Aunt Dorothy interrupted, "yer mom wants ya to build a fire in the furnace and get the air out of the pipes so the house can warm up. I am gonna build a little wood fire in the fireplace in the living room till the steam kicks in, but for now it is nice and warm in the kitchen. The oven is almost ready for the first batch of bread, then I'll make the rolls. Maybe we will have time for a little sit down with rolls and honey by the fire this afternoon, between you getting the radiators going and me baking. You can go over and get the Rupp boy, and we'll have ourselves a little visit."

Bill, knew that Aunt Dorothy was queuing up for a good tale about her latest encounter with something strange from the spirit world. He was only too happy to get started with getting the furnace going, knowing it would remain in some state of readiness all the way through the coming winter. He was more than happy to think of the hot rolls with butter and honey with his pal, Butch, by his side listening to what is sure to be another ghost story. He could tell by the gleam in Aint Dorothy's

Spirits

eyes that she was already thinking about the story she was going to share with the boys.

"Here, Billy. Here is your egg with a piece of bread and some bacon. Eat it up then go get that ole furnace fired up and start tapping the radiators. With any luck, it will get warm in here by evening."

Bill knew it would take a while. He had done this before, but it was not hard work, and the activity was better than just sitting and waiting for the house to warm up. He finished his breakfast quickly and headed to the basement.

It was nearly noon when he reappeared at ground level. He first cleaned out the ashes and firebox of the huge old furnace then drained and refilled the water pipes that circulated through the "*monster*". He then had taken the old ashes and burned materials to the trash cans through the basement outside door. He found paper stacked in a metal can and a few sticks of wood, which he expertly got burning vigorously before adding a few pieces of compressed coal. The release of the sulfur from the coal was unpleasant, but the smoke quickly found its way to the chimney and the heat carried it upward. For a moment he stopped to remember how much he liked seeing smoke coming from chimneys of houses as he walked to school in the late fall. He then watched and listened for the pipes to tell him where the air pockets were forming so he could let the air out and better circulate the hot water into the radiators. He knew from memory that once he got the old furnace fired and banked to hold its heat, he would begin the process of tapping and clearing air from the eleven radiators throughout the two-story house.

Halloween Bedtime Stories

He was now hungry again and asked Aunt Dorothy if there was anything he could grab for lunch. She smiled and pointed to a small dish on the table where a piece of ham rested in a roll that had been split open. The steam was still rising from the roll. Bill smiled and thanked her. Then he explained that he was going to take the sandwich with him as he went to get the air pockets out of the radiators. He dashed out to the garage to grab a bucket and some rags to take with him in case some water spilled. He shouted thanks and that he should be done in about an hour. He felt the chill of the air, even though it was only about twenty-five feet from the back door of the house to the garage door. He grabbed what he needed and headed back into the house to get the radiators drained so they would heat up. He was relieved and happy to feel heat in the bottom of the first radiator and made his rounds quickly. Before an hour had passed, he came back through the kitchen. His brothers were up and happily eating some warm bread. Aunt Dorothy was telling them how cold it was, but that it would be a lot warmer in the house soon.

"In the meantime, you can color in your books and sit here in the kitchen with me. That way you won't have to worry bout ol' Missus Walker scaring you. You know how spirits are. They usually start actin' up when the weather changes like it is now."

They knew alright; they were pretty scared to go almost anywhere in the house alone within a few days of hearing one of Aunt Dorothy's stories about how the unfortunate Missus Walker had been either choked, stabbed, or had her head cut off, or been chained in the basement, and starved, or..... Bill had figured out long

18

Spirits

ago that the Missus Walker stories were just his aunt's way of keeping young kids entertained and controlled. If she did not want you in a certain part of the house, that would become the most recent site of the unfortunate Missus Walker's grizzly death and where Aunt Dorothy had seen her looking just like she did when the police found her. ("So help her, God.") It did bring to mind the hint of some afternoon fireplace time with his aunt and Butch.

He looked at Aunt Dorothy and asked, "Should I go and get Butch now and start a fire in the fireplace?"

"Let's give it about a half hour. Your mom is taking the boys down to the department store to get some new coats, and we can have some rolls and time to talk by the fire then. I didn't get to building a fire yet", said Aunt Dorothy.

"Well, it's still pretty cool in the living room so I'll start the fire now and put on a log so it can catch up a little and knock the chill." He went to the living room and started the fire, smelling the wood smoke and noting how much more pleasant it smelled than the coal which was burning in the old *monster* in the basement. He then dashed to the basement to check the water levels one last time, before leaving to get Butch. His mom pulled into the driveway as he vaulted over the railing on the back stairs.

"You're gonna bust yourself one of these days Bill....e." She was still having trouble calling him Bill but was obviously working on it. The "e" had trailed off quietly as she remembered he preferred Bill these days. "I am takin' Bobby and Ronnie to the department store for new coats. How is your coat? Does it still fit? And

19

Halloween Bedtime Stories

why aren't you wearing it? It must be nearly freezing!"

"Ma, I am just runnin' over to get Butch. I'll get my coat out when I get back, but it is not all that cold. Besides, my letter jacket will be in next week, and I'll have that to wear".

"OK, Bill, but please dress a little more warmly. I don't want any doctor bills or sick boys. OK?"

"K, Mom, soon as I get back." He was off jogging quickly to get Butch.

He knocked on the door, but did not need to ask if Butch was there. He could see him sitting in the big chair in front of the television watching a football game. Shelly, Butch's older sister, answered the door and smiled at Bill.

"Good game last night Bill. Y'all really did well especially at the end by blockin' that kick that would have tied the game." Bill did not want to take the time to explain to Shelly that the ball had not been blocked, but was so slippery from the rain that the holder had not been able to hang onto it. Instead, he said,

"Well, I am glad we won, but it was too close for comfort."

"I watched you last night, and you played really good throwin' those passes, and when you were playing defense, you made a couple of tackles that stopped them from scoring. I told the other girls, that's my neighbor. One of the girls, Kay, really likes you and will probably ask you to homecoming if you don't mind going with a girl older than you."

"I like Kay, and I think she is cute. Maybe the next time she comes over, you can let me know, and I will come over and talk with her. I would like that."

Spirits

"I will call you on the phone the next time she's here Bill. I know she likes you."

Butch turned around in his chair, "Kaaay likes Billeee", he sang. "Kaaay likes Billleee."

"Oh, shut up Butch," Shelly said. If you weren't so immature maybe some older girls would like you too."

"No thanks," Butch said. "I don't care to be liked by your dumb girl friends with all the giggling and yelling and secret groups. I am happy to like girls my own age. Besides, Mom says I am too young to be worried about girlfriends and all that anyway."

Shelly turned and headed upstairs to her room calling back that she would call Bill the next time Kay was coming over. Butch turned to Bill and asked, "What's up"?

Bill said, "You know how Aint Dorothy likes to sit by the fire and tell stories about the spirits when it gets cold outside. Well, I built a fire, she made some hot rolls, and it is cold outside."

Butch was up walking toward the hanger in the hall to get his jacket as the words came from Bill's mouth. He was pulling on his jacket and yelling toward the kitchen to his mom,

"Going over to Bills! Be back in a while."

"OK", came the disembodied voice from the kitchen. "Mind your manners, and don't bc a bother to Mrs. Wilson."

Butch looked toward the clouds and said, "Cold isn't it"?

"Yeah, it is, but it won't be for long. A little cold ain't too bad anyway. Aint Dorothy made some hot rolls,

Halloween Bedtime Stories

and there is a fireplace in the living room", Bill answered.

The boys walked the rest of the distance quickly and in silence until reaching the bottom of the steps to Bill's house. Butch spoke again.

"Halloween in ten days. I sure hope it warms up before then."

"Most always does. My Uncle Ken says that we always get that cold snap before Halloween to drive the colors and get folks in the mood for fall. It also gets the spirits waked up. I guess they like the cold or something. Anyways, it most always warms up for Halloween. Only been rainy or cold one year 'bout fifteen years ago Uncle Ken says."

"Well, I sure hope it ain't cold this year what with our plans and all," Butch said back. "I mean if it is cold or wet, we don't want to lay in that old mausoleum. It's gonna be uncomfortable enough as it is."

"Don't worry about it Butch. It won't be cold; besides, who cares if it's cold anyway? The mausoleum ghost will probably kill us before we have a chance to be there long enough to feel the cold."

"Keep that up, asshole, and you will need to find someone else to scare the girls," Butch shot back.

"I was just kiddin," Bill said and added, "Sorry".

The boys entered the warm kitchen and the mood brightened. Aunt Dorothy gave them her best toothless smile and said,

"Well.....I've got some hot rolls with a fresh mold of butter and a jar of honey. The fire in the living room is caught up and it looks pretty warm in there."

"I'm gonna check a couple of radiators," Bill

Spirits

said, dashing up the stairs. He was back in less than two minutes saying, "Good, they are working and feeling warm. They will soon be hot and warming the house."

Butch was already half way through his first hot roll. Aunt Dorothy was putting several rolls on a large platter with the butter and honey.

"Let's go sit by the fire boys. I have a little something that happened to me just last night during the storm that I would like to tell you boys about."

Bill felt it first…that little thrill along the spine when you just know a scary story is about to be told. The three walked into the dim room lit only by the windows on two sides. The dreary weather did not provide much more light than the fireplace did, but it was comfortable and warm, and the rolls smelled like a piece of heaven. Aunt Dorothy took her customary place in front of the fireplace in a large wing-back chair. Butch sat on a rocker to her left while Bill plopped into an overstuffed leather chair on her right. They each buttered a roll and took a bite.

"They're good this time," Dorothy ventured. The boys munched quietly at first then Bill blurted,

"These are my favorite food, and this batch is the best I've tasted in a long time."

Butch mumbled his approval adding in a muffled way, "I'd like another one please."

Dorothy passed the platter to Butch. He took another roll and buttered it watching the butter melt into the bread. He turned to Dorothy,

"What happened last night that you were going to tell us about?"

Dorothy leaned into the fire holding her hands in

23

Halloween Bedtime Stories

front of the crackling log, rubbing her arthritic fingers together. She shifted so that Bill got a full-on look at her old face. Deep wrinkles, crystal blue eyes, a pointy nose that seemed to almost rest on her chin, especially when she was not wearing her teeth. Her hair was completely gray and wispy on the edges. She looked old, and when the fire dimmed and brightened, her features took on a slightly scary look. She continued to rub her hands together and began.

"Well, sir, I was cleaning up after cooking dinner last evening when I got the strangest feeling that someone was looking at me. You know when you get that feeling that someone is looking right at you, then you look around and sure enough someone is watching you?"……
She paused for the question.

Butch obliged, "Who do you think it was Aunt Dorothy"?

"Well, I got that feeling while I was standing at the sink. I looked around behind me, and no one was left in the kitchen but me. I went back to washing the dishes, and the feeling that I was being looked at got stronger and somehow seemed more eerie knowing that no one else was in the room. I glanced around again, this time looking more carefully, thinking maybe it could be a spirit what with the storm going on and all. Still nothing. In fact, as I turned toward the room the feeling went away. That is when I realized that whoever was looking at me was outside the window looking *in* at me. I turned back to the widow, but it was pretty dark outside, and, of course, the lights were on in the kitchen. So, whoever was watching me could see me, but I could not see them.

Spirits

I finished the dishes and put them away. I then walked
over to the light switch to turn off the overhead light
before I shut out the wall lamp by the sink. It was dark.
It took my old eyes a minute to adjust, but then I looked
out the window. I could see something or somebody out
on the street between me and the streetlamp, but I could
not see any detail. I heard someone in the living room
say something and looked toward the door to the
hallway, but when I looked back outside, whoever it was
had gone. I could not see anyone, but I still had the
feeling I was being watched. I could feel those eyes
looking right at me, but I could not see them. I turned on
the lights. About then, Bill's mom had come into the
kitchen to see why the lights were out, thinking I had
gone home. I told her about the feeling that someone was
lookin' in the window from the street, and she just said I
was being silly. She told me I needed to stop telling
those old ghost stories, that I was scaring myself. I
thought maybe she was right, but I also remembered that
I had seen something out there in the dark silhouetted
against the street lamp.

     I finished up in the kitchen and decided to sit
down and watch a television show with the rest of the
family before going out to my house. We watched a
funny program and I started feeling tired. I knew with
the storm I would need to light my little kerosene heater
to keep my little place warm, so I got my jacket and my
umbrella and I headed across the lawn to my little house.
I got right up to the door and started to put my umbrella
down when it stepped out of the shadows under the
willow tree. A female voice that was more in my head
than my ears said,

Halloween Bedtime Stories

"Don't be afraid. I will not harm you. I want to tell you something important".

"Well, sir, I was scared, and I opened the door and walked in. I started to the lamp and turned it on, then turned to shut the door. Just then, I saw her full on; her face was terrible distorted. She seemed to be in agony. She cried out loudly and said,

"Dorothy, you must listen to me. I am here to save two lives, and if you don't help, they will surely die. You must hear me."

"I told her that I could hear alright. I also said, "I don't know what kind of spirit you are, but you have scared me nearly to death."

"I am sorry to scare you so, but I can only appear now as I did when I left life as you know it. I was once beautiful, but when he buried me alive, I was doomed to look like this forever."

"I knew that I had never heard anything about anyone from anywhere around here being buried alive. So I asked her who she was and what she wanted with me."

She explained, "I am Evelyn Crawford. I was the wife of Charles Crawford. We were married for over five years with no children. I was worried that maybe we could have no children and wished to find a way to get help. I met a doctor's wife who belonged to a secret sorority in high school and college, and who believed that one of the ceremonies practiced by the sorority may help me to conceive. I was desperate and agreed to meet with the sorority to seek help. Charles became suspicious of my behavior, and the secrecy of the sorority did not help. He devised a plan to follow me to

Spirits

see if I had another lover. One time, when I was with the sorority, he sneaked up on a secret ceremony. From that day on, his sanity was gone. His attitude toward me changed, and he devised a way to kill me. He administered a potion which put me into deep sleep. He called the doctor who examined me and thought me to be near death. Late that same night, Charles buried me six feet deep in the family cemetery, which is part of the current city cemetery. He acted the part of the grieving widower, and no one was the wiser. Of course, for me awakening in a dark coffin, the panic was overpowering. I scratched, clawed, screamed until I became what you see before you now. That is how I became what you see, but I am here about the ceremony that the sorority holds. I am here to warn someone close to you Dorothy, someone who may see what Charles saw, and, if they do, it will destroy their mind and their lives. I know their plan because they made it by the old mausoleum in the cemetery. The mausoleum that Charles built after he did what he did to me. The mausoleum that is designed to prevent anyone from being buried alive and suffocating under six feet of earth. I know that there are two boys close to you who are planning to spy on a meeting of the same secret sorority that Charles spied on. I know the boys are just planning a Halloween scare, but if they listen to the secret sorority meeting, they will die just as surely as I did. Poor Charles knows it too. He knows all too well that the secret sorority ceremony will take either your mind or your life or both. He could not help his actions once he heard the ceremony he was doomed to kill me, the only woman he ever loved, and to suffer insanity. He lived only long enough to build the

Halloween Bedtime Stories

mausoleum that holds his bones and mine and has space for two more. Those two will be the next who hear or interrupt the sorority. You see Dorothy, the sorority is a very secret group whose origins go back to a darkness that has been long lost through the ages. No one knows how it started until after they leave this life, and even then, we are not allowed to tell. And lastly Dorothy, tell Butch and Billy that they must not go through with their plans."

The hair on Bill's arms was standing on end, and he was almost too frightened to speak.

"How did you ever know what we were planning to do"? he asked as he looked accusingly at Dorothy. "We have not talked to anyone about any of this except to ask a few questions from girls in the sorority. We did not even ask the same girl too many questions because we did not want them to know about our plan. How did you know?" His tone was accusing and irate.

"Now, son," Dorothy said. "I am just saying what the spirit asked me to say."

"My mom is right about you," Bill shouted. "You are just a crazy old lady who gets a kick out of scaring the hell out of kids."

Dorothy lowered her eyes and said, "Bill…, Billy I am sorry if I have scared you. I am just doing an errand for the spirit that came to me, but more importantly, I'm trying to help save your life. Are you and Butch planning something? Because if you are, I think you are in real danger."

Bill looked at the old woman with something almost like hatred in his eyes and said, "I don't know how you do it, but you have always been able to just

Spirits

scare the hell out of me and Butch."

Butch now found his voice, "Boy, Aunt Dorothy, that was the best ghost story I ever heard. It was really good how you worked us into the tale and made it even more personal."

Dorothy said, "I know that you boys may not be believers, but I will say what I always do. I am only saying what the spirits gave me, so help me God."

Silence filled the room.

Bill finally spoke, "Butch is right Aint Dorothy. That is probably the best scary story I have ever heard, and I don't know how you found out, but you are gonna have to keep it a secret too."

"I will only say this one more time boys. I don't know what your plan is, but if it involves a sorority or that old mausoleum in the cemetery, you better call it off and find something else to do. The spirit says you will die, and I believe her. Please, boys, don't do anything to upset the spirits of the Crawfords. I have never heard anything about them before, but that story scares me as much as it does you, so please…."

"You did it again Aint Dorothy", Bill exclaimed. "You scared two nearly fully grown guys. You are still the best story teller in the whole town."

"Not a story", Dorothy protested, but the boys were walking toward the door with the last of the hot rolls in their hands.

The next two weeks passed quickly, and, as Uncle Ken has predicted, the weather turned fine again and the days warmed into the low 70's and the nights remained comfortable. Butch and Bill had not talked much about the scary story Aunt Dorothy told them, but

Halloween Bedtime Stories

it did come up once when they were doing what they referred to as a "recon visit".

Bill said, "Do you think any of that story Aint Dorothy told us could be true? Or do you think she somehow just is messing with us? I have had my parents say they hear me talking in my sleep sometimes. Maybe she heard me, or one of my brothers told her. I have to admit, it makes me feel a lot more scared, especially when I stand in front of that old mausoleum and read CRAWFORD on the door. I never noticed the name until after she told us that story, then, sure enough, it was CRAWFORD just like she said."

"Let's just forget the whole thing," Butch said. "After all, no one will know that we got scared and quit except us."

"Not scared," Bill said back loudly. "And, by God, we are gonna do it just like we planned."
Butch looked at him right in the eyes and said,

"OK, Bill, but if we are gonna do it, then shut up about the goddamn story because it gives me the willies, and I am the one who is gonna be laying in there with them bodies that old Aunt Dot says she was talking to. So just keep a lid on it or I am out."

Bill looked at Butch and said, "You are right Butchy Boy. We don't want to scare ourselves out of pulling the all-time best Halloween scare ever in the whole damn county. Let's just sort out the rest of it on Halloween day just before the girls come down to do their stupid ceremony. Two days to zero and counting."
He smiled that big Bill smile, and they both walked over the hill to school together.

The night before Halloween, October 30, Butch

30

Spirits

and Billy told their families they were going to walk around the neighborhood to look at decorations and scout out where to send Bill's little brothers for the best treats. You could always tell which houses would give out the best stuff because they had good decorations. Pumpkins, witches and cornstalks all meant good treats. What they really wanted to do was to make their final plan for the big scare. They talked as they walked. Butch asked the first question.

"Did you decide whether Larry should be included in this deal, or are we just gonna do it ourselves? I think it would be better if more people were involved or at least told about it so they could see the fun. I mean, what good is it to do it if no one but us gets to see it"?

"You're forgetting there will be ten or so girls there to see it," Bill responded.

"Yeah, and what if they start beating the hell out of us, or what if they just tell everyone we are lying and that it never happened"?

That thought had never crossed Bill's mind. He stopped walking and looked at Butch.

"Look, Butch. We have been talking about this since we missed out on the duck joke last year. The stupid sorority will be there at the CRAWFORD mausoleum tomorrow night, and they will remove the blindfolds and place one or two of the initiates inside the door of the vault. They will then march around the mausoleum one time, which takes about 30 seconds, and open the door and let them out. They will be singing some old song or chant or something. Once they have done that, they will hold hands and stand in front of the

31

Halloween Bedtime Stories

mausoleum and say something secret. Then they go to the leader's house and drink cider. But this year, old buddy, when they open the door and start to put the girls in, you are gonna be laying on the slab across from the cement vaults and start talking real loud, telling them to get out of your tomb. When they start screaming and running toward the road I am gonna spring out from behind the big corner post beside the mausoleum in my hooded robe and act like I am grabbing one of them--- probably one with a blindfold on. When I jump, the string around my foot will trip the camera just as you step out the door in your mummy outfit, and we will start talking to them in our normal voices. I wish we could trust someone to take a picture or see the fun. But it might spoil the plan, so I think it will be just us, like we planned."

"How long do you think we will have to wait by that creepy damn mausoleum before they show"? Butch asked.

Bill was talking fast now, "We know they will walk up the school lane, then turn onto the cemetery entrance and straight down the road to the mausoleum, cross the fifty feet of grass, and be there. I think we should be dressed and ready. We can wait till they are coming up the school lane and get in place. I think about seven to eight minutes will put them in front of the mausoleum, and we wait for whatever they will do till they put the first ones in the door. The good part is that we won't be alone once they get here so it won't be so bad."

Butch grunted and said, "I wish I had not agreed to this. I mean I am starting to get the willies, and I can't

Spirits

help but to think about what Aunt Dorothy said."

"It will be fun, Butch, and think of it, we will be the talk of the school. It is the best Halloween stunt ever."

Butch exhaled deeply and said, "OK, but I wish it was over. I didn't mind lying in there on the slab when we practiced in broad daylight, but doing it in the dark dressed like a corpse gives me the creeps."

"Well, wussy, you can take your little flash light, but it has to be off in not more than two minutes after you are in place," Bill taunted.

The two then walked the rest of the neighborhood enjoying the Halloween decorations like they had when they were the little kids on the block. Butch even got excited a couple of times when they saw a house that looked like a good prospect for Trick-or-Treat.

Halloween morning broke beautiful and sunny. Autumn had moved into the valley and the trees along the sidewalks were in full color. The elementary school kids were all walking along the streets on the way to school in full costume and excited about the Halloween parade. The older kids who were too old for such silliness, looked wistfully at the costumes and thought about the Halloween days of the past.

The teachers, wisely, did not try to accomplish much on Halloween. The little kids had their parade and the high school kids walked along to help keep the little ones safe and fix costume malfunctions. The day went quickly. As the sun set and the colors faded, porch lights began to come on in anticipation of the hosts of characters that were expected to arrive. Bill and Butch packed their duffel bags and each left his house

Halloween Bedtime Stories

separately. They met on the footbridge that crossed the creek into the back side of the cemetery. It was just getting dark.

Bill spoke first, "Bout a half hour till they get to the school. Let's walk up the hill while we can still see good, then when they start up the drive from the school, its places, then lights, cameras, and action." He noticed the slight quiver in his own voice, but hoped that Butch would not.

Butch noticed, "You are at least a little scared too, ain't you Bill"?

"I'm just a little nervy; ain't scared," Bill said.

They walked to the driveway where the school drive intersected the cemetery drive and waited. The girls arrived at the school and assembled under the awning where kids waited for busses when the weather was bad. Two were in hoods; the others in long dark brown robes.

"We didn't know about the robes," Butch whispered.

"Yeah," Bill responded, "wonder what else we didn't know about"?

The girls started up the drive from the school, and the boys walked back to the mausoleum and waited.

There have always been two versions of what happened next. The local newspapers screamed in large headlines:

TWO BOYS DIE FROM STUNT IN LOCAL CEMETERY. The story went: William Allen Wilson, age 16, of 743 Kingston St, Strasburg, and Richard "Butch" Rupp, age 15, of 798 Kingston St, Strasburg, were found about 11 pm, October 31, in Strasburg

Spirits

Memorial Cemetery. The Rupp youth was deceased when he was found, and the Wilson boy, who was hysterical, was transported to Woodstock Hospital. The two were dressed in Halloween garb and seemed to be part of a ceremony held by a sorority that dates back to at least Civil War days in Strasburg. The sorority spokesperson claimed that the boys had nothing to do with the sorority and that the sorority does not know why the boys were in the cemetery where the sorority holds an annual ceremony. Some thought that the two boys were attempting to frighten the girls or surprise them due to the way the boys were dressed in their Halloween garb. Others thought the boys were spying on the girls to try to discover the secrets of the ceremony. Police investigators believe the boys were probably spying on the girls as a camera was found near the Wilson youth.

While details remain elusive, the police believe that the two boys went into the cemetery with the idea of watching a girls' sorority ceremony. The boys hid in and near a mausoleum as to not be discovered by the girls. The Rupp youth was found inside the CRAWFORD mausoleum and apparently died of a heart attack. A large blacksnake was found in the mausoleum as well, and police think the snake may have surprised the youth causing him to be frightened and stopping his heart. An autopsy is pending for him at this writing. The Wilson youth was found alive but incoherent. He was babbling unintelligible words. He was wearing a costume, which was entangled with a large cornerstone and by a stake driven through the cape of his costume. He was taken to the hospital for observation. He was placed in a room, and, when the nurse went to check on him, found that he

Halloween Bedtime Stories

had jumped through a third floor window and impaled himself on a signpost below. Investigation is continuing, but police believe that the Wilson boy felt guilty about the death of his friend and jumped to his death in grief.

Of course, many stories and investigations followed, but the main facts remained pretty much as they were reported on Nov 1, 1959.

The second version and the real story of the happenings were told to me by Dorothy Wilson, William Wilson's great aunt. It was a cold November day just a little over a year after the death of the two boys. The rain was about half snow, and the clouds seemed to be stuck in the tops of the trees. It was dark, and the story I was researching made me feel as somber as the day. Here, then, is what Dorothy Wilson said:

"Well, sir, here is the story of what happened to my Billy and my sweet little Butch. I don't like to have to tell it, believe me. One evening last winter, long 'bout January it was, when I was walking across the lawn to my little place over there. She pointed to a small building. I heard someone saying my name"…….. she paused ……

"Go on," I said, "please continue."

She cleared her throat and took a drink of hot tea, then started again in her crackling old voice.

"It was a young man's voice I was hearing, and he called me Aint Dorothy. I knew it was Billy who was talking to me. I did not want to look at him because I know how he died jumping through that glass and running that post through his body. I looked the other way. He sounded sad and said he was sorry that he did not listen to me. I looked at him then, and, I tell you

36

Spirits

mister, it was one of the worst spirits visions I ever saw. That poor boy's body and face was a mess. It was obvious from the look in his eyes that he had died completely crazy. He was cut and bruised and had a hole in his lower chest the size of a grapefruit. But it was his eyes that was horrifying. I knew from experience he had something to tell me and he surely did. Billy's voice was coming out of this poor creature so I listened."

"Aint Dorothy, I have to tell you about what happened so maybe it won't need to happen again. Me an' Butch saw the girls coming up the drive from the school, and we went to the CRAWFORD mausoleum to wait for them. We picked the latch open, and Butch took his flashlight and lay down on the slab across from the two coffins. I drove my stake which held the string that would trigger the camera. We were talking back and forth for about a minute or two then we decided to be quiet till the girls came. When we stopped talking, in about thirty seconds we heard them coming down the cemetery road toward us singing an old-sounding song. They walked along, the older girls leading the ones in hoods. They were all dressed in long brown robes. They then stood in a semi-circle in front of the old mausoleum. One of them, who seemed to be the leader, started hollering real loud...stuff about demons and the wrong done to Evelyn Crawford... which made me get real scared. I remembered the story you told me and Butch. Then there was this presence with them that came and stood among them that can only be described as '*all the evil in the world combined*'. Once a human looks at it, that human is not long for the world. To look at it causes something like insanity, but much deeper and

37

Halloween Bedtime Stories

much more complete. Then, the girls started to chant, and, right then, I heard Butch screaming from inside the mausoleum. He was screaming like a girl or somebody gone crazy. At first, I did not know what he was saying but then I heard him clearly he was sayin,

"Billeeeee, Crawford has ahold of my arm and won't let go. Help me. Help me."

It was just then that she appeared in the back of the mausoleum. The one that you told us about Aint Dorothy. Evelyn Crawford. She came toward me, and breathed out a vile smelling breath in my face saying,

"Charles has your friend, and I have you. You were warned and now you are mine."

I tried to run, but she had a hold on my cape and would not let me go. Butch was still screaming and banging around in the mausoleum. When Butch first started screaming, one or two of the girls screamed too, and they all took off together. The hoods came off, but once I saw Evelyn, I forgot who those girls were. In fact, I don't remember much at all. After about a half hour Butch got quiet and did not answer when I called to him. I knew they must have him. I tried to get up and run again, but she must have grabbed my cloak because I hit the ground hard, and cracked my head on the rocks around the edge of the lot. The next thing I knew was that I was in this awful place being told that I am one of the guards that stands with all the other spirits and protects the secrecy of the sorority ceremony. You would be surprised, Aint Dorothy, how many of us there are standing invisible in cemeteries and only showing ourselves when some fool threatens to try to interrupt the ceremony when the great evil acc........... I cannot tell

38

Spirits

you why; I cannot say more."

Dorothy Wilson looked at me and said,

"Well, Mister, you can believe me or not believe me, but I am telling you the story just the way the spirit gave it to me, so help me God."

Halloween Bedtime Stories

Happy Halloween, and if you ever get to Strasburg, tour the Memorial Cemetery on the south side of town on a hill overlooking the school and the Shenandoah River. Walk the road around the north side of the cemetery and look northerly barely down the hill to your left. You will see a mausoleum, old, with vines covering one side. The mausoleum has bricks where there used to be an iron door. On the bricks a plaque is attached, it says *CRAWFORD*.........Do not be there when it gets dark on Halloween.....I cannot say more.

PRINCESS OF SUMMER

Jimmy had been dropping small rocks off the jetty pier watching the ripples increase in size until the next wave moved them toward the shore. As one set of ripples went out of sight, he would drop another rock and watch again. It was nearly time to head back to the condo where he knew his mom, dad and his twelve year old sister, Jennifer, would be gathering for lunch. He was looking forward to getting lunch over with so he could meet up with Donny and try some more boogie boarding. He looked down at his hand and saw just two more rocks.

It was just as he let go of the first rock when she said, "Hi; Whatcha doin?"

He turned to see the most beautiful girl he had ever seen in his life. She was about five-feet five-inches tall, very tan with blue green eyes, and light brown to golden blonde hair. She was very well developed and moved like an athlete. She was carrying a very nice digital camera and a cell phone. He had noticed someone taking pictures near the end of the pier but paid no attention until she approached him.

He tried to answer quickly and to avoid staring at her, "Oh nothin' much, just killing time till lunch and waitin' for the surf to come up so I can go boardin' with my friends."

She walked toward him smiling and extended her hand. "Introductions first, my mom always says. I am Wendy and I live here. I live in the big house near the rides at the end of the boardwalk. Where are you staying?"

41

PRINCESS OF SUMMER

Jimmy was a little flustered. He was not accustomed to having girls his age just walk up and start talking to him. He stammered a little and told her he was staying near the pier at the condos just across the first street from the boardwalk.

"Why, we are practically neighbors," she smiled. "Now, tell me about the boarding you are doing when the surf gets up."

Jimmy was starting to feel a little more at ease and started talking about how he and a couple of new friends he met two days before had rented some boogie boards and were learning to ride them in the surf. He began to smile and laugh as he told of being tossed around by the waves and how much fun it was to get a ride that lasted more than twenty feet.

She seemed excited by his descriptions of boogie boarding, and said she would like to try it again. She asked where he was going to meet Donny and if she could come along too. Jimmy was not sure how welcome she would be with Donny, Billy and Larry, but he was not going to tell the prettiest girl he had ever met in his fifteen-year life that she could not join them.

He told her he had to go get some lunch but would meet her back at the pier in about an hour. She agreed saying that she needed to take her camera home and download her pictures, and she would be back here in one hour. They could go find Donny together.

She smiled and said, "OK, see you then."

Jimmy started to walk toward the condo and heard her running up the pier behind him. He turned and she said, "What is your name? You didn't tell me."

42

HALLOWEEN BEDTIME STORIES

He flushed a little and said, "Jimmy. Jimmy Wheeler", thinking to himself it sounded like the movie when Tom Hanks said…. 'Forest, Forest Gump'.

She smiled and said, "OK, see you in an hour back here then." He put the last rock in his pocket and jogged toward the end of the pier toward the condo.

Lunch was actually a fun time for the Wheeler family. They were all interested in the activities of the others. Jimmy's dad, Bob, had been learning to navigate the coastal waterways and canals surrounding Ocean City with a friend. He was enjoying learning the skills of piloting a boat around and catching some fish. Molly, the mom of the family, was taking scuba diving lessons, and Jennifer, the freckled little sprite of a sister, was taking lifeguard classes and was nearly certified.

Jimmy had been the one family member who didn't have any planned agenda. He was decidedly too cool for kid activities but did not yet have his driving permit. He was big for his age---nearly six feet tall--- and did not feel that he fit in well with younger kids. He had been happy to just walk the board walk, swim, and work on his tan. He secretly longed for the fall semester back at Roman High, where he had a great shot at being the starting quarterback. That was until he met Donny and the guys who were into boogie boards. Now he was transformed and loving the beach, the water and his new buddies.

The family was busily eating some grilled crabs that Bob had caught that morning and exchanging information about the morning's adventures. When the conversation lagged a moment, Jennifer wrinkled her

43

PRINCESS OF SUMMER

cute little nose in a smile and said, "Jiimmmmy, aren't you gonna tell us about your girlfriend?"

Jimmy flushed very red and looked at Jennifer. "I don't have a girlfriend Jennifer. What are you talkin' about?"

Jennifer said, "I saw you on the pier when the bus dropped me and Kristin off from our class. You were sure standing close together and smiling a lot. She is *very* pretty, and I think you should be proud of her."

"Well," Jimmy responded, "you are right that I was talking to a girl, and a very pretty one, but I just met her this morning. We are hardly boyfriend and girlfriend."

Jennifer pressed for more information about this pretty girl and wanted to know her name, how old she was, and where she lived. Jimmy told Jennifer that the girl's name was Wendy, she lived somewhere up near the rides at the south end of the boardwalk, and that she was going to join the boogie boarders after lunch.

Jennifer asked if she could go along but Jimmy didn't want her to tag along and cramp his style with his new friends and especially with Wendy. He told Jennifer that he wanted to go alone this time, but promised to take her in the next day or two after he got to know his new friends better. Jennifer seemed satisfied with that arrangement, and they started talking about Molly's scuba experiences of the morning.

The hour with his family passed quickly. They were all heading off in different directions for the afternoon. Molly had decided to take Jennifer to the rides park and maybe do a little shopping. Bob was off to check crab pots and try for some flounder for dinner.

44

HALLOWEEN BEDTIME STORIES

Jimmy was carrying his red and blue boogie board and walking toward the pier.

He crossed the street and turned back to wave at Molly and Jennifer as they drove off toward the pier at the south end of the boardwalk. He walked down a walkway between houses and came to another street that bordered the boardwalk. He entered the boardwalk walk and stopped to admire a longer and wider version of a boogie board.

EXTREME BOOGIE BOARDING,
the sign proclaimed.

Jimmy stood and let his imagination run wild. He was cresting a tall wave and rising to his knees. The wind was in his hair, and the spray of the ocean was sprinkling his face. He was moving fast and everyone was watching his ride.

"Gonna buy that board"? Jimmy turned to see Donny grinning.

"I sure would like to, but I'm sure it will have to wait till next year. After all, there is only a little time left this season. Besides, my dad just got a new boat, and I hate to ask for anything this expensive right now."

Donny considered the board and said, "You know it would not do you much good to get a new board right now anyway. You are just learning, and once your skills get better, you will find a board that is right for you. I know they look good in windows, but I've always heard that you never buy a board till you've tried it. Once you have had it in salt water, it will never be that shiny and pretty again."

"Yeah," Jimmy replied, "let's go surf"! They started toward the beach side exit of the boardwalk and

PRINCESS OF SUMMER

once on the sand started to jog toward the water. They were only about fifty feet from the water when Jimmy pulled up short and yelled to Donny. "I forgot I'm supposed to meet a girl at the pier. She wants to come and meet the guys and surf with us."

Donny stopped and walked toward Jimmy. "A girl? C'mon man. You know that taking a girl surfing will slow down *your* surfin'. She'll take up all your time and you won't get nearly as many rides in."

At some level Jimmy felt that Donny was right. He did not want to offend the guys, but he certainly did not want to fail to meet the most beautiful girl he had ever seen in person. He said to Donny, "This really pretty girl came up to me and she seemed kinda lonesome. She wanted to boogie board with us and I said OK. Wait till you meet her. You'll see. She's cool, and even if she can't board at all, she'll be worth knowing. I'm just sure of it."

"I don't know about you, but, OK, go get your girl. I am gonna stay here and get in a couple of rides while you find her. See, she is already costing you surf time." he chided.

Jimmy glanced at his waterproof watch and saw that it was fifty-seven minutes since he had agreed to meet her in one hour. He ran quickly up the beach. He covered most of the quarter of a mile in the three minutes. He was waving and calling to Wendy as the second hand swept past the last minute in the hour.

"Punctual I see." she said smiling. "That is a good thing. Where are we going to surf"?

"Back down the beach where I just ran from." Jimmy answered. He hadn't noticed her board lying at

46

HALLOWEEN BEDTIME STORIES

her feet until she stooped to retrieve it. It was the board from the shop all new and shiny and beautiful.

"Wow, a brand new board!" Jimmy said.

"No, actually it is an old one I have had for the whole season. They sell them on the boardwalk."

"I know, I've been drooling over one and it nearly made me late to meet you," he replied.

Wendy looked at Jimmy and smiled a knowing smile. "Yeah," she said aloud, and, "I know," she thought to herself.

They started walking toward the dip in the beach where Donny and all the guys would be riding. Wendy carried her board easily and looked toward the ocean. They walked into the water and the coolness felt good. Jimmy said, "C'mon out, let me introduce you to the guys that are here. More of them will show up for the next hour or so, and we will probably ride till about six this evening when we have to head home for dinner."

"What are you all doing after you have dinner?" Wendy asked.

Jimmy said, "Oh, I don't know. Sometimes we go for walks along the boardwalk and buy some stuff like ice cream or something. Sometimes we play hide and seek or tag or go look at surf stuff in the cool shops. I don't know what the guys will want to do tonight."

Wendy bit her lower lip just a little and looked straight at Jimmy. "I am not asking about what the guys are doing tonight after dinner really," she said. "I am asking what you are doing after dinner Jimmy Wheeler"?

Jimmy felt like he was blushing again. He said, "I don't have any plans yet," as he turned toward the water.

47

PRINCESS OF SUMMER

Wendy walked into the ocean beside him and pushed onto her board with the greatest of ease. She paddled out a short distance, leaned her upper body onto the board, and looked toward the ocean waiting for Father Neptune to provide her with a ride.

Donny came over and said to Jimmy, "This the girl you told me about"?

"Yeah," Jimmy answered. "Wendy, this is Donny Gordon and Donny, this is Wendy".......he looked at her.

"Wilcox," she whispered. "Wilcox." Donny paddled over looking at Wendy.

"Wilcox like the name of the boating company down by the fishing pier?" Donny asked. Wendy looked dreamily toward ocean then looked back to Donny.

"Yeah, the same big Wilcox family," Wendy smiled.

Donny was visibly impressed and whispered to Jimmy, "I don't blame you for bringing her, and look at the board. It's the same as the one in the shop, and she bought it just for today."

"No," Jimmy said, "she told me she has had it for a long time."

"Well, it doesn't look like it's ever been wet, especially with salt water."

Billy and Larry came paddling up to Donny and Jimmy. Larry asked, "Are you gonna introduce us to the sweetie or are you gonna keep her for yourself?"

Billy leaned toward the guys and said, "Yeah, how about introductions"?

Jimmy looked at them and then said to Wendy, "These two guys are some of the friends I told you about

HALLOWEEN BEDTIME STORIES

earlier. The red head there is Billy Johnson and the good looking one is Larry Zakarius."

"Hey," Billy protested.

Wendy smiled that beautiful smile toward Billy that made the water around you feel warmer and said, "Don't mind Jimmy. He was just kidding, and besides I like red hair."

Billy smiled back at her and pulled a face at Jimmy. They all sat bobbing about four hundred yards off shore when Wendy took over the conversation saying, "Here comes the best one since we have been here and for the next couple of hours. Get ready guys."

They all looked toward the ocean and saw a nice curling wave headed toward them. Jimmy noticed that Wendy seemed to be a different person when the wave got close. She looked determined and focused. She deftly paddled away from the other surfers and pushed into the front of the wave with power and grace. She seemed to become the leading edge of the wave. As she pulled to the top of the crest of rushing water, she placed her knees expertly on the board and rose to face the beach. Jimmy noticed that her hair didn't even look wet. She seemed like a bronze and blonde goddess, her hair blowing slightly from the speed she was moving across the face of the wave. Her blue-green eyes focused and concentrated on the water.

Billy was the first guy to pull out of the wave about one hundred yards from shore. Larry and Jimmy were still going pretty fast. Jimmy decided to pull out of the wave and watch at about seventy-five yards, and Larry was dashed head and shoulders first into the sand, as the wave crossed a small hidden rock ledge. Each one

49

PRINCESS OF SUMMER

of them had just had the best ride of his life. Wendy just rode on until the wave deposited her, still mostly dry, on the beach in about six inches of water.

She gingerly bent and picked up her board and held it against her rounded breasts and walked toward the guys. She came to Larry first. Larry was getting up and rubbing his shoulder. "Are you OK?" Wendy asked seeming concerned.

"Not hurt, just a dumb move. I forgot the little rock ledge. I know better, just forgot." Wendy smiled at Larry making him feel warm and causing him to forget the scrapes on his shoulder.

"I think you made a great ride," she told him.

"Thanks," he said, "but compared to you, I looked like a beginner."

Jimmy walked up waving his arms saying, "Wow, you two got great rides. I wish I was good enough to do that."

Wendy did not hesitate. She looked right at Jimmy and said, "Jimmy Wheeler, I will teach you to do that and more. By this time next week, you will be able to ride to the beach every time Father Neptune provides us with the incoming tidal wave. I'll teach you how to recognize the wave and to ride into it. In just a few days, you can ride a lot like I do."

Larry asked, "What about me Wendy; can you teach me to ride like you"?

Wendy looked at Larry and said, "I don't know Larry. You are already pretty good and know all the techniques. Your only problem is you didn't pay enough attention to the details that you knew were there. It would be harder to make you better. In the first place

HALLOWEEN BEDTIME STORIES

you are already very good, and in the second place, it is not a lack of skill but a lack of attention to detail. That is much harder to teach. Jimmy, on the other hand, is just a beginner and has some basic skills but does not have to unlearn any bad habits."

Billy came walking in toward the beach saying that they should head back out and catch another wave. Wendy explained to all of them that this had been the best wave until about mid incoming tide time, and they could go bob around in the water and talk or go get a coke and come back in a little while without missing much.

Billy was the first of the boys to question her expertise and obvious leadership. "How do you know so much about the ocean? We have been coming down here all summer, and we get some pretty good rides from time to time. Why should we give up after one ride? I mean I know you made a great ride and all, but maybe the next wave will be better."

Wendy turned toward Billy and gave him a look that, to the others, seemed to be a frown, but to Billy, seemed to threaten his very existence. Her eyes seemed to flash and she said, "I know so much about the ocean because I am part of it, and I live here. I have learned its secrets and its pleasures. I know its moods, and I am able to become part of it instead of struggling against it. You can go out and wait for waves and get small rides all afternoon. You can swim and play to your hearts delight. Father Neptune is providing a good day for beach people today, but you will not get a great wave to ride until about 3:10 this afternoon. Do as you wish."

51

PRINCESS OF SUMMER

She then resumed her pleasant smile and turned toward Jimmy, "C'mon, let's go get a coke. Then we can come back, and I can show you some things that will help you surf better without going all the way out."

Jimmy looked at the guys. A line had been drawn and they knew it. Billy started back to the ocean saying he was going to ride, because that is what he came for. Donny decided to ride some more with Billy. He had missed the big wave and was anxious to get some rides in.

Larry had been warmed by his compliments from Wendy and said to the others, "I could use a coke. I'll be back to join you soon." Wendy, Jimmy and Larry walked toward the boardwalk. Billy and Donny waded toward the ocean.

The girl behind the window in the hot dog stand looked enough like Wendy to be a sister. She brightened when Wendy approached the counter and said, "Hi, Mama. What are you all gonna have"?

Wendy flared up, looked fiercely at the girl and said to her, "I've told you before not to call me that. You know how I hate slang expressions. Do you want me to call Mr. Wilcox and have you explain to him why I am not going to buy any more items from you?"

The girl behind the window lowered her eyes and looked hurt. "No, I am sorry that I offended you. I just forgot. Please forgive me, and don't call Mr. Wilcox."

Wendy said that it was OK. She then turned to Larry and Jimmy and asked what they were going to have. Jimmy was reaching into the pocket of his surf pants to see how much money he had when Wendy said that she was paying for this treat.

HALLOWEEN BEDTIME STORIES

"That is great because I forgot to get more money, and I spent mine this morning," Larry said.

Wendy looked at Larry and said, "There go those details again."

Larry said that he appreciated her buying and offered to buy the cokes tomorrow.

"Deal," Wendy said.

The girl behind the counter looked at her helper who had been blending something in a food processor and asked if he was ready. The boy nodded.

Wendy said, "They want cokes," nodding toward Jimmy and Larry, and I will have my usual." The boy at the processor poured the contents into a large coke cup, and the girl drew two cokes from the fountain. She set the three containers on the stainless steel counter and pushed them through the window. She had a concerned look on her face and once again whispered that she was real sorry about what she said. Larry who overheard the exchange said to the girl behind the counter that it was OK, and no harm was done.

"After all," he added, "she is a pretty hot mama." Wendy smiled an icy smile toward Larry that actually made him feel cold, and he stopped talking immediately.

They were drinking their cokes and talking when a white Cadillac Escalade with gold trim and towing package pulled alongside the curb. A good looking, older man got out of the car, walked up to the window, and asked how things were going. The girl behind the window spoke with him gesturing toward Wendy and the boys. The older man looked toward the trio and nodded. He looked sad and maybe a little tired. Wendy acknowledged the nod with a wave of her hand that

PRINCESS OF SUMMER

could have been the way one waved off an unwanted fly. The man turned and got back into the Cadillac.

"You know him?" Larry asked.

"Yeah, we are related," Wendy replied, "but right now I don't want anything to do with him."

"Isn't he the Jim Wilcox who owns the boat store and the launch area?" Larry asked.

Wendy looked right through Larry and answered, "Details Larry. He is the Jim Wilcox who owns most of Ocean City. About half of the businesses here, the real estate, and the new hotels are all his. He understands this place, and knows exactly how to get what he needs from it. He is an expert boater, surfer, fisherman, and loves the beach. Jim Wilcox is almost as much a part of this place as I am, but he is getting old and the time is coming for him to step aside."

Larry was impressed with Wendy and said, "Gee, how are you related to him?"

"I guess you could say that now I am his oldest daughter. I don't want to talk about Jim Wilcox any longer. Let's go paddle out and catch a couple of little waves before the mid-tide wave comes. We can ride it, then I have to go home. I have more pictures to take."

Jimmy had been listening which was normal for him. He heard something in the tone Wendy used that told him that Jim Wilcox was very special to her. He couldn't quite put his finger on it, but he was sure that she knew something bad about Jim Wilcox, like maybe he was ill or maybe dying or maybe retiring and leaving the ocean. He wondered to himself what it was but, as usual for Jimmy, kept his thoughts to himself until he could ask his questions discreetly.

54

HALLOWEEN BEDTIME STORIES

Wendy smiled at Jimmy like she knew what he was thinking and she appreciated his approach. She nodded knowingly like she would be happy to explain more when they could talk alone. They were communicating non-verbally. Jimmy sensed it, and she was confirmed in her judgement of him. He was smart enough to spend some time with. She was sure of it.

The remainder of the afternoon was about like the first part had been. They bobbed in the sunshine and water and watched Wendy perform another fantastic ride on her gleaming board. The boys all did better than they had in the first run, but no one improved as much as Jimmy. He rode to within fifty yards of the beach and stopped in water just above his knees.

Wendy said, "Just think what you will do when I teach you what I know." The words came from her like they were familiar. Like uncomfortable words in a script. Jimmy didn't notice. He was basking in the warm feeling that he felt whenever she turned her attention on him.

Larry was the first to say he had to leave because he was meeting a girl named Sandy and going to the rides park for rides and hamburgers. "Why don't you ask Wendy if she would like to come with you, and you can come along with us."

Jimmy blushed and said he had not gotten to know Wendy well enough to ask her for a date.

Wendy joined in and said, "OK then, I'll ask you Jimmy. How about joining up with Larry and Sandy for some fun on the boardwalk about six-thirty this evening?"

PRINCESS OF SUMMER

Larry laughed and Jimmy said, "I'll have to check with my parents, but I would really like to do that."

Wendy said, "deal", and stuck out her hand toward Jimmy to shake hands. Larry headed off toward his parents' house on one of the canals. Billy and Donny were the last to give up the surf and came into the shallows where Wendy was explaining to Jimmy about tides, times and wave sets. Donny said he was going to go down by the rides park and hang out with Billy, maybe play some tag or maybe even bring his skateboard to practice at the board park. Jimmy explained that he and Wendy were meeting Larry and Sandy for burgers and rides.

Donny looked at Jimmy and said, "Once a guy gets a girlfriend here, you don't see much of them anymore, but if you want to surf some more tomorrow, we will be back out here."

Jimmy felt uncomfortable and was about to assure Donny that he was definitely surfing tomorrow when Wendy spoke up. "Donny you are not losing a friend. You are gaining a new one. We will *both* see you tomorrow. I can't make it until afternoon because I have my work to do in the mornings, but we will be there tomorrow afternoon if Jimmy wants to."

Jimmy felt strange as though his life had been a little bit taken over by this beautiful girl. He wanted to talk about it, but the look Wendy gave him told him she understood and they would talk about it later. Jimmy looked at Donny. "Sure, see you tomorrow."

They all headed off in the directions of their homes. Jimmy took a lot of kidding from his sister and

HALLOWEEN BEDTIME STORIES

parents when he asked if he could have some money to take Wendy to the rides park and for hamburgers on the boardwalk. Jennifer was relentless in asking to go along and meet the pretty girl. Molly, in a kidding way, teased Jimmy about needing to take his sister for an evening on the boardwalk so the she and Bob could go out to dinner alone. Jimmy thought for a while that she was serious, then overheard her laughingly telling Bob. Jennifer said she wanted to meet Wendy and ask her about her pictures.

Jennifer said, "I have watched her all summer, and she takes pictures of people every day. Not a lot of people, just one every once in a while. She usually talks to them first, then takes their picture and always makes a call on her cell phone. Sometimes she walks back toward the boardwalk and sometimes over toward the boat launch place. I wonder why she takes the pictures, and why she calls after each picture? When I get to meet her in person, I am gonna ask her."

Jimmy cautioned Jennifer to not be a pest when she met Wendy. "She will tell us about herself when she gets ready. I know she will." He must admit he thought Jennifer had been pretty observant, and his own curiosity had been piqued by her knowledge of Wendy. He also had to admit he had a very strange feeling about Wendy. He thought she was beautiful, and she made him feel warm whenever she talked to him. She knew just about everything about the ocean and Ocean City. She was fun to be around and she seemed to really like him too. He wondered about the feeling.

He went upstairs to his bedroom and looked through his summer clothing. He wanted to look good.

PRINCESS OF SUMMER

After all, this was the first girl he had been to the boardwalk with this summer. He had met some girls there and hung out with them. They had been on rides together and even a clumsy kiss or two in the Tunnel of Love, but this was the first planned date. He decided to wear a blue pullover skater shirt and his baggy off white shorts with his electric red vans. He looked like every other "dressed-up" teenager in Ocean City when he left the condo.

One major difference was that Jimmy Wheeler was truly manly and handsome. He looked a little older than he was, and he was a nice guy with a great attitude toward people. He was well spoken and polite. He was just exactly what Wendy Wilcox was looking for.

Jimmy had more fun than he had ever had in his life. They went to the boardwalk and rode some rides. They even went into the Tunnel of Love two times. The first time it had been difficult for Jimmy to work up the courage to ask Wendy for their first kiss. So, in typical fashion, Wendy took over and asked him if he was going to kiss her or just sit there and wish he could. Jimmy seemed a little shocked at first, then he wondered how she read his mind so well.

He scooted closer and said, "Since you put it that way, I would like to have a kiss please." It was magic. He never wanted to stop feeling the feeling of kissing her. She seemed to be enjoying it too. The first ride ended all too soon, so, after a short time of walking around with Larry and Sandy, Wendy announced that she and Jimmy were going to take another ride through the Tunnel of Love. She told them that she felt like maybe there were a couple of kisses still left in there for

HALLOWEEN BEDTIME STORIES

her and Jimmy. Jimmy just blushed red and followed her toward the tunnel.

The second time through, no time was wasted. They kissed from the beginning until the end, when the kid working the ride said, "Sorry guys but the ride is over."

Wendy looked at the guy and said, "Its OK, let us go through one more time".

The guy looked like he was in a trance and mumbled, "Ok, one more time." They got a second trip through the tunnel free.

All too soon the evening ended. The boys and girls walked to the entrance to the south end of the boardwalk. Jimmy offered to walk Wendy home, but she explained that she had not told her dad that she was going out with a boy. She thought it best that she went home alone until she could explain that she had a boyfriend now.

Jimmy looked at her and smiled broadly, "Boyfriend! I never thought I would be the boyfriend of a girl as beautiful as you Wendy, but I would sure like the job."

She leaned in and kissed him one more time. He was not shy this time even though Larry and Sandy were there. He kissed her too and whispered, "See you tomorrow."

She breathed softly into his face, "Many tomorrows Jimmy Wheeler. Goodnight for now."

Jimmy watched her walk toward the pier area for a minute. He turned to Larry and Sandy and said, "Well, I better be heading home. See you tomorrow?"

59

PRINCESS OF SUMMER

Larry couldn't help himself. He looked at Jimmy and smiled, "Many tomorrows Jimmy Wheeler."

Jimmy blushed just a little and headed off toward the condo. He jogged all the way to the front door. His parents only had to visit with him a short time to know that Jimmy was smitten with the pretty girl he had met that day.

The remaining week and a half of the summer went too fast. Every day was pretty much surfing, and the nights were walks on the boardwalk or the beaches. Jimmy and Wendy were a regular couple, and everyone thought they were just made for each other. Of course, everyone thought it was puppy love because of their age. But Jimmy knew that he loved Wendy in a way that would last forever.

It was the other guys in the surfing group that first noticed some of the strange things about Wendy. Like the way she protected her camera and would never even let anyone else hold it. They also thought they saw her kissing her dad one time when she got into the Cadillac. They heard other workers at other hot dog stands calling her Mama or Mom.

Larry was the first to bring up some of the suspicious things witnessed by the boys in the surf group. He told her that Billy had been certain that he saw her kissing her dad when she got into the Cadillac. Wendy flashed up and glared at Larry. She was turning red, and the air around them grew cold. She looked directly into Larry's brown eyes and raised her voice.

"Do I have to explain kissing my... she hesitated, then stammered... father"? She was obviously shaken.

HALLOWEEN BEDTIME STORIES

Larry continued, "Billy says it wasn't like a daughter kiss. It was like a Tunnel of Love kiss. We just wondered if your dad is one of those guys who abuses you and if we could help. Wendy's demeanor changed. She saw that Larry was being concerned and trying to help her.

"No," she said, "Dad was just upset and hurt because he got some bad news. I was just hugging him because of that." Larry seemed to be satisfied with her answer.

It had not gone nearly as well when Donny asked her about the camera a few days later. She had gone into a rage. She told Donny that he had better not ask too many questions about the camera or he would be doing himself some real harm. When he continued to want to know why she took pictures, she screamed loudly at him, "You had better just hope that I don't need to take your picture you nosy little twit."

She turned and ran toward the boardwalk and disappeared into the crowd. About five minutes later, a cloud passed over the beach and a freak thunderstorm ended surfing for the day. The boys sat on the dock at the back of the condo where Jimmy was staying and talked about Wendy and her camera.

"I wonder what she meant and why she sounded so threatening," Donny said.

"Maybe she works for the CIA or something," Billy offered.

"Maybe she has a job and has orders to not discuss the specifics," Jennifer chimed, sounding older and wiser than her years. Jennifer liked Wendy and had

61

PRINCESS OF SUMMER

no intention of letting these boys be mean to her in her absence.

Jimmy said, "I don't care about her camera; I think she is the coolest girl in the world."

Billy brought up the question of why the "hot dog stand Wendy look-a-likes" all seemed to call her Mama or Mom. "It's like the kids at Ocean City have strange ways of talking to each other that we don't get," he said.

Jennifer looked at Billy and said, "Yeah, maybe it is just the Ocean City way of saying 'you're a pretty girl, like a red hot mama'."

"Maybe," Billy yelled back. "Maybe she is some kind of alien with lots of children here getting ready to take over our planet." Everyone went silent.

Donny said, "Well, she is a little too perfect the way she can do everything better than anyone else."

Jimmy said, "You guys have been watching too many reruns of the Twilight Zone on TV."

"Well, you have to admit, it is strange the way she can never show up in the morning because she is taking her precious pictures. And it is strange that we can never go to her house. And it is strange that no one has ever seen her in anything but a bathing suit and maybe a cover up or a towel, Donny continued."

Jimmy was not concerned by the talk, but he did have to admit that some of the questions the guys raised were interesting. He thought to himself that he would try to find out a little more about Wendy so that when the subject came up again, he could defend her better.

The day after the thunderstorm, Jimmy went back to the pier just to watch the waves and think. Wendy was

HALLOWEEN BEDTIME STORIES

already there and was talking to an older couple. She was explaining to the man that she wanted to take a picture of his wife in front of the pier. The man didn't seem to like the idea, but finally Wendy leaned in to him and said something that changed his mind. He walked his wife to the spot in front of the pier and moved to the side. Wendy took several quick shots. She thanked the couple and turned toward Jimmy.

"The look on your face says you are going to start asking questions."

Jimmy said, "I was just wondering who those people are and why you are taking their picture?" He already felt guilty like he was prying into the business of Wendy, but also thought the question was innocent enough. Besides, he would like to know more about her, including the work she was doing.

She said, "I really don't know them, Jim, I was just sent down here with their description and told to take the picture. I did talk with them and told them that the picture may be used for Ocean City promotions or that it may not. I told them that it would be nice to have some older people in some of the materials. When I need to take the picture of the man, I say we are trying to appeal to the many widows who come to Ocean City. When I need the picture of the woman, only I usually say we are appealing to the large number women who come to Ocean City alone. I really cannot say more about the job than that." She looked at him shyly and added, "You know the saying, 'if I told you more, I would have to kill you'. I don't want to have to kill you Jim."

He wanted to ask her more but she sounded just serious enough to get his respect, and, besides, she had

PRINCESS OF SUMMER

said that was all she could say about it. Why make things difficult between them over a summer job? They surfed again that afternoon and all went well.

Wendy had kept her promise to teach him a lot about the ocean, and he was learning very well. They were both getting great rides and had even started to talk of borrowing his dad's or maybe even her dad's boat to learn some about navigation in the area. The other boys and girls in the surf group were getting better too but not as good as Jimmy.

It was a couple of days later when Wendy, Larry, Sandy and Jimmy were walking the boardwalk looking at all the surf shops for cool attire and boards when Larry challenged Jimmy to finally find out where Wendy lived. Jimmy decided that maybe he would double-back and follow Wendy. He had started walking toward the condo as usual, and when he got to the corner he simply stopped. He waited in the dark listening but hearing nothing. He peeked around the corner and saw Wendy crossing the street heading back toward the boardwalk. He watched as she waved, and saw a car coming quickly out of the evening fog toward her. It was the Cadillac, and Jim Wilcox was driving. He could see their faces, and he definitely saw the long embrace they shared. He watched the kiss that lasted for nearly a minute. He thought Wendy suddenly looked older. He was hurt, and he sure did not understand the relationship here. He thought about it all the way home.

Little did he know that he may have gotten the biggest break of his life. The time remaining at Ocean City was getting very short. The next day he decided to tell Wendy what he saw and ask her what was going on.

HALLOWEEN BEDTIME STORIES

He didn't know how to start so he decided to just go ahead and ask. He saw her walking toward the pier and walked toward her to meet her. She saw him coming and knew what he wanted to ask her before he got to her. She tried to explain again that her father was feeling down and she was just trying to cheer him up. Jimmy was not buying it. He told her that he didn't think fathers should kiss their daughters like lovers. It's just not acceptable. She became angry, and told him he just did not understand. He agreed that he did not understand, and asked her to help him understand. The more she talked, the more suspicious Jimmy became. The more questions he asked, the angrier Wendy became.

She finally just turned and yelled toward the ocean, "This is just not working this time." She then turned and ran back toward the harbor.

There was only a couple of days left before the Wheelers were going to go home, and Jimmy did not want to leave without trying to see Wendy and talk to her again. He believed it would be best to let a day pass before trying to talk about her problem and find out what was going on.

Donny had decided to get the surfer guys together at his house on a canal in north Ocean City. He invited everyone and called Jimmy last. Jimmy was glad to have something to do with the group. He had even agreed to ask his parents if he could spend the night with Donny and maybe one or two of the other boys from the "gang" that surfed every day down by the pier.

His parents had been planning for a night out with some of their friends and were only too happy to let

65

PRINCESS OF SUMMER

Jimmy have this night with his buddies. Jennifer had already made arrangements to stay with Kirstin. They were going to the ride park and ride every ride at least once.

Jennifer had told her parents, "I will need lots of money because we are gonna stay till they close at 9:30."

Bob and Molly had planned to go with some of the boating friends that they had made during the summer. Bob had been talking about how lucky they were to be invited to such a nice party, and "Just imagine, it is with Jimmy's girlfriend's parents," Bob had said. Jimmy stopped cold and told his dad that he was happy that they were going somewhere with someone but, that as far as he knew, Wendy had only one parent, that being her father.

"Well, maybe the old boy got re-married because he definitely included his wife in the list of attendees."

"Wow," Jimmy said, "that will be interesting. Take a picture of Mrs. Wilcox. I would like to see her."

"OK," Bob promised. "We will get a picture, and that way you can tell if it is Wendy's mom or if Mr. Wilcox has remarried. Have fun tonight, and we will see you tomorrow morning."

"Yeah," Jimmy responded, "see ya in the mornin'. Good night Mom and Dad." Jimmy grabbed his surf pants, a clean shirt, a jacket, and some vans. He threw a towel and bathing suit in his duffel bag, and headed for the strip where he was going to catch the bus to north Ocean City.

He was standing on the corner just across from the condo and could still see his parents moving around inside the house when he saw the white Cadillac with

HALLOWEEN BEDTIME STORIES

Mr. Wilcox driving and a woman older than, but definitely related to, Wendy. The woman seemed to recognize him and turned quickly away from his view as the car sped by. Jimmy wondered why Wendy had told him her mom was dead, and who this person, who looked so much like her, was. He was definitely going to call her tomorrow after he got back from his friend's party.

Jimmy had been the last one invited, but he was the first to get to the Gordon home. The weather had turned cool for this time of year. He was glad he brought his jacket.

Donny's dad answered the door and said, "Hello Jim. I guess you are here for the big shindig tonight. It is strange that the weather changed so much this afternoon. I guess we can roast up some crab and have a lot of fun anyway. If it gets too cool, you guys can take over the screened-in porch on the canal and whoop it up to your hearts' content."

Jimmy smiled, "I don't know about whooping it up, but we always have a lot of fun when the guys from the surf pier get together. I feel bad that it's getting cold already, because I was hoping for a couple of more beach days before we have to leave. It's only four more days here, then back to Hagerstown and school. This is the first time all season that it has felt like summer is coming to an end."

Donny heard his father talking to someone and realized that some of his friends were starting to show up. He pulled on his favorite shirt and bounded down the stairs.

67

PRINCESS OF SUMMER

"Hey, Jim," he boomed, "I am really glad you could make it. I have not seen as much of you since you met Wendy and wondered if you would be here or on another date. Larry even said he told Sandy he was coming to be with the guys tonight. The whole gang will be here."

Donny seemed really happy about all of the "surf gang" guys making it. Jimmy was glad too. He told Donny that he was happy to have something to do, because he and Wendy had not been getting along. Something had changed, and he really wondered about some of the things she was doing. When they had tried to talk about it, a fight broke out and they stopped talking. It looked like maybe he and Wendy were going to part for longer than just the winter.

Donny said, "Well, ol' buddy, you will still have the other surf dudes---that is, until they all meet girls."

Jimmy smiled and said, "Maybe we are too young for full-time girls anyway. Sometimes I would rather just hang out, surf, talk and have fun. It looks like your family is grilling brats, crabs and plank potatoes. How could I be anything but happy?"

The boys talked, joked and laughed. As the other boys arrived, the mood seemed like a party. They talked, teased and generally laughed a lot. They played their favorite music too loud in the background. After they ate mounds of brats, plank potatoes and grilled crab, they decided to go out on the dock and light the nearby fire pit and talk.

Larry was the first to suggest that since it was cool and there was a fire, that they tell each other ghost stories. Billy told an old Irish tale about Banshee's

HALLOWEEN BEDTIME STORIES

howling as the weather changed and before someone dies. Larry took the stories in a different way when he suggested that there were all kinds of modern ghost stories right here in Ocean City. He then told a story about a spook that frequented the Tunnel of Love. The spook scared would-be riders away and kept people off the rides. He looked like a normal kid until certain people got in the tunnel. When *they* were in the tunnel, this kid would turn his face to people getting on the ride and, for just a split second, they would see him as a ghoul with rotting flesh and red eyes. But it only happened when certain people were in the ride. Everyone laughed and Jimmy started to try to think up a spooky tale. All he could come up with was the Legend of Sleepy Hollow, and when he started to talk about it, all the other boys complained.

"Well," Jimmy said, "I admit it is hard to follow Larry's story. I wonder how he ever came up with a story so good."

Larry looked at Jimmy and said, "It was easy, that ghoul appears every damn time Wendy Wilcox gets on the ride. Everyone else just backs off, and she goes around until she feels like getting off. Haven't you ever noticed how many free trips you get when you and her are in there making out?"

A cold shiver passed through Jimmy. He looked at Larry and said, "You make it sound like it's not a story and that it really happened."

Larry said, "Well, Wendy was the one who insisted that I start noticing details. I will leave it at that." All the boys applauded. Larry seemed to bask in

69

PRINCESS OF SUMMER

the limelight. Jimmy was left wondering, but only for a short time.

In another part of Ocean City the Wheelers were being introduced to the Wilcox couple that owned the boating company, the marina, and most of Ocean City. Bob had whispered to Molly earlier that he noticed a strong mother/daughter resemblance between Mrs. Wilcox and Wendy. Bob and Molly were both taken back a little by the fact that Mrs. Wilcox was wearing a bathing suit with a very nice, but inappropriate, cover up. Molly said it was more than resemblance. It was uncanny. They looked identical, talked alike, and absolutely hung onto the men in their lives.

When they were formally introduced, Wendy seemed very uncomfortable. Molly told them that they knew her daughter, and that they were both amazed how much they looked alike.

"And to think you are both named Wendy." Wendy seemed cool and aloof. She smiled and nodded but did not have much to say to Molly. Bob remarked to Jim that he was a lucky man to have such a young, lovely wife. Jim told Bob that he was, indeed, a lucky man, but that he and Wendy had been married much longer that most people thought.

"Maybe it is the stress of business, but I know that I show my age a lot more than Wendy does. But, as funny as it may seem, we were both just sixteen years old when we got married."

Bob was astonished. He wondered how in the world Wendy could look like she was a young thirty-five and Jim looked all of seventy. Jim broke the conversation off by saying that there were lots of people

70

HALLOWEEN BEDTIME STORIES

who had bought boats from him that summer, and he needed to go pay attention to some of them too.

Bob and Molly were incredulous at the Wilcox couple. They wanted to ask more questions, especially about the Wilcox children and, specifically, the daughter who was dating their son. As the evening wore on, Molly tried to gain some of the information she wanted by talking to other people at the boat and yacht club. About the only thing she heard were expressions of amazement at the fact that such a young woman would be married to rich old Jim Wilcox. It seemed that Molly was one of the very few who understood that Wendy and Jim were the same age.

The evening was about over. Bob and Molly were headed toward their van when Molly overheard a young looking couple talking about Jim and Wendy. The woman was saying how romantic it was that Jim and Wendy had been married all that time and were still so much in love, and how it was a shame that they had no children. Molly wanted to go and ask more about it, but Bob assured her that someone had misunderstood. After all, they had met one of their children personally.

Molly said, "Yeah, we did mention knowing their daughter. Did you notice how uncomfortable that made them?" Bob and Molly were suspicious.

It was over breakfast the next morning that Bob asked Jimmy about Wendy and her family. Jimmy explained that he and Wendy had argued and pretty much stopped seeing each other. He explained to Bob what he thought he had seen. He told him of the argument he and Wendy had over her actions toward her dad. Bob told Jimmy about the party at the yacht club

PRINCESS OF SUMMER

and how strange it seemed to meet a woman who could have easily been the same Wendy they had met before only maybe twenty years older. He also told Jimmy what Molly had heard about Jim and Wendy Wilcox not having any children. They were both puzzled enough that they decided to go and pay the Wilcox family a visit.

"After all, it is a chilly day, and you guys probably won't go surfing today. I don't want to be on the boat much in this chill and fog." Molly had poured a cup of coffee and was sitting at the table with Bob and Jimmy, listening to what they said.

"I agree," she said, "I think it is only fair that we get to meet the whole Wilcox family in one place at one time. Jimmy and Wendy have been dating all summer, and we are a good customer. Let's drive over to their place this evening and get to know them better." Molly agreed to call Wendy and arrange it. She was a little surprised when Wendy immediately agreed to have them over and gave Molly the address.

Jimmy spent most of the afternoon walking from shop to shop on the boardwalk with Larry and Billy. Donny was at home helping clean up from the party and couldn't join them. They talked about how most of the hot dog stands were gone and about half of the rides in the park were shut down for winter. They talked about what they were going to do at home. Most of all they talked about how much they looked forward to next summer and surf riding.

It was about four when Billy decided to head home. He told them this would be good-bye, because his family was leaving for home in the morning.

HALLOWEEN BEDTIME STORIES

As Billy walked out of sight, Jimmy said, "Well, I guess this will be it for me too. We were going to be here another day, but with the fog and cool, Dad has decided to head home too." Larry held out his hand to shake with Jimmy, but Jimmy grabbed Larry and hugged him.

"One thing I would like to know, Larry, is how did you ever come up with that ghost story?"

Larry looked all around him as if maybe he was afraid. He dropped his voice and said, "Jim, I told you the truth last night. I was in line behind you and Wendy. She said something to that ride guy, and when he looked at me, I saw it. God help me. I saw it, and I have not been able to get it out of my mind. Sometimes I feel like I am going to go crazy, but, thank God, I never saw anything else. Still, I can't help but see it when I am alone or drifting off to sleep. I have been afraid all summer. Telling the story last night was an attempt to get it off of my mind. I think it has helped. I know you and the others don't believe me, and I hope you won't think I am nuts. I told the story because I saw it happen."

Jimmy felt a cold shiver again. His mind was linking all the strange things about Wendy together, and he was no longer looking forward to meeting the Wilcox's. The boys said their good byes and parted. Jimmy jogged home.

It was just getting dark when Bob, Molly, Jennifer and Jimmy got into the van. Bob asked if they would rather go to dinner before or after they went to the Wilcox house. Molly said it had better be before because they were not expected there until about eight,

73

PRINCESS OF SUMMER

which is an hour and a half. They drove down the strip toward the Crab Shack. The mood during the meal was a little down. They didn't know if it was the fog, the cool air, or just the end-of-the-season blues. Whatever it was, it was melancholy and a little sad.

When they loaded back into the van, they drove toward the marina and south end of the boardwalk. They drove up to the address that Molly had been given over the phone.

"It's a boat house," Bob said.

"Well, it is the right address, so let's go up and ring the ship's bell hanging over there," Molly answered. "Besides, I have read that some of these old warehouse places are really grand on the inside."

The family got out of the van and walked down the steps to just above water level. They were almost up to the door, where the shiny brass bell with a velvet cord hung, when a flash temporarily blinded them all. They stood motionless for a moment waiting for their eyes to adjust. Jim Wilcox's voice came from the darkness.

"Sorry about the flash, but Wendy had to take your picture." That was another thing Jimmy wanted to know… what was with the pictures and why take their picture now?

The door opened and the Wheeler family was invited to enter. As they walked in, they were very surprised. The inside of the warehouse was even more run down and deserted looking than the outside. As they walked in they saw a beautiful old sailing yacht. The name across the back was "Wendy, The Princess of Summer". It was in bad repair and looked almost abandoned. If these people were rich, they obviously

HALLOWEEN BEDTIME STORIES

spent most of their money on boats and not on this dingy house lit with only a small lamp in a corner.

They could see Wendy walking toward them, and suddenly they felt very cold. For a reason he could not explain, Jimmy felt afraid. Jim Wilcox just stood and looked old and sad, and Wendy started speaking.

"Curious. One thing that is a real fault with you humans is that you are just curious. I guess I can take a little time to explain. As you have figured out, I am not what I appear to be to you. I am a creature of the ocean, as I told you Jimmy. I did fall in love with you but realized that it could not be. You see, I am a Water Sprite, sometimes referred to as a Sea Sprite Demon. In old stories, you will see us referred to as Mulisina. I fell in love with a human the first time just over five hundred years ago. I married him and lived with him until he died. You see we live about a thousand years, and we do not age. We are the same from about a week after our birth until just before we die. When we love humans, we have to know that we have to find a new mate about every ninety years. I was alone for the portion of time I spent on land until I met and fell in love with another human. Each of these men have become very wealthy and are looked up to in the place where they live. They learn so much about the ocean from me, that they get into businesses that provide the things humans buy to go play in the water. They are helped by the spirit world to have success. The success they have helps them fill the empty time while I am away with Father Neptune. Once I realized that my human partners were only going to live about eighty or ninety years, I have started looking for a human to fall in love with as my current mate

75

PRINCESS OF SUMMER

approaches death. Though it pains me to say it, Jimmy Wilcox is very old now---about ninety in your human years---and he will die soon. In fact, he will die very soon."

"I saw you, Jimmy Wheeler, and fell deeply in love with you. I hoped to get you to leave your family and marry me. I know it seems like we are young, but that is just a fallacy of modern society. Humans are old enough to fall in love at your age, and, as you can see with Jimmy Wilcox, can live a long, happy life with a very young and beautiful wife."

"I live on land from April till the end of September. While I am here, my sea children come and live here near me. They can be near me without being too far from Father Neptune. Some of them are Sea Sprites like me and some are Sea Demons. I think your friend, Larry, saw one of them showing off at the ride park this summer, when I was trying to get you to fall in love with me Jimmy Wheeler."

"My Jimmy Wilcox is now very old and tired. He needs to rest, but he wants to hang on long enough for me to find a new........."

Jimmy interrupted, "I did fall in love with you Wendy. It was just"......

Wendy held out her hand in a stopping motion. "I realized it wouldn't work when I got my orders for the last week's pictures. I am like all of the other Sea Sprites who live on land. I am just one of many. You will see us on every beach in the world. In the winter, you see our land-locked sisters at the ski resorts.

Because we are spirit creatures, we have to take on a very undesirable job while we are here on land. It is

HALLOWEEN BEDTIME STORIES

our punishment and our burden. I have to document the new-comers to the spirit world. I am sort of the 'Welcome Wagon Lady' to death, during the time I am here on land. My camera is not really a camera, although it does create a flash. In the first few centuries that I was here, I had to actually write down the names. In the past hundred years, I have been able to get the information translated from film. Even we spirits have some technological changes. You see, when I take your picture, it means that you will die within the next twenty-four hours. It is amazing how many people have watched me take a picture that condemned another to death and thanked me for doing it. I must say, it is a little funny, but now the season is over, and I have to leave. The land fairies will send the winter camera keeper tomorrow.

I took your pictures because I was ordered to. It had nothing to do with me. I just picked the wrong boy this time. That was when I got upset with Father Neptune and told him this was not working out. I had just gotten the order to take your pictures this very evening. By the time you walk up the stairs to your van, you will see that it has exploded in a freak incident that has killed you all.

She looked sad and said, "Sorry, Jimmy Wheeler." She then aimed the camera at Jim Wilcox and said, "Sorry, Jimmy Wilcox."

As the camera flashed, she laughed that cold, mystical laugh that only Water Sprites can laugh. She placed the camera on a complicated looking stand. She then turned and said, "Time for Wendy to ride the

PRINCESS OF SUMMER

waves. I'll be back in the spring and find my new Jimmy. He will become the new King of Ocean City."

She appeared to shrink before their eyes, and, as she grew smaller, her features contorted and became demonic. Her voice became small, but her little demonic shrieks were still loud and piercing. The water in the boat house slot teamed with life and many Sea Sprites danced around on the deck. Wendy began to glow a yellow-orange and dove into the water.

Bob spoke first. "I don't know what the hell happened here, but let's get out of here now!"

Jennifer was the first to reach the car and climb in.

Jimmy was right behind her, but stopped and said, "What about what Wendy said about the explosion?"

"I think the Wilcox's have played some kind of weird prank on us," Bob said as he climbed into the van.

"I am not so sure," Molly was saying.

Bob was already starting the engine when the explosion occurred. Bob and Jennifer were in the van. Molly was hit by flying metal that tore most of her head off. Jimmy thought he had escaped, when the concussion of the explosion knocked him into the air. He floated toward the pier, his head hitting an iron rail. He did not feel his body sinking into the water. He did not feel the small bites as his body was the main course of the fall feast of the sea fairies.

.....................Happy Halloween........

HALLOWEEN CRUISE

Ben slowly opened his eyes and reached across for the alarm clock. He flipped the switch and lay back to enjoy the silence. He could hear the coffee maker going through its noisy last cup routine out in the kitchen. He listened for other sounds but there was only the coffee maker finishing up with a steamy pop. He got up and walked to the window and looked outside. It had been raining hard when he went to bed and now the only evidence of last night's storm was a few glistening drops of water on the leaves of the roses. He enjoyed the small rainbows reflected onto the windows and couldn't resist opening the drapes and watching the rainbows dance on the ceiling of his bedroom. He smiled and remembered his dad showing him how to let the reflections of the rainbows into his room. It had been one of the few good memories in an otherwise bad relationship with his father. When Ben realized he was thinking of his father he quickly muttered a curse under his breath and walked into the kitchen to pour his first cup of coffee. He added his usual half spoon of sugar, dash of skim milk, and took a sip.

"I wonder why I ever think of that son of a Bitch at all", he said aloud to no one there. Well, enough of this he thought. I better get ready for work.

He was expecting a busy day. After work, he would run some errands and put the finishing touches on the plans for the Halloween Costume Cruise. He

HALLOWEEN BEDTIME STORIES

was more excited about Halloween this year because he received an embossed invitation anonymously. The invitation simply said dress like a famous person that you admire, or come as yourself. The platform will be reserved and the train will depart the station at 6pm sharp. Everything you will need to enjoy yourself will be furnished. We look forward to seeing you. Enjoy the cruise!

In the past when he was still married he would not have dreamed of responding to such an invitation. But now that his marriage had become the last casualty of his fall from power, he just didn't give a damn about much of anything. So, if he could rent a costume and go drink Martinis all night, and, perhaps, find a Washington lobby whore to spend the night with, why not do it? After all being a straight arrow guy with a no- nonsense approach had taken him as far as he was going on that particular ticket. If he was going to have any other adventure, he better start soon.

He glanced at the clock, picked up the remote to check his stocks on the television and dressed in his usual dark suit, white shirt and dark tie. He had gotten used to this mode when the cameras waited outside his house to see what new piece of dirt he was going to charge the president with. He had been told to look modest, somber and serious for the cameras and he had carried out his orders perfectly. He had never disclosed the meetings with notable "religious leaders", deposed former speakers of the house, and strategists whose names had not yet become household words. But that was all past and once his mission was accomplished, he was placed in a legal research team. It was really

HALLOWEEN CRUISE

nothing more than a group of eager, mindless followers who followed any piece of negative information about any political opponent anywhere. The machine he worked for had become so powerful and ruthless that it could involve itself in local elections to vilify any opposition to the cause. He had never really understood the cause totally but he had blindly accepted that notable religious leaders, guys and gals with their own churches, and television ministries would only do what was best for their cause. And people who publicly went against the sanctity of marriage and flaunted their girlfriends in front of cameras deserved to be put through hell.

That was all behind him now and his job had become boring and uneventful. He was going through the motions and beginning to question whether focusing his working hours on destroying the political viability of others was the right thing to do. He had been to this point once before back when he was in the news daily. He had doubted his mission. He had questioned whether to bring down the office of the presidency over a few sexual encounters was the right thing to do but had been put back on track. This time it was different. He was a *nobody* again and when he lost his focus and doubted the mission, no one noticed or, worse yet, no one cared. That is until the invitation came. It was a very impressive envelope and he knew that the sender was rich, secretive and wanted him to show up with or without costume. Maybe there was something big brewing that he hadn't heard about. Maybe... At any rate he would know tomorrow night.

HALLOWEEN BEDTIME STORIES

He finished his second cup of coffee and headed out into the beautiful, sunny, fall morning. There were no cameras. He knew there would not be cameras but couldn't help think about the way it had been. There was the earthy smell of the fall leaves lying in colorful splotches on the green grass. The rain had brought the full odor of early fall to the Potomac basin and the slanted rays of the morning sun lit the world in a way to capture the attention of everyone. People seemed upbeat and refreshed by the cool crisp air that followed the storm. This was going to be a good day. He had sensed a change coming and now he could feel it, almost taste it.

Washington this time of year was always quiet. Everyone had to go home to stand for election and all the work had been done. The last few days before the election is a time to wait. Washington insiders understood and no matter what, it didn't pay to do anything one way or the other. Every action could be challenged by a newly appointed department head if the elections created a change in leadership. Now was a time to polish up the resume, frequent the watering holes in Georgetown or on the fun side of Capitol Hill, speak to the people who are on the other side. Let it be known that one could represent the minority view or perhaps even score a big job like special investigator for a minority position. Ben had dutifully pursued the standard pattern for politicos along the Potomac. Things were different this time. It almost seemed as if the war on the other side was subsiding. There was a feeling of "We Won". There is little left to do but figure out how to get rid of the religious right who

HALLOWEEN CRUISE

couldn't bring themselves to take the next logical step of creating a church for the truly gifted, wealthy, leaders and one for the followers. He knew enough about many of those guys to create a real hell on earth for them and perhaps that explained the invitation.

"I need to stop jumping to conclusions", he said aloud to no one there. This is a time when I need to stay loose, attend the small gatherings, and cruise the watering holes that all the Washington crowd knows about. See who is hiring lobbyists. Who needs the kind of knowledge and dogged persistence that he can bring to the table. Anything, even a political loss which seemed very remote, would create a better situation than what he had been assigned to these past six years. He was once a patient man but recently had actually considered suicide. He had a hard time being in the situation he now found himself in.

His wife had left for a more interesting man and to add insult to injury he was from the other political side. Emma was a good woman and had tried many times to save the marriage. She was convinced that he was being used and told him on more than one occasion that he came across like a trained ape doing the will of others who were hiding behind a shield of secrecy. He was shelved into the cubbyhole of a job he now had and was forbid to write about his time in the limelight. He was being saved in case they needed to retread the same ground again and it had become apparent to everyone that he was baggage. Perhaps instead of volunteering his knowledge of the religious guys he once wined and dined, he should go to them and offer his services. After all if he knew a lot about

HALLOWEEN BEDTIME STORIES

the leaders of the religious right, he knew tenfold more about the political people who had furthered their cause and now sought to divide the flock into haves and have not's.

He walked up the steps to his office. No one greeted him. He walked into his small glass enclosed office. He was grateful that so far he hadn't been put in a cubicle. That would be too far to fall. He never liked cubicles and had vowed to end his career or even his life rather than to go back to that level of anonymous existence. He checked his voice mail and had a message. Getting messages had become unusual. It was a follow up to his invitation to the Halloween cruise. It was an imitation of Marilyn Monroe in her famous happy birthday "Mr. President" voice singing the invite. At the end she said, "I look forward to seeing you there". No other messages. He turned on his computer the contents of which could turn the political world on its ear if he ever decided to. He checked his e-mail and found a similar message to the voice mail. This one showed a beautiful young woman dressed in a suit. She slowly stripped revealing underwear with a printed invitation. The top said see you, the bottom said soon and when she turned the back bottom said Ben. Under the stripper was the time and platform number at Grand Central Station. Ben smiled and thought that this was the most elaborate invitation he had ever seen. He was getting excited to go.

He decided to go to Georgetown to follow some investigative matters up with Georgetown University and as long as he was there anyway stop by

HALLOWEEN CRUISE

the biggest costume shop in D.C. He needed to decide on his costume. There was a suggestion that he use a link on the invitation to input his costume and see if anyone else would be dressed like him. This was obviously to avoid too many people demonizing the current political leaders in Washington. He would lean in a different direction with his costume. He would try to be surprisingly original. It even crossed his mind to come as the male counterpart to the stripper who appeared on the email invitation. He was really getting into this party. He remembered that he hadn't been to a costume party since his early days of marriage before they had moved to Washington and he had, as Emma said, "sold his sole to politics". This was going to be just what he needed... intrigue and social activity. Maybe he was going to have a second wind and once again be the darling of the conservative set.

He walked to the metro and again couldn't help but notice the beauty of the trees. Many of them were still glistening with moisture from the rains the night before. This was the first real day of autumn. This was the time just before the exciting beginnings of all the new people who would arrive in Washington. Everything was loose and ready to change or to defend the lack of change. Everyone was waiting for marching orders and had been given a beautiful, perfect fall day to enjoy. The Metro was crowded for mid-morning. It was as if people were all taking the day off. Even the young people who would normally be in class at the one of the universities were on the train and in the parks. It was as though the world was celebrating an upcoming change. Nature was showing

HALLOWEEN BEDTIME STORIES

off its ability to display beauty and peace even in the midst of this city polluted with political power. It was almost like a scene from the old musicals that had galvanized a generation. He actually found himself humming a tune, "The Age of Aquarius". It felt like something new was about to begin. It felt like the storms of the past several days ending with the storm last night had cleansed the earth of something and that it was new again.

Ben walked up the long escalator at the Foggy Bottom stop on the Metro and headed toward Georgetown. He normally would hail a cab but the walk would feel great today. He walked past some of the newly renovated hotels at the end of Pennsylvania Avenue and noticed that they were not busy. These hotels were lobbyist favorites and were nearly vacant waiting for the outcome of the elections. Only the hardcore bureau lobbyists or the extremely naïve were here to conduct any business with the government. The doormen stood relaxed outside the doors and enjoyed the day. Traffic was light and the air was cleaner than he ever remembered. He stopped where the bridge crossed Rock Creek Park and looked down at the small stream and the beautiful trees lining its banks. He saw it as he never saw it before. It is funny how much beauty there is in this old city that escapes the view of the busy politicians who are clamoring to control the world. He thought of the time he stood on the same bridge and waited to meet an informant who had secret information more than ten years ago. He had not noticed the beautiful little stream then.

HALLOWEEN CRUISE

His attention was brought back to the here and now by the sound of a fire engine rolling out of the station across the street and heading back toward downtown. He strolled the remaining two blocks and started window shopping at costume shops and other stores which lined M Street. He walked very slowly past a popular restaurant where many political aides and lobbyists often met for lunch. He recognized several of the people seated at various tables enjoying the fresh air. The restaurant had opened its pop out windows. This allowed the patrons to have the ambience of a sidewalk café, and equally important to many of the stressed lobbyists allowed one to enjoy a cigarette before and after their meal. Ben watched the careful dance of the political aides whose jobs may be gone in a few days with the lobbyists who may need to work with them or avoid them within the next week. He knew that many of them knew who he was but avoided making eye contact or acknowledging him. He knew in his heart that he had once been the darling of many lobbyists but was now political poison. Today he no longer cared. He was once again invited to an occasion and was about to open the book to a new chapter of his life. He speeded up his walk and went into Georgetown Costume Mall.

He was surprised at how busy the shop was and thought of the possibility that he may not be able to find a costume this close to Halloween. He had in mind that he would like to go as a famous historic figure like George Washington or Napoleon. He quickly found that those costumes were gone or were not available in his size. The sales staff was no help.

HALLOWEEN BEDTIME STORIES

Once or twice a sales person would approach then look as though he wasn't there and go help another patron. He was about to give up when he remembered that he had an old costume at home. He used it for Halloween office laughs in the past, and if he couldn't find anything else, it could do nicely. After all he made it somewhat famous by parading out of his condo wearing it in front of the cameras. He made a sign for his briefcase which said "don't monkey around with the law", donned his ape costume, added an oversize business hat and went to work. It wasn't his idea but it did get great press coverage and furthered the cause of his finely orchestrated investigation. He could re- live that time and it would serve the two purposes listed on the invitation. One he would be in costume and two would be coming as himself. His chest expanded with pride that he was going to cleverly do both. He turned and walked out of the shop into the warm afternoon sun. He whistled as he walked past the late lunch bunch at Clyde's and didn't even bother to look over to see who was ignoring him now. He was smug and happy. He was ready for the party.

Upon getting back to his office he noticed that the mail had been delivered and stacked on top of the stack which he had not touched for the past several weeks. He turned to his computer and saw something about an update cleansing some files. He would need to look into that, but first he wanted to check his e-mail to see any new messages. There was only one interdepartmental memo that he didn't even open. He revisited the stripper e-mail also on his computer, and clicked on the link. He was asked about his costume.

HALLOWEEN CRUISE

He typed in "Ape in business hat with briefcase stating don't monkey with the law". "Excellent" came back the reply. Then the email said "to limit exposure to uninvited guests the mail will self-destruct". Ben watched as the stripper walked to the center of the screen. She burst into flames then the whole screen burst into flame and the screen went dark. Next he got the inbox of his email which once again reminded him of an interdepartmental memo. When he searched for the invitation he found nothing. Strange he thought but whoever this is has a lot of money and ability to be able to reach into government computer banks and control e-mail devices. He thrilled to think that he was on the verge of a possible new adventure with some powerful players. He longed for the limelight again.

The rest of the day passed uneventfully, and Ben took the Metro back to its stop in Arlington. He truly enjoyed the walk to his condo and the beauty of the autumn afternoon giving way to evening. He walked past his overflowing mailbox and into his living room. He turned on the television and walked into his office and turned on his computer. This was the machine that had all the real dirt on many that he had not even shared with his most intimate friends. He was going to look back for the files when he wore the ape suit and be sure to duplicate the effect. It would be a bit like costume trivia to let people guess who he was imitating and a real gas to then expose himself as himself at the climax of the evening. He smiled to himself again as he watched the video of himself walking toward his party provided station wagon in his big monkey suit. He watched some news on television

HALLOWEEN BEDTIME STORIES

and settled in to a great Steven King Halloween thriller, a re-run of The Shining. He loved that movie and completely understood how one could lose all in pursuit of elusive fame. The main character in The Shining was trying to become a famous writer and thought he had tapped into a major ghost story. Only those around him could see that he was coming undone by his lack of interaction with other people.

Ben thought about how he felt very much isolated and the fact that no one had even spoken to him today or maybe for two or three days. He didn't care any longer and had become used to it, but he didn't want to become a raving maniac due to lack of human interaction. He was glad he received the invitation and really looked forward to being among those who could appreciate him. After all they had spared no expense in inviting him to the party. He fell asleep that night thinking about all the pretty girls that would be dressed in skimpy costumes and laughing and joking with him once they realized that he was a guest of honor. One who could even dress as himself. He dreamed dreams of socializing with powerful friends and being approached by lobby whores willing to do anything to get some of the information that he knew. He dreamed of the soft green glow of the limelight.

Halloween morning he awoke the same way he did the day before reaching for the alarm. He listened to the coffee maker finish working. He went in for coffee. He turned on the television to check his stocks. He got the news and saw that the media people were capitalizing on Halloween by appearing in costume

HALLOWEEN CRUISE

and showing old news clips of notables appearing in costume. The newscast focused mostly on current names in the news dressed in costume but…….there was an old clip of him…..coming out of his door in the ape suit that now lay draped across the recliner. It had no voice over just a banner saying Ben Barr famous for ….everything else had been deleted. He felt bad at first that no one would get to see the whole story but when he thought it over he decided that at least he made television today. He wondered how many of those vain assholes who failed to acknowledge him yesterday on his stroll through Georgetown would see the news. He wondered how many of them had ever achieved such fame even if it was fleeting. He felt smug again and thought he would watch the news and record the piece to use as an intro to the cruise tonight. Surely it would turn heads to know that he had been on the news this very day. He decided that it would not be necessary. Think of all the trouble the party givers had gone to sending a hand embossed invitation and the messages and e-mails. They didn't need to be reminded who he was and for him to do so would diminish his importance. When you are important you don't need your press clippings. Something his dad had told him back when he was in the limelight. He remembered that he had just thought of his dad yesterday and wondered how long it had been since he remembered that old bastard twice in two days.

"Anyway, he is in hell where he belongs now", he said to no one there.

Ben dressed in his usual just in case and picked up the ape suit and props. He headed for the Metro

HALLOWEEN BEDTIME STORIES

stop. He hoped to catch the eye of a cabby and ride to work today with his extra load, but none saw his waive or acknowledged it by stopping. He made it to the Metro quickly and was managing the costume well. It was another great day, even better than the day before. This was the perfect Halloween. The kids and moms would have perfect trick or treat weather. The party should get rolling to a perfect sunset over Chesapeake Bay. Ben was excited. He walked briskly from the Metro stop to his office. He thought he saw several people stare at his costume. He looked around and noticed that at least several other people were carrying costumes and others were decked out in full costume already. So while he may have drawn a little attention it was nothing to be concerned about. He was probably imagining it. He had gotten so used to being stared at or pointed at during the heyday of bringing down the president that he often thought people were looking at him years after he stopped being the focus of attention. Emma had said it was wishful thinking that being noticed was "only a dream for him now".

The day seemed to drag by. He once again walked into his office. This time he noticed that someone had taken his chair. He continued to ignore the stack of mail except for the top item. There was another invitation. He fumbled it open and saw it was a confirmation. It said Ben, see you at platform 30. Look for the Halloween Cruise Train, be in the costume and bring your invitation. "Don't monkey around". See you soon. He looked at his email but saw nothing new there. He decided to click on the interdepartmental memo. This was strange. It gave a

92

HALLOWEEN CRUISE

list of computers that were going to be removed from the circulation of memos and legal documents. He looked at the names and numbers on the list and couldn't suppress a sharp intake of breath as he saw his own name and the computer number listed there. He decided to fire off an email to the technical chief to see just what the hell they were thinking of. He wanted to show understanding because he knew it was probably a mistake. He was none the less pretty damn mad and it seemed like another swipe at his career and an exclamation point on his lack of importance to the current administration. He pushed his chair back and thought through his approach. He then took a deep breath and decided to give them both barrels. He wrote a scathing letter to the stupid son of a bitch in charge of the computers here. He let them know that he could still draw some attention that they may not like to the whole bunch and that only this morning he was on the CNN news clips. He finished it and placed it in his document file and knew that he would review it and send it later.

Right now he wanted to walk through the break room and see how many of his co-workers had seen him on television this morning. He wanted to enjoy a short walk outside in this gorgeous fall weather and forget how unimportant he had become here. He may just extend break into lunch. He circulated through the break room and heard several people comment about seeing ol' Ben on the tube this morning. But probably due to the elections and the changes that always accompany the announcement of the results everyone still seemed to be looking away

HALLOWEEN BEDTIME STORIES

from him. He smiled to himself that he was being remembered and cursed under his breath the type of town he worked in where people were afraid to be identified with anything. He knew things would get better from here as the ebb and flow of Washington changed with elections for well over two hundred years. Still it was hard to feel like he was an outsider.

He exited the building at his usual door and walked toward the Capitol. He was going to head for the fun side of Capitol Hill and see who was having lunch at Bull Feathers. He felt like having a good lunch and a drink, maybe two. He was in a party mood and may just get started early. He knew he was doing a little too much starting early the past several years, but since Emma left, no one including him gave a damn.

He didn't get back to his office until nearly 3 p.m. and the office Halloween party was in full swing. People were in costume and the booze was flowing. Not publicly of course, but everyone knew which closets and which abandoned offices held the libations. There would be the usual sneaking in for a paper cup full of cheer and the usual couples seeking privacy in a closed office.

Ben was shocked when he walked into his office and saw Audrey and John kissing and groping each other. He was really upset that they ignored him when he asked them just what the hell they were doing in his office.

He picked up the costume and walked into the men's restroom. He changed into the ape suit and immediately felt better. He placed the oversized hat on the ape head and picked up the labeled brief case. He

94

HALLOWEEN CRUISE

walked into the now-raging party and everyone suddenly stopped and applauded him. It was like they suddenly could remember how popular he had once been. He felt great. He forgot all about the couple now fully involved in sex in his office and took a brief bow. He went around the room greeting people. Everyone said how great it was for him to imitate Ben Barr. He said,

"Imitate hell ---I am Ben Barr".

They laughed even harder. He was the hit of the party. After one time around the room, the party seemed to be losing steam. Ben decided to go to his office and pick up his invitation. John and Audrey were not even aware he existed as he entered. They were naked and on the couch. The two were fully involved with each other *only*. Ben stopped and cleared his throat. He thought sure this time they would stop and they did.

They both immediately broke into laughter and said that "it was funny, if a little sick, to dress like good ol' Ben".

He wanted to ask them about screwing on his couch but noticed the clock, and knew he had to make a dash to get to the station on time. He turned and left the two still laughing. He was aware that they stopped laughing and were back to kissing and fondling again as he left the area.

He was in his ape suit with the hat and the briefcase stating "Don't monkey with the law". People were remembering him and pointing as he passed through the gates and using his Metro pass boarded the train to Grand Central Station. He got to

HALLOWEEN BEDTIME STORIES

the station with just more than thirty minutes to spare. He walked to platform 30 and was greeted there by someone who looked vaguely like the stripper he had seen on the e-mail.

He walked around the platform and was astounded by the depth of thought and the accuracy that had gone into the costumes around him. There was a guy who looked like Joe McCarthy. There were some past presidents of the United States. There were lots of people in costumes of every description. Ben was excited to talk to them and to see who they were and was already building anxiety toward the unveiling which he knew would happen sometime around the witching hour of midnight. In the meantime he longed to get on the train and have a Martini.

At about 5:45 p.m. a train car rolled toward the group on platform 30. A court jester appeared at the door and said he would need for each person to enter through his door and show their invitation. He said that there were two cars. Both would be full.

"There is always a big group from Washington. The train will push us out to the main track where we will hook on with the other cars. You will then be able to walk to the bar cars and party with everyone on the entire train. When the unveiling happens you will be asked to come forward and receive your reward. Enjoy!"

The entry onto the train and the ride to the main track was quick. It was nearly sunset, and the train headed northeast. It was only a few minutes until the sunset over the Chesapeake came into view and drew the attention of the entire train full of partiers.

HALLOWEEN CRUISE

They were talking about the most beautiful sunset they had ever seen, and all agreed that this had to be it. Ben couldn't wait any longer; he stood up and headed for the bar. He ordered a Martini and took a long swallow.

"This is great", he thanked the bartender and pulled a five dollar bill out of his ape suit and placed it in the tip jar.

"Thanks", the bartender said.

Ben then turned to face a woman who was incredibly beautiful and looked and sounded like Marilyn. He complemented her on her costume and on her beauty. She thanked him and smiled at him. He was amused when a new arrival to the bar dressed like a baseball player shouted, "Hey Marilyn, come over here, I want to introduce you to Joe". The ball player looked like Ty Cobb. He even talked like the Georgia Peach with an even drawl on each word. He immediately put his arm around the Marilyn girl and took her toward a taller thinner guy in another baseball uniform. Jocks, thought Ben, no one appreciated intellect as much as athletic ability. And while that thought was still present in his mind a blonde woman with a heavy German accent said

"Well Ben Barr, I am glad to see we are not all athletes and actors on this ride."

Eva Braun introduced herself and smiled at Ben seductively. Ben can almost sense the score coming and orders two Martinis from the busy but attentive bartender. She tells him there are at least two other bar cars and they start walking onward through the train where they meet many others. Near the next bar car, Ben is greeted by an Italian man who says he

HALLOWEEN BEDTIME STORIES

is Benito and another Italian looking man who speaks fluent English who says he is Al Capone. Ben is amazed at the accuracy and attention to detail of the characters on this cruise. He is more certain than ever that these folks have a lot of money and influence and cannot wait to see what they have in mind for him. He orders drinks for himself and his new found friends. He realizes that he has not had this much attention in several years and is starting to feel as if he is really in his element. Eva jokes with Al, and they turn to talk to some other people who are ordering drinks.

Ben becomes aware that people in "non-human" costumes are in the extreme minority. He is also thinking that the ape suit could become a real problem if the evening progresses the way he is hoping for. It would be pretty hard to show your full charming side while dressed in an ape suit. Of course they had recognized him because of his little stunt all those years ago when the news covered his "human interest side" showing him dressed up for Halloween on the way to his office. He leaned over to Eva and said

"Ms. Braun, do you know a place where I could go and change into something more comfortable?"

She looked at him then smiled and said

"Ben darling, you need to stay in costume until the unveiling. Don't worry everyone knows who you are and what is under that costume. The invitation was clear that we could dress in costume or come as ourselves."

Ben said, "Yes, I understand that, but so many of you have done such a great job of duplicating the

HALLOWEEN CRUISE

look of a famous human that I feel a little out of place duplicating the look of an ape."

Eva shrugged and smiled right at him, then she asked, "Ben, are you doubting that I am Eva Braun? I sure hope not because I do not doubt for one second that you are Ben Barr."

Ben was not sure how to answer this, and he sure as hell didn't want to lose contact with this beauty that was so obviously attracted to him. He quickly decided to drop the issue and blurted out loudly,

"How the hell does an ape get a drink around here?"

The bartender quickly handed him a Martini with exactly the same contents. Ben took the drink and said,

"How did you know I was drinking Absolute with a garlic olive and a twist of lemon rind"?

The bartender said, "I watched you walk in and have watched you drink your other drink".

Ben was starting to feel the effects of the Martinis. He said back to the bartender,

"You sure look a lot like the other bartender. Are you guys brothers or what?"

The bartender said, "Well, sort of brothers I guess. Hey, don't get tipsy and forget my tip".

Ben said "Yeah, and that's another thing; how did you know about the tip?"

The bartender was mixing another drink and talking to another patron but turned and answered,

"The same way I knew about the drink; put the tip on the bar thanks".

Ben didn't really like being dismissed like this,

HALLOWEEN BEDTIME STORIES

but Eva's smile drew him back to a more pleasant set of thoughts. She indicated a chair for him and pulled one toward herself. She sat down and crossed her lovely legs giving Ben a glimpse of her garter belt. He was beginning to feel the heat of the ape suit and looking forward to regular street clothes. As he and Eva sat and talked about "her role in Nazi Germany" the room took on the noise and din of a real party.

The revelers were definitely feeling the effects of the booze. "Ty Cobb" had found an umpire to start an argument with, and from the sounds of the language, it was about to become a brawl. Marilyn and the tall ball player were locked in an embrace, and his hands were well up under her skirt. Ben was just about to reach over and hug Eva when an Adolph Hitler look-alike burst into the room and looked at Eva saying,

"There you are".

Ben said, "You people are really good", and they both looked at him and shrugged. He was about to ask Mr. Hitler some questions when the court jester who had taken the invitations sprang into the car and catapulted his way onto the bar.

He said, "It's time to remind you that the unveiling is starting in five minutes in the front car. When all are unveiled, we will switch the cars onto their final destination. Please stay with the immediate groups you are now with while we go through that process".

Thank goodness, Ben thought. I can get out of this suit and into my regular clothes, then, hopefully, get Eva out of her clothes.

HALLOWEEN CRUISE

The groups became quiet and some muttering was heard in different quarters as everyone converged onto the number one bar car. The court jester was speaking loudly saying that he was going to proceed through the new comers alphabetically

"You who have been here time and again will just need to be patient while I introduce those who you may not know."

Ben waited patiently until a few people who he had not heard of were introduced. He jumped up and down and made monkey sounds when the jester said.

"Welcome Ben Barr who made a monkey of a president and an ape of himself". The crowed jeered, laughed and applauded wildly. Ben cleared his throat to say thanks but noticed that his attempts to speak loudly were hampered by the costume. He reached up to unzip the head gear and could not find the zipper. He asked Eva if she would mind helping him out of the suit.

She answered "Ben darling, sorry, but you are going to be in that suit forever".

Ben was confused. "I don't understand. What do you mean forever"? He looked at Eva waiting for an answer. As he stared at her, he could suddenly see a demonic glow behind her eyes, and her voice became high and thin.

She said, "Some of the others get to be switched into purgatory to await an outcome, but you, Ben darling, get to come with us. You will be the first pet in Hell". The car erupted in laughter.

Now... he remembered the pain in his chest a couple of weeks ago, the vacant feel of his office, the

101

HALLOWEEN BEDTIME STORIES

absence of conversation with anyone for days, and the surreal invitation to this cruise. This is All Hallows Eve, and those who have passed in the past year are sent forward......

He started to scream, but the only sound that came from him was the wail of an ape......

TALL TREES

The trees on the mountain top seemed to reach well into the deep black/purple night skies. The clear unpolluted air gave the stars the appearance of sitting in the tops of the trees. In places where an opening in the forest occurred, the sky seemed sprinkled with thousands upon thousands of stars. A passing jetliner roared overhead leaving a silver-white trail. The beauty of this night almost made Becky forget that she was bone tired and a little depressed.

This was her sixth night on the mountain helping search for a lost boy, and, once again, today there had been no news---good or bad. Even though she was tired, she had been restless this evening. She was wondering how a place as beautiful and peaceful as this forest with its abundant wildlife, beautiful lakes and clearly marked trails could become a place for a Boy Scout to lose his way and, perhaps, die.

Becky kept remembering the childhood hikes she had been on as a small girl. Her mom usually placed her in the middle of the line of siblings. Her dad would take the lead and point out the pretty patches of wildflowers or, perhaps, a grazing moose. Once they had even spotted a cougar. Her parents were visibly shaken by this experience, and it had been the only time in Becky's life when she felt threatened while in the forest with her mom and dad. She could still remember the tension in her dad's voice as he tried to sound strong and confident.

"We should turn back and take a longer look at those chipmunks we were watching down by the lake in the meadow," he suggested.

HALLOWEEN BEDTIME STORIES

"I thought we were going on up to Blue Cloud Lake," her older brother Brian chimed in.

Her dad had thought quickly and said, "Okay, I didn't want to scare anyone, but I just saw a large cougar on the rise in the trail about two hundred yards ahead of us. I don't have a weapon, so let's not panic. I think we should stick together, turn around and walk quickly back to a more open area like the lake in the meadow".

The kids understood almost instinctively and the line reversed with Dad picking up a huge broken limb and lagging behind, checking over his shoulder and trying to sound confident.

Becky understood how the forest could turn from a happy-go-lucky search for wildflowers and chipmunks to a scary escape from imminent danger in just a few seconds. She wondered what had triggered the disappearance of the boy they were searching for. Had it been a cougar, bear or just a grass covered boggy spot?

She had once watched her older sister step onto a green grassy spot in the forest near a spring, where they had filled their canteens, and sink in up to her waist very quickly. But how could an experienced Boy Scout simply disappear without a trace? Becky knew but couldn't bring herself to say it out loud.

She remembered when she had first heard the reports of the boy missing and thought, "I know that place. I've spent many days and nights in that very area." She even remembered thinking that she may have some special ability to help, because she had memories of playing hide and seek in the very forest where Joey had been last seen. If anyone knew where a child may go to

TALL TREES

see new things or hide out from others, it would be Becky.

She thought back to her phone call to the TV station asking how to volunteer. She had packed her outdoor gear into a back pack and made a quick stop to get some food, water and basic mountaineering supplies. She drove to her office and waited for her administrative assistant and her boss to arrive. She explained that she felt she had a real connection with this missing boy, because she knew the area so well. Her boss encouraged her to "get involved and bring him back alive", and she was off to the mountains.

The first part of the drive was pleasant enough. The weather was high clouds with temperatures in the low 70's. It was cool for late August---even in the mountains. She knew what this meant and was happy that she had believed the reports of heavy weather in the search area. The reporter had talked of snow, rain, and cool temps. Becky knew all too well how quickly and dramatically the weather could change at over ten thousand feet in elevation.

As she drove into the foothills, the clouds which had seemed high, got closer. She was climbing right into the storm. She first encountered hard rain at about sixty-five hundred feet. At eight thousand feet, the rain developed a noisy character, and small ice crystals clung to the windshield of the new burgundy Grand Cherokee. In less than five minutes, she was driving in an all-out, heavy, wet, hard snowstorm. Visibility was down to near zero, and slush was forming on the pavement.

Becky knew the road, and that she had a pass to cross over before dropping downhill to the search area.

HALLOWEEN BEDTIME STORIES

She drove patiently and carefully as the snow silently fell. She thought of trying the four-wheel drive of the new Jeep and pushed a button on the dash. A light came on indicating 4x4 in green. Becky smiled to herself, and had to wonder if she was really in four-wheel drive, or if it was just a light to instill confidence. The jeep took her safely through the snow to the top of the mountain where the storm reached its greatest intensity. As she dropped into the basin where many natural lakes formed, the snow gave way to a steady, moderate rainfall.

She heard the search area before she saw it. The "blat, blat, blat" of helicopter blades and the sounds of muffled voices over loudspeakers shattered the stillness of rain falling on mountain lakes.

Her first sight of the trailhead was quite a surprise. Becky had never seen more than four or five cars at the trailhead except for one time on a Labor Day weekend. The scene now looked more like the grand opening of a major grocery store or Wal-Mart. There were easily one hundred cars and trucks and many horse trailers and camp trailers. The vehicle traffic was, in fact, the immediate problem. There was not enough room to park all the vehicles without stringing them along the narrow two-lane road. She was so engrossed in the scene that she nearly missed seeing the man in the yellow slicker waving frantically. She lowered her window and turned the CD player off.

"You up to help look for Joey?" the man yelled over the helicopter noise.

"Yes," she said. "What do I do to get started?"

He grinned and said, "Not to sound obvious, but I think you better find a place to park and walk over near

TALL TREES

the center of the parking lot. That's where they are handing out instructions and forming teams."

"I may as well park back here and walk to the lot. It looks like a lot of people are here and lots more on the way. Any word on the boy yet?"

"No, and with the weather, time is real important. By the way, my name is Ted Avery. I work with the Summit County Sheriff's Department."

"I'm Becky Emery, and I have spent many happy days and nights in the forest here with my family. I feel like I know the place well enough to be of some help finding Joey."

"Right now, we need all the help we can get. You probably know that in this weather hypothermia is one of the biggest concerns."

Becky remembered the forecast she had listened to describing the search area outlook for the next three days and knew that every minute would count. Ted was now waving him arms frantically, getting the attention of the next new arrival. He smiled and waved as Becky backed the jeep onto the rocky bank beside the road.

She looked around for some raingear and found her red slicker and hooded rain poncho. She quickly got herself weatherproofed, clipped her cell phone onto her belt and placed a map into her dry interior pocket. She checked her backpack for food, water, matches, flares and a notebook with pencil, then started the half-mile hike to the parking area.

The noise of helicopters and airplanes and the drone of news media generators, with lights glaring and reporters talking excitedly, gave an atmosphere of near festivity to the area. There were people in huddled

HALLOWEEN BEDTIME STORIES

groups deciding where their assigned areas were. There were horse posses and search and rescue teams.

At first, it seemed very disorganized and like they may be wasting time by not getting out there and help look for this little boy. However, the knowledge of the size of the area, and the fact that this is one of the biggest remaining wilderness areas in the world, justifies the time spent in organization. It was true that you could drive right into this area in a car. It was also true that you could start off walking from a point in the parking lot, and walk a straight line for 312 miles and not come to a house or a cabin or any other indication of modern life unless you came across a lost hiker.

Becky forced herself to stop thinking and to listen to the voice on the loudspeaker. The voice was saying that new arrivals needed to sign in at a Sheriff's trailer on his left, and then be assigned to a group. Becky headed for the short line and waited. She was soon assigned to group that was on foot, and all were familiar with the lakes and meadows areas. (This is where the boy was last seen late yesterday!)

Her search team consisted of twenty experienced hikers who were all well-equipped for being outdoors in the first snow of the coming autumn. They spent about an hour mapping an area, extending between the exact spot where Joey was last seen and the area where Joey and his dad had been camping.

In less than two hours from the time Becky arrived, she was in the deep forest near the lake. Pete was working between her and the edge of the water, and Alice was working about fifty yards into the forest. They had decided to keep sight of each other at the outset,

TALL TREES

because they didn't want any area to get over-looked. They wanted to be sure every inch of ground was looked over by a searcher's careful eye and that nothing was missed.

The first afternoon had passed walking, calling out "JOEY," and slogging through wet snow about three to four inches deep. Lots of things were found: fishing gear, pocket knives, socks, flashlight batteries, a flashlight, a tackle box, and even some condoms were brought in dangling from the end of twigs. There had been no sign of Joey or anything that had belonged to him.

It hadn't been until the second day, about the time they all came back to the lake area for lunch and an update of searched area, she had first spotted the two men fishing. It was strange, she thought, that two old guys would be fishing right here where the search area headquarters were set up. They seemed to be having a great time even though it was raining pretty hard. She would hear them talking back and forth (sounded like they kept calling each other boy). They were sure pulling in the fish. She had never noticed anyone catching more fish any faster in her life. They were talking and laughing and seemed to know nothing of the search. There were a few other isolated fishermen scattered around the lake, but the only people that were catching fish were the two white-haired men.

"Ha ha," one of them laughed. "I caught two on this cast."

"Yep, it never fails," the other said. "It takes a long time to know how it's done, but when you know the secret"...... "Boy, look, now I have two" ...

109

HALLOWEEN BEDTIME STORIES

The loudspeaker voice was talking again now about the search, and Becky was drawn into the plans of the second afternoon. It was another day of wet and cold and no luck at finding Joey. The search teams were starting to discuss hypothermia and the probability that Joey was not going to be found alive.

On the third day, the weather started to clear. The clouds were higher over the trees, and there had been some bright spots in the skies. The rain had stopped falling and the talk now was of a night of extremely cold weather if the clouds lifted. Sure enough, along about sunset when the teams gathered in the lake area to discuss the afternoon search, the sun broke through the clouds. The sunset was beautiful with its gold and pink sky.

Becky had just built her campfire and started to heat up a can of soup as she heard the two old fishing buddies leaving the lake.

"Tomorrow?"

"Yep, we better catch all we can while the conditions are right."

"OK then, see you tomorrow."

Becky looked over just in time to notice each had a full stringer of prime trout. Some people can ignore almost anything. She thought about how the two old men could ignore the plight of this lost boy to come and fill their freezers with trout.

It froze hard that night, and the temperatures dropped into the low twenty's for nearly two hours before sunrise. There was a thick layer of frost on everything when Becky woke up. As the sun started to rise, it was the first time she noticed the reddish glow

TALL TREES

around some of the tallest trees. It is funny, the things that occur in nature that we all miss until one day we just notice it.

Pete had announced that morning that today was his last search day as he had to return to his job.

"Besides," he shrugged, "Joey is probably dead by now anyway." Becky's cheeks flushed red, and she looked sharply at Pete.

"Just because you are going to give up, doesn't mean that the job can't be done. Even if he is ...well, not alive, we should try to find him for his parents sake."

"I'm sorry. I guess I'm just tired and frustrated."

"It's OK," Becky said. "I guess I'm a little sensitive because I was lost up here when I was a kid, and spent a night full of fear and bad dreams. I can't stand the thought of a kid being out here alone."

Alice had been listening to Becky. She told both Pete and Becky that they needed to stop arguing and get ready to search the rocky hill area above the lake where cougar and bear dens were known to be located.

Pete said, "OK, but tonight I want to hear Becky's story about being lost in this very forest oh so long ago," he laughed.

Becky said "OK, smart ass, tonight I'll tell you about things in the olden days."

They covered a lot more ground the fourth day. The good conditions and clear sunlight gave them better spacing and lifted spirits. At the end of the day, they had found nothing.

Pete was packing everything into his Ford F-150 4x4. Becky was cooking a big pot of stew. Alice was

111

HALLOWEEN BEDTIME STORIES

trying to hang some wet gloves out to dry from the previous two days.

"More like freeze stiff," Pete had said.

The two old fishermen were, once again, laughing and dragging huge stringers of fish off toward the road where they were parked.

"OK," Pete said. "You owe us a story Becky."

Becky began, "Well, it isn't really that much of a big deal. When I was eleven years old, my dad brought us up here for a weekend of hiking and fishing. He loved to be here in the high country and wanted his kids to love it as much as he did. We got here early afternoon on a Thursday, well ahead of the usual weekend rush. Dad parked the camp trailer just off the dirt road along the stream that flows into the lake, then gathered big rocks and wood for a campfire. My brothers, my sister and I played along the edge of the water and watched the fish create pools in the lake as they jumped up to eat bugs off the surface of the still water. Mom and Dad got the camp set up and started a small fire.

Dad had asked who wanted to go fishing, and all four of us excitedly shouted, "I do!" We had learned to love fishing the clear, cold lakes in the high mountains and had been taught to actually catch fish, where others with less outdoors expertise failed. We grabbed fishing gear and bug spray, then headed for the lake."

Becky pointed, "Its right over there near where those two old geysers have been fishing all week."

"We fished until the sun started to go down. Each of us had a nice stringer of pretty Rainbow Trout, Grayling and even a couple of Albino Trout. We were

112

TALL TREES

proud of ourselves and our dad was about the proudest dad you have ever seen."

"Honey, look at these mountaineers! They're practically able to fend for themselves," he bragged to Mom."

We cooked some of those trout and had a nice meal. Then we sat around the fire and talked of night skies, trees growing at high altitude, and of the "Keepers of the Trees".

Dad told us that of all the places in the world, this was one of the last places on earth where there was such an expanse of forest. He said that the altitude and the kind of trees had a lot to do with the fact that this was one of the last, true wild places. He said that the "Keepers of the Trees" also have a lot to do with it. There is a legend that sometimes, at intervals known only to the trees and their keepers, a sacrifice is made to keep the forest strong and alive. It is a legend shared only with certain people and is sacred.

"Oh yeah," Andy said, "then how do you know about it?" Dad thought for a moment.

"You're right," he said. "I've said too much. Let's just say the "Keepers of the Trees" told me about it when they taught me how to fish the lakes in this forest."

We all wanted to hear more but Mom said, "No. Let's have some S'mores and get some kids in their sleeping bags. The sun comes up early here."

The boys wanted to sleep in the bed of the truck and watch the stars. Becky wanted to sleep out there too but was tucked into her bunk in the trailer instead.

"We got up with the birds the next day and went hiking into a lake up near the top of the hill to the east. It

HALLOWEEN BEDTIME STORIES

was that Friday, all those years ago, that I was lost. I was fishing the lake with my dad and brothers; my sister had stayed behind with Mom. I kept seeing fish rolling up to eat off the top but wasn't able to get them to bite. I kept moving around the edge of the water to get a better angle to cast toward the feeding fish.

I hadn't noticed when I lost sight of the boys or Dad. I did notice that it was very quiet and that the sun was setting. Suddenly, I had the feeling that I was alone. There was not a sound or a ripple on the lake, and the sun was down behind the peaks. The evening birds were making their perching noises.

DAD! Where are you? BRIAN! Come on you guys; talk to me. ANDY! Surely Andy would answer. *Nothing. Not a sound.*

It was like I had been pulled into another place where no humans were around, and I was alone. The fear did not come on slowly as it sometimes does with other kinds of trouble. It came on fast and hard. I just knew that I was with my dad and brothers, and we were all right here."

The lake was less than five hundred feet across and less than two thousand feet long. While there were large fir and pine trees around the edge of the water, you could see the shoreline almost all the way around from just about any spot on the lake.

She had just walked a short distance to try to toss her fishing line toward some circles on the surface where a trout had just eaten a bug. Now it was getting dark, and they had left her. She loved the lakes and the forest, but the thought of spending the night here alone frightened her to the very core. Meantime, her dad and brothers

TALL TREES

were becoming worried. They had noticed Becky was
nowhere in sight about an hour and a half before sunset.
They walked the shoreline together at first shouting her
name, and thinking that she must be playing hide and
seek with them. Her dad had lost his sense of humor
after about twenty minutes and after realizing there was
no one around the lake except himself and the boys.

He had told the boys to stick together and walk
the shoreline toward the far end of the lake. He would
take the other side and meet them at the rock ledge on
the other end. It only took about twenty more minutes
until they had walked to the meeting point. They had
called her name all the way and did not see or hear her
anywhere.

"I'll bet she went back to camp," Andy said.
"She was probably tired of not catching anything, got
bored and just walked back".

"I don't believe Becky would dare walk in the
forest alone," Dad said. "I think she still remembers the
time we saw the cougar too well to take chances here".

Brian said, "I don't think Becky is afraid of
anything Dad, and she loves this forest more that anyone
I know. Besides, we know she isn't here, so we may as
well head back the way we came and look for her there."

Dad had a feeling something was really wrong,
but, truthfully, didn't have a better idea.The three guys
started toward the camp trailer as the sun was going
down.

A quote came to Becky's youthful mind, "No one
knows how or why these things happen, but sometimes
people just disappear into thin air."

HALLOWEEN BEDTIME STORIES

She decided to head back down the trail in the gathering darkness. She was going to really yell at her dad and brothers for leaving her there all alone. "Boy, are they gonna get an ear full when I get back."

Becky stops the story and announces that the stew is ready, and Pete and Alice help themselves to a large bowl.

"The story," said Pete. "Get back to the story."

"Yes," Alice joined in. "Let's get back to the story."

"Not really that much to tell," Becky offered. "I wandered the forest all that night, the next day, and another night. I had bad dreams. I nearly froze at night. I walked around the woods, fell on rocks, got all cut and bruised, and didn't eat for over two days. My parents thought I was dead, and searchers must have walked within a few feet of me several times without finding me. I started walking back to the trail that my brothers, my dad and I had used to get to the lake.

I knew something wasn't the same. The direction of the trail was different, but it was the same trail. I started down it several times and got to a place that seemed unfamiliar and strange. When I felt that way, I headed back to familiar territory. I knew better than to pursue a trail that was unfamiliar, especially when it was getting dark.

After about ten starts down the ever-changing trail, I just decided to spend the night beside the lake under a large tree, where I could see the trail and much of the lake. I gathered up some branches with leaves and evergreen sprigs on them to cover myself so I wouldn't get too cold. I found some dry wood, but I set my tackle

TALL TREES

box too close to the water, and my matches had gotten wet. I knew that it would be a long, cold night, but I didn't count on becoming delirious.

I found a dry spot with a good view of the trail and pulled the branches up around me. I drew myself up into a ball and tried to keep warm. I fell asleep, but it wasn't long until my sleep was interrupted by the dream of the talking trees. The tallest trees in the area started talking to each other in "people" voices.

"She could be the one," a large Douglas Fir tree said.

HALLOWEEN BEDTIME STORIES

"I don't think so," another then chimed in.

"The chosen ones must love us and our place or the formula doesn't work," a stately Sugar Pine observed. "All the others have been males of their species".

"Stop it!" Becky had screamed at the trees." "What are you doing talking? Trees can't talk."

"Well dear," a stout, heavy limbed Oak with a husky, feminine voice said. "We don't often get a chance to talk, but that doesn't mean we can't. You see, we are the chosen trees that guard and protect the forest. About two hundred thousand years ago, we were selected to grow tall and big and old. We were given the ability to select a loved one who could, through an unselfish sacrifice, become part of our forest forever."

"This is silly," Becky interrupted herself. "It is the wild dream of a lost child."

"No, tell it," Pete insisted.

"Yeah," Alice chimed in. "Tell it Becky."

"The tree told me that they could tell when a human child of *not more than 12* loved the forest very deeply. They said that about every ten years, they had to select one such child, and that the child would become part of the forest. The child would feel nothing and would simply take up their life on another plane. The child would be lost to all they knew and would never be able to go back to their families or their lives. The forest tried to select a child who would rather just stay in the forest due to their strong love for the forest and, when possible, they tried to select a child who didn't have a good home life to begin with.

TALL TREES

Well, I told them they had made a big mistake with me, because I love my home life and my family and I wanted them to send me back".

"Oh dear," said the big Oak. "It isn't that easy. Besides, while you feel nothing, your earthly body is used to create the "*ingredient*" to get the fish for the mulch that keeps us all vibrant enough to protect the entrance to the largest natural forest on the earth."

Becky had gotten angry at this point in the dream. She demanded to know what they meant by earthly body being used.

"Tell me what you're talking about," she had demanded".

"Now, let us not get so excited here," a gnarly, twisted, old, Lodge Pole Pine said. "Besides, I think we may have made a mistake for the first time in our lives."

"A mistake!" The murmur went up through the forest.

"Yes, a mistake. This one is a female of her species, and the "*ingredient*" has to be made from a man who loves the forest like his own life. It takes a young man who would rather live in the deep forest forever than to see the forest die. This young one loves us enough but it is a female and cannot produce the formula for the "*ingredient*."

"What are you talking about" young Becky demanded?

"We have a formula for life that must be followed closely, or we will all perish".

"Yeah, we become floors or tables and chairs or firewood," a sapling Birch said. "You humans all want us to stand here and wait for you to come and admire us

HALLOWEEN BEDTIME STORIES

or run into us with your machines or cut us and kill us with your saws. You want us to make oxygen for you to breathe in so you live, and only a few of you appreciate us and love us in return. It is an unfortunate rule of Mother Nature that we can only get our secret formula to life from among the few who love us.

About every ten years, we have to select a young human to live among us forever. We have ways to bring them across the dimension from their world to ours. With time, they become comfortable among us.

"The trees said some other things about how they got to live, but it has become such a faded memory, that I can't remember it all. I do remember that just before I woke up, the old Lodge Pole Pine boomed, "But it must be a male of their species".

"I woke up lying under my branches, and it was morning," Becky said. "It was actually two days later, and people swore they had walked across this very spot many times and had never seen the pile of branches or the little red coat I had pulled up around my face. I told the searchers about the trees and the *"ingredient"*, but they called it delirium. They took me back to my parents' camp trailer, which was still parked where it had been all along. My parents were relieved and happy and we never stayed in the woods overnight again."

"Nice story, Becky," Pete said. "Now, tell us a story about the two old farts who've been up here fishing all week"!

"Pete, it was a dream," Becky said.

"I know but ... well, never mind. I have to head back to go to work tomorrow anyway. Good luck you two, and I really hope you find Joey alive."

TALL TREES

"Pete makes me wonder about the two old men fishing here Becky, and maybe your adventure was not a dream," Alice said. "Have you noticed the pink glow around the moon the last couple of nights?"

Becky decided to not say anymore and to just get some rest. Talking about being lost as a child always put her in a down mood, and today was no exception. She had decided that this new question of Pete's needed some looking into, and tomorrow she was going to do it.

She was going to pay a visit to the two old guys fishing at the lake. She thought to herself that they probably wouldn't even show up. However, as she reached to pull the flap down on her tent, she noticed for the first time the pinkish color that seemed to be illuminated in the halo of the moon. Funny, how you don't notice things in nature which were there all along until someone points them out.

Becky did not sleep well. Dreams of the trees and comments made by her companions caused her to be restless and remember more clearly the voices of the trees, voices that often sound like the rush of wind or the bubbling of water. She also felt a little guilty for not telling her two search mates the whole truth of the dream, but then it was only a dream.

She awoke to a beautiful clear morning. There was no frost and not a cloud in the sky. It was just turning light and the oranges of the sunrise were beginning as small streaks in the east. Becky watched a young buck approach the shoreline of the lake and drink. The deer walked right between the old guys who were already fishing in the lake without even noticing them. Yet, a noise from the area where she was camping

HALLOWEEN BEDTIME STORIES

seemed to catch the attention of the wary buck. He looked carefully across the lake at the movement near the flap of a tent. He must have sensed danger because in a moment he turned and disappeared into the forest.

"What a beautiful morning," Alice said. "If we are going to find Joey, today should be the day."

"Yeah," Becky said, "But first I am going to go and talk to those two guys about their fishing. I have never seen more success at catching fish and wonder what they are doing with them all. In fact, I think I'll walk over there now, while everyone is around, and visit with them. If I'm not back in half an hour, come and get me OK"?

Alice laughed, "I think you can handle yourself around those two. They must be a hundred."

"Just the same, only half an hour." Becky said.

"You want me to go along," Alice asked?

"No, just keep an eye on me, and come get me if I'm not back in half an hour. I told you before, I've been lost in this area with no explanation, and I don't like losing sight of people. I don't want to seem too needy, and I'm building my confidence by doing this on my own. So, please just check on me in a little while".

"OK", Alice said.

Becky approached the two older men and smiled, "Hi, I'm up here with the search group, and we have been watching you catch fish from the lake all week. I just wanted to come over and see how you do it."

The smaller of the two men looked intently at Becky and smiled back, "You ain't a game warden are you"?

122

TALL TREES

"No, just a searcher looking for a lost little boy," Becky said.

"I know," he smiled. "We been watching you all week too. You ain't gonna find him you know."

Becky looked at the man, and anger flashed in her. "How can you know that?" she demanded.

"Same way you know it," he returned. "Now, you better get back over there before we have the whole camp over here messing up the fishing. Your half hour is about up."

Becky felt fear. How did he know? She wanted to ask, but knew that she was too afraid to get her voice to work right anyway. She turned and rushed back to the edge of her camp.

"Alice can you see me"?

"Well, I hope so! You're wearing red, and you must be, what, about twenty feet away"?

"Sorry. I just had a bad thought and got myself scared," Becky explained. "I'm going to talk to those two some more when the search is done today".

"Yeah," said Alice, "let's hope it is early and with good results."

The search did not end early. Once again, nothing was found, and Becky knew now that nothing would be found. She was not looking forward to the evening, but she needed to be brave and find out once and for all what she thought she already knew.

There were very few searchers left now. Only about ten tents compared to the sixty or seventy that had shared the opening in the forest when Joey first was listed as missing. The search director had told them at the lunch break that the search was now considered a

123

HALLOWEEN BEDTIME STORIES

recovery operation. That means that we are looking for a body.

Many searchers had simply pulled their belongings together and headed down the road. Becky stayed because she felt she had an appointment with the two old "boys". She looked toward the lake, and sure enough, the joy of catching fish was evident.

"Look at the size of this one. He's one of the biggest yet."

"Yeah, but we better get them while the getting is good. Another day or two, and it will go back to normal."

"Well, I'll be ready for the rest myself."

The old guys were having fun but were getting tired of the all-day fishing.

"So, why do you do it?" Becky asked boldly from behind the shorter and more active of the two men.

"Told you this morning. I think you know, or did you choose to forget that part of the lesson you call a dream"?

Becky was startled and started to run away, but remembered that there was no getting away until the forces of the forest released you. She knew they would release her as they had before.

"What do you mean?" she asked again, this time with anger in her voice.

"I mean that we are the caretakers. You know, the caretakers of the trees that guard the entrance to the last forest on earth that isn't fouled by the presence of humankind."

"Caretakers?"

TALL TREES

"Come on. You remember, the old Lodge Pine told you. When these young ones who are raised to love the forest come to live in the forest forever, the earthly body had a function."

Suddenly, Becky remembered the part she had chosen to forget all those years ago. The part of the story that she had been afraid to think about.

She was catapulted back through time to the side of the lake in her red coat. She was clutching branches up around her to keep warm and to keep something from grabbing her. She was hiding from the trees. The trees knew she was there, and had tried to tell her that she was going to be OK.

They tried to tell her that they were using a force of nature to protect themselves and to rescue forest creatures who had been placed into the wrong body at birth. They had been so sure she was one of them that they had acted without remembering that it only occurred in males. That is how they knew they were wrong. They had told her that when the forest creature was restored to its rightful existence such as a moose, a cougar or a large elk, that the human body was quickly decomposed and absorbed in the roots of the protector trees. The trees then emitted a reddish pink mist into the air. If you see it in broad daylight, it looks like a small colorful rainbow. If you see it at night against the moon it looks reddish. The mist falls into the surrounding lakes and streams and enhances the eggs of Trout and Salmon in the area. Those eggs are carefully harvested by the caretakers and used as bait to catch the largest Trout and Salmon. Once the fish are caught, they are buried at the bases of the guardian trees. This cycle allows the trees to

HALLOWEEN BEDTIME STORIES

live for hundreds of thousands of years. It gives them the knowledge and wisdom required to protect some of the last wild places on earth.

The last thing they had told her was that she was going to go back, and that she would always love the forest. They told her that sometimes human families had such strong emotional ties that it was easy for the forest dwellers to get confused. Becky did not know what they had meant.

"I still don't know what they meant," she said defiantly.

"Well, little one, you have most of it now. I don't think it will hurt for me to tell you some of the rest. Have you ever wondered how you and your family caught so many fish when no one else was doing very well? Remember your dad telling you there was a secret that you would know the answer to someday?

Caretakers are selected pretty much the same as the young boys are except that they have no misplacement at birth. They are humans and destined to be humans. They are selected to live unusually long lives, and they are given vital information about how to help save the forests.

I was selected as an older man and am ready to soon move on. I am your great uncle Boyd, and, over there, the quiet one, that is another great uncle Roy. Next time this happens, your dad will be up here doing the work. Now you know the whole story.

One last thing…the nice buck you saw walk between us the other day, let me introduce him to you. I want you to understand that life goes on, and there is nothing to fear.

TALL TREES

Joey, come on out and say hello. A magnificent buck walked out of the edge of the forest.

It looked at Becky and spoke, "Let them know I'm OK."

It turned and ran back into the woods where a few other deer waited. Becky could hear the sound of children laughing as the darkness closed in.

The taller old man came up to the two and said, "Hey, Boyd, we better get these fish taken care of."

"Yeah, Roy, we better get at it. Don't forget us, and don't forget to clean your fish where and how your dad told you."

Becky was shaken and almost in shock as she walked back over to the camp area.

Alice waited and said, "Well, are you going to stay one more day, or are you going to quit too"?

"Oh, I think I'll spend one more day in the forest."

"What did the two old guys say"?

"They said that the fishing is great, and that we should enjoy our time in the forest."

"Why are they fishing and not helping with the search"?

"They say they are just keeping everyone mindful of the good things that happen in the forest. They are sorry Joey is gone, but they know that if he were here, he would be right down at the lake with them. Besides, with the way that kid loved the forest, he will never be gone as long as the forest is here."

"Anything else"?

"Yeah, they told me how to catch fish the way they do."

127

HALLOWEEN BEDTIME STORIES

"Really"?

"Yeah, but I can't tell you. It's a secret, and you will have to ask them yourself."

Alice stood up to walk over to the lake where the men were just in time to see them disappearing into the forest.

"I'll ask them tomorrow," she said.

"Yeah, tomorrow," Becky said absentmindedly. "Then I think I'll call my dad and see if he wants to go fishing."

The search went on at a much lesser pace until winter snows blocked the entrance to the forest area. Of course, Joey was never found. But sometimes in the dusk of a quiet mountain lake, you can hear kids playing off in the distance. You can't quite make out the names, but, be assured, they are all there just as they should have been all along.

FLIGHT

Sometimes you don't understand what it is that draws you to a place. MUGSY'S BAR in New York City is such a place. It is one of those places where everyone seems to understand why you are there except you.

Jim had nearly finished his last cup of thick, cold coffee and looked at the clock. It was six-thirty, and he was alone in the office. He had not looked up since just after lunch, when the afternoon mail drop was placed on his credenza. He took a deep breath and thought about having a quick drink. He was finally able to start putting his tough day behind him.

He had worked at engineering a new fiber optic link that would tie several buildings together from Wall Street to the Park area, then back to the main office. He had struggled with the mechanics of leaving room for future expansion and access that would become world-wide. This job was his first global fiber optic project. He really enjoyed the challenge of figuring how many conversations could be placed simultaneously on a single fiber (A piece of glass slightly smaller than a small fishing line, or about the size of a strand of human hair). He had been so engrossed in his numbers and layouts, he had worked past normal quitting time.

He called Cindy and told her he was pushing to finish the project and would be late coming home. He looked at her picture which was taken just a few weeks earlier at a 4th of July picnic with Tommy and Lindsey. For the first time that day, he felt like a person and not

HALLOWEEN BEDTIME STORIES

just an engineer. Cindy's smiling face was beautiful, the blonde hair and blue eyes, the look full of promise and life. He could see Cindy in both kids; although, he had to admit, Tommy looked more like him with the dark hair and green eyes. He realized that this was the first thing he had noticed all day that was not part of his job.

He had worked so long, that he was like a man in a trance. He did not notice the feel of the humid air from the bay, carrying the coolness of the water, as he came out of the building and crossed the street. He was walking along a familiar route, which took him past one of his favorite men's clothing displays in the city. He did not even look up at the new fall offerings. In fact, he did not notice much of anything until he walked up to the front of the large window with the door just off to the left. He looked at the sign over the door, and, for the very first time, noticed that the place was established just two years earlier. Funny, he thought, it had the appearance of a place that had been there forever. He stepped to the window and looked in. He then reached in his pocket to be sure he had one more cigarette.

Through the lettering that proclaimed MUGSY'S, he saw Charles standing and gesturing to another patron. He thought, "There goes Charles telling another story and doing all the hand motions to help make his point." Charles was truly one of the people that Jim knew who couldn't talk if he couldn't use his hands. In fact, Charles usually used his entire body to make points and express the emotions contained in his colorful, explicit stories.

Jim shook his head gently as if clearing cobwebs. He thought about how much he was looking forward to

FLIGHT

his two drinks and his last of three daily cigarettes that he allowed himself to enjoy. He paused on the step and took a deep breath. He thought briefly about Cindy and the kids, and decided he needed this daily ritual especially today. He promised himself that he would not linger at the bar; just have a couple of pops, a smoke and head for the subway.

He received the usual greeting from several other regulars as he walked in the door. "Hey, Jim how is it goin?"

"Hey, Jimmy, how 'bout the Yanks?"

"Jimmmmmyyy." He smiled and nodded to everyone. He waved across the bar to Charles without speaking because Charles was in the middle of telling his story.

Gibson, the old bar tender, walked toward Jim and smiled. He said, "You want your usual, Mr. Donnegan?"

"Yes, Gibson, thank you." Gibson set the scotch near Jim's right hand, smiled and walked back toward Charles, who was getting loud and very demonstrative. Gibson obviously wanted to hear the end of the story Charles was telling. Jim lit his third and last cigarette of the day. He took a sip of scotch and waited for the laughter and exclamations, which came almost immediately. He then drank the remainder of the shot and signaled Gibson for his second drink. Gibson came over, still smiling broadly from the effects of Charles story.

He said, "That Charles ought to be in comedy! He is pretty good at it. You would never know he had a care in the world the way he goes on. You would never

131

HALLOWEEN BEDTIME STORIES

suspect that he actually spent time... he trailed off and looked furtively at Jim.

"What?" asked Jim. "Actually spent time what?"

"Oh, sorry Mr. Donnegan. I was just rambling. You know, running off at the head, like sometimes when you talk to yourself. I don't think Mr. Evers, that is Charles, would appreciate me saying everything I know. Besides everyone in here has some story they would just as soon the world did not know."

"Now you have got me curious, Gibson. What is it that Charles spent time doing that is such a secret?"

"Well, Mr. Donnegan if you promise not to say anything else about it, I will tell you what happened to Charles. Remember that every person in this place has at least one such story that I know, except maybe you, Mr. Donnegan. You see, Mr. Donnegan, Charles had an accident years ago. He was driving himself home after a few drinks right here in the bar. He did not notice two boys in the crosswalk as he approached an intersection about two blocks from his house. Well, the long and short, Mr. Donnegan, is that Charles hit those boys. One of them died, and the other is damaged for life. Charles had to spend almost a year in county for reckless driving and driving intoxicated. He has never talked about it. He would not even talk at the trial except to answer questions. You would almost never know anything happened the way he came back to being himself. But he carries a sad secret with him, Mr. Donnegan, and every once in a while, he says a word or two about that little boy to close friends or bartenders. So anyway, Mr. Donnegan, that is the story about Mr. Evers, and I would

FLIGHT

appreciate it if you would kindly forget that you know it now."

"Yeah, sure Gibson," Jim responded absentmindedly. "I am sorry for Charles to have to live with that image." The ring of his cell phone interrupted his thought. He glanced at the back of the phone remembering he had worked late and was ready to apologize to Cindy for not coming straight home, but the number being displayed was not home or her phone. It simply read RESTRICTED.

He answered and heard a feminine voice say, "Jim" ...then nothing.

Hmmm, he mused. Then, quickly finishing his second drink, he swung off the soft bar chair and stood up. He handed Gibson a ten and said, "Keep the change Gibson and thanks." Gibson smiled. Jim walked quickly to the door and angled toward the subway.

He was home in about twenty minutes. He loved his street near the Park area in Brooklyn, the huge trees that lined the sidewalks, and the brick row houses with steps down to the street. It was the neatness of the brick homes and the sanctuary provided by the trees that made Jim feel comfortable enough to tolerate the city at least for long enough to finish this project and move his family back to the wide open spaces of western Missouri. It made him a little nostalgic to think of western Missouri. He always thought of the way the lightening bugs would blink right after dark and how the soft yellow glow points would create hundreds of little yellow splotches of light. He missed the open fields and small towns. He missed something else that he could not

133

HALLOWEEN BEDTIME STORIES

put to words. But he was here now and needed to finish this project.

He and Cindy wanted to come to New York to experience the city. They wanted to see some plays and take subways to various points in the city. They wanted to walk down through the theatre district at dusk and watch the lights come on. And now, after nearly two years in Brooklyn, and facing the fact that little Tommy was going to start school next year, he was ready to finish the job and get back to Missouri. He wanted his kids to have the experience of growing up in one town and going through school with the same group of kids from beginning through high school graduation. He felt that the experience of coming to New York was a good one, and that he and Cindy had grown up during the past two years. He had started feeling comfortable with his job and confident that he could now take the latest technical knowledge with him wherever he worked. Yeah, he thought, New York was a good job and we got to see it all. Now, let's get the hell back to Missouri!

He walked up to the door, and, as he reached for the knob, he heard Tommy yelling, "Mommy, Daddy is home". He could hear Tommy's footsteps running to greet him. He opened the door and saw Tommy running full steam toward him. He stooped and picked Tommy up and held him over his head. "Hi champ. How are you doing today?"

"Great, Daddy! Mommy took us up to the park today. We played and got a milk shake from Mr. Smoothie. And, we are having hamburgers for dinner Daddy. Can we play for a few minutes before dinner?"

134

FLIGHT

"Sure Champ," Jim said, "what do you want to play today?"

"I want to go hide, and you see if you can find me. Oh, and Daddy, Lindsey is already hiding so find her too OK?"

"OK, Champ, I will close my eyes and you can go hide." Jim closed his eyes and only opened them when he felt the kiss on the cheek Cindy gave him.

"Hi honey, long day?" she whispered.

"Yeah," Jim said, "but once I get to the front porch, it's worth it." He called Tommy and said, "Here I come to find you".

He had only taken one step when the phone on his belt rang again. He looked at Cindy, then at the back of the phone. RESTRICTED it said. He pushed the talk button, and once again heard a female voice say, "Jim?"

"Yes," he said.

Then he heard the voice say, "I need to talk…..then nothing. The phone blinked off and was dark. He pushed the storage to see where the call came from and saw RESTRICTED.

He looked at Cindy and said, "I don't know who is trying to call me, but that is at least two times today that I tried to answer my phone and some woman gets out a couple of words then the call drops. I guess it is some person trying to call on a cell phone where the signal is poor. He then said loudly, "Now, where is Tommy and where is Lindsey? I haven't seen Lindsey all day. Where can she be?"

He heard the soft, high laughter coming from the clothes hamper (her favorite hiding place). He said loudly again, "Well, I guess I can't find them, so I better

135

HALLOWEEN BEDTIME STORIES

just put my coat in the closet." He opened the closet and pretended to not notice the legs under Cindy's raincoat. He reached for a hangar, and with a burst of noise and yelling, Tommy came out of hiding. Lindsey, hearing the commotion, climbed out of the clothes hamper and ran toward Tommy and Jim, yelling, "Daddy couldn't find me".

They all laughed and played on the floor for a few minutes until Cindy walked in and asked, "Who is hungry?"

"We are," they all answered on cue. They ate and visited and talked about each other's activities for the day.

The extra time spent on the job caused the evening to be shorter than normal. It seemed that story time for the kids came early. It had become the custom in the Donnegan house to have a story for the kids before they went to bed. Cindy had insisted upon it. Her reason was that sometimes the kids would watch a television show with violence or a negative plot. She wanted to insure that the last thing they heard before they went to bed was a positive story with a happy ending. Jim pointed the remote at the television and switched to ESPN news to get the latest update on the baseball scores. By the time he got caught up with the sporting world and switched the channel to scan for movie choices, Cindy returned dressed for bed. He thought it seemed early, but a glance at the time on the television told him it just seemed that way because he had worked late. He patted the couch beside himself, and Cindy sat next to him. He put his arm around her neck, and told her that he had only about one month left

FLIGHT

to finish the project he was on and would be eligible to return to the firm's home office in north Kansas City.

Her smile was instant and genuine. "Good," she said, "let's focus on getting ready to move and finding a place in a small suburb or town like Smithfield within easy driving distance to the city. Jim, I am so happy to know we are going back home. I know this job has meant a lot for your career, but I am really ready for a dose of Midwest hospitality."

"Well, it will be about five weeks until we actually go, but I can give you some Midwest hospitality right here in Brooklyn tonight if you play your cards right," he said.

She looked at him and said, "Well, are you going to talk about it, or are you going to do it?" He reached for her and kissed her fully and long. He reached inside her dressing gown and stroked her inner thigh.

She pressed against him and said, "Let's go to bed.....now." He pushed the remote, tossed it onto the chair, and walked with her to the bedroom.

Six-thirty came early the next day. Jim fought waking up by rolling over and trying to go back to sleep, but Cindy said, "Remember, only five more weeks to go". He woke up, made his way to the coffee maker and poured a cup of coffee. Cindy was right behind him and smiled at him saying, "Good morning honey. I am so excited to start preparing to move home, I woke instantly this morning without even having coffee. I guess I am ready to leave New York and go live a boring, happy life in Missouri."

"Me too," Jim said. "I only have one or two more tough days on the project; then, the rest is drafting

HALLOWEEN BEDTIME STORIES

and presentation. A few minor changes always come at the end. Then I can hand it off to the construction engineer, and I go back to the home office. We go back to open spaces, wild animals, clean air, drinkable water and people that smile and say good morning when you walk past them on your way to work. Back to"…..

He trailed off because a negative thought had crossed through his mind. He did not know what it was, but something troubling about returning to Missouri. Not really Missouri, but a place nearby…a place where he had grown up. Troubling, and he could not put his finger on the feeling.

Cindy saw the darkness pass across his face and asked, "What is wrong Jim?"

He glanced at her. "Oh, nothing really," he said, "every once in a while I get a strange misgiving about going back home. Don't even know why." He shrugged and finished his coffee. "Well, I have to be at my desk in about an hour, so I better get to the subway. I sure look forward to driving a car to work again and being on my own schedule instead of the schedule designed for an entire city of over nine million people."

He walked up the stairs and quickly changed clothes. He picked up his briefcase, then looked in on the kids, still asleep. He kissed Cindy on the lips, and walked toward the door. His cell phone rang again. He looked at the screen and saw RESTRICTED. "Look, Cindy, another one of those calls."

He flipped the phone open, said hello and heard a feminine voice through lots of static saying, "Jim? Jim? Is this Jim?"

"Yes," he said, "this is Jim. Who is calling?"

FLIGHT

"This is"...then static.

Once again the screen flashed RESTRICTED. Jim looked at Cindy. "Seems someone wants to talk to me, but I didn't recognize the voice. If some girl calls here, see if you can find out what she wants and call me.

Cindy looked right into Jim's eyes and asked, "You don't have a girlfriend do you, Jim?"

"No honey," he said, "If I had a girlfriend, I would not give her my work cell phone number. Only you and people I work with get that. But, believe me, I don't want any other woman in my life in a romantic way. You are the woman I need and, besides, I am in love with you. See you later sweetie. I have to run."

He made the subway and got to work. The day passed uneventfully for the first two hours. Then, his cell phone rang and the RESTRICTED appeared on the screen. This time the voice asked if it was Jim again, and when he said yes, she asked if it was Jim Donnegan. Again, he said yes, and the voice said "I have been trying to talk to you for a long time. I wonder if you even remember me."

Then the connection was dropped and static and the RESTRICTED flashed. He was starting to get very curious and started to think about any women he knew from work or socially. Maybe he did not know them too well, because she had said she wondered if he would even remember her. He was mystified. He could not think of anyone who even sounded like this girl. At least she sounded like a girl. She did not have the depth and fullness of a mature woman speaking. More breathy and staccato, like a high school girl.

139

HALLOWEEN BEDTIME STORIES

He was starting to be distracted from his work. He took a brief break and grabbed a can of juice and a cookie. He walked back to his desk and got back into the project. He began to realize that he was gaining more on the project than he had realized. A couple more days and he could start the approval and funding phase. He would spend about a week less in New York than he thought. He stopped only briefly for lunch and was on his way to the deli across the street from his office when his phone rang again. He glanced down and saw the RESTRICTED. He got angry, but controlled his temper and answered. "Hello, this is Jim Donnegan. Who is calling?"

The voice was clear. "Jim, I am glad that I got you. I have been thinking about you a lot lately, and I need to talk to you." It was the same young girl voice, but this time it was confident. She said, "I still bet you don't remember me, do you?"

Jim answered that he did not.

She said, "Well, I am calling to talk about our time together, and although you might not remember, I sure do. I am going to be in town, and I want to talk to you in person alone. I know you will remember me when you see me."

Jim said, "Look ...... I don't know who you are, and I am not interested in meeting with you. I am married and have two kids and a job that keeps me busier that anyone should have to be. I am sorry to seem offensive, but I honestly do not know who you are or what you want. If you can't tell me more about yourself, I am going to ask you to stop calling me." Static and then RESTRICTED. Jim was frustrated. Who could this

140

FLIGHT

be? He started to think about young people he had met recently and, other than a couple of baby sitters from the neighborhood in Brooklyn, he had no young girl acquaintances. This girl did not have a Brooklyn accent, and he had not known any young girls since he was a boy himself.

He selected an egg, cheese and tomato sandwich and a ginger ale. He sat at the table near the door of the deli. He watched people walking up and down the street in front of his office and thought about how much he longed for a place where he could have some space to himself. He wanted to be in a place like western Missouri. He needed a place similar to the part of Iowa he grew up in. He wanted to be in a small town or a suburb, where you could see the sky, trees and the horizon. A negative thought about small towns or something in his past floated through his mind, something that cast a shadow on his dreams of wide open spaces. A thought that was creeping into his consciousness but not fully developed. He was not a man given to paranoia. He was not usually one to fear any unknown. But this was something known. This was a memory that was just out of reach, just beyond the conscious mind.

He didn't know how long he sat thinking, but he was late when he got back to his office. Janet, his personal drafting clerk, was waiting with some technical questions. Janet was a small, intelligent girl with a nice manner. She was great to work with. She was living with her boyfriend and had become good friends with Cindy on the few occasions when the two had been together. Janet got her questions answered, and Jim got

HALLOWEEN BEDTIME STORIES

busy with his work. The rest of the day flew by, and he found himself well ahead of schedule again at the end of the day.

Completion of the job ahead of schedule was now a certainty. He felt good and was in a lighthearted mood when he walked into MUGSY'S BAR. He waived at Charles who was telling another story and caught Gibson's eye long enough insure that a scotch was on the way. He took his first sip of scotch and looked around the bar. He noticed Sue sitting alone at the corner chair and observed that she looked upset. When Gibson brought the ashtray over, Jim stopped him and asked, "What is wrong with Sue"?

Gibson looked at Jim and said, "It's like I told you, Mr. Donnegan, all the folks that come in here got some, shall we say, issues? They got some bad stuff that they done, and sometimes it comes back on them, that's all. I don't know what brought you into this bar, Mr. Donnegan, but my guess is that you may have one of them stories too that you ain't so proud of." Gibson dropped his voice to a whisper and glanced over his shoulder, "Sue there was married to a guy named Bob, and she caught him having an affair with a woman that lived in their building. I mean she caught them in the act. She went wild and crazy, Mr. Donnegan, and she got into the kitchen, grabbed a knife and stabbed her husband and cut that other woman up so she wouldn't be attractive to no man ever again. Sue was eventually let go because they said she was temporarily insane. Today is the fifth anniversary of that day, and Sue is having some bad memories. They, that is, the patrons here, tell me that anniversary days are the worst. They actually

142

FLIGHT

have visits from the people they have killed or wronged. Now, I never see them, but they say they do. Yeah, Mr. Donnegan, Sue is having her tough day today, and tomorrow it will be somebody else. It is always someone who is reliving the awful thing they have done, and the others, they just hang around here because they know they all got problems and they sort of understand each other. I wonder, Mr. Donnegan, what it is that you have done. I wonder when your anniversary will be and who you will have visiting you."

"Don't be silly, Gibson. I don't have any secrets or any bad stuff in my background. I just work across the street, the bar is convenient, and I like the people who come in here. For the most part, they are a fun group. I sure never knew about any of their past until yesterday. I don't know what they have all done, and, honestly, I don't care because, Gibson, in less than one month, I am done with my project. I'll be going back to the home office in Kansas City. One more scotch, Gibson, and I am off to catch the train to Brooklyn."

Jim finished his cigarette and second scotch about the same time and headed out into the late afternoon sun. He glanced back at the bar and noticed that Sue was now talking with Charley. Next to her was a horribly disfigured person, and sitting on the other side of her, a sad looking man. "Funny, he had not noticed them while he was inside," he thought.

He pushed through the crowd wondering if he could do anything to speed up the job and leave New York faster. His next phone call came just before he reached the corner of his street in Brooklyn. This time the voice was a little sad but a lot more insistent. She

HALLOWEEN BEDTIME STORIES

went through the 'you don't remember me'. Then she said something that caused Jim to remember something.

She said, "If you don't even remember me, how many were there? How many times did you force someone to lie down while you"....... Static and RESTRICTED.

But this time Jim remembered something negative and terrible. He had thoughts of walking into a house somewhere. A house that was nearly empty except for an old sofa, a cheap dinette set and some cleaning materials. A house he could not fully remember, and there was someone else in that house. There was a girl there. She was a pretty girl with dark hair and a sad look in her eyes. But who is she, and where is this place? His hand was turning the doorknob, and Tommy was jumping into his arms before the thought left his mind.

Jim was scared. He did not know why really, but he was feeling like he was remembering something that was destined to frighten him. He did not know if it was real or something from some old creepy movie, but he knew that he would find out soon. He decided to turn off the cell phone and try to relax and gather his thoughts and his memory. He absentmindedly played with the kids, and after they were in bed, he confided to Cindy that something strange was going on and that it was causing him to doubt himself. He explained about the phone calls and told Cindy about Gibson's strange story. She said that as far as she knew he was as normal as apple pie, and that since she had met him in college, she could not think of a man as solid and trustworthy as him. She said that, honestly, many of her friends had

FLIGHT

cautioned her that this guy seemed so normal and laid back that he would likely not be a very exciting or romantic partner. Of course, they could not know Jim the way she did. While he was a quiet unassuming man who could be borderline dull, he had a passionate side that was like something out of this world. All in all, she could not think of anything in his past that was even borderline bad.

"I wonder why, then, that Gibson said that everyone there had a bad thing they had done in their past, and he expected to soon hear what bad thing I had done. And why was I seeing that house all empty except for a couple of pieces of old furniture and that girl. What does that girl have to do with all this, Jim thought out loud?"

"Maybe she is the one calling. Maybe you have to meet up with her like she suggested and find out what this is all about. As long as it doesn't interfere with your job, you may as well meet her and find out what she wants, said Cindy."

Jim looked at Cindy, "And you would be OK with me meeting another woman to talk about something in my past?"

"Sure," she said, "I trust you, Jim. You have earned that. I just want you to solve the problem so you can focus on the job and get us back to Missouri."

Cindy walked into the kitchen still talking, "My folks were real excited about it when I told them today, and the kids don't remember living in Kansas City. They remember Grandma and Grandpa, and they are excited too. So, go on honey, and get this behind us. Besides,

145

HALLOWEEN BEDTIME STORIES

now I am curious about this mystery lady. Maybe she was your first love."

Jim sat bolt upright. He looked at Cindy and said loudly, "I told you one time a long time ago there was no one before you."

Cindy looked back and smiled and said, "OK, but I just thought you were being a gentleman. I just assumed that we would not talk about our experience, and we never have."

"Experience!" Jim exclaimed. "Look, I don't like talking about this stuff, it always makes me feel like I was some kind of inexperienced geek, and you were the love interest of most of the boys in your school."

Cindy held up one hand and looked at Jim. She was hurt. "Jim, we agreed a long time ago not to talk about this stuff, and I am sorry that the phone calls are happening to you. I do want you to figure out what it is about, and as long as it does not affect us, we will put it behind us. Please don't hold things against me that happened when I was an immature teenager. We have too much going for us to do that."

Jim felt himself calming down. Cindy was right, he thought. It would be best to get this "mystery" solved. It would be best to finish this project and get on with the rest of our lives where we want to be.

That had been on Friday. The weekend passed without any calls, and he was beginning to believe he had imagined it all. He spent most of Sunday packing things he was sure he would not use for the next month and planning the early stages of their move back home. He was tired and had spent most of Sunday evening napping and watching some mindless sitcom on the

146

FLIGHT

television. He went to bed and slept a restless sleep, punctuated by dreams of the dingy, nearly empty house and the girl. He wanted that girl. He did not know why or hadn't even looked at her closely, but he woke up with an erection, and he knew that he wanted her. He had been awakened by the sound of the phone ringing again, but he had turned it off. It was ringing, and in the glow of the screen on the phone he read RESTRICTED. He looked at the phone and pushed the power button. The phone came to life and the icons lighted. It was still ringing RESTRICTED. He turned it off again and yet it rang. RESTRICTED.

"Hello," he said, forgetting that he had not turned the phone back on.

"It doesn't need to be on," he heard the feminine voice saying. "You remembered me, didn't you"?

Jim thought then said, "No, I did not remember you".

"You wanted me, I saw it."

Now he was afraid, "Look, I don't know who the hell you are or what you want, but I want you to stop bothering me."

"I can't do that," she said. "I have to see you. I have to meet you, and we need to talk about what you did to me and why you did it. I can't stop calling until you talk to me. You have to realize what you did and what it caused and, Jim, you have to pay."

"Money! Is that it; you want me to pay you money"?

"No, Jim. I want you to introduce me to your friends at the bar where Gibson works, and I want them to know our secret."

147

HALLOWEEN BEDTIME STORIES

"But I don't know myself. I don't remember."
"You will remember. I will make you remember
because I have to. I will call you again. I will tell you
what you did if you don't remember by then and before
tomorrow night, because tomorrow night, you see, is the
last night before the day of our anniversary. Think about
it, Jim, twenty years ago. Remember, you wanted me.
Bye." RESTRICTED.

Then he heard nothing but silence. He looked
and the phone was still turned off. He began to feel
frantic. He had to remember. He was trying to
remember.

He could only think of the house. There was
the sofa, the dinette, the cleaning materials and Linda.
Linda, that was her name....but Linda who, and what
was the connection? He quickly explained the call to
Cindy. He told her of the dim memory of some place
that seemed negative and even sinister. He told her that
he remembered a girl named Linda, but he could not
remember why. Cindy was full of questions and was
worried. She had wanted to talk more, but she knew Jim
was running late. He kissed her quickly, agreeing to talk
more after work then went off to catch the subway. He
was able to focus amazingly that morning and got the job
all the way to the final stages of completion. He had
completed two weeks work in one morning. His mind
was working as fast as he could write. Hell, it was even
faster than that. He had to speak into a recorder to keep
up with the speed of his thoughts. He had always had
periods of time when his mind worked very quickly, and
he was almost on auto–pilot. He would quickly go
through these times barely remembering. It was as

148

FLIGHT

though he became a passenger in his own body. It was like the first time it ever happened to him. It was a time that he had not remembered. A time he had been counseled to forget. A time that had been put so far out of his conscious mind that he almost thought it had not happened. He called Janet into his office. He explained that he had finished the job entirely and had made the necessary notes and recordings to allow her to draft the final. He told her he had some personal business to take care of, grabbed his cell phone and walked out of the office.

He walked until he came close to the Battery Park entry. He spotted a quiet bench and sat down. He thought about the first time his mind had raced uncontrollably. He suddenly knew who Linda was, and remembered why he had to talk to her. He gazed into the water and remembered……..listening to the boys on the football team laughing and talking about Linda.

One particularly homely, tall boy with thick horn-rimmed glasses said, "Man, that Linda, I did not know what she was like when she was drunk, but for her to just take off all of her clothes in a car full of boys!"

Another much more handsome boy named Robert spoke, "She was just trying to fit in by drinking, and I don't think she ever drank anything before that. She was just out of it. Besides, she didn't take everything off. She still had on her panties."

"Yeah, but she took off those clothes then left them off for the next half hour. I thought we were all going to get some, but then she started to get upset and wanted us to take her home."

149

HALLOWEEN BEDTIME STORIES

"Just real drunk, I would say," a guy named Dave was saying.

"I think Linda was scared and embarrassed herself nearly to death. She would not even speak to me the next day at practice."

"Well, she sure has a great body, and the whole car full of us can swear to that."

Jim had not moved while the boys were talking. He just sat quietly and listened intently. He knew Linda, and he could just imagine her nearly naked in a car full of boys. He had not thought of her as that kind of girl, but the thought of it made him excited. He put his books in his duffel bag and walked almost half way home before he realized where he was. The story of Linda was running through his mind. He knew Linda Halladay well, and he thought she was nice. She was not his type. They had never dated or shown much interest in each other, but this new information made him nearly obsessive in his thoughts of her. He had heard of girls doing this kind of stuff in other places, but never anyone here, never anyone that he knew. He began to think of her in the car surrounded by boys, imagining her taking off her clothes. Only in his thoughts, it did not stop with taking off the clothes. He imagined every boy in the car having his way with her. He thought about her for days.

One scrimmage day when he was on his way to another part of town to pick up a book from a classmate, he saw Linda going into a small house. She was alone and dressed in denim jeans. She wore a flannel shirt with worn tennis shoes and an old hat. She looked like a young, well-built, pretty, cleaning lady.

150

FLIGHT

He waved and said, "Hi, Linda. What are you doing here?"

Linda explained that the house was a rental owned by her father. It was her job to clean it between occupants.

"I know that I look like some kind of scrub woman in this get up, but I did not expect to run into any friends in this neighborhood. What are you doing over here anyway, Jim?"

Jim explained that he was away at a football scrimmage, and that Billy Johnson had agreed to bring his physics book along home so Jim could pick it up when the team got back into town.

Linda smiled and said, "Well, I better get busy. This place is rented for tomorrow, and it won't clean itself. See ya, Jim."

She went inside. Jim walked on over to the Johnsons' house and got his book. As he walked back past the rental house, he saw Linda through the window. She was moving like she was sweeping the floor. He suddenly remembered the story the boys were telling. He walked up to the door and knocked. Linda answered. He walked in and told her about what he had heard. He could see that she was embarrassed, but he didn't care. He wanted her. The rest was the first one of the times when his mind was on auto-pilot. He did not realize or think about what had happened until he was almost home. Then he remembered what he had done. He remembered how she begged him to not hurt her, to not do this to her. He remembered her tears and her pain. He remembered everything. He remembered that she had been so ashamed, she had not come back to school.

HALLOWEEN BEDTIME STORIES

He had never heard a word about any of it. She must have decided to not tell.

He developed nightmares and nervous ticks that people wrote off to teenage hormones until he was met and treated by Victor Samson, a physician who treated mental disorders. Dr. Samson had talked with Jim until the secret of Linda was revealed. Jim continued treatment until he had put the episode completely behind him, and, only now, sitting in the Battery Park, staring at the bay and watching sea gulls swoop around a man standing at the sea wall, did he remember her and the way he had hurt her and violated her.

The phone rang RESTRICTED.

"You remembered me, didn't you? I saw it in your eyes."

Jim looked around himself and realized no one was within thirty feet. "How did you see anything in my eyes?"

"I will explain that tomorrow, Jimmy. But for now, we have a date. You need to meet me at MUGSY'S BAR, and we need to tell Gibson why you are one of the regulars. Don't worry, Gibson is not judgmental, and he does not care what one has done. He just provides a place for gatherings. Sort of helps people remember. You go on back to your office now, and when it is your regular time for your scotch and your third daily cigarette, I will be waiting on the corner bar chair for you. See you then, Jimmy." RESTRICTED.

Jim wanted to call Cindy and tell her what had happened and tell her that he needed her help. He wanted to tell her everything, but he could not. He believed that if he tried to explain this to Cindy, his

FLIGHT

marriage and his life would be over. What could Linda want? It had been a long time ago, and he had completely lost touch with the entire town of Haybrook. He had lost track of all the positives and negatives of his life up to the point of meeting Doctor Samson. He knew that he had to go and meet Linda and take whatever life had in store for him, because now he remembered. He knew that whatever Linda wanted, he had it coming, and he knew that it would not be easy. He was truly a changed man, and, because he was, he understood the depth of his crime and that he must pay for it in some way.

It was with great apprehension that he walked into MUGSY'S and caught Gibson's eye. Gibson sat the scotch at his right hand and reached for an ashtray.

He pushed the ashtray to the corner chair and said, "She said you would be sitting next to her."

Jim looked and, as if from nowhere, there was Linda Halladay sitting on the chair. She was easy to recognize because she had not aged a day in the twenty years. He was starting to show some gray hair and a few crows' feet around the eyes, but she looked as if she was still seventeen. He lit his cigarette and took a drink of his scotch.

Linda spoke, "Such discipline, and especially from you, is a real surprise. I watched you smoke your three cigarettes a day, your two scotches a day. The way you are always at home on time. I see the loyalty, the sheer discipline and control which you practice. I sure am surprised after the way you treated me. You could not control yourself at all when it came to me, Jimmy. You could not even face me to see if I was OK when you

153

HALLOWEEN BEDTIME STORIES

were through with me. You didn't even check to see if I was still alive when I did not show up for school. You denied me all of your life.

Why, only a couple of days ago, you said to Gibson that you only chose this place because it was across the street from where you worked. Well, Jimmy, let me tell you how this works and how it is. You see, this place is here because of you and because your office is just across the street. I am here because you are here. I had to come and fill in the part of your memory that is missing.

You have noticed that I look young, and you have noticed that Gibson and the patrons here are ………well….. strange. I came to help you solve the problem with your memory. I came to fill in some of the missing facts that you never knew. Yes, Jimmy, this is all about you facing up to and paying for what you did to me.

It was shortly after you left the house that night when you raped me. I was very emotional. I was confused about why those boys told you about the night in the car. I was confused about why I had done such a thing, and I decided that maybe what you did to me was my punishment for being the way I was. I decided that maybe I deserved it. I got myself cleaned up and went home. My mom knew immediately that something was wrong because I had failed to button my clothes correctly.

She pressed me until I told her what happened. She told my dad. As we all talked about it, it came out that you had been the one who raped me. Of course the story about my drinking and undressing in the car came

154

FLIGHT

out too. My dad said that with the story about my undressing in a car full of boys being common knowledge, there was no use in claiming I had been raped. He said that most any judge would say I was asking for it and enticed you. In short, my parents were mortified. They decided that I should not return to school but should go and live with my aunt in New Harmony. I was placed on the bus the next day. My parents followed within the month."

"My dad got a new job, and my mom was trying to adjust to the new place. I became listless and did not adjust well to the new place. My parents were always fighting over money, the new job and the new house. They started to blame me, and I just realized one day, about three months after our time together, that I could go no further. I took my own life." She looked longingly at Jim and said in a louder voice, "Did you hear all that, Gibson?"

"Yeah, Linda, I did. Now I know why Mr. Donnegan is one of our regulars. Like I said, everyone here has some bad thing that they have done, and here is where they come to forget it and to remember it." Gibson looked at Jim and shoved his second scotch toward his right hand. "Mystery solved," he laughed.

Linda was looking sad now, and she seemed to be hanging her head. She said, "Now, Jimmy, is the hard part. You have to meet me for coffee tomorrow morning. You can tell your wife or you can choose not to. It won't matter because tomorrow you will find out how you will pay for our time together and what you did to me. I suggest that you enjoy your time at home with your family. Wake up at your normal time and, instead

155

HALLOWEEN BEDTIME STORIES

of going down stairs to your office, meet me on the ninety-ninth floor coffee shop. That will be the last time I bother you. I promise. Gibson, would you please hand Mr. Donnegan back his real cell phone. There will be no more calls."

Gibson reached under the bar and withdrew a cell phone. He took the one sitting in front of Jim and placed it under the bar. He then looked at Jim and shrugged, "I had to help her. I know you don't fully understand today, but by tomorrow, you will know why you all come in here. It is my job to provide a place for the gathering. That is all I do. No hard feelings Mr. Donnegan."

Jim was in a stupor. He felt disoriented, like he had entered a dream world. He nodded to Linda and mumbled that he was sorry for what had happened. He looked toward Gibson who was now busy with a new face at the bar. Some Middle Eastern type he called Atta. He felt confused. Was Linda real? Was any of this real? How could he talk to Cindy? How could he have done such a thing, then put it out of his mind? Why was it all happening now? He had suddenly become a downtrodden soul, a man with more questions than answers.

He walked into the early evening street. He headed for the train as usual, but this time he did not look back and give his usual wave. He did not notice that the window proclaiming MUGSY'S faded into a blank concrete wall as he headed for the subway. He drifted through the evening as though in a trance. He felt like he should talk to Cindy. He decided that he would tell her, but he would wait until he knew for sure what

156

FLIGHT

Linda wanted. She had promised that he would know tomorrow. He would find out what she wanted, and then he would tell Cindy everything. It also occurred to him that, perhaps, his mind was going. Maybe he had experienced a nervous breakdown. Maybe he was imagining the whole thing. After all, not many sane people think they have conversations with a person who claims that they have been dead nearly twenty years. But come hell or high water, he would know tomorrow. Tomorrow he would get it settled, and he would come home and ask Cindy to help him get through this nightmare. He did not sleep. He lay awake wondering if he was going insane. He even wondered if maybe it was all a dream.

The next morning he got out of bed early and dressed. He kissed Cindy and said a quick prayer over his kids. His subway ride was quick. He walked up to the front door of his office and remembered that he was supposed to meet Linda at some coffee shop on the ninety-ninth floor. He wondered if Linda had been real or if it was just a trick his guilty mind was playing on him. He remembered her all right. He remembered that he was guilty of losing control and raping her, but the part about her killing herself and then showing up, was beyond belief. He had never heard about her dying, or had he heard and forgot? Anyway, whatever was going on, he decided he needed to try to meet her, as she had demanded. Maybe then, all would be explained, and he would understand. Maybe then, he could get back to the life he loved so much with Cindy and the kids.

He got on the elevator. He stood quietly looking at the digital display as the floors flashed by. He saw the

HALLOWEEN BEDTIME STORIES

doors open on the ninety-ninth floor. He stepped into the large, open lobby area around the elevators and looked northward. Nothing much he hadn't seen before. Just some airplanes and a sunny morning. He looked up and saw Linda. She was with Gibson and several people ....no, EVERYONE from MUGSY'S!

They motioned him to come over. He walked up to where they were standing under a digital clock that kept time to the second so workers could time their coffee breaks. They were pointing toward the side of the building where a plane was flying nearby. The digital clock blinked. The sign flashed the following message:

Welcome to North Tower, Tuesday, September 11, 2001, 8:45:13 A.M. Have a Nice Day...............................Happy Halloween

A very special THANK YOU to Judi, she takes my rough story lines and turns them into readable material....B

DREAMS OF HALLOWEEN

Willie was a small blonde child. He had lots of energy and loved to use his status as the youngest child and only boy in the family to have his way. In a word, he was spoiled, and from his perspective that was just fine. He loved to run through the house pretending he was sword fighting with a dragon or shooting his toy rifle at unseen armies of enemies, his overly long, curly hair bouncing as he ran.

He was a typical boy in most ways and loved all the games and toys that went with being a boy. He was considered a little too young for formal classes, but the people in the household used every opportunity they could find to further his education. Since he was the youngest person in the home at that time, nearly everyone there taught him something important. As with many privileged children; along with being very spoiled he was very smart and mentally developed well ahead of any normal five year old.

Willie was a social child who liked to involve everyone in the adventures he was having. He would often insist that some of the household help would participate in his "wars", sometimes as fellow soldiers and sometimes as the enemy. The maids and even the kindly, old gardener usually declined to participate as an enemy because sometimes Willie pressed his attacks of enemies to the point of pain. Even the most polite friends of the family often referred to Willie as high strung, or stubborn and unruly.

Willie's father thought Willie was a lot like he had been as a boy: bright, active and full of life.

HALLOWEEN BEDTIME STORIES

Willie's mother simply thought Willie could do no wrong. Willie's grandmother was so happy with Willie that she often said he was in line to become a king.

As the summer days began to get shorter and the hot days began to yield to cooler mornings and evenings, there had been a lot of talk about Willie's birthday coming and how much fun the celebration would be. The family was inviting cousins from all over, even other countries. There were plans for a huge cake and lots of activities, especially for children. There were going to be clowns and entertainers. This birthday was going to be much better than the last year, and Willie thought last year's birthday was even more fun than Christmas. He was looking forward to a whole day where the house would be overflowing with people, and every eye and ear would be focused on him. Willie loved it when he was the center of attention. He was more excited than he had ever been, and he had spent most of his life to that point excited about something.

He was so consumed with thoughts of clowns, children his own age to play with, and being the center of attention that at first he did not pay much attention to the dreams. Besides, dreams were silly when they did not make sense. Father had said so. It was only when the dreams became frequent that Willie and his parents started to become concerned. The first time that a dream seemed to happen over and over, Willie began refusing to go to bed. When his parents asked him why, he told them about the dreams. He dreamed in great detail of one of the women who worked as a maid. The woman was one that Willie barely knew

160

DREAMS OF HALLOWEEN

because she was not a maid who worked in the house but was a maid who did laundry, cleaned cookware, cleaned chickens, and prepared meats for cooking. Although Willie did not know Hilda well, he had dreams about her every day for the last two weeks.

He would dream that Hilda was working cleaning clothes and hanging them up in the laundry area. She would reach inside of a cupboard, and a mouse would run up her arm. She would scream, jump back and bump into the pot holding the scalding hot water, and it would tip and spill onto her leg. Willie would wake up standing up in his bed holding his leg. Even though his dream would begin to be about Hilda, as it progressed he became one with Hilda and experienced the dream as though it was happening to him. Once Willie was fully awake, he would be able to go on with his day as normal but did not ever actually forget the dream.

When bedtime came, he dreaded the thought of going to sleep, knowing he would again wake up in pain. It became such a problem that Willie's mom had decided to talk to Hilda to see if she could find out why Willie was dreaming about her. Hilda was a large country girl with plain features. She was a good worker and loved having her job. She had an honest face that reflected the honesty of her life. She had acted very surprised when Willie's mother approached her and talked about Willie's dream. She shook her head up and down and smiled. She said that for some reason Willie seemed to be having the same dream that she had been having for some time.

HALLOWEEN BEDTIME STORIES

She told Willie's mom that she had always been somewhat afraid of working around the large tubs in the laundry. It was fear she was conquering, but she did often dream about something happening to cause her to injure herself. She went on to say that recently she had dreamed of a mouse causing her to become startled and to hurt herself. As the story unfolded, she explained that she had actually seen a mouse in one of the storage cupboards one day and she guessed that the incident of seeing a mouse and her fear had created a dream that was disturbing to her. She had actually bumped her leg recently against a fence post while she was carrying recently gathered eggs into the house. Her leg was still a little sore from the scrape against the post.

She figured that her dream had occurred as a combination of the pain in her leg, her fear of the hot water vats, and her run in with the little mouse. She laughed at herself and said to Willie's mom,

"Now that I have said all this out loud, I'll bet I stop having the dream." Sure enough, Willie slept in peace that very night.

Willie's mom did not sleep as well because she was wondering how Willie had been having the exact same dream as one of the maids. She developed a mistrust of Hilda thinking that something must be wrong with her because Willie was sharing her dream. She preferred to believe it was the maid's fault rather than to question whether Willie may have a problem.

It did not take long for that suspicion to subside because only a couple of nights later Willie was having another dream that was waking up the whole

162

DREAMS OF HALLOWEEN

house. This particular dream did not seem to be one that involved fear or negativity. Willie awoke laughing loudly. He would shout out with joy and jump out of bed laughing. This dream happened a second time a few nights later. When his mother asked him about what he was dreaming, Willie told them that he dreamed of Bob the old gardener when Bob was a boy. He was riding a neighbor's pony for the first time and having a wonderful time. Bob was laughing loudly as the pony broke into a trot. Willie's mom asked Willie if he felt like he was Bob in the dream, and Willie said he did not know but he did feel like he was riding the pony. In fact he wanted to go back to sleep so he could ride some more.

Willie did not know how it happened that when he was asleep he became other people. He could feel their thoughts, their surroundings, and even their beliefs. He was able to experience joy or pain as another person, and, as he awoke, he slowly became himself. He remembered how he felt in the dreams. He was confused at times because some of the feelings were very adult. The beliefs were far too developed for the mind of a five-year-old child, but Willie felt them all the same. He did not want to think about this right now. Right now he wanted back on the pony enjoying the ride.

Willie's mom walked to the garden early the next morning. Bob was busy trimming the dead tops from some flowers that had passed their peak of bloom.

"Good morning ma'am," Bob said.

163

HALLOWEEN BEDTIME STORIES

"Good Morning Robert, I have a strange request today."

"Anything I can do for you would make me happy ma'am."

"Well, Robert, Willie has started having dreams about people who work here around the home. He actually seems to dream the same dreams others are dreaming. I know it may sound strange, but recently he had dreams about you riding….."

"On a pony", Bob finished.

"Why, yes, Robert, that is exactly it."

"I don't know why, but when I have happy dreams, ma'am, it is usually about the pony that my neighbors all those years ago used to let me ride. I guess it was one of the best times of my life, and when I dream good things, the pony ride is usually included. You know, I even wake myself up laughing sometimes."

Willie's mom was now sure that in some way Willie was seeing into the dreams of others that were around him. She wondered what to do about it and decided to talk to Willie to see how often it happened and try to determine if it was going to be a real problem for him. She also spoke to her husband to see if, perhaps, a doctor should be involved. She spent much of the day thinking of Willie and how best to deal with the strange thing that was happening to him. She decided the best first step would be to talk to Willie.

It was almost Thanksgiving and she would be responsible for the feast and the guest list, which would count in the hundreds this time. Of course, then

164

DREAMS OF HALLOWEEN

Christmas would take center stage, and there was always a whirlwind of activity around Christmas with official parties as well as numerous family celebrations. She wanted to give all the time necessary to ensure that her family had a wonderful holiday season. She decided that she would watch Willie closely, learn all she could, and talk to him on January 27...the day of his fifth birthday

Thus, it was on the morning of Willie's birthday she sat with him as he ate his breakfast of fruit and raisin toast.

She started, "Willie, do you know what day this is? This is your birthday, and you are five years old. We are so proud of you and love you very much."

Willie was used to hearing this from his mother and replied with his usual, "I love you too Mommy."

She went on, "Willie, we have noticed that you seem to have lots of dreams at night, and we are worried that it will interrupt your rest, and that it may even weaken your health. Would you mind if I talk to you about some of the things you are dreaming?"

"I like the dream about the pony the most", he said.

"Do you dream you are other people often Willie?"

Willie thought, he seemed to be very quiet, and his answer very mature. "Mommy when I go to sleep at night ".....he trailed off.

He did not want to say what he was thinking because, even to Willie's young mind, it seemed strange. So he just got quiet which was extremely unusual for Willie. Even if he did not say it aloud, he

165

HALLOWEEN BEDTIME STORIES

was thinking, realizing that he was seeing the dreams of others. He could not remember if he ever had a dream of his own. He was thinking that when he went to sleep he became other people. He had always thought that everyone did this until recently when his mother had started to seem to not understand why he would awake at night.

Willie did not understand completely, but he knew for certain that he was sharing the dreams of others, the good ones which made him laugh, the bad ones that made him cry, and many that he did not understand at all, at least until he was much older. He was five years old today. He held up his hand and counted five, and he was seeing other people's dreams. He realized for the first time that seeing other people's dreams were not what everyone did when they went to sleep. He wondered why he was different in his own small child's way. First it was his arm and now something in his dreams. He seemed to perk up very quickly and said.

"Yippee, Mommy, today I get to see all my cousins and all my friends and the clowns. I am glad to be five; it will be fun." It would be years later when he would wistfully remember the time that he first realized his "gift".

The birthday was all it should have been for a very wealthy child. The guest list included important people from everywhere. Cousins came from other countries, and even a few crowned heads were present to celebrate. Willie was five and had all the promise that wealth and position can give to a person. He was destined to become a very important man. His fifth

DREAMS OF HALLOWEEN

birthday ushered him from being a baby or very small child into boyhood. It was time to recognize that Willie was going to be important to his family, his country and to the world. Next year would begin his official education, but this year he could be a boy of five.

His grandmother held him on her lap for pictures. She whispered into his ear what a wonderful boy he was, how proud she was to have him. Willie grew impatient having his picture taken with everyone and wanted to play. He had cousins here to play hide and seek and to chase around the house. Most of the cousins here lived fairly close by, but his favorite cousins were Georgie, who lived in a place far away that Willie had visited one time on a long train ride, and Nicky, who lived in another far-away place but usually came to visit on a boat. Georgie, Nicky and Willie were not only cousins, they were fast friends. They loved to play the same games and really enjoyed their times together.

The day was glorious. It was winter and the entire party, games and entertainment had to be done indoors which was no problem in a house with more than 50 rooms. Willie's mom had decided with the other parents that the children should have all the delights possible and have the run of the house to "chase off their excess energy".

"After all, they will be indoors for most of the next three months so let them enjoy this chance to run and play together."

The boys and girls had a wonderful day together. They played the organized games tentatively

167

HALLOWEEN BEDTIME STORIES

at first, and later they started having fun at it. They shrieked with laughter at the clowns who were, surprisingly to Willie's mom, very talented.

But the most fun was when Georgie, Willie, and Nicky took off running through the long hallways commanding their imaginary armies. They played for a couple of hours before their mothers called them together to say good-bye to some of the other guests who had been playing games and enjoying the clowns. Willie's birthday was coming to an end, and it was time to thank everyone for coming and bid them farewell.

Willie became sad; he did not want this day to end. He wanted to keep playing, but after a brief talk with his mother, he knew that he needed to stand by the door in a line with Mother and his other family members. Nicky and Georgie would be in the line too saying their good-byes to the guests. Mother had reminded Willie that Nicky and Georgie would be spending a couple of more nights before they returned to their far away homes, and that they could all play together tomorrow.

The servants had nearly cleared away the decorations by the time the guests were in their carriages on their way home. The tables were once again glistening, and everything in the dining hall in order. The clowns had departed before the guests had started to leave. The house was back to normal except for Nicky's large family of mostly girls and their mom and Georgie. When the last carriage door closed, the boys looked at one another and bolted for the playroom. Their mothers looked at each other and

DREAMS OF HALLOWEEN

smiled. Nicky's mom spoke first; she thought it was good for Nicky to have some boys to play with. The others agreed and left the boys to do the things that only little boys can enjoy.

That evening there had barely been time for a quick snack for the boys, then right back to their play. When it was bedtime, not one of the boys was willing to go to sleep until their mothers agreed to let them all sleep in a room together. There was lots of noise from that room until quite late, but when Marie went to her room, she looked in the door to check on Nicky who had very fragile health. She just had to know he was alright. She looked at the little boys and marveled that here in front of her was the future of the world. These three who were tired little boys, had a future that they had not even guessed at. She was saddened too to think that Willie would soon realize that with his arm problem that he would not be able to do many of the things which Nicky and Georgie would enjoy.

It was after two am when the house was awakened. Willie was screaming loudly in a language that he did not speak. As the house awoke and people hurried toward the noise, only Nicky and Marie understood what Willie was saying. He was crying about Nicky's pet rabbit dying, and he was shouting about his poor pet. Nicky was especially confused because he was awakened by the same dream. Nicky whispered to his mother that he was dreaming about poor Puff, the rabbit, and Willie woke up shouting about discovering Puff cold and dead the exact way Nicky had found his pet a few days before leaving to

HALLOWEEN BEDTIME STORIES

come to Willie's birthday. Once Willie was calmed down, they all returned to sleep.

The next day the boys talked about the dream. Georgie had barely been awakened during the night. He had sleepily sat up in bed then lay back down and drifted off to sleep missing most of the excitement. Nicky and Willie talked about both having the same dream at the same time. It slowly came to Willie's mind that he had become Nicky during that dream, experiencing the loss of a pet. It was the first time Willie realized that he could know things about people, what their fears and experiences may be. He could guess at things that would cause them to be upset or to want to hide away. He could know secrets that they did not want to tell. He never forgot that his ability could be useful after that night. On January 28, 1864, Willie realized that he could see into the lives of others by sharing their dreams. He did not know what it meant, but he knew that it was as special as it was annoying.

As Willie grew, his hair color changed to a medium brown. He grew in height but became short for his age by the time he was ten. His arm never got better; it grew but at a slower rate than the rest of his body. It was difficult for him to master riding a horse but he loved it so that he worked at it until he was able to ride with even the best riders. He learned that with special training, a horse could be taught to make up for his disability. He had grooms constantly working to specially train horses for him for the next fifty years. Willie realized that his arm was not ever going to be normal or useful in the normal way. He knew that he

DREAMS OF HALLOWEEN

was physically damaged and unable to use his arm hardly at all.

He also knew that he was born to a position where his leadership was needed, and he would assume authority when the time came. In many ways, he remained a spoiled child even as he became an adult. He was viewed as "full of bluster, rude, and crass". He was talked about even in his family circle as "being completely convinced that he was born with God-given authority to rule".

Willie never lost his ability to see the dreams of others. He never lost his ability in dreams to become the other person. He learned what it felt like to have two good arms through his dreams. He learned about sex and what it felt like to both men and women in his dreams. He learned what his teachers and tutors thought of him through his dreams. He learned to like the dreams and to treat them as a special gift given to him by God above to compensate for his unfortunate arm. Willie used his dreams to exert his will on others as he grew older.

When he was thirteen, he dreamed that he was one of the cooks' assistants. She was, at the time, a lovely girl of eighteen. She had dark brown hair and beautiful green eyes. She worked at the estate for the past two years. Willie awoke to a feeling he had not experienced before. He was thrusting his hips wildly and he was experiencing a wonderful feeling in his lower body. In the dream, he had become Greta and had been in passionate lovemaking with one of the grooms who worked training horses. This was not the

HALLOWEEN BEDTIME STORIES

first time that Greta and Louis had met in this way, but it was the best time for Greta.

There had long been rules against the workers being sexually involved with each other, especially in a barn or a closet where a young family member may inadvertently walk in on them. Willie had wanted to have this dream again and did several times until it finally occurred to him that he could use this information to have Greta the way the groom did in his dream. Yes, Willie's 'gift' was becoming useful to him. He planned his moves well.

He approached Greta as she was preparing carrots and potatoes for a meal. She was washing and cleaning the vegetables carefully. He came up and sat across from her on a kitchen stool. She avoided looking directly at him because she knew from the other house staff that he was trouble. Whenever Master Willie approached you, you had better be on guard. He was known to get servants into trouble with his parents or get them reassigned to other duties that suited his personal wishes for them.

He started by talking to her about her job. He asked if she was married and she said "No, I am single and have no plans to marry."

Willie said, "That is good, but what about Louis the groom that you have been meeting in the barn?" Greta blushed deeply then gained her composure and asked, "Whatever are you talking about Master Willie?" Willie pressed his advantage.

He said, "You know what I am talking about. The groom, Louis, who trains my jumping horses. You and he have been doing things together that you both

DREAMS OF HALLOWEEN

love to do, and you even dream about him. That's what I mean Greta."

She understood that he knew something, but how could he? They had been so careful to be discreet and to not even acknowledge each other in public. She also realized that she may be in trouble and that, perhaps, Willie was there to fire her. She looked at him as he sat perched and smirking on his kitchen stool. She wished that she were at least talking to an adult about this, but here was Willie, her scrawny master with his pointed face and twisted arm. He then softened his tone toward her and said,

"I have dreams that are the same as dreams that other people have. They are always true and always the exact same thing you dreamed, and, Greta, your dream is one of the best feeling, most fun dreams I have ever had. So much so that I want to actually do with you what you do with Louis."

She was speechless at first. She thought that Willie had not come to fire her but if she was hearing it correctly wanted to take her to the barn and have his way with her. She did not relish that thought, but it was better than being fired and disgraced by the master. She decided to take an easy approach and see if she could keep herself employed and try to avoid actually having sex with Willie.

She started a conversation, "You know, Master Willie, as you grow older and larger you start to have certain desires that go along with developing an adult body. I'll bet in a few years you will become so dashing that you will be able to have your pick of any of the girls in the whole country. It is well known that

173

HALLOWEEN BEDTIME STORIES

you will be king one day and nearly every girl would want to marry you."

"Of course, I am not talking about marriage Greta; just talking about lovemaking with you. You dreamed about it last night. I know you liked it, because I dreamed it as if I were you. I know you wanted it, and I am here to give it to you, only this time with me."

Greta tried telling Willie that there are times that are just not right for lovemaking, and that she believed she had too much to do to go off with him right now. He relented and told her to finish the vegetables that he would be back in about thirty minutes. He had to go and send the grooms over to the other barns on other errands so they could have the barn to themselves. In half an hour Willie appeared at the back door of the vegetable storage room. He motioned to Greta and she removed her apron and walked to him.

Once in the barn, he seemed to know exactly what to do. He knew because he dreamed it; he knew everything she felt and would feel as they kissed then made love. He had accurately dreamed of what she liked and what felt good. In short, she found him amazing, and Willie found a new way to use the information he got through his dreams.

It was also during his early teens that Willie started to have dreams of a different kind. He would have a dream about an event or incident that had not happened. At first he thought he was becoming normal just dreaming nonsense or disconnected facts, but when something he dreamed vividly came true to the

174

DREAMS OF HALLOWEEN

letter and color, he realized his dreams had added another dimension. He was starting to see the future.

As Willie grew to manhood, he started to take on the "duties" of his position and actually began to work at learning some of the things his father had always done. It was during his early military training that he began to have an extremely disturbing dream. It became a nightly dream during every day in October. It was fantastic and frightening. He would dream of himself as a much older man. He would see himself with his crippled arm posed to look normal. He would see himself with Nicky, then angry at Nicky. He would see himself with Georgie, then angry at Georgie. He would see himself using his dream gift to see into their plans and into their hearts. He would see and hear loud angry voices. He would see the flash of guns large and small, and he would see armies of young men in different uniforms, young men speaking different languages.

He would see himself, Nicky, and Georgie leading armies of men and horses and machines against each other. He began to visualize men dead of gunshots, bodies blasted apart. He envisioned men frozen to death from fighting a war in the winter. He would see the flames, hear the shrieks of women being told their husbands and sons had died in war. He experienced feeling his own family turn against him.

He knew by the incomplete nature of the dream that it was not fully developed. Some of the faces in the dream changed and the actions were different. The dream was still developing, but each development would make it worse. The death, destruction and

HALLOWEEN BEDTIME STORIES

stench of dead bodies got worse with each passing night.

The one theme that never changed in the dream was the murky beginning. Some men, three it seemed, were part of an organization called the Black Hand. They met on Halloween to plan the murder of someone that would take place during the early summer. Once the calendar changed to November the dream stopped and he went back to having his normal ability to see the dreams of others. He pondered why he, who had always prayed to have normal dreams that were just his own was now having those dreams, and they were scaring the hell out of him. As he achieved status in the military, he became known as "William or Willie" to many, seldom using his more official title.

He met Vicky at a dance that had been arranged by his parents. He was now officially in line for the throne and was expected to marry a suitable spouse. Willie was shy toward women of his own standing. He had been taught to believe that they were more mentally gifted than other women. He had been tutored to know that women of proper lineage where always intelligent, religious, loyal and did not like lovemaking except for the production of more people of proper lineage. He never once dreamed about what Vicky was thinking and could never see into her thoughts. He thought she was a pretty enough girl, and he knew it was his duty to marry and settle down.

For a time after the initial meeting, Willie would send letters to Viktoria as he now called her. The letters would ramble about his military activities. He described his contact with his cousin George

176

DREAMS OF HALLOWEEN

regarding some future possible alliance. He rarely spoke of his feelings except to always open the letters with *my dearest Viktoria* and to close them with *most affectionately yours*. Willie had learned to separate his feelings of love toward a proper spouse and his duty to produce future children who would rule future generations, from his more basic desire to experience sex with those women around him whose dreams he looked into.

Willie and Augusta Viktoria were married and took up the life of a princely couple and began to have children. William, as he was now called nearly all the time, became a model military leader until his dreams once again caused him problems. For all the apparent normalcy in their lives, William continued to dream, especially in October.

Every year in October the murky dream of the men of the Black Hand would begin to hold their nightly meetings in his dreams. They would plot and plan to murder a Royal, and that would start a chain of events that led to the rest of the dream. William would dream that dream every October night for all of his adult life.

He would see himself riding one of his fine horses at the head of a column of men dressed in uniforms. He would then watch as his cousins, mounted on their horses, took position at the head of their columns of men in uniform. He would awake in horror as he saw large guns erupt in smoke and fire and large projectiles land among those uniformed men and explode tearing away flesh, arms, legs and even the heads of some. He could smell the seared flesh. He

HALLOWEEN BEDTIME STORIES

could even smell the chemical bombs being used by soldiers to kill other soldiers. He even remembered the English term for the smoke that floated out of the bombs searing flesh. They had called it "Mustard Gas". Much later he would remember the term and tell a Prussian general about the dream. November would dawn and William would resume his normal life.

Wilhelm (William or Willie) had been King of Prussia for some time when the rumors of his instability started to circulate. His own family had long whispered of the possibility of his dreams being connected to the "problems" some family members had experienced. It was talked about openly in England where George V (Georgie) was king, that the German King was mentally ill like many of his predecessors.

Wilhelm had tried openly to form alliances with his Anglo cousin but had failed. They had discussed how they could work more closely but had disagreed over Wilhelm's intractable position on the rights and obligations to rule Europe through the monarchy. Willie had even shared some of his October dream with George. The two men became distant and avoided one another.

Cousin Nicholas had continued to visit much to the delight of Wilhelm, but their relationship became strained as Wilhelm stubbornly renewed alliances with some of the lesser kingdoms that were giving Russian allies problems. It was in October of 1908 when Wilhelm had tried to explain to Nicholas the importance of his October dream. It was the day before Halloween that Wilhelm experienced a complete

178

DREAMS OF HALLOWEEN

nervous breakdown. It was also on Halloween night that the dream became crystal clear. Unfortunately, Wilhelm's explanation of his dream to others was discounted as the babbling of one suffering from a nervous condition. Wilhelm tried one last time to explain the future events to his wife.

In the dream he sees a group of shadowy political figures calling their organization the Black Hand. He watches as they form an alliance to further their own financial desires. He sees them agree to kill those who may stand in their way or discover their true nature. He watches them plan to kill his old friend Ferdy. They think Ferdinand knows too much, and they will kill him when he visits Serbia in the early summer.

Wilhelm dreams he is in the crowd when the coward fires the shot that kills the Archduke. He sees the activity that quickly escalates the murder to a matter of state and treaty protection. He sees George and Nicholas talking by telegraph about how the coming crisis must be handled. He watches as Nicholas is told by his overly aggressive Russian Generals that Russia must mobilize. He is in the room when George states that should France be attacked or invaded England will throw her full support to oppose Germany and their Kaiser.

In his dreams, Wilhelm observed in horror the way George belittled and made fun of his withered arm and his mental breakdown. He slowly, as the dream progressed, became very angry.

In his dreams he would experience some of the worst days of the coming war. He would see the

HALLOWEEN BEDTIME STORIES

horrific sights, sounds, and smell the death and decay of nearly all of Europe. He would always end his dream with the significance of October and Halloween. In his dream things always came to a terrible end for himself, Nicholas, George and the very European Monarchy they were all a part of. It would be twenty more years in the future during October.

The Bolsheviks would overthrow Nicholas, and Nicholas Romanov would abdicate his rule of Russia only to die a terrible death a short time later. It would be during October that Kaiser Wilhelm Albrecht von Prussia would desperately try to arrange an abdication that would save the Monarchy, only to fail and to communicate with countries around the world that his reign was ending.

It would be in October that the English Parliament would officially assume rule from King George V Windsor. A plan created on Halloween night of 1913, the night before All Saints Day in Serbia, would unfold in June of 1914 creating a four year long war of nightmarish proportions. In October of 1918 the royal houses of Europe would turn over the rule of the countries under the Monarchy to common people.

The October dream that started with a young boy would unfold in the most savage war in history. It would play out beginning on Halloween and ending five Octobers later. Strange that so much happened in October, strange that Willie was five when he first realized about his dreams, and strange that from beginning to end October to October World War I was five years long.

DREAMS OF HALLOWEEN

Sometimes history tells us Halloween stories that we never imagined and they are too good to be fiction. No fiction can match the fantastic revelations of Truth............ But I keep trying .....Happy Halloween.............B

THE CROWNING OF A QUEEN

Norma is a pretty woman. She has a nearly olive complexion and the light green eyes that you usually only find in colored contact lenses. Her coloring, along with many of her attitudes and emotions, come from her Italian mother. Her cool aloofness and pin point logic come from being educated at Brown University. Her inquisitive nature and athleticism come from her overly doting father. Like many other people born to fulfill a specific purpose, she had no idea that there were strong forces at work in her life.

Norma graduated with honors from her political science major at Brown and was accepted at Yale School of Law. It was with difficulty that she decided to opt for an MBA instead of completing law school. By then, she had focused on a career idea. She considered working for someone in the U.S. Congress or Senate but did not like the small salary that most of them offered. She had served as an intern one summer for a congresswoman that she especially liked. She really enjoyed the job, but the lack of money created hardships.

Norma had become friends with several of the "lobbyists" while working for Congresswoman Johnson. She had seen them in Georgetown when she was out having drinks with her friends. They were nice people who were working for causes that they believed in much like the interns on "the hill". She quickly understood that they had plenty of money for very nice clothes and to spend on entertainment.

When Norma graduated it was with the thought that she would find a job working for an association

HALLOWEEN BEDTIME STORIES

representing some business lobby in Washington D.C. She was certain that her MBA with emphasis on Political Science and two years of law would qualify her to be involved in the development of legislation. She was excited to find an employer who was working for a good cause. The job offered an opportunity to travel and work with rural communities developing infrastructure. Something was placing Norma just where she needed to be.

Norma worked two years developing requests for funding and regulatory support for the development of jobs in some pretty rural areas. She traveled often and was quickly recognized as a real contributor to the success of the projects she worked on. Her good looks and quick wit served her very well in the halls of Congress. She was doing so well as one of the staffers that she hesitated at first to apply for the Meetings Coordinator job when it was announced.

Norma looked at the duties of the job and the salary it commanded. She believed she could excel at the duties. People in the organization and even the Executive Vice President were encouraging her to apply. She did not know why, but she knew she must take this job when it was offered. Her ability and the unknown forces working in her life landed her the job.

Her new job was everything any young successful person could want. She made a great salary. A big part of her job was to locate places where the association could hold large-scale meetings with five to seven thousand attendees. She would look through information about large hotels located in sun-belt locations.

THE CROWNING OF A QUEEN

Conventions must be in good weather locations to get the best attendance and to keep the association popular with the membership. After all many of those attending were doing their only travel of the year other than their vacations. These conventions were meant to accomplish a little work and a lot of fun. Norma would create options based on her personal research and the board members elected by the members would choose a location. They nearly always followed her recommendations.

Norma developed her recommendations by selecting several locations with good to great weather. She then found facilities that could accommodate the meetings and displays of associated vendors. She had to make sure to find adequate up-scale hotels to accommodate the thousands of attendees. It was real work, but it was pleasant work. She knew from her early experience that there were only about 15 to 20 possible locations for the annual meetings with many thousands of attendees.

The regional meetings were much easier and usually consisted of several hundred attendees. First she found the appropriate size of location, and made a personal visit to confirm the quality of rooms, food, catering and meeting facility. She would then tour through the typical accommodations by the hotel and convention specialists. She took various tours of the cities in order to arrange activities for spouses of meeting attendees.

It was her job to travel to the location, sample the restaurants, attend and evaluate the tours, experience the hotel facilities and to recommend a site. She was making

HALLOWEEN BEDTIME STORIES

a very high salary of which she spent very little. It was her job to be demanding and to make sure her trade association's members got the best treatment possible when they attended the annual meetings. She was the person the hotels, tour guides, entertainers, and catering services had to impress to land the opportunity to host an annual convention for over five thousand people. She became accustomed to being treated like royalty, and the role fit her perfectly for more reasons than she ever realized.

Norma traveled a lot because she had two national level meetings with thousands of attendees and from seven to nine other meetings in regional locations ranging from Florida to Alaska and from Maine to Southern California and everyplace in between. It was a job requirement for her to attend all of the meetings to make sure everything went as planned and to solve any problems that may happen.

She learned if she wanted the actual event to be successful she should arrive several days early and plan on staying a day or two after each meeting to tie up any loose ends. The meetings were something she really enjoyed because it was her busiest time. There were always issues regarding reservations with hotels, catering, and facilities problems like heating and microphones. She and her staff of two were on the run making the meetings run as smoothly as possible.

She spent about fifteen to seventeen meeting weeks each year with regional meetings, annual meetings and special meetings for educational purposes. She spent another similar amount of time traveling alone setting up those events. She was out of town about half

THE CROWNING OF A QUEEN

of the time not counting her three weeks of vacation. The main downfall of this life was that she had very little time to cultivate friendships and to get to know anyone where she lived. She managed to have good friends at work and often went to Georgetown with the people at work. She even tagged along to Capitol Hill for legislative visits when she had time.

She liked her apartment and was lucky to share it with an employee from another trade association. Nancy was a lobbyist who was always writing language for legislation and calling on congressmen and senators to have it included in a bill. Nan was a fun person, and she and Norma got along extremely well. Often when Norma would return from a ten or more day trip, Nancy would give her the executive overview and bring her up to date with what was going on in "the old town". A term used by Washington insiders to describe Washington during the legislative season. Norma had even started dating one of the politicos who was working at a top level staff job for the Federal Emergency Management Agency (FEMA).

Mike was a pretty good guy but had two problems. He did not know when to keep quiet and he was a republican. The latter was forgivable because everyone in Washington was something, and the longer you spend there the more you realize how much the same they all are.

Norma was excited when she walked into Clyde's Restaurant and Bar in Georgetown. She spotted Mike and Nancy sitting with Laura, a congressional staff person for a highly ranked congressman. They were not talking business; they were just having a good time. As

HALLOWEEN BEDTIME STORIES

she approached the table she was met by the waitress who offered to help her with her jacket and asked if she would like something to drink. Norma ordered a glass of Merlot and sat down. As she joined in the conversation she had a warm sensation of friendship.

Just the experience of a place so alive with conversation, friends, great food, and drinks made her feel good about herself. She was happy to be so involved in a place where decisions are made that affect the lives of nearly everyone in the country in one way or another.

She loved the heady atmosphere and rubbing elbows with the nation's decision-makers. She loved being able to watch the development of laws that effectively set the direction of nearly every aspect of life in our country. She felt lucky to live in a place where one can have access to the highest leaders in our country.

She really did not want to take the trip to New Orleans that was scheduled to begin next Monday and leave all this behind. But there were forces at work in Norma's life, and she could not know yet in her conscious mind that everything that had happened in her entire life was leading her to New Orleans. While she was in Washington, she would soak up the "Old Town" atmosphere.

She knew that she was going to have a great evening. She knew she would go home with Mike and make love, and she knew she would be on the plane to New Orleans Monday morning. She decided to relax and enjoy the warm atmosphere of intellect in Washington.

The plane ride to New Orleans was uneventful. She talked briefly with a businessman from New Orleans

THE CROWNING OF A QUEEN

who explained that the upcoming week in New Orleans would be fun.

"This is the week when the krewes are formed. You know, the krewes that compete for royalty in the Mardi Gras. There will be lots of tourists and lots of "homies" returning for the festivals. You picked a good time to get a flavor of the big party to come later on."

Norma was not really interested in the wild, raucous Mardi Gras. She was curious, and decided that if she had to be here anyway, it would be good to see what the big party preparation was all about. It was with a mixture of wanting to be back in Washington and willingness to experience a city new to her that she walked through the airport. She hailed a cab and told him to take her to the Marriott on Canal Street.

The cabbie smiled and asked if she was "comin inta town fo the krewes competitons"?

Norma smiled back and said, "No, I am here to plan a convention coming into town, but from what I hear, the krewes competitions will be a fun extra."

"Yeah, fo us, dis betta dan dee big party is mo local mo like jus fo us," the cabbie responded.

Norma mused at the driver's deep southern accent. She enjoyed listening to him speak.

Once in the hotel she was greeted by the desk clerk that set her up with a room, had a bell man take her bags and contacted the business services supervisor. The clerk, a friendly efficient black lady, did all this professionally and in less than two minutes. Norma was impressed, but was aware her presence had been expected and that Marriott wanted this convention. She checked into her beautiful room at the top of the hotel

HALLOWEEN BEDTIME STORIES

overlooking the Mississippi in one direction and Canal Street in the other. She could see the corner of Canal and Bourbon near the base of the hotel. About two blocks distant was the River Walk shopping and restaurant area. "It looked very tourist friendly", she had written in her notes. First impressions were very good, and the locals, with their easy southern approach, are sure to please visitors.

After several hours of meetings, she decided to take a mid-afternoon walk down Bourbon Street. She suspected that she should do it in daylight at least the first time. Even the hotel staff, who wanted her business very badly, cautioned her to be careful going out alone at night. So it was that Norma Pearson was walking down Bourbon Street in New Orleans on the opening day of Krewe Week. The sun was shining and the temperature about 80 degrees. The city was in full-on party mode.

MONIQUE
Monique grew up in New Orleans. Her mother's family had been in New Orleans since the first slave boats started arriving in the 1700's. They came from Africa by way of Haiti. Her father, a Cajun/Creole, was from a small swamp village just up river from New Orleans. Mrs. Didier, pronounced Da-yay, owned a small shop about four doors off Bourbon Street. Samson Didier worked as a teamster on the docks of the second busiest port in the country.

Monique was a typical (for New Orleans) girl. She attended public schools and excelled at her studies of history, music, Spanish, French, and English. She was a born communicator, but her first love and greatest area

THE CROWNING OF A QUEEN

of interest was her mother's business, which was also the family's hobby and religion. Monique was an expert at voodoo and could read about and discuss it fluently in five languages while still a child.

Monique had her father's light olive coloring and slight build; she had her mother's deep dark eyes. She was a strikingly beautiful young woman and was still attending college classes while working in her mother's store.

Monique hoped to increase the size of the actual store and buy or rent a larger space to teach classes about voodoo for visiting tourists with a more in depth option for those who became true believers like herself and her family. She wanted to take voodoo from the side streets to some of the main thoroughfares in New Orleans. She saw the craft as more than a tourist pastime, more than sales of fake shrunken heads and alligator teeth. She knew things about the craft that proved beyond doubt that it was not just a belief. It was and is a process with specific outcomes. A properly thrown hex could do more harm or good to a person than all the words in the world. She had personal experience with the craft, and knowledge that it is not a belief; it is a certainty.

In most ways, Monique was just like any other beautiful, smart, young black woman in New Orleans. She did not wear voodoo on her sleeve. She was typical. Her boyfriend, another Cajun from up-river, was working in a law firm as a clerk while studying for his bar exam. He also played Cajun music on Bourbon Street about three nights a week. Monique did not particularly like Cajun music, but Raymond was worth suffering through a little musical inconvenience.

HALLOWEEN BEDTIME STORIES

Monique had great news when she walked into the "Island Treasures Magic and Voodoo Shop".

"Mom", she said, I got a chance for us to buy a shop with a bigger front right on Bourbon Street".

"Giirrlll Chile we goin ta hafta talk bout tha wit you pop. Monique knew from her mother's deep southern accent that there must be customers in the store.

She quickly got the hint and said, "Yessum" and walked into the back of the store where the office was located. The office consisted of a smallish desk with three drawers and enough room for a small lap top computer. When she heard the rattle of the shrunken heads she knew the door of the shop had opened to let the shopper out.

Her mom walked into the office smiling and said, "Honey, that's great news you brought about the larger store. I hope we can have a back room, basement or upstairs room to hold classes too. It would be great to be able to pull the tourists in right off the grand march. But you have to remember when we are talking voodoo to tourists, most of them expect to hear us talk like we are under-educated, superstitious, black folk. If we disappoint them we could lose their business."

"I know Mom," Monique responded, "but I was so excited I forgot."

Her mom relapsed into the shop talk that they both used. "Come in heah soundin like a New York lawyer, an people won think you kno nothin bout th craf. Bettah to let them think they dealin with real voodoo girls. Ya kno, the black ones tha aint got no school."

She was smiling as she chided Monique, and they both laughed when she finished talking.

191

THE CROWNING OF A QUEEN

Monique could not wait to tell her dad about the new location and see what he thought. She valued his cool, logical approach to business and his ability to dig into investments to see if they were good. He could have never been showman enough to work in the store, but he could have done about anything else in life he wanted to do. He was genius intellect with an outdoors physical job that suited his energy level. Monique knew he would not only approve of her find but expected him to be excited about it.

They all knew that the growing interest in their craft was going to bring many more students and followers. They also all knew that the more followers a group had, the stronger the effect of the spells, hexes, incantations and impact. They suspected they were on the verge of becoming amazingly powerful practitioners of their craft.

Her dad knew all about the family business and was involved in many of the family decisions. He was generally flexible and open to investigating nearly all aspects of their opportunities. The only time he ever became inflexible or agitated was when any one was about to do something against the "rules of the craft". Then he would be very firm and measured and could cast a look that told anyone within visual contact that he was not to be questioned. When it came to the practice of the craft it was a religion to him and must be adhered to down to the smallest intonation of a chant. Samson was, after all, a true member of voodoo royalty. He understood the lineage of Mary his wife and his family.

Mary had a long family history of voodoo from West Africa and Haiti. He had the Spanish Creole

HALLOWEEN BEDTIME STORIES

voodoo lineage, and their daughter was one of the very few who had both lines of royalty. It was nearing the celebration of the crew selection in the city, and the upcoming Louisiana Voodoo and New Orleans Voodoo meetings would start in a couple of weeks. It was going to be a busy time, and the Didier family would have a lot of activity in the coming weeks.

The powers of the religion were strong upon them at this time. Samson wondered if it was time to talk to Monique and Mary and to say some of the things that he knew. Monique was absorbed in planning the layout of a new larger space. She could have entire isles of gris-gris, a section for dolls and a back room for serious members and practitioners. She could finally have a place to teach incantations in native Spanish or Creole.

New Orleans Krewe Week

It was on this Monday afternoon that Monique would meet the remaining piece of the puzzle that would allow her to see a bigger picture. It was destined that she would meet a customer that would change both of their lives forever. She kissed her mom on the cheek and told her she could go on home. She dropped into her voodoo store lady accent.

"Youn can git on hom mamon I don got this sto work covered. See ya back aa da hous".

Mary chuckled at her daughter, grabbed her purse and walked out on to the street. It was relatively quiet, but a few doors away on Bourbon Street lots of tourists were making their way through the hubub that was typical of Bourbon Street nearly all the time. She felt a slight rush of excitement to think that she may finally

THE CROWNING OF A QUEEN

have a storefront where many more people passed by than her current location.

As she turned on to Bourbon Street to make the seven block walk up to Canal where she would catch a trolley car home, she was humming a happy tune under her breath. She had always been interested in people and looked into the eyes of nearly everyone she passed by. When she spotted Norma, she noticed first her eye color and that she was very pretty. As she made eye contact, she noticed a feeling somewhere in the pit of her stomach. She smiled and nodded to the young stranger. Norma to her surprise found herself nodding back and smiling. She did not know this pleasant looking black woman and could not guess why she dropped her big city demeanor and was speaking to a stranger.

She heard her own voice saying "hello".

Mary was a little less surprised because she often had the effect of having people acknowledge her presence. "Lo mam," she smiled back.

Norma used the connection as an opportunity to ask some questions about shopping and other activities on Bourbon Street. Mary used the opportunity to have a tourist with money to spend, stop by her store. She told Norma about several great bars with music and entertainment for tourists. Lastly, she told her about the " bestus voodoo shop in Nawlens".

Norma did not know why but she instantly liked Mary and was anxious to visit the places Mary described to her. She was thinking how lucky she was to meet this wonderful native of New Orleans to guide her search for future excursions for people who would attend her

HALLOWEEN BEDTIME STORIES

meeting here in about eighteen months. Most of all she wanted to see the "bestus Voodoo Shop in Nawlens".

She thanked Mary and headed off to the next corner and turned right, counting doors to find the Island Treasures Magic and Voodoo store. Mary watched Norma walk away, and the feeling in the pit of her stomach told her to be careful. Norma saw the gold lettering outlined in red and decided to go on in and see what this little shop had to offer that made Mary speak so highly of it. She did not immediately notice the family resemblance between Mary and Monique. She did notice a very beautiful young black woman was sitting on a stool near the cash register. She approached Monique and explained that she was a tourist who came to town to arrange for a future convention. She told Monique she could mention her shop in meeting brochures as an interesting place to visit while in New Orleans. Monique was interested in this opportunity. She said to Norma.

"Wel ah would preciate having folks com to de sto and can git extra hep to spen time wif dem folks yall kno teachn dem de hex an th chant and th spells tha go wif dese gris gris and dolls."

Norma was struggling to understand Monique, and since Monique was so good at voodoo, she knew exactly what Norma was thinking. Monique quickly changed her manner. She cleared her voice and spoke in perfect English.

"I was demonstrating part of the show that most people expect when they walk into a voodoo store. You know the "ignorant black woman superstitious thing". We dun lik ta give th visitas to ourh faihr city they mon s worth".

195

THE CROWNING OF A QUEEN

Norma smiled and laughed a little. She said "This is great. The lady I met on Bourbon Street is right. This is a great shop.

"Sounds like you met my mother, Mary," Monique said. They both laughed out loud. Norma spent the next half-hour looking though the artifacts of voodoo---both real and fake. Monique, sensing a real opportunity, treated Norma like a trusted friend. She patiently explained nearly every piece Norma asked about and even gave a little insight to the spiritual aspects of voodoo. Norma knew that she had discovered a treasure in the little shop and the mother and daughter who ran it.

She knew she needed to get back to a late afternoon meeting with Marriott business people. She promised to return to the voodoo shop to talk more about all the things of interest she had discovered. She was strongly thinking about having Monique address a spouse session about voodoo and pay her for it. Of course, Monique could use that opportunity to plug her place of business. Once again, it seemed that Norma had placed herself in just the right place at just the right time. She marveled about it as she walked the few blocks back to the Marriott.

She was excited to spend more time with Monique. She was intrigued about the obviously intelligent, beautiful, young black woman. In the short time they were together, she had learned that Monique was fluent in several languages. She was feeling like she was a lot more interested in the diverse cultures of New Orleans than she expected. Her homesick feeling for Washington was fading, and she was feeling the

HALLOWEEN BEDTIME STORIES

adventure of a new city with some new discoveries about some very old things.

She was intrigued by the thought of discussing voodoo with an obviously intelligent person near her own age. Voodoo, she thought, had been pretty much a bad joke. It was a way for white people to make fun of ignorant black people, by showing the black culture as superstitious and uneducated. She did not know anything about voodoo or voodoo shops when she had first walked through the door of Mary and Monique's shop. She now was feeling a real thrill at the thought of learning more about this obscure religion and its practices. She was looking forward to tomorrow afternoon when she could meet with Monique to discover more of New Orleans and voodoo. She was wondering if, perhaps, she could share some of her craft with these practitioners of jungle magic. She was thinking of how much fun it would be to share her new found knowledge with her friends. She could not know how wrong she was.

Norma made her meeting with James Randeaux . He was a pleasant man with a soft southern accent like most of the people she had met in New Orleans. They ran through the general concept of meeting rooms for various size break-out groups and large venues for the entire convention to participate in. It was nearly 6:00 pm when James apologetically explained that he had to leave. His wife was expecting him home for dinner with another couple, and he did not want to be late. Norma said, "That's great James. To tell the truth, I am pretty done in for today myself. We can put the touches on this tomorrow morning, then I can meet with catering on

197

THE CROWNING OF A QUEEN

Wednesday. I am booked with Monique Didier tomorrow afternoon for some planning of activities in the city."

A dark look passed across James' honest face. "You know that Monique is a voodoo lady?" he asked.

"Yes, I find it very interesting, all the diverse beliefs and cultures here in this one city," she answered.

"You be careful she don't put a hex or a spell on you. Monique Didier is not one to play with."

"Aw, you don't really buy that bayou stuff, do you?" Norma asked.

"Well, not so much I guess," he answered, "but you be careful about that voodoo stuff all the same. You see some pretty strange sights around those shops when those voodoo witches get upset or offended. More than one time, I have seen otherwise normal people walking around barking like dogs, or just repeatedly running into the side of a building like a stuck windup toy. Yeah, some strange stuff takes place with those voodoo folks".

Norma felt a slight chill run up her spine as James pulled on his jacket to leave. He turned and said,

"Oh yeah, and in case nobody else told you, don't go to those voodoo places before sunrise or after sunset. While I am at it, you be as careful as heck if you go down on Bourbon Street alone after dark. It's a pretty wild place, especially during crew weeks. See you tomorrow, Ms. Pearson. You have a good evening."

Norma decided to stay in the hotel and order room service, watch a movie and get to bed early. Tomorrow would be soon enough to resume her adventures of discovering New Orleans. Perhaps she could get Monique or James to show her around, or have

HALLOWEEN BEDTIME STORIES

someone else guide her to potential activities for her conventioneers. After dinner she walked to her balcony and looked toward the river. She could see traffic on the bridges and see lights shimmering off the water. She could smell New Orleans. It was the earthy, almost dirty, richness of the delta mixed with Cajun cooking. As she looked back toward Bourbon Street, it started to rain. The warm droplets on her forehead soothed her, and she felt sleepy.

A NIGHT VISIT

She did not remember when she went to bed. She watched the soft rain falling and watched the people below raise their umbrellas or dash to the awnings for protection from the rain.   Suddenly, she found herself dreaming a strange dream. There was an older, light skinned, black man. His handsome face and intelligent eyes reminded her of someone she knew. He told her that he had something that he must tell her, and she should listen patiently because at the end of his story it would all make sense. He also told her that, for the time being, she would not hold this in her conscious mind but only in her subconscious mind or in dream state. She nodded her head, and Sam began to talk in a soft voice.

He told her he would introduce himself, and then he would tell her the rest. He told Norma that he was the father of Monique; the same one she had spent a part of the afternoon with. He explained he was the husband of the very woman who had directed her to the voodoo shop. Norma sat bolt upright in the bed. She thought to herself, James was right! I have been hexed or something. Sam interrupted her thought, shaking his

THE CROWNING OF A QUEEN

head and softly saying, "No, Norma, you are not hexed. In fact, you cannot be hexed. It is impossible. You are not really dreaming either, but it is the best way to say the things that must be said to you so that you can understand your true self, and why you have been lead to us. I know that you do not know it yet, but when my story is done, you will understand everything.

You see, voodoo started a long time ago on the African continent and moved through the Egyptians into Europe. It flourished in Spain, Italy and even France. There were lots of African people who migrated to Europe long before America existed. The voodoo craft sort of merged with the pagan religion for a time and even crossed over into some forms of Christian beliefs.

The 'craft', as it became known, flourished best in Italy. The Italians became masters of developing the spiritual side of the art and of passing the traditions through the lines of royalty within the craft. They gave us the way to keep the craft renewed without ever losing any of its strength. In the old times, the craft used to have to be physically passed from generation to generation, but in Italy some of the practitioners learned a way to extend life for several generations. Oh, people still die. They just live several centuries instead of several decades.

The Europeans also learned to use certain people to carry the craft through times of trouble and to renew it when the time was right. Like, for example, when the popes first came to power in Italy, the craft went underground because Christianity was too strong for voodoo to compete with.

HALLOWEEN BEDTIME STORIES

So the craft got sent to Spain, then to France, and finally on to the new world where it once again flourished. It was the Italians who learned to suspend the craft then bestow it on a new person to carry it safely to the next regeneration. There were times when the churches and the governments were hunting our people to kill them in order to stop the craft. There were times when it got too dangerous to even admit that you knew someone in the craft. As a result, the men and women in the craft devised a way to suspend the knowledge for a time. Sometimes it was even close to fifty years.

They would keep that information out there in the hands of an experienced old voodoo queen and wait until a child with all the right things came along. The child had to be smart, had to have the blood lines that connected them to the ancient queens. They had to have that certain coloring and an extremely intelligent mind. Most of all they could NOT know about what they were able to do or the treasure they carried. They had to believe they were normal people. They would only find out that they were part of the craft when the moment arrived that their knowledge, which had been planted by the ancients, was about to come into play.

Another way to put it is that the "maker" would only be able to know that she was the maker, when the time drew near to crown the next queen. The queen would rule for a long time, maybe a couple of hundred years. The maker would wait in that special place between life and death for the right person to be born. They would then inhabit that person, remain quiet and undiscovered until the time was right. I am telling you, Miss Norma, that you are the maker. It is coming to you

201

THE CROWNING OF A QUEEN

in a dreamlike state so your unconscious mind can allow your conscious mind to adjust to the knowledge. It will feel gradual and quite natural to you that you will realize who and what you are to the voodoo (voudoux) peoples.

You will gradually come to know over the next couple of days about your true self and will be able to access the knowledge you have to crown our next queen. Now, this is critical Miss Norma. You are the only person who will be able to do this ceremony and crown Monique. Should you fail, we will have no queen until another child can be found with all the attributes to pass the secrets through. You will realize that you are the maker before Monique realizes that you are the maker and before she knows that she is to be crowned this very week. You are very special to us. You are not only one of us, but you are critical to our sect. We need you to perform the ceremony and crown our queen because you, Miss Norma, are the maker. You have carried the keys to voodoo magic from over a hundred years ago since your birth.

One last thing I have to say Miss Norma. You need to know that once you have done your job as maker, you will have a few days to live among us and be part of our lifestyle. After those few days, you will be placed into a trance, and you will remember all this as a dream. Your job with us will be done. In a couple of hundred years, Monique and her man will plant the information you carry with another child of the right cast and age to keep the magic going. Now, you get some sleep Miss Norma. I have done my job as the informer. It is up to you to do the rest."

HALLOWEEN BEDTIME STORIES

He then leaned forward and kissed Norma on the forehead and patted her shoulder. He murmured some unintelligible words. In her dream she suddenly felt powerful and strong. As Sam left looking back over his shoulder at her, he could not help but to see her beauty. He longed to touch her, but knew that now was not the right time. He would get his chance before all the ceremonies were done. Sam walked out the front of the Marriott Hotel whistling softly and disappeared into the heavy fog toward Bourbon Street.

Tuesday, when she woke up, it was nearly 7:30 am. She felt rested and had enjoyed a great night's sleep. The rain pattering on the windows had helped her drift into one of the most restful nights she had ever had. She ordered some coffee with chicory, New Orleans style. She did not like the taste of chicory and showered and dressed quickly to head downstairs to get some real coffee. When the waiter in the hotel coffee shop asked her if she wanted the New Orleans style with chicory, she said, "No thanks. I tried it and don't like it." He brought her a good, real cup of coffee and she enjoyed it.

She spent the morning riding on tour buses and trolleys looking at old mansions, art galleries and shopping malls. It was just past noon when she arrived back at the hotel. She quickly went to her room, changed into some blue jeans, casual shoes and a light blouse. She grabbed a cup of red beans and rice from the fast food joint next door to the hotel and walked toward Bourbon Street to meet with Monique. She stopped along the way to watch some younger boys, about 11 or 12 years old she guessed, tap dancing for change. They were very talented and had their own little group of

THE CROWNING OF A QUEEN

musicians playing jazzy tunes for them to dance to. She tossed a couple of quarters in their box when one of the boys looked her way and smiled a big open smile. She saw the hole in the back of his pants as he bent to pick up the coins and motioned him over and handed him a dollar bill. He thanked her and kept dancing, not missing a step.

She walked past several joints where different kinds of music wafted out through the doorways. She heard some blues tunes, some old jazz, some Cajun music and even some old style piano. There were lots of people on the street and even more jammed into the small bars and stages where performers were present.

She was once again amazed at the constant state of partying on Bourbon Street. She did begin noticing other businesses besides bars and strip clubs and restaurants. She saw a couple of stores selling art-work and souvenirs.

She walked into the Island Treasures Magic and Voodoo Shop. There were several customers in the shop, and Mary and Monique were busily talking to them in their voodoo shop lingo. Norma nodded at Monique and just started browsing around the store. The customers were waited upon one by one and, after about fifteen minutes, the shop was empty except for Norma, Mary and Monique. Mary spoke first, "I hope you don't mind me sending you to my own store, but I knew you were looking for some New Orleans type experiences, and I told you the truth that this is the best voodoo store in town".

HALLOWEEN BEDTIME STORIES

Norma smiled and said, "Well, it is fine, and I am grateful you guided me here as long as you didn't put a hex on me or something like that."

Mary smiled widely and said, "Well maybe jus' a lil teeny bit to get yo biness at ouah sto." All three women laughed.

Norma and Monique were fast friends, and Mary had been filled in on the potential that the business opportunity with Norma represented. It was Mary who suggested that Monique and Norma visit in the office for a while. The two women talked about how they would work together to provide a great New Orleans experience for the conventioneers.

Monique suggested that they do a little shopping around and look into some other voodoo shops, art stores, and souvenir shops. She suggested that she develop a talk about some great little places to shop and include her own store. She could also offer a fun look at voodoo for a spouse half-day seminar. Norma loved the idea and the two agreed to proceed. Norma would get the paperwork to Monique before leaving town.

Monique suggested that they go to dinner in The Quarter to celebrate, and later they could stop by The Ragin' Cajun to hear her boyfriend and his band play a few tunes.

"We might even get to do a little dancing if the mood hits us," she suggested.

Norma said, "It sounds like fun, but I was warned to stay from Bourbon Street at night alone."

Monique said, "Honey, we aren't going to leave you alone on Bourbon Street. Ray and me will walk you home whenever you want us to."

THE CROWNING OF A QUEEN

Norma brightened and said, "Ok, I guess I will get to have an experience on Bourbon Street that I never expected."

Norma felt like she had gotten the feel of New Orleans. She drank the remains of an O'Briens Hurricane while walking past Resurrection Hall listening to jazz played by the Resurrection Hall Boys. It was just after midnight when Ray and Monique said goodnight to Norma in the lobby of her hotel. They were all ready to get some rest after a fun night of listening to bands and bar hopping around Bourbon Street. Norma felt at ease with Monique but a little less so with Ray.

It seemed to her that Ray was more interested in her than Monique would appreciate. Maybe it was just her imagination. She went to the elevator and was probably almost to her room 17 floors away when Monique turned to Ray and asked, "Just what are you doing trying to hit on this girl? I told you she is important business to me Ray, and, besides, I like her. Don't you mess this up boy or I'll"… she stopped there.

"What," Ray asked, "you gonna what? Put a hex or a spell on me? Shit, woman, you must know by now I ain't afraid of you."

"Well, Ray, you had better be afraid because I will not let you screw this up for me. I don't care how important your momma and daddy are to the voodoo people in Baton Rouge. You need to understand that we are on the verge of something big here."

Raymond looked down at the ground and muttered, "Sorry."

"Sorry don't get it man; just leave that woman alone. You can have her after we get our work done.

HALLOWEEN BEDTIME STORIES

Right now she is mine and Mary's, and I know you don't want to mess with Mary."

Ray shook his head and said, "OK, she is probably worth waiting for anyway."

"We like her Ray, and we won't harm her none."

"She is a real smart woman and real educated too. She may just be the type to catch on if anyone would try to mess with her, then you lose all this stuff you are working on with her."

"Well, honey boy, you just let me worry about that. Now, take me home and make some of that wild Cajun voodoo love to me. All this dancing has got me going in a big way."

"Yes ma'am," he answered. "CABBY!" he yelled out the door at a mule drawn carriage. "We need a ride."

"Glad to do it," the cabby replied. "Hop on in."

Norma stood on the balcony of her room and watched the cab glide into the fog on Canal Street and disappear. She took a deep breath.

It was nearly 8:30 on Wednesday when Norma got up. She only had an hour before her meeting, but, thankfully, it would be in the hotel. She ordered American coffee and wheat toast. She was dressed and headed for the door when the phone rang. It was Mike.

"Hello," he said, "how are things going in the big easy?"

"Good," Norma answered, "but I am running late. Can I call you back in about two hours?"

"I'll hurry," he said, "I've been talking to the office down there, and I am coming down today for a little business and, hopefully, later tonight a lot of

207

THE CROWNING OF A QUEEN

pleasure. Can I share your room, or do I need to book my own?"

Norma said, "Mike, I have lots left to do and won't have much time for fun. I cannot allow any guests in my room except maybe my mother and get away with it. I can make sure you get a room on my floor with a great view and all the amenities."

"All?" Mike interrupted.

"Well, most," Norma said. "I told you I have work to do, but I met this nice young couple who would probably be fun to hang with in the time we do have. Now, I have to run, really, so see you later?"

"Yeah later," Mike answered. "You at the Marriott on Canal?" But she had hung up and was gone.

Norma breezed through the details of featured speakers large group venues and even the vendor showcase area. She was surprised at the speed with which things fell into place. The hotel staff she worked with seemed to anticipate and be ready for her questions. Well before her estimated time of 2:00 pm, she had finished her Albacore Tuna sandwich and was standing in the lobby of the Marriott calling Monique on her cell phone.

Monique's voice was robust as she said "Norma, how good to hear from you. I hope we didn't dance you too hard or keep you out too late. And I hope Raymond did not drool too much on you. I swear that boy has a roving eye, and I am sure you must have noticed the way he fawned over you all evening."

"Whoa!" Norma said. "Take a breath Monique. Yes, Raymond was a little overly attentive, but he is cute and very interesting. To be honest, if he wasn't your

HALLOWEEN BEDTIME STORIES

beau, I would be interested. But he is your beau. Besides, Mike, my beau from Washington, is coming down for some business today and wants to meet you two tonight. Will it be OK if we all go to dinner and then out together? And before that, I need to meet with you. I have most of the meeting venues arranged. I also have the contracts for your engagement to offer two spouse sessions, complete with bus tours to your business, with allowance for a two hour shopping tour while there."

"Now, you whoa girl," Monique said. "You already have contracts ready for me to teach classes, then bring busloads of people to my shop?"

"Well, not just your shop," Norma interrupted, "but to start at your shop and have two hours to shop in the neighborhood around your shop before returning to the hotel."

"Wow, girl, you good," Monique responded. "You damn good, but we did not set fees for the seminars. I guess if we get that many people with two hours to kill near our shop, I won't be able to charge much. After all, we will get lots of business from them."

Norma said, "Monique, that is why I need to see you now without the boys around. I have a range of prices that I can negotiate within, and we need to discuss some of the loose ends. I cannot give you a number, but am authorized up to a certain level which I cannot disclose."

"Good," Monique said, "lets meet at Brennan's on the veranda, have a fruit juice and talk some business."

THE CROWNING OF A QUEEN

"Now, don' yo taa 'vandage of dis Nawlens colored gal, Miss Norma. I'se gwine ta see ya'll theah in 'bout half houah. Bye now."

Norma chuckled to herself and wondered if Monique had ever negotiated for a speaking fee before. She suspected not. She decided she would be fair and try to help Monique through the process. Both women headed for this meeting feeling that they each had the advantage over the other.

They arrived at Brennan's Restaurant---one of the finest eating establishments in the entire country. Brennan's has long been famous for their large extravagant breakfasts complete with fish bowl sized Creole Bloody Mary cocktails. Their dinners were too numerous and too extravagant to describe with flaming desserts and after dinner liqueurs.

The lone waiter in the front of the restaurant walked over to the two striking young women and said, "I'm sorry, ladies. We are closed for a couple of hours to prepare for our dinner guests."

Monique looked at the waiter. She had never seen him before. She spoke slowly and extremely clearly. "Bobby," she said, "we really prefer the veranda while you folks go about your dinner preparation. We will only need one clean table and some fruit juice. We can discuss our business in private and you can forget we are here."

The young waiter was transfixed. He mumbled, "Yes, of course, we can seat you on the cleaned portion of the veranda, bring you some juice and leave you to your discussion. Yes, very well then, let me show you to our veranda."

210

HALLOWEEN BEDTIME STORIES

"That is a good boy Bobby," Monique purred.

Norma was a little surprised at the ease with which Monique seemed to be able to get her way. Once they were seated a carafe of apple juice and one of mixed fruits were placed on their table, and Bobby walked back into the building leaving the two women alone.

Norma had thought of offering the waiter a tip to seat them when he first stated they were closed, but, obviously, Monique knew this young man too. She wondered if Monique was taking her to places where she had "plants" to make her look good.

Monique thought to herself 'be careful, she is starting to question how all this is falling into place'. Be careful. She was also gloating to herself. She did not know this waiter at all. She had simply opened his mind and looked in to see how to get what she wanted. She could not tell Norma that or Norma would become impossible to deal with. She needed to let Norma think that she had the upper hand.

Norma had decided to be fair to Monique because she liked her. She also liked the idea of being able to schedule an activity that would be truly memorable and out of the ordinary.

Monique was very happy about this opportunity and knew that Norma actually liked her. She also knew Norma was very smart and capable and was used to making decisions quickly on her own. Monique "read" that Norma could become very hard and challenging to deal with if she were treated unfairly or crossed.

Monique thought it best to admit that this would be her first time to teach a session to an entire group of strangers from out of town. She had taught many classes

THE CROWNING OF A QUEEN

in voodoo, voudou and crafts of the religion to small groups in the store after hours or in small church meeting rooms. But to teach a bunch of white women with lots of money from places all over the country about voodoo in a huge room in a top of the line hotel was pretty heady for her. Monique started the conversation.

"Norma, I really appreciate getting to know you and I really appreciate the opportunity to teach something of my knowledge of voodoo, our craft and religion, to others. I want you to know this is my first time to do it for a large group and my first time to teach it in a larger venue. I have done it many times for groups of up to twenty, but for hundreds this will be a first."

Norma smiled broadly, "Well, I have to admit that I was pretty sure that was the case. But your ease with people, well, it just let me know that you are a natural at being able to express yourself and have everyone get it. Now to cases, how much do you want to get paid to do this?"

Monique looked at Norma and tried to use her powers to look in but could not seem to at the moment. Monique had experienced this before when people were being guarded. It was much harder to get a look in. She would try guile and the direct approach. "Can you tell me the usual fee someone gets for this kind of talk, or give me a clue what I can expect to get?"

Norma smiled, "I am sorry, Monique, but I have to be true to my job and follow the company negotiation guidelines. I can say yes or no or tell you if you are out of range if you ask too much. Above all, you need to believe I am here to help you in many ways."

212

HALLOWEEN BEDTIME STORIES

Monique tried again to look in to Norma's thoughts. Again, it was murky.

"Perhaps you would like to talk to your mother about this," Norma offered. "After all, we are only considering one alternative other than you for this group. Worst case, we can get them if you decide to charge too much or cannot make the obligation once we agree."

Monique reminded herself again to be careful. She was surprised, but she was feeling a little challenged by this young woman in front of her. She was feeling a little angry wondering what Norma meant by "cannot make the obligation once we agree". Something in the manner Norma talked today was causing Monique to doubt her control of the situation. Norma had offered to let her talk to Mary. Was she just being nice or was this girl from Washington trying to play with her? Monique brightened outwardly and smiled at Norma, "How about we meet again tomorrow for coffee? I am not sure I want to talk to Mom about this, but I would like to think about it and investigate speaker fees at similar functions."

"Great," Norma answered. "Now, how about you taking me to the art shop you told me about over on Royal Street."

Monique looked at Norma and looked in to her mind again as she had before. She was getting information about the art shop and somebody named Mike. Monique decided it was probably just a matter of focus. When Norma was focused on a point, she seemed to be able to block any transmission of signals that would tip her hand. Monique was intrigued. For the first time since she was a little girl, she was a little confused.

THE CROWNING OF A QUEEN

Something she could not put her finger on was just not right.

They walked the short blocks in The Quarter and were on a pretty old street with gardens on the balconies overlooking wrought iron rails and black metal fencing. The sun was shining and the feel and smell of the old south was overwhelming. They walked onto the slightly elevated, brick overlaid porch of the old-looking shop and through the doors.

"Good afternoon ladies," the shop keeper said. "Are you new to ouah faiah city?"

"Visiting from Washington," Norma answered. "My friend, Ms. Didier, is from here."

"Well, welcome to my shop. Come in and look around. I'll leave you to yourselves and will be at my desk near the door here if you need help with anything. We have quite a collection of local artists and some old paintings of New Orleans from artists who have long since passed on."

Norma was so carried away with the memories and overwhelmed by seeing Royal Street that she let a thought slip out that really confused Monique. Norma thought to herself "I have always loved Royal Street."

Norma was drawn to a painting depicting Royal Street in the 1800's. It was a great rendition of horse drawn carriages and people dressed up strolling the French Quarter. Everything in the painting looked wet from a light, warm, spring shower and the title was <u>Reflections</u>. Norma walked over to the shopkeeper and brought him back to the painting. After a couple of questions, she said she would take the painting and asked to have it mailed directly to her home in Washington.

HALLOWEEN BEDTIME STORIES

The shopkeeper told her it was one of his favorites. He pointed out to Norma that one of the young women in the foreground of the painting had coloring and eye color very much like her own---very unusual in this part of the South.

Norma agreed, then added, "Artists are that way. They usually paint the *unusual;* it sells better."

It was the only one he had left of that particular scene at that time except the one on the wall at his place up near Lake Pontchartrain in the Ninth Ward. He took down her personal information.

Norma looked at her watch. "Oh, my gosh," she said. "I forgot Mike is coming in to town today. I better get back to the hotel and connect with him. I will call you as soon as I talk to him, and we can figure out where to go to dinner. Then I would like to go to that Ragin' Cajun place where Raymond plays and do some more dancing."

"You really did like Raymond, didn't you?" Monique asked.

"Yes, I do like Raymond, but please don't hold that against me. I am far too wise to try to take a boy away from a voodoo lady. You probably have a spell on him anyway I'll bet."

"Well, maybe a little one," Monique laughed. "See you this evening. And thanks, Norma, for the help with the contracts."

"Sure," Norma smiled back. "After all, we have to stick together." Norma had raised her hand and stopped a carriage cab. "Later," they both said together laughing.

THE CROWNING OF A QUEEN

Monique strolled further down Royal Street before turning toward her shop. Suddenly, she seemed to be thinking more clearly. She wondered about the coincidence of the lady in the painting; she certainly did look like Norma.

"Hi baby," Mary said as Monique entered the shop. "How did your afternoon go? I've been busy here and selling good luck charms and dolls like crazy. This year many of the krewes are trying to hex the king of the other krewes. Of course, they all want a good luck charm to help them win the competition or at least win a spot to march in front of the horses." Mary laughed at all the novice talent that would be trying to cast spells and throw a hex in New Orleans this evening.

Monique told Mary about the meeting, and Mary was thrilled that they would get a chance to become part of the entertainment for visiting conventions. She had never entertained the thought of having a marketing person address the tourists to help send them her way, but she certainly was astute enough to latch on to the idea when it was served up on a platter as this had been. She felt good that her powers had led her to send that little slip of a girl with the 'out-of-town clothes' down to her shop off of Bourbon Street.

She felt like they were about to bring voodoo back into the popularity it had once had in New Orleans. She felt like she was on the verge of seeing a new voodoo queen crowned and the city laid before her feet. Mary was feeling pretty positive about their opportunity.

Monique shared that she had started struggling with reading the thoughts Norma was having. She said

216

HALLOWEEN BEDTIME STORIES

she even felt like Norma was intruding on her thoughts at times. They talked at length about Norma.

Mary told Monique, "Be very careful with Norma. Norma may be from somewhere else, but she is very important to us, and she is doing us a big favor. It was almost too easy to send her here to the shop. But I could tell she is very smart and very special. If you look at her coloring, you know she is indeed something special. If I didn't know better or had met her as a native here in New Orleans, I would try to see if she was one of us. I had this feeling in the depth of my soul when I first saw her and the thought to be careful. She is very special. The other thing I am positive about is that she likes us."

Norma was hoping to get to her room before seeing Mike, but he was waiting for her in the lobby. "How about this. I was able to get a reason to come to New Orleans while you were here. We could be in for some real fun. I know this town real well."

"Mike, you know I am here on business and obligated to take care of that business first. I hope we can get in a little partying, but I cannot let it interfere with the real reasons I came here." She gazed into his eyes as she talked, and he began nodding before she was half way through her sentence. "I suggest you go set up your meetings for tomorrow, and I will catch up with the paperwork I need to do. We can get together about 7:00 pm and meet a couple who have agreed to show us the town tonight. She is a person who I am doing business with for my firm. He is a musician; you'll like them."

"Great," Mike mumbled, nodding his head and heading for the elevator.

THE CROWNING OF A QUEEN

Norma marveled at how easy it had been to get Mike to do her bidding as she went to her room and showered. She sensed that she was changing, and she began knowing of the other side of her life. She was becoming aware that she had powers beyond normal mortals. She was thinking about how to help Monique land the opportunity to speak in a fair way. She could not know yet that this was the last test Monique needed to pass. Monique must be able to successfully handle a situation without the aid of magic. Monique must trust a person she believed to be an average human being.

The phone rang and Norma answered, "Hello."

Monique said "Norma, I have been talking with my mom, and she says that we should trust you. She says you are on our side. So, I want to tell you that I am ready to accept whatever offer you make to me so we can do business together, and, most of all, so that we can be friends."

Norma felt warm all over. Monique had just done the thing she needed to do to land the contract, and, in the voodoo world, Monique had just done much more. She had trusted a young stranger based on her feelings. She had shown the confidence in herself to become a Queen. Norma was pleased and relaxed. Her convention would have a great speaker. Norma was also 'awakened'. She knew that there would be a greater purpose for coming to New Orleans than just her job. She knew everything and that she was a Queen sent to crown another Queen.

"I know we are going out in about an hour and a half with the boys," she said to Monique, "but can you please run over and sign these papers? I will get you

218

HALLOWEEN BEDTIME STORIES

$5,000 for each session and guarantee you at least two full busses of people with money to spend. It will give you enough cash to move to your new store, and you can start commanding the $5,000 fee when you address other conventions in New Orleans. It is truly a win-win. Come on over and sign it, and I'll fill you in on the details. "

Monique felt a sensation of a slight chill. She knew for sure Norma was her friend, and she knew for sure now that Norma was more than she seemed to be. Norma was something special.

It took Monique about 20 minutes to be standing in the doorway of Norma's room. The first thing she did was to offer her hand. Norma took her hand and shook it.

"We have a deal," she smiled, "Now, come on over and sign these papers for me." Monique signed the papers. The two women hugged. Norma thanked Monique and reminded her that they only had about an hour before going out with the boys.

Monique took her copy of the contracts, placed them in her purse and said "Boy, am I happy and grateful to land this deal. Thank you Norma."

"You are welcome dear; now, let's spend the night celebrating. There is much more to talk about, but we have two days left before I need to leave. I apologize in advance for my current boyfriend, but sometimes we just have to do the best we can. Mike is OK, but I honestly didn't expect him to be a part of all this. He just decided to show up on his own. I guess last Saturday night was more impressive to him than I guessed."

Monique said, "We may both have to watch our boys then, because Raymond is more than a little impressed with you."

219

THE CROWNING OF A QUEEN

Norma answered, "We will talk about that tomorrow over lunch. I have to give you all the paperwork you will need to file with the organization anyway, and we can talk about our beaus."

"See you soon," Monique said.

It was about a half an hour after midnight when Norma suggested that they all order one last drink, and then she needed to get to bed. Mike had been having a wonderful time and really liked Ray. He could not take his eyes off of Monique.

Ray ordered a round of Hurricanes for the table and winked at Norma. "After we drink this I'm gonna need to go to bed with somebody, and if you are the first one to finish, maybe I'll just go with you Miss Norma."

Norma winked back at Ray. "Now, Ray, you don't want to get in trouble with Monique. After all, she is a voodoo lady."

Mike had been listening to the banter and said in a bit of a slurred way, "Voodoo, schmoodoo. It's obvious ol' Ray wants to get some of you Norma."

Monique looked at Mike and said, "Well, you have been taking my blouse off all night with your eyes, so you can't say too much. I don't mind the attention, mind you, but I can't let you bad mouth voodoo so be careful white boy from Washington, be careful."

Monique gazed at Mike and he became quiet. They drank the Hurricanes and danced. Ray was dancing with Norma, and Mike was dancing with Monique. Both men were being more familiar than they should be with each other's girl. As they walked toward the hotel they all hugged.

220

HALLOWEEN BEDTIME STORIES

Monique and Norma had agreed to meet for coffee and planning. Mike had announced rather loudly that he had some business to take care of regarding levees near the lake. Ray had agreed to take Mike on a guy's tour of Bourbon Street after he finished his business, and they could all meet for dinner. The plans were set.

Ray leaned toward Norma and kissed her. Monique glared, then leaned over to kiss Mike. Norma whispered to Ray, "Later. Good night Cajun boy."

Ray was taken aback; he looked at Norma in a different and hopeful way.

He hooked arms with Monique and said, "C'mon baby. We have to get some sleep---big day tomorrow."

They parted company when Ray hailed a mule drawn carriage cab, all yelling "good night" to each other.

"You were pretty worked up by that pretty voodoo lady, weren't you Mike? You want her, don't you? I'll bet you are wondering what it would be like to sleep with a lady who can do that kind of magic. I'll bet you are thinking about seeing her naked right now."

"Welllll, OK, something about her turned me on, but something about you turns me on too." He reached for her and pulled her close. She gazed into his eyes. He did not know why, but he suddenly wanted to make wild Cajun voodoo love to her. He was thinking wild sensuous thoughts about Norma and Monique. He was transported to a level of passion he had never felt before. Norma was happy.

Morning came a little later for all of them the next day. Mike had his wake up call and was off to tour

THE CROWNING OF A QUEEN

the aging, crumbling levees of New Orleans. Ray was lazily having breakfast with Monique, and they were planning what to do this evening. Ray talked in low tones to Monique.

Monique said, "I think she is someone special. She may not be one of us exactly, but something very special. Mom and I both get that."

Ray said, "Yeah, I get that too. She definitely communicates with me on more than one level at a time. What do you make of Mike?"

"Mike is a completely average human being with an average IQ. He likes to party and may be some fun. I am not sure why Norma keeps him around. But he is easy to hex."

Ray chuckled, "That poor boy had hexes flying at him from all directions. Wonder he didn't get crazy last night."

"I got a feeling he did get crazy," Monique smiled. "I can't wait to have coffee with her this morning and get our business out of the way so we can talk like friends. I will also ask her about some other things that have me thinking. You want her don't you?"

Ray answered, "Yeah, I do, and I can tell she wants some of this boy too."

When Norma and Monique met, they got the business portion of their meeting done quickly. All the contracts were signed and put into the appropriate brief cases.

Monique looked at Norma and tried to look in. Norma smiled and said aloud, "Only when I let you or want you to."

Monique smiled broadly.

222

HALLOWEEN BEDTIME STORIES

"OK, it is time to let me in on the secret. Just who are you really, and what is going on?"

"I am a friend who has come to give you your final test and to place a crown on your head. I am a sister in the craft. I am of the Wiccan people. I am of the witches of Europe who came to the Northeastern shores of the United States. I am one of the two queens required to crown a new queen. I have administered the final test. You needed to trust a human being and deal with them without your craft. You needed to prove that you can accomplish important things without magic in order to receive greater powers. And now you have passed the test. There will be great celebration among the practitioners of the craft. There will be many happy witches from all over the world. We can talk to Mary and plan the ceremony for tomorrow. Your dad and Raymond will be very happy. Your dad has been planning for this day. Come on. Let's go talk to your family. I can wrap up all this mortal business, and we will be off."

With a flourish and wave of Norma's left hand, all the papers and computers placed themselves into a travel case. There was only one device left. It was a recorder with its microphone activated. It was running and had recorded the entire meeting between the two. The machine had initials M.D. on it.

"Uh oh, looks like Mike has made himself a loose end. I was worried about him being a little too curious about my business and friends. I will let that problem be your first to solve as our queen." Meanwhile, she pointed at the machine. It burst into flame. Both women laughed.

223

THE CROWNING OF A QUEEN

Mary could tell by the smiles on the faces of Monique and Norma that their meeting had been a good one. She was curious about the details. She was just about to attempt to gain knowledge by gazing into the mind of their guest when she suddenly caught a bolt of recognition

Norma had looked into Mary and silently said, "Sister, I am here to help crown a new queen."

Mary smiled, "I knew you were something special. You can't hide that supernatural coloring under a business suit and phony glasses. Glad you made it sister. Welcome to our home. Please come and share our place. I bet you are Wiccan."

"Queen Norma at your service," Norma bowed. "I am here to join you in the deserved crowning of Queen Monique. Tomorrow night we will complete the ceremony. There will be practitioners from all over. We can be pretty much at ease because the mortals will be busy with the Krewes' competitions. When the ceremony is over, I will head back to my place in Washington.

You and Monique can start getting your new location ready. Voodoo may have a chance to become a much larger religion than it has been for the past couple hundred years. Get your sacrifices ready; tomorrow is the big day."

The rest of the day and evening were much like the day before (that happens a lot in New Orleans). It was late and Mike, Ray, Monique and Norma were drinking and dancing at the Ragin' Cajun. This time when Ray made his pass, Norma said yes.

HALLOWEEN BEDTIME STORIES

She looked at Monique who smiled and said, "OK and I will have Mike." She gazed at Mike and said, You do want to come home with me tonight, don't you? You want to experience a voodoo lady."

Mike grinned and said, "Voodoo schmoodoo."

Monique said, "I told you to be respectful of voodoo."

"Yes. I am sorry," Mike blurted out. "Don't want to get one of those pins stuck in my ass do I?"

Norma leaned over to Monique, "Remember, he is easy to hex, and you can make him whatever you want in bed."

Monique warmed at the thought and said, "c'mon Mike; let's take a walk." Those would be the last words Mike remembered hearing that night. He would remember some of the sexiest dreams he had ever had in his life. Monique had forgotten the thrill a 'well-under-control' mortal could provide.

Friday morning came later than the other days that week had come. It was a little after 9:00 am when Ray left the room. Monique called and said she had enjoyed her night with Mike and had adjusted his memory before depositing him in his room. Norma thanked Monique for sharing her lover.

Monique said, "You are welcome. This has long been a favorite custom among witches, and, after all, you returned the favor."

"I just hope my favor does not become a burden for the rest of the time here. I still have not talked to him about that little recorder he buried in my briefcase."

"When you do," Monique added, " give him some instructions about his little smart ass statements

225

THE CROWNING OF A QUEEN

about our craft. If he says voodoo schmoodoo one more time, I may turn him into a toad or something worse."

Norma said, "Oh yes, sorry about that. I will see if I can fix that. I am not sure what I am going to do with him during the ceremony. I may have to cast him into a little spell. We can think about that tonight. See you at 7:00 at the shop."

Mike woke up hungry. He wondered how he had gotten home. It was not the first time in New Orleans that he awoke somewhere not knowing how he got there. He had been with Norma, Monique and Ray. He must have had too much to drink. Ray had probably put him in bed. His clothes were scattered all over his room. He had a headache. He thought again about his dreams of sex with Monique. She was stunning, and he had been with her in every imaginable position for the whole night. He was tired. He dialed Norma on the phone.

"Good morning," she said. "How are you feeling this morning?" He knew then he had drank too much and probably made a fool of himself.

"I'm OK," he lied. "How are you?"

"Good," she said. "I have a few wrap-up things to do this morning, and then I am going to take a nap this afternoon. I have some plans that I need to take care of tonight on a personal basis. I cannot take anyone with me. I will need to do this myself. I thought maybe we could have a quick breakfast today, then I will see you back in Washington."

"OK," Mike stammered. "I guess I can finish my work in a couple of hours and catch a plane back tonight."

HALLOWEEN BEDTIME STORIES

"Meet you at Brennan's courtyard in 45 minutes?"

"Great," Norma said. She walked into Brennan's right on time as usual. Mike was standing talking to the same waiter, Bobby Martin, who had waited on Monique and her just a couple of days earlier. They were laughing.

"What is so funny?" Norma asked as she approached them.

"Oh, nothing," Mike had said. "Bobby here was telling me about his krewe going to this voodoo shop and buying up a bunch of trinkets to try to hex the other krewes and win the competitions. He says they all have dolls and gris-gris and shrunken heads."

Bobby was still laughing, and he said, "Yeah, and then Mike said voodoo, schmoodoo, and we started laughing."

Norma said, "You better be careful, both of you. This is a very big voodoo weekend and lots of shamen, warlocks, witches, voodoo princes/princesses and even some queens in New Orleans. It would make them very angry to hear you belittling their religion and their craft. It is very disrespectful."

Mike looked at Norma, sneered a little and said, "OK, I won't offend your new friend. I still think that voodoo junk is a bunch of mumbo jumbo. I mean, how can a pin cushion doll, a few frog skeletons and some plastic shrunken heads have any effect on anything? If those people really believe that crap…."

"Enough, Michael Downey!" Norma's gaze burned. Her eyes seemed to enlarge and contract, and something like electricity ran through Mike's body. He

THE CROWNING OF A QUEEN

started to shake and became very nauseated. He turned for the street and staggered, collapsing onto a bench for waiting customers near the door. He gasped for air and his eyes became bloodshot. Norma quickly sat down beside him and took his hand.

"We are going to have to go back to the hotel a little early. We need to get you ready to head home, and I have a little work to do. I am going to have to rearrange your priorities. I will re-program you some and will set a trigger. You will not want to see me any longer. You will not remember me. You will not remember any of my friends. You will jumble the information from this trip, and it will get you into big trouble. I just hope you were not doing anything important."

Norma took Mike back to her room. She left him sitting in "staring straight ahead position" while she went through his electronic devices. She managed to erase everything about herself and any reference to her friends. She wiped his computer clean. She smiled when she ran across a memo he had been sent via email that afternoon congratulating him on his promotion to head of FEMA. Mike was going to be the head of FEMA even though he had just given up a good percentage of his IQ. She got onto his computer and found his plane reservations. She just had time to call for a cab, pack him and get him to the lobby. She was in a hurry now and needed to make sure Mike was on the plane and out of here. She did not want him in town when Monique became a fully powered voodoo queen.

Monique would not stop at a few IQ points, a jumble of memory and messing up his silly levee report. Monique would turn this guy into a toad. Yes, Norma

HALLOWEEN BEDTIME STORIES

thought, Mike would be much safer if he were away from here. Voodoo people do not take kindly to being made fun of even if it is by accident. Only a few more things in the brief case to fix, then she could put Mike on the plane. He would arrive back in Washington thinking he had a quietly successful trip to New Orleans.

She looked intently at the files in her hands. There were many little red tabs. She opened one and read, "This levee is in severe need of quick repair. A storm surge will certainly cause it to fail, bringing a flood of lake water into the Ninth Ward area. Norma shrugged and waved her left hand over the paper. The red tabs disappeared. The typing on the page changed on the page she was holding. It now read "Levee is OK". All the notes had been changed. Nothing unusual would be noted. Everything would be fine. She was certain she had completed her work.

She walked Mike to the door of the boarding area and kissed him on the cheek. "Bye, Downey," she whispered as he walked onto the plane.

She was anxious to get to the coronation. She was excited to explain to Monique how she had found someone very like herself the subject of an artist and had bought the next to last canvas left. She wanted to explain that her face got on that canvas because of a time about a hundred years back when another "maker" had come to town to crown a young woman a voodoo queen. She wanted to explain why "makers" who are of Wiccan Queens do not age.

The ceremonies of the evening were a huge success, and there were members of the craft from literally all around the world. She was able to perform

THE CROWNING OF A QUEEN

all the duties of the maker and to help establish the new queen. The coronation of the queen was a great party, and everyone there enjoyed all of the excesses of food, drink, and, later on, sexual pleasure in a way only known to the practitioners of the craft. The parties continued on for several days and nights. Then came the time that all would part and return to their own homes.

Norma knew somehow that once she left this experience that she would resume her normal life again. She seemed to know on some level, that her time in the glow was short and near an end. She hoped she would remember it but sensed that she would not.

She meant to tell Monique about Mike's reports which she changed so that Monique could use the appropriate magic on taking care of that problem. It was the one thing that slipped her mind. She became so involved in the ceremonies, she forgot to tell Monique about the changes she made on the reports on the old levees. But then, to magical folks what did it matter that some old levee in a place called the Ninth Ward needed to be fixed? And what harm to have one more incompetent buffoon in charge of yet another government agency?

As promised by the informer Norma awoke in her room at the top floor of the Marriott with a more than severe headache. She felt like she had made love to every man in the bar the night before and was feeling just plain ill. She only started to remember the strange surreal dreams a few days later. She felt tired and wanted to go back home to Washington.

She called Mike's room and was told that he had checked out. She thought it strange that he had not said

HALLOWEEN BEDTIME STORIES

good-bye but she had noticed the way he and Monique sneaked away from the dance floor at the Ragin' Cajun. She remembered feeling angry and embarrassed at his behavior and finding his "bug" in her briefcase. She remembered thinking that Mike had proven himself to be more of a burden than an asset.

She was glad he was gone and would avoid making contact with him again. She completed her work in New Orleans and went back to Washington where she could participate in and tweak the government. Once home, her memories of New Orleans seemed pleasant and productive. She had arranged some great meetings and wonderful tours that would give a flavor of New Orleans as the intriguing city it is. She dreamed strange dreams that she attributed to meeting Mary and Monique and being interested in their practice of voodoo. She even dreamed of herself as a witch participating in a ceremony with nude men and women. She usually woke up spent but satisfied after those dreams.

She only had a brief twinge of memory as she listened to the weather reports on August 23. The weather girl talked of a hurricane headed for Bermuda, a bad one named after a mean and violent old queen, Katrina. Katrina. The name sent a shudder through her nervous system. She seemed to think there was something important about to happen that involved something dreamlike and murky in New Orleans.

She watched in horror, as much of the country did, as New Orleans became filled with water. But she never remembered why those levees in the Ninth Ward failed. Mike Downey could never believe he missed noticing the condition of the levees that he inspected. He

THE CROWNING OF A QUEEN

knew he had not been himself during his visit to New Orleans but thought it was because he drank too much at O'Brien's.

The meetings that Norma planned while in New Orleans were cancelled, but the Island Treasures Voodoo Shop continues to grow and thrive.

It all happened just as it was supposed to......Happy Halloween.

THE COLLECTORS

It was a glint of sunlight that caught Jim's attention as he drove past the old Wilson Dairy Farm. He slowed down and looked into the overgrown field that had once been a manicured farm lot. It was definitely a car, and it may even be a convertible he thought. He must have driven past here a thousand times in the past couple of years, but he never saw the car until today.

He was already late getting home because of Betty. She had waited for him in the parking lot as she had before. She wanted him to take her for another "drive". Jim was starting to get nervous about his relationship with Betty. After all, she was just a senior in high school and he was thirty-five years old. It all started when he was asked to drive the baby sitter home from the Maxwell's. She was a very aggressive young woman in a high school girl's body. Now, a year later, he was in over his head and didn't know how to get out.

One thing they had definitely worked out was, that she was not to come to his place of work again. Today he told her about his obligation to his family that night, and that she would have to wait until one day next week to see him.

By the time he got started home, he was nearly late. He drove faster than usual and was enjoying speeding down the country roads with his radio blasting 50's rock. There was usually no traffic anyway, so he was making up for lost time when he had spotted something shining through the tangled blackberry bushes in the abandoned lot. He decided to stop and take a quick look and started to slow down. He felt a distinct

HALLOWEEN BEDTIME STORIES

chill, and the sun slid behind a cloud as he pulled up in front of the old, red, wooden gate. He turned off his car and started to get out for a look. Just then, his cell phone rang. He answered, "Hi, Jim here."

A feminine voice quipped back, "Janice here! Jim, where"?

"Just driving past the old dairy farm and spotted a car in the old cow lot. Stopping to take a look."

"You better not honey," she said, "we are already late come on home and let's go look at the car tomorrow."

"OK," he said backing away from the gate. As he aimed his car toward home, the sun reappeared. He pulled away, and stepped on the gas pedal picking up speed and casting one backward glance toward the potential prize he had just spotted.

North Central Indiana was just about as pretty as it ever got. Early October usually brought the colors into full view. The trees were glowing as though the light was coming from within them. The grass was still vibrant and green, and the cornfields were standing golden and ripe for harvest. Jim was really enjoying the beauty of the day and of his surroundings. He wished he had the courage and the discipline to tell Betty that their affair was over. But each time he was alone with her, she quickly made the occasion a sexual fantasy come true. She was a Natalie Wood look alike. She often teased him that they were just like the couple in the old movie Rebel without a Cause.

As he drove home, he cleared his mind of Betty and began to focus on his surroundings. Each hilltop revealed a new vista of fall splendor, and around each

THE COLLECTORS

curve there lay a new picture of nature at its fullest. One more hilltop, then he could see his house. It looked beautiful to him too. He noticed how the large Maples, Oaks and Gum trees formed walls of color around the property. He could see the red brick and gray shingles of the roof and the flowerbed out front that Janice took so much pride in. I am lucky to be here in this pretty place at this time. I am lucky to have a great wife and two wonderful, over achieving children.

"I am glad we are here," he heard himself saying out loud. "I am glad we came to Indiana."

He pulled into the garage and shut off the car. He got out of the car and walked to the back door and stepped in. He paused then gave it his best Ozzie Nelson, Ward Cleaver, saying "Honey…. I 'm home."

He heard Janice reply from the direction of the kids bedrooms and stopped to pull off his shoes. He paused to look at the new leather sofa and love seat in the large living room and wondered if Janice would ever let him put his car trophies on the shelf in the corner. Janice kept the house very clean and seemed always ready for and happy to have company. She liked to decorate but did not have full appreciation for Jim's car trophies. Her true love was more for natural beauty. Jim often thought he must be crazy to be involved with Betty when he had Janice. He then walked toward the west side of the house listening for a clue as to which room she was in. He heard a noise from Billy's room and looked in the door.

"Hi dad," Billy said. "Are you and Mom coming to the open house at the school to meet Miss Gooding"?

235

HALLOWEEN BEDTIME STORIES

"That's right. It is Oct 11; the school open house. Miss Gooding huh? I don't think I know her. Is she new"?

"Yeah, Dad, she is new and boy is she pretty."

"Sounds like you have a crush on her already."

"No Dad, but she is pretty. Hey Dad, you want to see this really cool picture of this car I found today? Look, it's an old sports car like the race drivers and big movie stars used to drive. I think it's a Porsche, but it says something else. See if you know what it means."

"Ok, Billy, let me see the picture." Jim studied the picture and read the description. He slowly analyzed the lines of the car and thought it was more of an artist's rendition than the real thing. The description said: 1956 Porsche limited production RS (Rally sport) Beck 550 Spyder. The car was set up for race and looked enhanced. "I am not sure this is the real car or someone's drawing Billy."

"Oh yeah, Dad, it is real. It says so in the story. In fact, that is a picture of one that somebody famous owned or something it says in the book."

"A picture huh? Well, I am not so sure."

"You guys stop talking cars and get ready," came the feminine voice of authority from the room down the hall. "We are going to be late if you don't get on with it."

"Sorry Mom," Billy said just as Jim started to say sorry. "I wanted to show Dad the car in the book I told you about."

"Cars, cars, cars. Sometimes that's all you think about," they all said in unison and started laughing.

THE COLLECTORS

"Well, c'mon. Let's get ready to go see the fabulous Miss Gooding and the steady Miss Rydell."

"Robin got Miss Rydell?" Jim asked, then added, "Great, she will be more at ease with her. It is good that she already got to know her through Sunday school. I think I am going to enjoy this conference. Both kids have teachers they like, and the weather couldn't be better for an excursion to a nearby car discovery tomorrow."

"Auto excursion huh, where to this time?"

"Not far. Remember I just told you about it at the old dairy farm."

Billy's eyes lit up. He was really excited.

"This time, Dad, can I go too?"

"You sure can son. After all, you already have the fever; you may as well get involved in the hunt for the perfect old collector car."

"OK, boys, now let's get going and get ready for school then Dad will buy us dinner at Ray's Diner."

She smiled and shrugged at Jim. He immediately took the hint and said, "I would be honored to escort these two lovely young ladies to Ray's, wouldn't you Bill"?

"Yeah, Dad, but I would rather take Miss Gooding than Robin."

Robin acknowledged Billy's dig by sticking out her tongue and crossing her eyes. She said, "Yeah, and I would rather go with just about anybody but you dog breath, but I guess we are stuck with each other, so let's just make the best of it."

"Robin do you like having Miss Rydell as your teacher"?

237

HALLOWEEN BEDTIME STORIES

"Yeah, Dad, I do like her, and I think it will be a good year."

Jim walked into the bedroom and looked into the mirror. He was still wearing his sport coat and tie from work and decided to just leave it on and make a favorable impression for the sake of the kids. He quickly brushed his teeth, then his hair, adjusted his clothing and walked to the front of the house where Janice and the kids were talking about what they would have at Ray's after the school open house was over. He was taken by how adult his kids seemed now. It was only a short time ago that they would have been happy with a quick burger at McDonalds, but now they were looking forward to a great fifties diner as a reward for their efforts in school.

The drive to the school was only about two miles and uneventful. The school building was a nice, one-level, brick structure. It had very nice grounds and was situated with open fields behind it. It had the latest in desks and materials and even offered a computer in every classroom. Once there with the car safely parked, the Miller family walked into the school together just as they always had.

Robin wanted to have everyone stop by her classroom first. She was in the seventh grade this year, and it was her last year to have a "room". Next year would be Junior High School with home rooms and class changes. This was her last year as a "kid"; next year she would be a grown up Junior High student with all the trappings. Robin wanted this to be the best of her elementary years and had worked hard to make a good start. She hoped that if she did real well, her parents would let her become a cheerleader for the 7th grade

THE COLLECTORS

basketball team. Miss Rydell was smiling as they walked into the room and anxious to tell Jim and Janice how wonderful their oldest child was to have in school, and how bright and dedicated Robin was in her schoolwork. They covered the report with Miss Rydell and offered to help where and when needed. They thanked Miss Rydell and headed for Billy's classroom where they were about to meet the new teacher Miss Gooding.

Billy was right. This woman was a knock-out, and looked more like she was ready to start a modeling career than teach school in a small Indiana town. But there she was, and she seemed to be totally involved in the experience of teaching 5th grade and the children of that age group. She was excited to talk about Billy and how he was doing very well in the early stages of school, which was mostly review to this point. She talked of Billy and his social skills and his ability to excel at the schoolwork. She spoke like a veteran teacher and quickly let the Millers know that she was more than just a pretty face.

Jim appreciated the meeting with the teachers but he was getting hungry. When he told Janice that it was about time to head for their dinner reservation both Robin and Billy cheered. Janice gave a small impatient look in Jim's direction, but he had looked at the kids and was walking toward the door with Robin and Billy in front of him. Janice looked at Miss Gooding and said, "Well, the family has spoken so the mother must go too. It was nice to meet you Miss Gooding."

The lovely young teacher stuck out her hand and said "Please call me Sam, but not around the kids. We are new in town and are anxious to meet some people

HALLOWEEN BEDTIME STORIES

near our own age. I am sure my husband Rob would enjoy meeting Jim."

They shook hands and parted. Billy was already standing beside the back door of the car when she walked outside. Jim and Robin were standing near the doorway waiting for her. Janice started talking before she got to them, "I think "Miss" Gooding is going to be a real asset to our community. I am anxious to get to know her and her husband better. I think we should invite them over for a visit soon."

The Miller family drove to Ray's Retro Diner, and as they looked in the parking lot for a space to park, Billy said loudly, "Wow, Dad, look at the cars on that transport."

Jim looked at the rear of the lot and could hardly believe his eyes. He saw an auto transport truck nearly fully loaded with classic cars. There was an Austin Healey 100 S with original racing colors. There was a '57 Chevrolet Bel-Air convertible. There was a '47 Mercury convertible, a '49 Mercury sedan as seen in the movie Rebel without a Cause. This truck full of cars must be worth several hundred thousand dollars, but what was it doing in Marion? The drivers must be inside. Jim hoped to recognize them and strike up a conversation about the collection of cars being transported.

Once inside, Jim looked around the crowded restaurant. The waitresses in their poodle skirts were busy moving around the crowded dining area.

"Obviously we were not the only parents with great kids who deserved a meal at Ray's Diner," Janice said.

THE COLLECTORS

"Yeah," Jim said absent-mindedly. He had spotted two men dressed like transport drivers. He elbowed Billy and said, "I'll bet those guys are the transport drivers."

Billy was already walking toward the men asking in his deepest 11 year old voice, "Are you hauling all those neat cars"?

The men both smiled and said, "Yes."

"Wow," Billy said. "I'll bet it's fun just looking at them and talking to all the people who are curious about them."

"Well, it sure is a good conversation starter and never fails to get attention," the older man of the two said. He smiled at Billy and Jim who had joined the conversation. He offered his hand to Jim. "Dave Merkin," he said.

"Jim Miller," Jim answered. "Where are you guys taking the cars, to a special show or something"?

"Well actually, we can't say because the owner is funny about saying where these classics are stored," Dave answered.

"Well they are sure beauties. Would you mind if my son and I took a closer look at them"?

"Of course you can get a closer look. It is the usual with classics".

"I know," Jim said, "look, but don't touch. Billy and I are used to it. We have a little classic of our own".

Dave's companion moved closer and offered his hand. "Robert Benson," he said shaking Jim's hand. "What kind of classic do you own? Our boss is always looking for a couple of new cars to add to his collection."

241

HALLOWEEN BEDTIME STORIES

"I have an old Porsche Speedster Coupe," Jim said. "It's rough and has a lot to be done, but it is all there".

"Say, Jim, we are actually here following up a lead on a possible addition to our boss' collection. Do you know where the old Wilson Farm is?"

Jim hesitated, but Billy blurted out that they sure did; it was pretty near their place over by Fairmount. Robert smiled, and asked if he could get their phone number in exchange for a tour of the cars.

Janice cleared her throat loudly and said, "Someone here was pretty hungry about 20 minutes ago."

Jim immediately came back to earth. He quickly asked where the men in the transport were parking for the night and promised to come by after dinner for the tour, and he would leave his phone number at that time. They all agreed, and Jim and Billy joined Robin and Janice just as a cute brunette waitress in a light blue poodle skirt offered to lead them to their table.

"Jim, isn't that the babysitter from Maxwell's last year"?

"Why yes, I believe it is," Jim answered. He tried not to look directly at Betty.

Janice was already saying, "You may remember us. We are the Millers, and my husband drove you home from the Maxwell's where you were babysitting last year for them. I believe it was the car club Halloween party."

Betty looked at Janice slowly and said, "Sure, I remember. It's not every night that a girl gets to be taken home by James Dean."

THE COLLECTORS

"I nearly forgot. Jim did go as Jimmy Dean. Well Betty, it is good to see you again."

They were seated where they could watch the two transport drivers walk across the parking lot toward the truck loaded with precious cargo. Billy wondered out loud if they may take one of the cars off the truck to let someone just sit in it. Jim told him he doubted it.

Janice said, "BOYS, please; that's enough talking about cars. Let's talk about what we saw at school and your plans this year."

"Ok, Mom," Billy said, "but those were pretty cool cars you have to admit."

"Well maybe, but I didn't like the looks of those two glorified truck drivers, especially the smirk on the one when Jim was talking about the old Wilson place."

"Oh honey, they are just a couple of guys trying to make a living by hauling expensive cars for some car-buff millionaire. They are probably good guys who have spent too long on the road."

"OK, but all the same, I'm glad they are just moving through the area because they look like they could be trouble to me. Call it a woman's intuition, but I got a chill when they were talking to you. That I didn't like one bit."

Robin chimed in, "Look at them now standing by the truck smoking cigarettes and talking to all the boys from the high school basketball team. I agree, Mom, there is something about them I don't like."

Jim looks at Billy and shrugs his shoulders, and Billy shrugs back.

The waitress who had been standing waiting all this time interrupted and said, "Hi again, I am Betty, and

HALLOWEEN BEDTIME STORIES

I am going to be your server tonight. The specials are the Ranch Burger with trimmings or Meat Loaf. They both come with drinks and fries."

"Great," Billy exclaimed, "I'll have the Ranch Burger, fries and a Coke."

Robin and Janice ordered Meat Loaf, and Jim decided to get a double cheeseburger with the works. They spent the next forty-five minutes eating and talking and enjoying the 50's tunes on the big juke-box. When the juke played Betty Lou got a new pair of shoes, their waitress walked to the middle of the floor in the dining area and did a few dance steps. Betty Parker could really dance. As she danced in the direction of the Millers' table, she was showing off her saddle shoes and a little too much leg to suit Janice. The 50's diner was all it was advertised to be, and the Miller family walked toward the door very happy with their meals, the service and the music.

They had nearly forgotten the transport, but as they walked toward their car, they noticed it was gone. Jim spoke up, "Girls, Billy and I told those men we would stop by their motel for a minute to give them directions to the Wilson Farm and to take a quick look at the cars. We promise to be not more than ten minutes."

"Good," Janice said, "that will give Robin and I just enough time to swing by the Tastee-Freeze and pick up two hot fudge sundaes. That way we can all enjoy the next fifteen minutes."

Billy looked longingly at his mom and she looked back shaking her head, "OK Billy, I'll bring one for you too, but your father is using up his treat by making this stop. You two be careful around those two

THE COLLECTORS

guys. They look like some pretty rough characters to me."

"Don't worry," Jim said as he and Billy got out of the car and walked toward the office of the motel. The desk clerk agreed to ring number 13, and Dave and Robert came out onto the low roofed porch. "Oh, hi there Jim. Are you guys ready to look at the cars"?

"Are we!" Billy echoed.

"This Healey must be one of the original racing cars from 1955," Jim was saying as he approached a beautiful purple and white small car with its windshield lying almost flat against its hood.

"Yep," Dave said, "I think Donald Healey himself raced it at Sebring".

"Who is Donald Healey?" Billy asked Jim.

"I will explain who Donald Healey is later, but you get the number off of that beauty," Jim said to Billy.

"Anyway, it's a really cool car," Billy said. They looked at each car for what seemed like just a few seconds when Janice and Robin reappeared in the driveway. Jim quickly gave his phone number to Robert and thanked the men for allowing a close up look.

"Oh, it's our pleasure, and the boss kind of likes us to show off his stuff anyway just not tell where he keeps it."

They parted and drove home. Jim was preoccupied all the way home with memories of the Healey they had seen. He was certain that car had been wrecked at Sebring. It was a complete disaster. Donald Healey had walked away, but a number of spectators had died in the fire caused by the crash. The car was burned beyond salvage. Maybe these guys were making look

245

HALLOWEEN BEDTIME STORIES

alike cars and trying to pull something over on the public. Janice was right. They were at least suspect looking. He was not positive and would have to do his research later. Billy was bubbling about the pretty colors and new appearance of the cars on the transport. He was talking about a deep purple Jaguar XJ-12 with a white top that Jim had not seen at all.

"Not like Dad's Porsche which looks like its old; these cars are old but look like brand new."

"Yeah," Jim said wistfully, "that is what you can do if you have lots of money to restore them. Billy tell me about the Jag. Where was it? I missed it."

Billy said he saw it up near the front on the right side. Jim wondered because he was sure he had seen a 1932 Ford five window coupe in that spot on the carrier. He was definitely wondering about the owner of all those cars.

"Home," Janice breathed, almost relieved to get the boys into the house and their minds on something besides cars. The boys caught the mood and no one mentioned another word about cars that whole evening.

When the morning alarm sounded, Jim could not believe he had gone to sleep. One minute he was lying beside Janice, listening to her breathing, and the next he was walking across the cool floor toward the noisy jangling alarm clock.

He got ready for work quickly because he was planning to stop by the Wilson Farm to verify that he really saw a car in the tangled blackberry patch that used to be a farm lot. He was just finishing his second cup of coffee when he remembered he had promised to let Billy go along on the hunt for the old car. He decided

246

THE COLLECTORS

to go ahead by himself then come and get Billy after work and re-discover the car with him then. He didn't like the idea of going by without Billy, but believed that it would be best given that the transport drivers were interested in something at the Wilson Farm, and he just may know what it was and where it was.

He drove quickly to the old farm and pulled up in front of the locked gate. He felt the chill again and a sense of trespassing. He looked around in the early morning sunlight and saw no one, so he climbed over the fence and walked toward the briar patch where he had seen a glint of sun shining on chrome if he didn't miss his guess. He looked hard into the tangled plants and leaves and saw the outline of a Porsche 356 Speedster convertible or a close resemblance of one. It was filthy, covered with the dark green blackish film that can only come from sitting in a place completely overgrown with plants. It appeared to be sort of white with a dark color interior.

And............it had numbers stuck on the side as if it were going to be raced. He was so engrossed in looking at the car that he didn't hear the other cars stop or the boys climb over the gate. He did hear them laughing and talking as they approached him. Larry Warner was the first to speak.

"Good morning Mr. Miller. I was bringing the guys I play ball with to show them this little beauty. I saw it last week and have been trying to find out who to talk to about it ever since."

Jim spoke back explaining that he had spotted the car earlier too, but didn't quite know what it was so stopped to take a look.

HALLOWEEN BEDTIME STORIES

Larry said he didn't know what it was either, but one of his fellow players spoke up saying, "I saw a picture of this car in a magazine or one just like it.

"It is a Porsche Limited Beck 550 Spyder Special. It was real fast in its day," Jim said. "I'm not sure about the Beck thing, but it is at minimum a 356 type Porsche which makes it worth quite a pretty penny."

They all pulled brush away from the car and admired its lines. Jerry, the team leader, said "Guys, it's time for school, and we don't want to get kicked off the team so let's get going."

The entire team scrambled into the two cars packing them full and headed off down the road toward town. Jim took one last look, and decided to spend his lunch hour at the courthouse looking at a way to find an owner.

The only thing he could find out for sure was that the Wilson family no longer owned the farm, and someone named Dean in California would need to be contacted. He wrote down the sketchy information.

That day after work he went home to pick Billy up for their car excursion. As he was leaving, Janice came walking toward the car, and said that she and Robin wanted to go along and look too. Jim explained that a gate had to be climbed, but when Janice pointed at her blue jeans and Robin's as well, Jim said, "OK family, let's go."

Things looked a little better when he pulled up in front of the gate. The sun was out, and the car seemed less covered with brush and blackness. It was clearly a white Porsche convertible around the 55/56/57 era. He could see the car better and tell that it seemed to be in

248

THE COLLECTORS

remarkable condition for a car that had been sitting in brush for years. Billy waded through the brush and climbed into the car.

"Dad, it is just like the one in the book I showed you. Can we buy it?"

Janice quickly said, "Now wait a minute, Mr. Money Bags, let's take it more slowly. You have to admit, he looks a lot like a 50's movie star in that car. In fact, he looks like someone famous, but I can't remember who."

"You know, Mom, the blonde guy with the blue eyes."

The family looked into the brush at the little car and talked excitedly about the prospects of fixing it up along with their other Porsche. Jim decided that he better get on with locating the owner because at least two other potential buyers were trying to get this car. The kids from basketball team were interested in finding the owner, and the transport drivers were looking for this farm. One look at the transport told any fool what they were interested in here at the old Wilson Dairy Farm. Jim knew he better hurry if he wanted a chance at this little car.

Once at home, he asked Billy to bring the magazine with the Beck Special Speedster picture in it. Billy returned holding his hand over his mouth saying, "Dad, this is the same car. It has the same numbers."

Jim had not noticed the numbers and certainly had no reason to believe the discolored hulk sitting in the berry patch was the shining, trim beauty in the pictures. He decided to read the article and discovered that this was, indeed, a real Porsche 550 Beck Special Spyder.

HALLOWEEN BEDTIME STORIES

The numbers were added as nostalgia. He was excited. This car in the berry patch just may be a real Beck Special.

The next morning when he was on his way to work, he was flagged down by one of the high school boys. It was Larry Warner. Larry asked Jim if he knew anything about the place or the car. He really wanted to find out if there was any chance of getting the car for himself. Jim decided right then and there to make Larry and offer. He told Larry that he too was interested in the car and that he too wanted to buy it.

He said, "Larry, if I get to buy that car, I will make you a real good deal on my coupe."

"Thanks, Mr. Miller, but I want this convertible. Besides, I found it first, and if I hadn't started pulling the brush away from it, no one would even know it is here."

"Larry, that may be true, but the other evening after the school open house when you and your team were at the diner, two guys in a transport asked me about the Wilson place."

"Yeah, Mr. Miller, I guess you're right. They asked me about the Wilson place too, and I told them a lie. I told them I didn't know where it was. Once they find the place and this car, they will add it to that collection for their boss."

" I think you are right, Larry, and no matter which one of us gets this car, I would rather have it stay in town than to be hauled away to some warehouse and never be seen again. I think we can agree to work together on it and keep it our little secret. What do you think?"

THE COLLECTORS

Larry smiled and said, "I think you are right Mr. Miller."

"Now that we are partners, call me Jim, OK Larry."

"Sure, Mr….. Jim."

They both laughed out loud. They took one last look at the bush pile and discussed perhaps coming back in the late evening to re-cover the car better to keep other curious treasure seekers from spotting it. They even talked about removing the Wilson Dairy sign. Jim told Larry that he had a lead, and that they could get together the next morning and see what they knew about the place and the car. Larry said that would be great. They could use the whole weekend to find out about the place and the car.

"By the way, Mr., I mean Jim, are you superstitious?"

"Why?" Jim asked.

"Well, today is Friday the 13th. You know, October with Halloween coming and the 13th and all."

Jim looked at the younger man and moaned,

"Woooooooooooooooooooooooo," then laughed as he walked to his car.

Larry was laughing too as he started walking back toward town. "Hey, Larry, come on; I'll drive you to town. It's on my way anyway."

"Thanks Jim."

Jim asked if Larry thought the team would be any good this year, and was impressed to hear Larry say that the team was ranked as one of the state favorites for the first time since the early 1950s. They parted with a

HALLOWEEN BEDTIME STORIES

reminder to keep their secret and compare notes the next day

Both Jim and Larry were of the belief that he had the upper hand on owning that car. Jim was certain that a high school kid would not have the money to buy such a prize. Larry was certain that no one realized that he had a large sum of cash paid to him to shave points in some upcoming basketball games. If worse came to worse, he could let Jim know that he knew about good ol' Betty. Hell, all the guys on the basketball team knew about good ol' Betty.

Jim arrived at his office on time and was happy to see that everything was going well. His assistant told him that everything was caught up, and that she may just leave early today. Jim stopped to fill his coffee cup then walked into his large office. He loved the furniture in his office. The cherry wood desk and meeting table suited his sense of style.

Once behind his desk, Jim took a little time to continue his research on the Wilson Farm. He actually found a phone number that looked like a piece of history because of the way it was stated. It said dial the California area code, then Hobart 5-5455. Jim looked at the dial on his phone and decided that Hobart 5 was 465. He dialed the number and the person on the other end, a man, said, "Yah."

Jim hesitated for a moment, and asked "Is this the Dean residence"?

"Yeah."

Jim stammered and said, "Well, I am calling about the old Wilson Dairy Farm owners."

"Yeah"? came the reply.

THE COLLECTORS

"I found an old car there, and wonder if I can buy it or something, or if you even are the right person to ask".

"Yeah."

"I found a rare Porsche Beck 550 Spyder, and I want to buy it."

"Oh, that again. Look man, I already sold that car, and the owner took it back to the Wilson place to store it. You will have to contact him."

Jim was getting a little angry because of this guy's tone and manner. He asked the person on the phone, "How can I do that"?

"Look in the jockey box man. You'll find all the papers. That will explain everything. You can call the guy who bought it. His number is on the papers too. Tell him Jim told you about it. Gotta go now. Bye."

Silence---then a dial tone.

"Son of a bitch hung up on me," Jim said to himself. He scratched Jim on the front of the papers he had obtained from the courthouse and got back to his work. He could hardly wait to see what was in the "jockey box" of the Porsche. He thought that if the papers are really all there and all signed, anyone could claim that car. He wondered if he should tell Larry.

Meanwhile, Larry was looking at the neat stack of papers he had pulled from the glove compartment of the little car. He did not understand how some of this stuff could be true, but there it was. A complete California title all signed. Everything was in order. He just needed to check the numbers to be sure, and he could get the car for nothing. He had intended to get the numbers that morning, but Jim had been there. Larry

253

HALLOWEEN BEDTIME STORIES

thought to himself that there just might be no way around the problem. He may have to tell Jim that he knew about Betty, and that he would make trouble for him.

By the end of the day, Jim was anxious to see the car again. It was as though he was consumed with trying to own that little Beck Special. He decided to go there directly after work. He thought about the transport and the cars on it, and was pretty sure who the voice on the phone had sold the car to. He remembered the Healey 100 S, and decided to look up that information. He found an Austin Healey Club listing and a link to the early race cars of Donald Healey. There on page 109 of Donald Healey's book, "My World of Cars" was number the number 45 100 S Sebring racer just hours before it was involved in that horrible incident. The book was clear in saying that the car was completely destroyed leaving Donald with five other Sebring cars. Jim felt a chill very similar to the one he felt when he first spotted the Beck Special. It was about two in the afternoon when his phone rang.

"Hello Jim," the voice on the phone said. "This is Dave. Robert and I are going to drive out to the Wilson Farm like we talked about at the diner. We need those directions."

Jim was thinking fast now and was trying to stall. He told Dave he was real busy right now and had someone in his office. He asked if he could call back in an hour with the directions.

"Sure, Jim. You just do what you have to. Robert and I have a car to pick up, but anytime today or tomorrow will work for us. Talk to you in a little while."

THE COLLECTORS

Jim was nearly panicked now. He called Janice and told her he needed to get over to the old Wilson Farm right after work and make some arrangements on the car. He had found out enough information to be able to own it if he played his cards right. Janice seemed excited too and told him to go ahead and get it. She had sensed that something was lacking in their lives and wanted to support her husband and her son in this project. She could hear the excitement in Jim's voice

Larry had a busy day too. He had talked to Clarence Kelly, the bus driver, and, in fact, even paid him a $20 bribe to drive the small team bus past the old Wilson Farm and make a brief stop. He told Kelly that there was an old car he wanted the whole team to see. He did not tell Kelly that he intended to tow the car out behind the bus, but that could be another $20 bribe later.

Kelly was glad he was taking the team to see a car and not to another one of Larry Warner's visits to "Blonde's Incorporated". Larry occasionally took the team to various strip clubs or "houses" for morale purposes. Kelly had already decided that Larry would not get him involved any further in team problems. Kelly agreed and called his wife to say he would be a little late because the team wanted to stop for a class project at the old Wilson Farm.

Larry intended to pull the car to his house, and since he already had the title, he would become the owner. If others had a problem with that, he could get team and community support. Jim couldn't do much because Larry could always tell Mrs. M. about Betty and Jim. The transport guys were no problem because the car wouldn't be there when they came, and since he had the

255

HALLOWEEN BEDTIME STORIES

title, he was the owner. He knew their boss would be mad because he had already paid someone for the car, but he didn't care. If their boss was stupid enough to pay for a car without having the title, he could just go to hell. Possession is nine tenths of the law he thought.

He hustled through basketball practice that afternoon. He pushed the team hard to improve the speed of the passes and to work the ball around perimeters. He encouraged each player to put forth an effort, and they would be rewarded with a special surprise on the ride home. A lot of the players were hoping for another visit to one of the strip clubs in Anderson or some other delight. Larry was being cagey. He would not say exactly what he had in mind. Near the end of practice he said, "OK guys, I'll let you in on my secret. We are going to get that little sports car out of the blackberry patch at the old Wilson Farm, and I will personally see that every one of you get to take her for a drive. I've already got the title and paperwork done---all we have to do is talk old Kelly into hooking a rope on the back of the bus and towing her a couple of miles to our place."

The boys were all excited and could hardly wait for practice to end so they could start the adventure. The coach had never seen the team look better. He knew these boys were special; they were definitely on the way to a state championship. He had looked the other way a number of times when they had kicked up their heels a little too hard. He had helped smooth over the low grades of some players and had even failed to follow up on some of the cheerleaders' complaints of sexual misconduct. But he was also worried. Today he had gotten a phone from someone he didn't know.

THE COLLECTORS

The man who had described himself as Dave Merkin had told the coach that Larry Warner, the star player on the team, was guilty of accepting bribes. He said that some gambling operations from Indy had paid Larry quite a sum of money and that they were onto him. Coach Thompson had asked who they were and told Dave that any such allegation had to be proved. Dave had told the coach that by Monday the score would be settled, and that the news of Larry's acceptance of bribe money would be public knowledge. Coach was wondering how to talk to Larry about the phone call. He decided that first he would call this guy back and find out more about just who he was and how he knew this information. He was not going to upset his best player because of one phone call which may just be some fan from another school trying to create problems.

Coach Thompson would just sleep on this information. Practice ended and the boys rushed into the showers. They emerged wet and loud and headed for the team bus.

Kelly saw the boys' half running through the doors of the gym and heading toward the bus. He crushed out his cigarette on the curb and climbed into the driver's seat. He opened the doors and waited for the team to load up. He was nervous about Larry's request to go by the Wilson place, but knew that it could only take a half hour or so at the worst.

He was counting on it not taking long because he had big plans for the evening. He was going to stop by Ray's about 9:30 and give the Parker girl a ride home. It was all arranged, and he knew he was going to have a good time of his own.

257

HALLOWEEN BEDTIME STORIES

He watched Larry Warner saunter down the sidewalk looking at some old looking folder papers.

Larry got on the bus, and said, "OK, everyone ready? We are heading to the Wilson place." He looked at Kelly, and in his loud manner said, "OK, driver, lets' go."

Kelly accelerated away from the gym nearly spilling Larry onto the floor. The boys laughed, and they were on their way.

Jim was just about to leave his office when he remembered that he had agreed to call Dave Merkin back. He knew where they were staying and called the motel. The clerk had told him that there was no one in Room 13 and that there was no transport parked there. He looked at the number Dave had given him, and it was a different number than the motel. They are probably waiting at a truck stop or diner or someplace like that he thought. He thought he should perhaps try one last time to be sure about the papers on the Beck Special. He found the numbers from the property search and called the number in California again. This time all he got was a recording saying "The number you have dialed is not in service, if you need assistance look in your directory or dial zero for the operator."

He tried it twice more getting the same message. He thought how strange it was only a couple of hours ago that he had talked to someone at that number. Probably didn't pay his bill, Jim thought. Serves him right. He was an asshole on the phone anyway. Jim looked at the number Dave had given him and dialed it on his cell phone as he walked across the parking lot toward his car.

THE COLLECTORS

The phone rang once and Dave's voice answered, "Hello, Dave Merkin here."

Jim said, "I am calling with directions to the Wilson place; do you have a pencil?" Dave said he did, and Jim give him the directions.

Dave said, "I think we will just go on over and load her up tonight. The boss is getting anxious to get these cars back in the warehouse."

"Say," Jim asked, "I wondered about the Healey 100 S on the carrier. I looked it up today and that car was destroyed in 1955 at Sebring. How did you guys ever find it? The book says that it was lost to the team and completely destroyed in the fire after the crash."

Dave hesitated and said, "Oh, that little car is the real thing alright---at least as real as any of them are." He chuckled adding, "You, car buffs are a strange sort. Drawn to these things like bees to honey. Well Jim, Robert and I are heading to the Wilson Farm. Do you want to come help us load her onto the wagon?"

Jim said he did want to be there and would see them there. As Jim ended the call his mind was racing. He knew that if he hurried, he could beat the slow transport there. If the papers were really there like the guy on the phone said, he could put up a good fight toward owning the car. Oh, he knew there would be a fight, but if he offered to compensate whoever the "boss" was, he may be able to pull it off. He jumped behind the wheel of the Mercury Grand Marquis and gunned the engine, leaving the parking lot at a high rate of speed. He would be sure he got to the farm before the lumbering transport could make it there.

The team bus was driving east on the old

HALLOWEEN BEDTIME STORIES

Fairmount road at about the speed limit when the transport loaded with a bunch of shiny collector cars overtook the bus and passed it.

Larry Warner saw it immediately and told Kelly to get his foot in it because they were going to have to get to the Wilson Farm before those guys got there.

"They are going to try to steal my car. I've got the paperwork, but the rich bastard they work for will figure out a way to beat me out of it once they load it on the carrier."

Kelly was hesitant to pass the transport but did speed up and stayed right behind it. The boys were chanting "pass it, pass it, pass it."

Kelly remained cool and stayed just behind the transport waiting for his chance. He knew the road and would get them on the straight near the Wilson place.

Jim was driving west on the old road to Fairmount at about 80 miles per hour when he saw the transport in his rearview mirror. It was gaining fast. He could see the faces of the two men in the truck and they were laughing. He pressed the accelerator to the floor, gaining speed. The big transport was going even faster and actually passed him. He was in a panic. If these guys got there first, he would have no chance to get those papers. It was then he noticed they had the Beck Special. It was sitting on the truck. It was right in back It was shining like new, and the interior was glistening. The numbers were crisp and very readable "33". He felt A chill again and wondered how the hell they had picked up the car so fast. He also wondered why they were racing toward the Wilson place. He flashed his lights. He again flashed his lights. He was getting

260

THE COLLECTORS

angry and accelerated again. They were getting very close to the Wilson place, and he wanted them to stop and tell him just what was going on.

He pulled alongside and was looking at the driver who was laughing and pointing ....Oh my God; he thought, a school bus. He swerved hard to the left, leaving the road. The transport stopped quickly.

Kelly finally saw his chance and floored the accelerator of the bus. He was right beside the transport before he saw the car coming straight at him. He swerved hard to the right.

Both Kelly and Larry scrambled from the bus running toward the car they had hit. Jim was dazed and shook his head saying, "What in the world?"

Kelly answered, "Lucky we are not all dead. Those bastards driving that transport nearly got us all killed."

"Yeah," Jim said, "they sure were driving strangely. They passed me must have been doing a hundred."

"Passed you?" Kelly asked. "They passed us about a mile ago, and we were going the other way. Are you sure you are OK"?

They stood and looked at each other for a full minute. Larry had started walking toward the transport realizing that the Beck Special was already loaded. He approached Dave and said, "Look Mr., I have the title to that car, and I am going to have to ask you to unload it".

Dave's laugh seemed like a howl. He said, "You, car guys."

He pointed toward the transport and his co-driver Robert got out. As Robert walked toward Larry, he too

HALLOWEEN BEDTIME STORIES

started laughing. He said, "OK guys, take one last look at the bait. The boss is gonna take it back now and keep[it till next time."

The sky was turning dark, and clouds seemed to be swirling around them. The sun was shining in the distance somewhere, but it was very cold and dark at the Wilson Farm. Jim had cleared his head and walked over to join Larry, Robert and Dave.

"What is going on?" he asked in a voice that seemed surreal. "What are you saying about the cars and bait"?

Robert said, "Listen, we only have a few minutes now. Those cars are about to go back into storage. If you want to take one last look, now is the time. I sometimes wonder how dumb you, car guys can be. You had all the clues in the world and were so blinded by the glitter of chrome that you didn't get it. Larry started to interrupt, but Robert held up his hand and looked at Larry saying just shut up and let me finish. It's important. Any damn fool should know that the Beck Special was destroyed in 1955 when James Dean ran it under a truck and burned it up. The Healey was destroyed in 1955. It burned up at Sebring. Those other cars, they are just whatever the viewer wants to see. It is all bait for car buffs with a streak of evil. It is their last greedy pursuit before we put them to work.

Nearly everyone who claims to be a fifty's fan knows that James Dean's Mom was a 'Wilson', and grew up right across the road there. Jim over there, was even given a rare treat and got to talk to ol' Jim personally through our special hook ups. You guys should have known for several days now that we were

262

THE COLLECTORS

not here for that car. It was here for us to lure you to this spectacular Friday 13th crash. So boys, take one last look at the cars and one last look at Indiana and one last look at those bodies burning in that crash. Come on boys; it's time for you and your friends in the bus to go. Hear those sirens coming in the distance. We have to go before they get here and see your bodies.

You are just like the cars. You didn't make it through the crash and fire. But you do have a place in eternity with the boss. The boss will sure keep you busy for a long time. His voice became high and steely, and he shrieked with laughter. Maybe next time the boss will have you boys drive the transport. Look boys the fire truck is coming over the hill. And……….. Here comes the boss and it's time for us to leave………..

Happy Halloween………Everyone!…….."

CRISSY BEELER

Dave Tompkins felt tired. He was alert enough to be driving but was becoming weary of the road. He felt every day of his sixty-one years, and as the days on the road passed, he longed for the comfort of his home. His suit coat hung neatly from the hangar just behind him. He had his tie loosened from the top and top collar unbuttoned. Dave was still a good dresser and kept himself at the perfect weight for his nearly six foot frame. He still had enough charm to get past even the most discerning receptionist.

The drizzle falling from the aluminum colored sky was becoming a little faster and thicker. A passing truck created a mist of water and fog that momentarily obscured his vision. He felt a slight agitation and thought to himself "Time to get off the road for today Dave. You are starting to become emotional, so look for a place to stay and call it a day". He had learned from many years on the road when it was time to call it a day. He decided to perk himself up by re-thinking some of the customer contacts of the day. Just then, the first billboard caught his eye. It read…..STRASBURG HOTEL..BEST FOOD…BEST DRINKS….HOSPITALITY SOUTHERN STYLE. I could use a little hospitality, southern style or otherwise he thought. Dave had not had much southern hospitality on his sales calls that afternoon, but he understood why.

The morning had dawned clear and beautiful, and his day began very well. His call home to Carol was good, and they were both excited about their grandson Timmy's (Tim these days) football game coming up next

HALLOWEEN BEDTIME STORIES

week. Dave knew he would be spending next week at his home office sorting out the orders from this week on the road, phoning customers, and planning his next round of face to face visits to his customers' location. Even though the day was beautiful in Virginia, he was longing to be in his home office where he could work from his desk and see Carol, by walking into the kitchen. He missed Carol when he was on the road. She is still a very pretty woman and as her brown hair turned silver it became very complimentary to her blue eyes.

His first customer visit of the day was a short drive from the motel. Bob Johnson, a rather tall at just over six feet and very thin guy was a great customer and old friend. He could always be counted on for a big order and a big breakfast at the Colonial House, where Virginia ham was the featured breakfast food. He could hear Bob now:

"They pick the biggest, juiciest ham; then they prepare it with brown sugar, black pepper and herbs. They still do it the way the early settlers used to do it; no refrigeration, no sir, don't need it. They wrap it in cloth and salt and hang it up. Every so many days, they give it a rub with the things they mix up. It's just delicious."

Dave had heard Bob's statement on Virginia ham so many times he was saying it out loud as he drove through the ever increasing drizzle. The ham had been tasty, if a little salty, for Dave's taste, but he knew Bob loved it and he really liked Bob. As always, Bob had given him more than enough of an order to justify the whole week of travel. That was why at least two times a year Dave found himself having breakfast at the Colonial House in Staunton, Virginia. The weather was beautiful

265

CRISSY BEELER

and warm with the leaves in full autumn splendor as the two men walked to the Buick. Dave drove Bob back to his office and said his usual,

"See you again soon Bob. Take care and thanks." They shook hands, and Dave was on his way to his next stop.

The clouds started to build off to the northwest as he arrived in Harrisonburg and made his way to Gleason Telecom. He could hear loud voices and laughter as he approached the entry. He was there to see Jerry Wilkinson, whom he had never met, and, hopefully, get some new business started with this new company. The building was impressive enough, but his first five minutes inside told him this particular stop would not be a big sale. He had walked in on a Halloween office party, and the receptionist, who was dressed as a rag doll, thought he would be the perfect judge for the office costume party. As he looked around the office everyone was dressed up for Halloween. He thought quickly and decided that declaring a busy afternoon would keep him from being the judge.

Dave learned long ago to never be judgmental or comparative with customers. In that way, he could find something special about everyone. He looked for some trait or feeling that made them special to him and allowed him to make them feel special. He worked toward being friendly to everyone because he liked people and liked to do business on a friend-to-friend basis. That was why he had chosen sales as a career in the first place. He enjoyed working with people without judging them or their motives. Since he avoided being a judge of the best Halloween costume, he could sincerely

HALLOWEEN BEDTIME STORIES

compliment each and every one on their choice. Besides he really did like nearly all of the costumes he saw that afternoon. He could do without the standard spooks and witches, but some of the people showed real creativity. That Daisy Mae girl ....now there was a costume. Not much material, but for her, it really worked.

Special events in offices always equal a fact: you are not going to sell much. You can make some contacts with the proper people, but the event will rule the day. Forty years of sales experience had taught Dave to take these events in stride. He introduced himself and his company to the people who would be ordering fiber optic supplies, then bought some soft drinks and cookies for the crew.

His meeting with Jerry Wilkinson was brief. Dave learned that Jerry was setting up a new supply system and not ready for a large order at this time. Dave got to know the younger man and established a good contact for future sales. He had also received a small order which would not do much for his quota, but was at least a start with a new client. Not what he had hoped for, but neither a strike out. The less than fully successful call, however, did take his mood down a few notches, and caused him to wish he was home in his office smelling the aromas of dinner cooking.

He knew he was behind schedule due to some extra-long visits, but he had the orders to justify the time spent. Besides, part of him still enjoyed the road and he still enjoyed "his" people, yet the older he got, the more he longed for those office days at home. He thought how much more he had liked the road when he was a younger man as he walked to the Buick.

267

CRISSY BEELER

As he sat behind the wheel, the first few drops of a light drizzle touched the windshield. One more stop then home he thought.

It was true he had one more stop, but the drizzle was now a light rain falling from a sky that had become foggy. He knew he would not drive the entire distance to Hagerstown this late in the evening, so ...STRASBURG HOTEL... it would be. Southern style hospitality and one of those best drinks would feel pretty good to help shake the damp, dreary feeling the day was becoming.

"But only one drink" he said out loud mimicking the Arkansas accent of his boss. Dave hated the new company policy of one drink in a 24-hour period while working. He had always bought drinks for clients as a sales tool to show appreciation and had never had a moment's trouble. He certainly didn't have a problem when it came to consumption of alcohol, yet management did not want to hear it. Instead they wanted to cover themselves legally. So, Dave bought the first drink for his clients then watched as another company's salesman bought the next two drinks and took his sale away.

With only one more year to go he had told himself, he could keep most of his customers happy by making the visit to their places. It's harder than going to trade shows or conventions and buying lots of drinks, but so far, his sales were not suffering much from the new manager's temperance movement.

Another truck passed this time with a larger even more blinding spray of moisture, making him think to himself that he had enough of the freeway in the rain for one day. He started to look for an exit.

268

HALLOWEEN BEDTIME STORIES

Maybe I won't make the Strasburg Hotel after all he thought. He spotted an exit sign proclaiming Woodstock, Virginia Exit - 2 Miles.

He took the exit, which placed him on old US Route 11 just south of Woodstock. He saw another sign. STRASBURG HOTEL... BEST DRINKS...BEST FOOD...SOUTHERN HOSPITALITY...JUST 12 MILES NORTH ON BEAUTIFUL SCENIC HWY 11. Ok, he thought, twelve miles without the trucks on the freeway won't be so bad.

This drive would have been breathtakingly beautiful at mid-day when the sun was bright and the colors of the Ash, Maple, Persimmon, Red-Bud and Walnut trees were ablaze with autumn. There were lots of farms in this area, and the animals in the fields added to the rural beauty of this part of the Shenandoah Valley.

Dave had driven this area on good days when sunshine spilled onto the mountains and lit up the entire

CRISSY BEELER

landscape with colors. However, right now in the light fog and misty rain it was all gray, dark and abandoned feeling. It is strange he mused how many of the old roads in this country take on the atmosphere similar to an abandoned old house no longer teaming with life.

No doubt this road had once been one of the major highways in the country. It was Virginia's primary north/south route. Now the freeway had pretty much by-passed the old highway, and the old buildings that were once alive with commerce and people now sat quietly at the side of an even quieter road.

He remembered the road as it was when the traffic jammed its three lanes, and it seemed a little depressing to see it be so lonely and quiet.

Dave's mood brightened for a moment at the news coming over the Buick's radio. The Y2K conversions were going well, his computer stocks had done very well on Wall Street that day, and his 401-k retirement looked very good. He decided to celebrate with a Marlboro. He didn't smoke much any longer but still had four or five cigarettes a day. He reached across the dash for his cigarettes and must have brushed against the radio controls because the Wall Street report was replaced by

.. ALL MY HUGS..ALL MY KISSIN .. YOU DON'T KNOW WHAT YOU'VE BEEN A MISSIN. OH BOY. WHEN YOU'RE WITH ME ..OH BOY.

Wow, he thought, Buddy Holley. It was one of my favorites when, I was in high school. He thought about reaching for the button to listen to the rest of his Wall Street news, but the music seemed somehow soothing and warming, and he saw a sign said only eight

HALLOWEEN BEDTIME STORIES

miles to Strasburg. He could almost taste the cold beer he would order before dinner. As he lit his Marlboro, another song from the past filled his ears. ...he half mumbled along with the words ...

"Daddy's home...Daddy's home.....to stay."

The rain was slowing down now, and the fog was not as thick as it had been. The sun had set, and wetness from the storm and the overcast sky caused the colors to remain muted and dull. A sign said "Tom's Brook" and still another sign proclaimed STRASBURG HOTEL..THE TRAVELERS' CHOICE.

He was ready to be at the hotel and out of the car. He didn't really notice much about the commercial on the radio advertising a big Halloween dance at the Moose Lodge in Strasburg Virginia, with a personal appearance by a new local singing sensation, Patsy Cline. He did notice the music when it began again playing one of his all-time favorite songs, "Theme from a Summer Place" by Percy Faith and the 1000 String Orchestra. As he listened he could still feel Nancy swaying in his arms at the High School Homecoming Dance his sophomore year. As the tune filled the Buick with music from Dave's past, he was cruising.

Another day almost done. Hotel in five minutes. He almost didn't notice the wave of something on the side of the road.

He slowed and squinted. There, on the side of the road was a girl waving something to get his attention. She was standing on a rise to the side of one of the old stone fences that dot the landscape in Northern Virginia. Dave was at full attention now. He could see that she was soaked to the skin and standing in wet grass waving

CRISSY BEELER

her coat. He pulled the Buick to the side of the road and stopped in the gravel. He powered the passenger window down and put out his cigarette. He spoke first.

"It's a pretty bad night out here for hitchhiking. Are you OK?"

"Yes," she answered. "My car has a problem and I can't get it started. I really need a ride into Strasburg. It is just a couple of miles. I need to get my dad so he can come get my car, or fix it or something."

"Where is your car?" Dave asked and added, "Maybe we can get it going for you. I don't know much about them, but it may be worth a try."

"Oh thanks, it's over there," she said pointing, "but I would rather just have a ride home and have Dad come and get it tomorrow. I am so cold I don't want to be out here any longer. It will be easier to come get it in the morning when it's light and warmer."

This sounded better to Dave than getting cold and wet and probably frustrated with the disabled car.

"OK", he said, "let me move my briefcase and stuff onto the back seat and clear a space for you. Then you can hop right in. You'll have to excuse the condition of my car, but I am a guy who uses his car for a traveling office. It's my home away from home, where I live and work during my waking hours. There now, I have a place cleaned off for you to sit. Again, I'm sorry for the clutter."

She smiled brightly at this and said, "I am just happy that you stopped to help me. It is so cold and dark, and I want so much to just be home".

Her words touched a place in his heart and caused him to think of his home. Several hundred miles

HALLOWEEN BEDTIME STORIES

away right now Carol would be sitting in her favorite
rocking chair in front of the fireplace watching
television. Taffy, the family's loyal Cocker Spaniel,
would be curled at Carol's feet. Her voice interrupted his
thoughts of home.

"May I please borrow your coat to warm me up?
I will try and not get it wet."

"Sure," he replied. "Don't worry if it gets a little
damp. This road trip is nearly over anyway, and it will
be at the cleaners day after tomorrow."

As she took his jacket he noticed how strikingly
beautiful this young girl was. She was very formally
dressed as though she was on her way somewhere
important when her car broke down. Funny, he thought
how styles come and go. This girl could be an ad right
out of a 60's magazine. I guess it proves what they say:
"if you keep things long enough, they come back into
style."

She spoke again softly, "Thank you for picking
me up. It is so nice and warm in your car, and you have
my favorite radio station on. It is a sort of local station
out of Harrisonburg, and I must be lucky because it
seems everyone that I get a ride with listens to it. They
play all the new songs, you know."

Dave pulled onto the road and glanced in her
direction.

"I haven't heard anything but oldies for the past
ten miles, you know, stuff from the sixties."

"Yeah," she answered dreamily, "I really like
Elvis and Buddy Holley, but my favorite is our new local
star---a girl named Patsy Cline."

He thought the conversation was becoming

273

CRISSY BEELER

disconnected, but shrugged it off as he passed the sign Strasburg-2 Miles.

"Well, only a couple of miles to Strasburg and my stop for the night. Some days on the road seem too long."

"You have no idea," she said, "but I am so grateful for the ride and to be warm if only for a little while."

He wondered what she meant, but decided not to pursue it. The Buick rounded a curve and approached a sign---Strasburg Pop-3532. A silently blinking yellow caution light flashed on a sign, 'SLOW'.

"I thought it would be bigger by now," Dave said.

"Ummm," she said. She seemed happy to be warm and to see town. She was smiling. Her voice was nearly a whisper when she said, "Could you please take me to my house Mr. .... I don't know your name."

"Tomkins, Dave Tomkins. I live in northern Maryland these days."

"Well, Mr. Tomkins, could you please drive me to my house? It is near the Strasburg Hotel. In fact, just up the hill past the hotel, on the same street."

"Sure," he replied. "I will be happy to take you right up to the door. You just tell me when to turn and what direction."

"Thanks. I sure will," she answered.

As the Buick approached a stoplight, which was red, Dave heard her say, "Right turn here Mr. Tomkins. The hotel and my house are just up this street."

The radio announcer said, "Well folks, its 8:48 pm in the valley, and the rain has stopped. Gonna be

HALLOWEEN BEDTIME STORIES

clear tomorrow, and now here is a new tune from our own songbird who hails from right here in the Shenandoah Valley, Nashville's newest female star Miss Patsy Cline. Now don't forget. There are still a few tickets available to hear Patsy in person at the big Halloween dance at the Strasburg Moose tomorrow night. That's right. Patsy is coming here tomorrow. Now here is her recording of her new release, "Crazy."

"Must be some kind of a retro broadcast thing," Dave said. The young woman didn't seem to hear him.

She was looking out the window and saying "This is the exact song I was talking about, "Crazy", and Patsy is coming here tomorrow to sing it in person. I am so excited; I can't wait."

Dave cleared his throat and said, "This must be a retro cast because Patsy Cline has been dead for over thirty years, killed in a plane crash. It must be a Halloween special broadcast or something like that."

"Oh, there is my drive. It says 300 East Massanutten Street. Turn right here, and... Mr., I just saw Patsy Cline in person and talked to her myself in August when they dedicated that new bank on the corner that we just drove past."

He glanced in the rearview mirror at a building surrounded by trees at least 30 years old.

She continued, "Patsy was here with Jimmy Dean, Roy Clark and ...oh, a light is on."

Dave looked to his left and saw the Strasburg Hotel, then drove on toward the porch light on the right. The homes on the street were nearly as big as the hotel and had obviously been mansions of the town's best families. Very fine big homes.

275

CRISSY BEELER

"Oh, goodie! I see Daddy through the window. Daddy is home!"

Patsy Cline was singing "Crazy" on the Buick's radio as they pulled up to the walkway to the house. The skies opened up with a flash of lightning, thunder and a torrent of rain.

She looked over and said, "Mr. Tomkins, thank you so much for bringing me home. I am sorry if you were offended by what I said about Patsy Cline, but you see, she is the closest thing to a celebrity we have had around here for a long time and well... we are proud of her. Oh, I nearly forgot. My name is Crissy... Crissy Beeler". She held out her hand.

He shook her hand then said, "It is OK about Patsy Cline. I guess there must be another one. I don't keep up with music much these days, and I'm sure there are lots of new people I don't even know about. But you are freezing, young lady, and we better get you into the house. I've never felt anything as cold as your hand, and look at you, you're shaking."

"Yes," she stammered, "Mr. Tomkins could you please go get my father to bring a dry coat and umbrella to get me into the house"?

"Sure, I uh... guess, I'll get him Crissy. You just sit tight. I'll get him."

He heard her say as he was closing the door to the Buick, "Thanks, Mr. Tomkins, for letting me get warm and listen to the radio. I hope to see you again sometime."

The door closed, and Dave wondered what she meant. He jogged to the porch and approached the door. He noticed his dripping clothes left puddles as he moved

HALLOWEEN BEDTIME STORIES

across the porch.

The front door was massive with an old-fashioned twist bell in the center of the door under the glass. Dave twisted the bell, and it rang loudly. He heard shuffling inside the house, and the door swung open. In front of him stood an older, very kindly looking man who appeared to be in his seventies. The man was very well dressed and well groomed. The man looked far too old to be the father of Crissy, but his blue eyes could definitely qualify him as a relative. Dave spoke first.

"Mr. Beeler?"

"Yes."

"Hello, I am Dave Tomkins. You don't know me, but I have your daughter or maybe your granddaughter in my car. You see, she had car trouble a couple of miles south of town. She was waving traffic down when I stopped to give her a ride. She is very wet and cold and wanted me to have you bring a dry coat and umbrella to help her into the house. I hope I am not startling you, but she is very cold and talking a little strange, so I thought I should try to get some help getting her into the warmth of the house." The old man looked at Dave and seemed suddenly very sad. His chin quivered as he looked at Dave through tear filled eyes.

"My God; not again. Sometimes I wonder how many times I can go through this. It is a cruel punishment to a father who loved his daughter so much."

"Listen, Mr. Beeler, this is for real. I've been on the road all day, and your child or grandchild is out there freezing in my car waiting for you to bring her in, so please come with me."

The old man drew in a ragged breath and gazed

277

CRISSY BEELER

out into the driving rain. He spoke softly, "I am Bill Beeler, Crissy's father. She was the most wonderful daughter a father could ever have. She was smart, talented, popular and active in the community, and you have seen how beautiful she was."

Tomkins blinked away some of the water that was running across his eyes and looked at Mr. Beeler, "You keep saying WAS."

The old man continued, "You see, Mr. Tomkins, Crissy did have car trouble near where the old stone fence comes down to the road north of Tom's Brook. She was trying to wave down a passing motorist for help when she was struck and killed."

Dave Tomkins drew in a sudden breath and felt light headed.

Mr. Beeler continued, "Since her death in 1961, she comes back every two or three years. It is always near Halloween and usually on a very rainy or foggy night. I was afraid when I heard the forecast for tonight, knowing that Halloween is tomorrow, that it may happen again. I even turned on the light. A local spiritualist says she is still trying to attend the Halloween dance she missed so long ago to see her idol, Patsy Cline. I am saddened that I have never been able to see her, or talk to her. Each of those who have come here before you tell of listening to an old radio station that has been out of business for over 35 years and talk of Crissy singing along with Patsy Cline. But each time someone comes, I go into the rain or fog hoping that tonight I will see her. Who knows, perhaps tonight I can. I am getting pretty old Mr. Tomkins, and I would dearly love to get to see her again while I am still here on earth. I would give

278

HALLOWEEN BEDTIME STORIES

anything to see her once again."

He reached to the side of the door and picked up an umbrella.

"Let's go, Mr. Tomkins. Let's walk to your car together."

As they approached the Buick in the pouring rain, they could hear the car's radio blasting loudly, the evening news with the stock market to follow. The Buick was empty, but when Mr. Beeler opened the door, he said ,"This is the closest I have come yet. The seat is still soaking wet and extremely cold."

The radio news was proclaiming seven o'clock. Dave reached for another cigarette. He shook his head and told Mr. Beeler he was sorry to have bothered him.

Mr. Beeler smiled and said, "I understand. Besides, Mr. Tomkins, I know she was there, and I almost got to see her."

As Dave backed out of the driveway, he saw his coat neatly folded and draped across the passenger seat. He reached for it and it was dripping wet and extremely cold.

In fact, Dave Tomkins' coat was still extremely cold as he finished telling me his story during his second beer at the Strasburg Hotel last October 30… the day before Halloween. For some reason I'll never understand, I did not bother to tell him that Mr. Beeler died three years ago, and the house was burned to the ground last year. I wonder if he happened to notice it as he left town the next day?….. Happy Halloween……

CRISSY BEELER

THE BUTTONS

Chapter One

It was a bright, clear morning in La Costa, California. The morning warmth foretold a sunny, warm afternoon. You could see the surf just beyond the lagoon about two miles away, and, if you looked intently, you could see Catalina Island about fifty miles distant in the blue Pacific. This was the kind of day that made Southern California famous. Dan looked toward the ocean and stopped to watch a flock of gulls swoop into the lagoon and land. He loved the view from his back patio and just wanted to enjoy it for a moment in silence. He took a deep breath and sighed as he exhaled. He lowered his gaze back to the ashes and rubble on his patio, where only five days before his lawn furniture had sat.

As he looked around the area where the Master bedroom had been, he tried to focus on looking for small items. The ash had caused everything to be gray in color and had to be sifted to reveal size. His blonde hair fell over his forehead as he worked. He spoke softly to Sue, his wife, when he found a possible item of value. Sue was still in shock, and he understood that he needed to be gentle with her and to try to be as calm as he could. He tried to not get, or even seem excited because the least excitement caused Sue to regress back to tears. He struggled to not raise his voice when he spotted a ring cradled in a small gray pile of ash. His blue eyes squinted as he looked intently at about two thirds of what had been a nice garnet stone ring he had given to Sue.

HALLOWEEN BEDTIME STORIES

He recognized the leaf design on the side of the ring but the garnet was no longer in the setting. He quickly picked it up and placed it in his pocket. He did not want Sue to find it. She did not need any more negatives just now. He was not really in a full search mood, so once again raised his face toward the ocean and let his thoughts wander.

His thoughts swung back to Monday. He had gone to work at his normal time. It was windy with very gusty Santa Ana winds blowing dust, and the trees were bending in a precarious dance. Sure it was windy, but he had seen it many times before and thought little about it as he began his work day. As he walked into his office, his administrative assistant had mentioned some fire danger warnings that she heard on the news before coming in to work, and they both acknowledged that fires are a normal part of certain areas in California in the early autumn when the Santa Ana's blow, and a spark from any source can turn the summer's vegetation growth into fuel for a wind-driven wild fire.

It was mid-morning when Sue called with the information that there was a wild fire burning a couple of miles from their home but that the wind seemed to be taking it the other way. She was at her job and had seen the information on the break room television when she stopped for coffee. Dan had been through fires being in the area before. After living in southern California for 20 years, he was a veteran of Santa Ana winds and the fires that had burned large strips of land nearly every fall. But this time when he heard Sue's voice talking about it being near but the wind taking it away from their place, he had a moment of misgiving. He thought about

282

THE BUTTONS

the possibility of fire coming near their neighborhood on top of the hill and was happy his place was about as far away from the canyon and the sage brush as you could get. He was glad his neighbors all had well watered lawns and nice green trees to help dampen the effects of the smoke and the heat. Still, something deep within him was troubled by the closeness of the reported fire.

Dan spent most of his lunch hour watching the television in the break room and watching live fire reports from around San Diego. He saw a brief mention of the fire between San Marcos and La Costa and saw that, at least for now, no homes were endangered. He had barely walked into his office from lunch when his children's baby sitter, who lived in their neighborhood, called and excitedly explained that some of the houses in the neighborhood were being evacuated because the fire had shifted. She said she thought that he and Sue had both better get home and make sure things were OK. She offered to meet them there in case they needed her help with anything. Dan hurriedly explained the situation to Diane, his administrative assistant, and called Sue who had gotten a similar call from Mindy just moments earlier. They agreed to meet at the hill just below their house. They thought they could, perhaps, help their neighbors or keep their part of the area watered down to help prevent fire from leaping into their area.

The deep gray and yellowish-tan smoke made it difficult to see exactly where he was as he pulled onto the street that led to the bottom of the hill. He still had about a half mile to go and could not see more than seventy-five feet. As he got closer, he could smell and taste the fire, and the heat was very palpable. He pulled

283

HALLOWEEN BEDTIME STORIES

to the curb at the bottom of the hill and Mindy ran up to the car.

"It's burning on your street," she screamed. "We have to get up there and get your stuff out! They are giving you about ten more minutes. Sue is there already, and I'm riding up the hill with you. Let's go!"

Dan pulled the car onto the roadway and drove steadily up the hill, losing visibility all the way. He pulled into the driveway and opened the door. He saw Sue coming from the house with pictures, clothes and some of the kids' toys. His mind raced...what to grab? A loud crack and burst of heat caught his attention as the house about two hundred feet away burst into flame. He heard amplified voices saying "evacuate now!" He ran into the house, grabbed the keys to his Austin Healey and his grandfather's rocking chair. He tossed the chair onto the seat of the car and ran back into the house to look for anything. He grabbed some of his clothes and a picture. He heard a police siren in the front of the house give a whoop and heard an amplified voice yell, "GET OUT NOW. It's coming in."

He raced to the garage, opened the door, and yelled to Mindy, "Drive! Take my car; the keys are in it. I'll drive this and get down the hill. Meet you at your place if it is safe."

He started his Healey and backed out of his garage. As he cleared the end of the garage, he saw the roof on his garage burst into flame and debris falling onto the garage floor. That was the last time he saw his house.

They made it safely to Mindy's house and decided how to tell the kids. They had called some

THE BUTTONS

family and found a motel to stay in for the present and called their places of work. Then they had collapsed in tears and shock for most of the next thirty hours. It was Wednesday before they could really regain their thinking process and talk about what to do next. Their families had offered money and help, but no one realized that they had lost nearly everything except a couple of armfuls of things gathered in shock and panic. Their entire list of remaining possessions could fit into the back seat of a Volkswagen.

The first time back after the fire, Dan was looking out over the beautiful Pacific on an ideal late October day, he could barely wrap his mind around the events that had unfolded in the past five days. He was looking through the rubble that had been his home and trying to find anything that was special or valuable. He was incredulous at the damage the intense heat had done to the home and its contents. There was virtually nothing left. He found a heap of melted metal about two feet by two feet that had been his refrigerator/freezer. He found some melted silverware that at first he thought was jewelry. He found melted tools from the garage and bits and pieces of charred materials that could have been almost anything. The devastation was nearly complete and nothing larger than the two foot by two foot refrigerator/freezer stood anywhere on the lot. Funny, he thought, he had never thought of it as a lot before. He had thought of it as his house and his lawn. But with nothing on it except ashes and rubble, it became his lot.

Sue walked to the street where a girlfriend from her office had just arrived. The two sat in the car crying, talking and hugging for a short time. Sue thanked her

285

HALLOWEEN BEDTIME STORIES

friend got out and walked toward Dan. They glanced at each other, and both started to tear up and choke up with emotion. It was hard to be brave when friends shared their loss. They hugged and sobbed together for several minutes.

Dan pushed away and said, "We have got to get on with finding what we can and get the insurance papers ready for the claims guy." Sue nodded numbly and started to bend and sift through what had been their lives.

They had been looking through ashes and debris for about an hour when Larry, a neighbor from less than a hundred feet away whose home had been spared from the fire, came over and offered them a cold beer. They both eagerly accepted the beer and all three wondered together how a fire can take one house and jump over another and take yet another next to the one it jumped over. The neighborhood had about half of its houses intact after the fire but still looked like a disaster zone because of the debris from all the houses that burned. Larry offered to help but honestly did not know what to do that could be useful.

Dan smiled and understood completely. "Just keep the beer coming and loan me your garage once in a while as we sort through all this," Dan said. "We are trying to see if anything survived and find what we can so we can meet with the insurance people. Someone suggested we try to find what we can or document any fragments that we find to help prove our claims. It seems to me that anyone who walked through one of these places and identified the refrigerator over there could understand that it is pretty much a complete wipeout."

THE BUTTONS

Larry nodded and said, "They are probably just hoping you find your fifty thousand dollar diamond instead of claiming it got lost."

Dan said, "Yeah, maybe I need to tell them how close they came to paying for my Austin Healey. If Mindy hadn't been here we would have had to watch it burn up too."

"I heard you just barely cleared the driveway when the garage went."

"Driveway hell, I just barely cleared the garage when the ceiling burst into flame!" Dan said. "Larry, mind if I have another one of those beers? I'm not doing much good here, and I may as well enjoy being outside in my backyard as much as possible."

Sue could not resist, "Don't you think we should set up a way to sift all this stuff and go through it while the weather is good?"

Dan shrugged and said, "Guess you're right. I guess I'll save the beer for later Lar. Have you got a bushel basket or plastic trash can we can borrow? I'll send Sue to the hardware store for a length of screen, and we'll sift through our belongings." He chuckled to himself and added, "Wonder if I will recognize any of my suits or good shirts?"

Sue got back with the screen, and they proceeded to sit and sift through the various areas where debris was stacked deeply. It became even more amazing how little had survived. There was virtually nothing of worth or even that could be recognized. They had taken turns crying and working, then crying some more. It was nearly dark when they decided to knock off for the night and move their pieces of rings, parts of melted

HALLOWEEN BEDTIME STORIES

silverware and melted kitchen articles into the trunk of the car. Dan knew he needed to get a rental house lined up and needed to meet with the rental agent. Sue was anxious to get back to the kids who were feeling shock of their own. They picked up their basket and their few recognizable items and put them in the car and drove away from their place wondering if they would ever find anything at all. It had been a very depressing day.

It would be fully three days before Dan made it back to really resume looking. He only came back then because of his sense of obligation to make another sweep of the place before he met with the insurance adjuster. It was Tuesday evening nearing sunset when he drove into his driveway and parked. It still shocked him to drive up his street and into his driveway and see a pile of ashes. He looked out over his view and saw some clouds over the ocean close to shore, and experience told him that in less than an hour it would be raining or a heavy mist and fog. He thought he better hurry. He knew that anything of real value would have to come from the bedroom where some of the jewelry was kept. He sifted through ashes there until it started to get dark. He found a couple more scraps of gold too small to identify and a few charred books that had burned down to the spines. As the sky turned darker he saw the fog forming down along the lagoon and knew soon he would be getting wet. He noticed that there was no moon and only a few stars were shining above. He remembered it was the dark of the moon and, with the fog rolling in, it was about to become a very dark night. Once again, he gathered up the scraps of metal and book spines he found and carried them to the car. When he tried to start the car it just sat

288

THE BUTTONS

there. He looked in and noticed that the girls had left a light on in the back which had drained the battery. He jogged across the street to Larry's house and borrowed a charger and some cord and plugged the charger in and brought it back to his car. He decided that while he waited for the battery to build up, he would find his basket. He walked cautiously through the debris, half-way feeling his way. He found the basket and the screen where he had left them. He picked them up and started back toward the car. The darkness was so complete that he really had to move slowly. He thought about the possibility of tripping or stepping on something sharp or harmful. For a moment he was overcome with his situation. Stumbling around in the deep darkness, wet, cold, and helpless in what had been his sanctuary. For just an instant, tears formed in his eyes and spilled down across his cheek. It was then that he saw a glimmer.

"Glimmer," he said. "How the hell?" But it was a glimmer. It seemed to glint up at him. He brushed away the debris and picked it up. He did not know exactly what he had, but something had survived. He was anxious to see it in full light but that could wait. He placed the object in his pocket, and, taking his basket and screen, went to the car. Once in the car he tried the switch, and it started right up. He disconnected the charger and returned it to Larry.

"Thanks," he said. "I am sure that is only the first of many things I'll have to borrow if we decide to rebuild this place."

"I'm glad to know you are even thinking about it neighbor. Most folks don't rebuild when something like this happens. They just move somewhere else." Dan

289

HALLOWEEN BEDTIME STORIES

smiled.

"Not sure anyone else would take us; anyway, we like the company around here, and damn, that is some view. I guess we will have to see what the insurance people have to say and let that affect our decision. Thanks again, Larry. I better go see how Sue is doing with getting things rounded up to move into our rental. It is just down the hill about a mile, and I will get you the address as soon as we get in. The phone number will stay the same. Sue is hitting all the thrift stores and sorting through the piles of donated materials at the relief center they set up at the school. We are both hoping to find a couple of changes of clothes till we get a minute to go shopping. It is pretty unreal how many things you take for granted till they are gone."

"Later," Larry said.

The meeting with the insurance adjuster the next day was a disaster. The adjuster was obviously there to settle for as little as possible and questioned every claim and statement Dan and Sue made. When Dan mentioned he had at least seven good suits and two good sport coats the agent questioned that.

"Seven suits--- isn't that rather a lot? Do you wear suits to work every day?"

"Yeah," Dan had answered. "I do wear suits to work every day except since the fire."

It was a long and painful negotiation, and when Dan got around to explaining that there were quite a number of antiques that had been lost, the agent rolled his eyes and said he would need some kind of proof as to the existence of these antiques and some documentation. Dan explained that he was unusually sentimental and

THE BUTTONS

collected items such as school pictures of his grandparents and great grandparents. He had some old musical instruments and some coins. He even had some old clothing items and some uniform buttons. In fact, some of those items have very interesting family stories with them.

The agent said, "I would love to hear those stories Mr. Sanders, but I am pretty busy what with several hundred home claims to settle in the next couple of weeks. Perhaps you can tell me about them another time when we both have more time."

Dan knew the negotiations were over with this person.

"Thanks. Come on Sue. This guy is busy." Looking over his shoulder as he walked toward the door he said, "Perhaps you will have time to talk to Mr. Allen, our lawyer. He has been alerted and will contact you tomorrow."

The agent asked the couple to wait and offered a half-hearted apology, but Dan just walked to the car and got in. He drove away without looking back. Sue was worried, but realized that they would be better off having their attorney deal with this matter.

Dan had known Bob Allen for several years. He first met the attorney during a tough contract negotiation. Dan's very first thought was that this well-dressed, black attorney was a good strategic move by a minority contractor. As the negotiations progressed, he could see that the attorney needed no advantage. He was completely capable on his own. Mr. Allen had been representing the opposition and doing a bang up job of it. Dan immediately liked Bob Allen and found him easy to

HALLOWEEN BEDTIME STORIES

talk to. They were able to sit together and work through very tough problems without losing their focus or patience with each other. Dan had always found it a little difficult to truly trust attorneys in general, but Bob Allen was different. Bob was equally fond of Dan for a reason he could not explain. He liked and trusted the guy. He was just comfortable with him. When the negotiations for the contractor were complete, the two men shook hands. As they were expressing their pleasure at working with each other, they decided to meet for lunch. From then on, Bob was Dan's friend and attorney. They often visited back and forth, and at least several times a year, planned a dinner with their wives and kids. Dan knew he could turn to Bob in a crisis.

The next day Dan and Sue sat with Bob Allen and talked about the losses in their home. Bob was the perfect attorney for them because he had been in their home several times and knew about many of the items that Dan and Sue described. He knew of Dan's habit of collecting antiques and family memorabilia. He even laughed about Dan grabbing his grandfather's rocking chair, the only piece of furniture saved and carrying it past a new computer on the way out of his house.

"These people will have to be convinced about the antiques, but I think we can do it. Still, I wish we could find at least one other thing that survived to help our story. Did you find anything?"

"Not much", they both said together. Dan explained that he had made several trips to the house. The last time he had finished in complete darkness, but had found mostly only parts of things that they sort of recognized but would have a hard time proving to

292

THE BUTTONS

anyone else what they were.

"I did find something I sort of forgot that night, but I don't know what it was. Just something shining in the darkness. I put it in the pocket of my jeans. I guess the jeans are still in the closet of the rental we are staying in. They should be easy to find; they are the only pair of my own jeans I still have. All the rest are possible fits from the shelter that I haven't even tried on yet."

Bob Allen cleared his throat, "Wow, he said softly. You folks have really been through a lot. It is hard to imagine you have lost nearly everything."

"Hey, we are healthy, alive and our kids are healthy. That is our standard answer, and we are sticking to it."

"Good for you", Bob said. "Still, it tugs even at the heart of an attorney to hear the level of your loss. It is going to be fun to go after THIS insurance company. If it goes all the way to a jury, I'll even have the judge crying. If we can just find a little proof other than hear say, I am sure we will win big."

They agreed to adjourn for now and let Bob initiate his filing, and Dan and Sue would search for any documentation they could find.

The next week kept them busy getting enough used furniture, clothing, and buying new clothing to continue on with their lives. Their families had helped with some emergency money to get them started. They found most things in the newspaper ads and through the shelter. By the end of the week they were into the rental and starting to settle back into life. They were still suffering from the losses and the post-traumatic shock of the situation but were both amazingly resilient and resourceful and things

HALLOWEEN BEDTIME STORIES

were coming together. They had both been called separately by the insurance company wanting to discuss a settlement offer, but had both responded as they had agreed with their attorney, Mr. Allen, would entertain all settlement offers and discussions at this time. They needed space until they had settled into the rental and gotten estimates together to replace their house and belongings. They both assured the insurance company that they were in no hurry, they needed to figure out all the losses and get good accurate replacement estimates before they attended any further meetings. Both Dan and Sue continued to sift through the rubble of their home for another ten days as time allowed and then decided that they were wasting their time and they were done. They would now wait until some decision was reached and have the remainder cleaned up and hauled away by professional disaster clean-up people.

Sue had called and written to family members asking for any pictures taken of their house inside and out. They both had family members that visited them in the winter and many of them responded that they had pictures and set about having extra prints made to send them. From the descriptions she had heard on some of her phone calls, many of the pictures had a good chance of showing some of the articles and items that would be worth the most money and would be hardest to get the insurance company to pay for. Dan had found several pictures in his desk of them dressed up for various occasions that showed some of the missing jewelry and some of the clothes in question. Both had lined up neighbors and co-workers to testify as to the dress requirements of their jobs and the condition of their

THE BUTTONS

home. They were going about proving to a questioning insurance company that their claims were real and reasonable and in the process seemed to be having to justify their very lives. Needless to say, they were becoming more than slightly angry and resentful. As their final series of meetings with Bob Allen approached, they were becoming more confident that they had much more proof of many of their claims than they had before, but both longed for a few more pieces or partial pieces of evidence.

HALLOWEEN BEDTIME STORIES

Chapter Two
Spring 1861

Lizzie, who was really named Elizabeth Ann Johnson, was about to turn sixteen. She was excited for many reasons. She would take her place as an adult on the plantation at sixteen. Her master, the plantation owner, Mr. Reid Johnson, would talk to her one day soon about what she would like to do and what he would like for her to do. She was anxious to tell her master all about her skills learned from her mama. She knew that her mama was one of Mr. Reid 's favorite slaves, and that she was considered the best and most organized housekeeper in the entire Baton Rouge parish. Lizzie was pretty like her mother and was very intelligent too. Everyone thought she would be assigned a "house job" working for her mother or maybe even be chosen as a nanny to Mr. Reid's children and personal assistant to his wife Anne.

Lizzie's Mother, Lucinda, had spent her life at Twin Creeks. She had been chosen by Mr. Reid's father, Samuel, to "keep this house in order and get the house servants to work together". Mr. Sam had known that the slaves would respond better to one of their own and had recognized Lucinda's ability to get people to do things for her and to have a good time while getting it done. Lucinda had been present at the birth of young Mr. Reid and had been one of his teachers as he grew up. She was more than just the head housekeeper at Twin Creeks.

THE BUTTONS

She was in a big way part of the spirit of the place. She was bright and organized and liked the work that she did. She knew that the Johnsons were good people, and she knew how to work with them. She was one of the few slaves who dared ask questions of the master and who dared offer suggestions about which person may be chosen to do certain jobs. Lucinda was probably as much of an overseer as Egan, the white field overseer, but she was much more respected by the black and white residents of Twin Creeks.

Lizzie was walking along the graveled path between the summer kitchen and the barn when she heard her mother calling her.

"Lizzie, then louder LIZZIE!"

"Coming Mama," she answered.

Her mother was acting busy in an official sort of way. Lizzie had seen her act this way with other adult slaves before but never with her.

Her mother was saying, "Mr. Reid, he wants to talk to you girl. He wants to talk about your job here and see if 'n you are what he has in mind. It is important, honey, that you please Mr. Reid cause sometime they take girls your age and they sell 'em off and we never see them anymore. Lizzie, this is important honey; you got to make Mr. Reid want to keep you here so you be sure you please him, and let him know you will do whatever he wants, but that you loves him and his family, and you wants to stay here with them. You understand me Lizzie? This is special important so you be careful. Now you go and wash yourself and put on your special Sunday dress 'cause Mr. Reid will be wantin' to see you right after supper."

297

HALLOWEEN BEDTIME STORIES

Lizzie took her time walking to the little cabin that she had shared with her mother for her whole life. She had never known any other place except this clean little cabin and the Johnson plantation. She wondered what life was like to some of the others who had been sold away from the plantation and where they lived with their new owners. She wondered if she would be allowed to have a man for herself and maybe even be allowed to marry, or if she would be taken away from the Twin Creeks Plantation and forced to work in cotton fields…or worse, sugar cane fields…or worse yet, as a prostitute. All this was going through her young mind as she was washing herself and dressing. She had just pulled the dress onto her body when her mother walked in and let out a low whistle.

"Girl, you sure are pretty. I'll bet Mr. Reid will want to keep you around to make his house look good."

Lizzie was nervous, but also anxious to see what her fate would be as she walked up the steps to the back entrance of the main house. Old Edward, the footman, met her at the door and smiled.

He turned and loudly announced, "Lizzie to see Master Reid."

Reid Johnson was a kindly, handsome man of 34. He had grown up on Twin Creeks Plantation and had known Lizzie since she was a baby and he was a boy of 18. He was proud of Lizzie and of her mother Lucinda. He had long ago decided Lizzie would be a resident of Twin Creeks as long as he owned the place but he also understood the importance of the official meeting he was to have with each slave as they came of age. He understood that it was his obligation to interview them

THE BUTTONS

and to listen to their thoughts about their lives. He never had liked it when he had to sell slaves and usually only did it when the population was too great for the plantation to provide for. When he did sell, he only sold to reputable farmers who he knew treated the slaves as he treated his slaves. Reid Johnson would have been happy to simply free his slaves and make deals with them about sharecropping the plantation, but he knew that if he did free them now, they would not make it more than a few days until some opportunist "captured them and sold them on the cane field market or prostituted the women". Reid was troubled about the talk of war that was rampant at nearly every social function and business meeting that he attended. He was worried that the South was about to launch into a war to keep people enslaved. He believed that if they entered a war on this premise, one that he believed to be completely wrong, that they were doomed to be defeated. It was the spring the war erupted that Lizzie turned sixteen.

"Good evening Elizabeth. How are you?"

Lizzie bent in a curtsey and said, "Good evening Mr. Reid. I am doing well, and I hope you and Miss Anne and your children are well."

"We are fine Elizabeth, and I am here to discuss your future with you. I will say right off that I have always liked your nickname and would prefer to call you Lizzie when we talk."

Lizzie smiled broadly and said, "It would make me feel better, Mr. Reid, cause you have always called me Lizzie, and when you call me Elizabeth, it makes me feel like I did something wrong or you are about to sell

HALLOWEEN BEDTIME STORIES

me."

Reid smiled broadly, "Lizzie," he began, "I have always been able to be proud of my home. Your mother does a fine job of keeping all the other slaves organized from the butler, to the cooks, to the maids. She knows how to keep things running and how to get people to do things correctly. I have always regretted that we were not able to save your father, but he was very ill when he died and was much older than your mother. I am sorry you never got to know Jonathan because he was a fine farm worker who did a good job managing the crops in his own right. Anyway, Lizzie, I want to keep you here with us and would like to have you start learning how to help Miss Anne with the children. I know there are times when your own mother could use you to help her with house duties too, and you would learn a lot from actually working with her. I want to call you a house servant and assistant to my wife Lizzie. What do you think?"

Lizzie smiled deeply and broadly. She was proud, and she had a glimpse of just how much power her mother had. It had happened just like her mama hoped it would.

Lizzie then glanced at the floor; she averted her eyes and asked, "Mr. Reid, may I ask one more question? You see, I been told by some other slaves from other farms when we go to town that masters always…she hesitated…well, they always do…sex to slave women when they come of age to get them started and to…"

Reid Johnson blushed; he held his left hand palm out toward Lizzie, "I do not do that Lizzie. I have heard of it, and I know that it does happen at times but not on

300

THE BUTTONS

Twin Creeks. In time, you may take a liking to one of the field hands here or want to jump the broom with someone or have a young one. We can talk about that when that time comes. In the meantime, you will be very busy learning all the things you need to know about helping Anne; I mean Miss Anne and the children. You will need some good house help dresses that you will need to make and you can start in training in one month. I value my people here Lizzie, and you and your mother are among my most valued. I am happy you are going to be with us."

"Me too, Mr. Reid. Me too!"

Mr. Reid continued, "Do you have any other questions Lizzie; are you happy with your job?"

"Oh, Mr. Reid, I am so happy. I will be a good helper and do the best I can to make Miss Anne happy. Thank you Master Reid, thank you."

Lizzie left the house with her heart light and her fate set. She was so anxious to tell her mama that she did not notice the rider coming fast up the lane. She heard some loud talking and thought something exciting must be going on. It was not until the next morning that she learned that Mr. Reid was going to be leaving the plantation to go and fight in a war somewhere far away. He did not want to go but knew he had to. Lizzie became worried about her master. She liked--maybe even loved-- him as her boss and did not want to risk him being killed in some war that she did not understand. She hoped that it would not happen; she hoped it was a rumor. It was two days later that Mr. Reid had called all of the slaves together---a rare thing at Twin Creeks. He told them himself that he was going to fight Yankees who were

301

HALLOWEEN BEDTIME STORIES

invading the South. He told them he would depend on them to keep their jobs up while he was gone and to listen to Miss Anne, Lucinda and Mr. Egan and to work hard to keep Twin Creeks the kind of home we all loved. Lizzie listened to this young man talk and was filled with desire to do all she could to help him. She wanted him to come back to Twin Creeks and raise his children and to be kind to his slaves and to be her boss. She knew she needed to do something...something very special. Something magic that assured that Mr. Reid would come home and that things would be the way she wanted them to be. She decided to use the magic she had been learning about and called upon her friend Noah to help her. She needed to be sure to protect Mr. Reid and the home she loved. She told Lucinda that she was going to talk to Noah about how to protect someone who was going to be in a war. Lucinda agreed that if anyone could figure a way to help or hurt someone that Noah would be the right person to see.

Noah, "jes' Noah," he called himself, refusing to take the last name of his owners. He was old. No one knew just *how* old Noah was, but some thought he may be the same one who built the ark that the Bible mentioned. Noah liked it when people thought he may be that same Noah and would reach back and rub the back of his head and say, "Well, I jes' cain't remember tha' long ago." Noah was good with animals and had been the plantation's animal and slave doctor for as long as anyone living could remember. He made potions and liniments from herbs he would find in the woods. He would sing and chant and use special salves to heal cuts and cure chest colds. He helped to birth babies and even

302

THE BUTTONS

set and repaired broken bones. He openly admitted to other slaves that he used voodoo magic and some other African magic that he was able to apply to dire situations. Noah always had a plan to deal with things that went wrong. Once he even cast a small spell on Egan, the white overseer, to stop him from picking on Paul, a large black slave who Egan seemed to despise. Noah told Paul to bring anything he could that Mr. Egan touched every day to him, and he would do the rest. Paul brought the leather reigns from the overseer's horse's bridle. Noah prayed and chanted and dropped the reigns into a boiling liquid. He pulled the reigns out and handed them to Paul. He smiled and told Paul things would get better. Paul took the reins back to the barn and waited. Egan did not see Paul for several days, but when he did, he smiled and told Paul to get the cotton bundled and to the wagon. Paul thought that was the first time he ever saw Egan smile at him.

He responded with a quick, "Yessir, is there anything else sir?"

Egan said, "Yeah, Paul, you been workin' hard this morning. Grab yourself a drink of water while you are at the wagon, and bring my cup over to me."

Paul took his drink quickly and took the cup to Egan.

Egan drank the water, handed the cup to Paul and said, "Put my cup back on its hook Paul, and uh…thank you." Paul and everyone else knew Noah had done his job well.

Noah was mixing a brew to cure chickens from some illness that they caught when Lizzie knocked on his door.

HALLOWEEN BEDTIME STORIES

She could see the fire burning through the cracks and heard old Noah's voice say, "Com'on Lizzie. I been expectin' you girl. Tell me about what you want to do for the Master."

Lizzie wondered how he knew but knew better than to question Noah. She understood that he just knew things. Lizzie told Noah that the master was going off to some war that he did not want to be in but had to go. Noah told her he knew all that but wondered what she had in mind. Lizzie explained she wanted to protect Mr. Reid and to protect the lives they all enjoyed at Twin Creeks.

Noah thought, then spoke, "Well Lizzie, I got a feelin' that nobody's life will be the same after this here war. I got a feeling lots of folks will die and black folks too. Yeah girl, this war is something those white folks been stirring up for a long time and it will be a long time before it's over. I expect that nothing much will be the same after it is done, but I think we can come up with a way to bring Mr. Reid back home in one piece. I will need something that he will wear every day during the whole war like his uniform hat or something, and I'll need it for a couple of days during the dark of the moon. Can you get me something like that?"

"Yes, Noah. I will get you something because we got to protect Mr. Reid."

Lizzie thanked Noah and visited for a few minutes about the new baby born two cabins away from his last night, then went back to her own cabin. She had made up her mind while she was talking to Noah that she was going to get him to teach her everything about the magic he knew. She was sure someone needed to know

THE BUTTONS

how to do those things, and she wanted to be the one.

Weeks passed, and news of the coming war was sporadic. For a time, it seemed like maybe it would not happen. Maybe Mr. Reid would not have to leave the plantation and go fight Yankees. Lizzie had taken her place learning the duties of her new job and working with Miss Anne. Anne had known Lizzie from the day she arrived at Twin Creeks and had come to love her long before Lizzie started her duties as her assistant. One day Anne told Lizzie that Mr. Reid's orders had come and that he would be getting a uniform and taking a position as a lieutenant in the Confederate Army of Louisiana. Lizzie could not help but to ask about Mr. Reid's uniform and if she could see it. Anne promised that when it came from the tailors that Lizzie could have a look at it. Several days later a wagon approached and several boxes were brought into the house, and a small white man wearing a black suit waited at the front door. It was Edward who let the man into the house and announced in his most official voice. "Mr. Ron Talbot, tailor, to see Master Reid, Mr. Ron Talbot tailor to see Mr. Reid." Anne responded to the door and offered to take the tailor to the study where Reid was working on orders to leave for the overseer and Lucinda. The two men exchanged a handshake and the tailor began opening boxes. He told Anne that "she would most likely want to leave as some of the measurements and questions of fit were personal to the man in question." Anne retired to the children's nursery where Lizzie was playing with the smallest boy, Tyler.

"New uniform is here Lizzie, and once it is all altered and done, I will show it to you."

305

HALLOWEEN BEDTIME STORIES

Lizzie decided to wait until she was actually seeing the uniform to tell Anne about her plan to protect Mr. Reid.

It was July 3rd when Anne summoned Lizzie to her room. Lizzie knocked, then opened the door when Anne told her to come in.

Anne spoke first, "Here it is, and he looks very handsome in it."

Lizzie gazed at the gray and gold uniform. She looked it over from the hat to the boots. After about a full minute, her eyes fixed on the brass buttons on the front of the jacket. She summoned all her courage and told Anne of her plan to try to put what she called a blessing on an article of clothing that Mr. Reid would wear every day to protect him.

Anne was touched but did not believe much in the superstitions the slaves practiced. She was reluctant, but she trusted Lizzie and understood that the young slave girl nearly worshipped both she and her husband. She certainly did not want anything un-Christian done to any of her husband's belongings. She could not refuse Lizzie's attempt to protect Reid. She definitely believed he would need all the help he could get.

After a brief discussion, during which Anne warned against any act of evil, the two women decided that Lizzie would keep the buttons for three days during the dark of the moon and then they would sew them back onto the uniform. Anne was so touched by Lizzie's enthusiasm to help her master that she clasped Lizzie's hands in hers then hugged her long and hard. Lizzie felt warm and valued, and she was determined to help Mr. Reid and Miss Anne.

THE BUTTONS

When Lizzie had dressed the children for bed and brought them to the nursery where Miss Anne and Mr. Reid would read stories and play with them, she was excused for the evening. She carried the buttons in her hand as she walked through the gardens of the main house to the gravel path that led to her cabin. She made a quick stop at the slave privy. She washed up and had a quick supper with Lucinda, all the while talking about having discovered a way to help Mr. Reid come home safely.

Lucinda warned Lizzie to be careful and not lose anything that belonged to the master. She also told her to be careful and tell old Noah that he could not do anything that would make the white people angry.

"White folks just don't believe in African magic, an' you certainly don't want to do anything that they would think of as evil."

Lizzie answered, "Well, Mama, sometimes white folks don't know how some things happen, and when they don't know, they believe in it. Noah says it's best to not tell anyone some of the things we do to help cause it would just scare them anyway. Sometimes if you tell people things, they feel like they have to *not* believe it because they don't understand it. But if you don't tell 'em nothing, they just go along and don't get in the way of the magic. Magic works better if you don't get in the way of it. Sort of jes' let it happen. That is what ole Noah says."

Lucinda knew very well of Noah's ability, and she was about as reluctant to challenge him as to challenge her master's.

She looked Lizzie in the eyes and said, "OK,

HALLOWEEN BEDTIME STORIES

Lizzie, but you and Noah be careful that what you do is to help."

Lizzie looked hurt and said, "Mama, I would never hurt Mr. Reid or Miss Anne; they love us and treat us good, and I love them."

Once again, as Lizzie approached Noah's cabin, he said, "C'mon Lizzie, I been waitin' for you. Now, let's see them buttons you carryin'." Lizzie held out her hand and Noah exhaled deeply, "Boy those are some buttons; bet that's one fine uniform."

Lizzie confided to Noah that Mr. Reid would stand before all the workers at Twin Creeks and bid them good-bye in his uniform, and he could see it then if he wanted to come.

Noah smiled and said, "That won't be necessary; we gonna get a good look at it tonight when we do this spell."

Lizzie said, "No, Noah the uniform is in the big

THE BUTTONS

house in the master's bedroom closet. We can't go in there."

"Don't have to," Noah muttered. "Gonna see it right out back in the pot when we drop them buttons in. You be ready girl; we gonna see some sights we don' get to see often. But when we done, them buttons gonna have power to bring Master Reid home in one piece and more."

The fire burned blue at times then flashed to red, sometimes with whitish edges. The pot had long since been boiling and had lots of things floating in the liquid inside. Lizzie saw some small skeletal bones from things she could only imagine. She smelled the pungent odors and watched the fire change colors. Noah had already taught her to build the "witchin' fire" that burned all the colors. It was a mixture of mosses and twigs from special trees and bushes. It burned low and hot and nearly invisible to anyone more than 30 feet away. It was soundless until you got in real close; then it sounded like rushing air, not like a fire at all. The contents of the pot, Noah explained, were types of salamanders, newts, frogs and a chicken's tail feathers. There were herbs from under certain bushes and some dill from the slave garden. There was one serpent that Noah tossed in live, and the last ingredients were three drops of blood from each of them. When the blood hit the water, the fire flashed black, then very white, then very red. As the fire turned to red, Noah whispered to Lizzie,

"Toss the buttons into the pot."

Lizzie wanted to question this move but did not dare. She held her hand directly over the boiling mixture and released two beautiful, shiny, brass buttons. She

309

HALLOWEEN BEDTIME STORIES

watched as they tumbled through the air into the pot and sank. She felt a sense of loss and a little fear, but was soon distracted by the gut-wrenching sounds coming from Noah. He was staring straight into the fire and chanting.

"Dark moon fire, put your magic into these buttons. Make them last for all time. Make them stronger than death. Make them protect the wearer of the buttons from harm. Use the bones to make them strong, the feathers to give them flight, the liquid to give them movement and the magic of the fire to make them timeless."

He spoke in rhymes, rhythms and chants for about fifteen minutes repeating some phrases and adding other words that he later explained to Lizzie as being African. He used a combination of Voodoo and African magic that white folks called Black Magic. When he got to the end of the ceremony, he leaned into the pot, motioned Lizzie to do the same, and pointed to the boiling liquid. He quietly repeated,

"Dark Moon fire, Dark Moon magic", and they both saw the uniform just as Lizzie had seen it with the buttons in place over the left chest pocket. "Now Lizzie, don't be afraid reach into the liquid and pick up those buttons."

The buttons had floated to the top and seemed to by lying on the uniform. Lizzie picked up the buttons, and her hand with the buttons dripped liquid, but she was not burned. The buttons felt cold, and were even shinier than they had been before the ceremony. Noah dropped to his knees exhausted and spent.

He said, "Don't have to worry now; they are

310

THE BUTTONS

protected, and you couldn't lose them if you tried. Only person can do anything with them buttons would be me or Mr. Reid or whoever he may give them to. I ONLY WISH I COULD BE ROUND AS LONG AS THEY WILL BE."

Lizzy helped Noah to his feet and hugged and thanked him. She told Noah she wished she could tell the master what had been done for him, but knew she could not do that.

Noah said, "No, girl, better not tell any of the white folks any more than you already have about those buttons. They would not understand, and they may get in the way of the magic, or, if they are afraid, they may even get hurt by it. Cause them buttons are here on this earth for a long time to come, and if Mr. Reid keeps his jacket on, he won't get killed no matter what. We got it started now, best jes' let it work."

Lizzie nodded in understanding. She walked with Noah to his door and then on back to her cabin. It was late, and she could hear Lucinda across the cabin breathing like she always did when she was asleep. Lizzie said a quick prayer to Jesus and fell asleep.

Lizzie awoke refreshed, and the night before seemed like a dream to her. Like something that she had not really experienced. She reached under her pillow and pulled out the two buttons. She looked at her hand which had been in boiling liquid and wondered how it had worked. She was sure it had worked and could feel a certain power coming off of the buttons. She got her morning chores done then walked to the big house to start her day with Miss Anne and the children. When the

311

HALLOWEEN BEDTIME STORIES

children were having their breakfast, Lizzie asked Miss Anne quietly if they could sew the buttons back onto the uniform. They quickly went upstairs and sewed the buttons in place. They both were a little astounded when the uniform appeared to glow for a few seconds then went back to normal.

Anne smiled at Lizzie and said, "I guess that was the *angel of protection* that you talked about."

Lizzie nodded, "It is the buttons doing their job of protecting that uniform. You just be sure to tell Mr. Reid to not take off that jacket till he comes home safely to you. Nothin' will happen to him as long as those buttons are between him and harm."

Anne assured Lizzie that she would caution Reid to leave the jacket on.

"After all, I have seen the affect myself; I saw the uniform glow with the protection when we placed those buttons on. I am going to tell Reid those buttons have been blessed and they are his Guardian Angel."

"Don't do that, Miss Anne. Those buttons will work better if he just wears the coat and don't know about how special those buttons are. Sometimes if you think about things too much or know too much, they don't work as good. Just tell him you had a dream or something, and that he must never take off his jacket. That way he will be home safe sometime soon."

Anne was a smart woman and knew that Lizzie was telling her to not question or disturb whatever presence she had witnessed. She decided that she would have to share her vision of the glow on the uniform with Reid as though she had seen it in a dream. She believed for the first time that Lizzie had some special power and

312

THE BUTTONS

her husband would be home safely. She told her husband at lunch about the dream and she knew it was a message of protection. He promised to wear the jacket even to bed when he was away from the plantation until he returned safely home. She slept well that night for the first time in a month.

Lizzie was more at ease about Mr. Reid leaving than she had been. The Civil War had begun, and Mr. Reid stood before the slaves gathered for the occasion and promised them he would do all within his power to protect their home and protect them from people who did bad things to slaves, and if it all went well, once this threat was over, he would work toward giving his slaves their freedom and hiring them as partners in a share cropping arrangement.

Noah shook his head and said in a low voice to Lucinda, "That man don't know what them confederates is up to. They won' never give us no freedom, and they won't like it if he try to free us. Only way we get free is if 'n them Yanks win and we live through the war."

Civil War in the United States raged on for more than four years. Reid Johnson fought from the Mississippi River to the Atlantic Ocean and from the farm fields of Pennsylvania to the swamps of Louisiana. He never took off his jacket except in a rare visit back to the plantation to wash it. His trips home became further apart as the South lost the war and lost territory under control.

Conditions at the plantation got pretty bad too as the money ran out. Many of the slaves at Twin Creeks wanted to stay once they found out the Yanks were winning because they knew Mr. Reid would be able to

313

HALLOWEEN BEDTIME STORIES

free them if the Yanks won. They could find jobs share cropping the land they already knew. Many other slaves from other plantations were leaving the area and tried to talk Twin Creeks' slaves into going with them. A few left, especially those that the overseer Egan did not like. But as the money ran short, Egan became afraid that the slaves would rise up, and he left the plantation. Once Egan left, the remaining slaves stayed.

Once Mr. Reid came home, the slaves were given parcels of what had been Twin Oaks land, and they formed a partnership and co-operative way of working with their former owner as free people. Lizzie kept her job with the Johnsons for several more years until she met and married a young man.

Little was said about the uniform until about a month before Lizzie was to be married. One morning there was a stir in the house, and Miss Anne was very upset that Mr. Reid's uniform coat had been taken. He had left it on the hanger in the back entry and it was gone. Lizzie helped search for the jacket, but it was gone.

That evening, old Noah got Lizzie's attention and told her the jacket had been stolen. He said "I feel sorry for that carpet baggin' fool who took it. He done accidental-like step into some very dangerous stuff. Them buttons ain't gonna do nothing but cause him grief, and they won' even do no one any good till they find they way back to dis family or they ancestors.

No one at Twin Creeks ever heard what happened to the jacket, and no one talked much about it or the war. They were tired of war and wanted to get on with life.

THE BUTTONS

Lizzie left the area and moved north with her new husband and became a very successful dressmaker.

Rumors came round about the carpet bagger who had been trying to steal some of the Twin Creeks land and take some of the sharecroppers' land and homes. A story was told that he was running away from police in Northern Virginia and rode into a tree limb and split open his head. But those were only rumors.

The Johnsons continued to farm until the economy of the area got too bad. They then moved north to a small town in Illinois. Twin Creeks was no longer a farm or plantation. The name was used as an old black man named Noah opened a country store. He sold dry goods, groceries, and genuine articles of magic. He called his store the Crossroads Grocery and Magic Shop at Twin Creeks. Last we heard it was still doing business.

HALLOWEEN BEDTIME STORIES

Chapter 3
Northern Virginia….Summer 1931

Charlie Sanders is a young farmer in the Shenandoah Valley with a pretty wife and a large family. The great economic depression was in full swing and times were hard. Charlie felt lucky that he was a farmer and a strong healthy one. He had good land and a good wife and enough strong boys to produce more than enough food. He worked his crops, cut some timber in the hardwoods of the nearby mountains, and watched his money closely. He was an honest man and never hesitated to help people who were struggling during the hard times. He did not have a lot of money, but he helped with food and with jobs for those less fortunate. He worked just as hard as any of his helpers or his sons and was known for his friendly, helpful approach to the people who lived in the area. He often wondered if the depression would get worse or if things would get better. He had experienced some personal losses that would have stopped a lesser man due to some dishonest bankers, and had developed an attitude of frugal conservation of his money and his resources. He knew first hand that he was going to have to get things done, and could not depend on anyone except those who he had control over. He was not cynical…just real, and, yet, remained optimistic and friendly. He had little use for church and even less for the constant requests for money which came from the churches in the area. He often thought too much of the money at churches went to buildings which were unneeded and unused except for a couple of hours a week. He also thought too much of the

THE BUTTONS

money went to keep the preachers who only worked a few hours a week and their families who did not work at all. Charlie was, simply put, a smarter-than-average farmer who was soft spoken and hard to take advantage of. He had a quick wit and a slow temper. He would often allow people to get by with treating him poorly and would not hold it against them. He seldom showed any anger, but when he did, it was best to not be in his presence. In many ways, you could say that in the early 1930's, Charlie Sanders was a middle class farmer in his community.

The farm the Sanders lived on at present was a large piece of land. It was partially wooded, partially rocky with limestone outcroppings, and partially fertile land where just about anything could be cultivated. They had sheep, cows, pigs, chickens, ducks, geese and even some stock dogs and horses to pull plows and wagons. Charlie had purchased a motorized truck which his wife drove most of the time. Charlie preferred horses. There were ten kids of various ages and some occasional farm helpers who worked the land. Charlie had negotiated a share crop arrangement with the wealthy owners after the banks had cheated him out of the place he had been buying. He could have been bitter and certainly he did have feelings about the way the banks had taken his money and his land. However, he did not let it stop him from being a successful farmer who provided well for his family even through the great depression.

The best and most fertile fields where along drainage bottoms between ridges of woods. Many of the better fields were not within sight of the house so the workers would leave home with a sandwich, a water pail

317

HALLOWEEN BEDTIME STORIES

and the horses and plow in the morning and only return in the evening.

The Shenandoah Valley had become prosperous with very good farm ground, furniture making, pottery making, and animal products like dairy and especially Virginia Hams after the Civil War. The towns in the valley were hard hit with this new threat of economic depression, and most people in the area were struggling. Yet, there were certain activities that were such a part of who they were and their beliefs and those continued even when the money was very short. Churches continued their social roles with lawn parties where patrons would donate food and desserts to be sold to attendees. Musicians would provide music and the children would run and play and buy a sweet treat when their parents could afford it.

The other big social events were those times when the communities would celebrate the honorable war dead from the Civil War. It was nearing July when normally a parade was held in the nearby town of Strasburg to celebrate the Civil War dead (from both sides locals were quick to point out). Strasburg had changed hands about ten to fifteen times during the Civil War years as the armies had raged back and forth through the valley. However, most locals were actually still great southern sympathizers and just knew that if not for a few bad days, the South would have won the war and damn near did. Such were the times in the summer of 1931 in Northern Virginia.

"How ya doin' Charlie?"

"Pretty good, Bill. I'm getting my north fields up enough to run the plows through them again and will

THE BUTTONS

probably do that tomorrow."

"Surely not tomorrow Charlie", Bill replied. "Tomorrow is the big parade. You won't wanna miss that."

"Well, I don't have much choice about when the fields get ready to work, so I guess I will do the plowing myself and let Mary take the kids to the parade. I'll go and meet up with them there once I'm done. Besides, that may give me the chance to stop by the High Spot for a quick beer on the way. I can kill two birds with one stone. I can get my beer and Mary won't have to worry about it."

Both men chuckled. Bill knew Charlie well, and knew he truly enjoyed having two quick beers more than most people enjoyed a turkey dinner.

"It sounds like you have er all worked out Charlie. How are your corn crops looking this year?"

"They are pretty good Bill. I think we will get plenty to eat and enough to feed up the stock through butcher time. If prices hold and we don't have any tough luck, we ought to do pretty well."

"Glad to hear it Charlie, and, by the way, I would like to order another two of your hams early this year. In fact, I can pay you some toward them early if you want."

"I will be happy to hold two of them for you Bill, and I don't want any money till you are ready to take the hams just like always. I would not want to take any money till I get them ready; that would like countin' my chickens before the hens hatch the eggs. During these times I have found it is best to only count on what you have in your pocket."

Bill respected Charlie and understood why he

319

HALLOWEEN BEDTIME STORIES

was a successful farmer and provider, especially when he shared a tidbit that gave insight to the way he thought about things. Charlie bought a plug of tobacco to cut the dust from the plowing he would do the next day and a bag of sugar. He paid cash and told Bill he may see him tomorrow at the parade if the plowing went well.

People all over town were getting ready for the parade and the celebrations that would be after the parade. Several churches were holding picnic type dinners where meals could be purchased. There would be a band from the high school at the park playing marching tunes, and kids could play on the school yard swings, teeter-totters and sliding boards. Folks would dress in their best, and would stroll around to find shaded areas to sit and sip lemonade which could be bought for two cents a cup. Kids would spend their pennies on sweet candy or cupcakes, and everyone would take a day away from work. Ladies were preparing their dishes for the church sales, and men were counting their money to see how much they could spend and still get through the coming week.

Charlie walked onto the back porch and sat on a chair by the door. He took off his boots and unbuttoned his work shirt. He then reached to his side to grab the dipper from the bucket of cool water. He poured the dipper into a tin cup and drank. Three times he drank the cup empty then he picked up the bag of sugar and carried it into the kitchen.

"Oh good, you got it." Mary said. "I am just getting the last touches on supper so wash up and we will eat."

"Sounds good to me; I'm hungry."

THE BUTTONS

"Are you gonna be able to make it to the parade tomorrow?" she asked.

"I hope I can make it, but I may be a little late. That north field is ready to plow, and I don't want to miss the chance. If we get a rain or something, I could miss the chance to get the weeds out and work that dirt. So, I'll head out to the north field early tomorrow and then back here to put the animals away then meet you at the parade."

"Well, I know that you have to work those fields when they are ready, but when you come to meet us, don't stop too long at the High Spot. You wouldn't want to miss the marching band."

He winked at her and said, "Will do dear, will do."

The rest of the evening was filled with excited young people making plans for how they would celebrate their day off, and how they would spend their pennies at the big lawn parties in town. It was the highlight of the summer, and the boys and girls got into their own groups to talk about how to dress, what to buy, and where to stand to see the parade the best. They stayed up until their parents reminded them that the sun had been down for an hour, and it was well past nine o'clock. Then they trooped off to bed still talking loudly and excitedly. Charlie could still hear voices about half an hour later when he lay down next to Mary.

"You kids don't sound very tired; maybe I ought to keep you here with me and work you a little harder tomorrow so you can quiet down when you go to bed." Silence....

As always, Charlie awoke exactly when he

321

HALLOWEEN BEDTIME STORIES

wanted to… about half an hour before daylight. He did not own an alarm clock. He simply told himself when to get up as he went to sleep, and it happened.

He patted Mary on her shoulder and said, "Don't get up just yet. I'll grab a biscuit and some butter and a piece of cured ham and get on out north. See you at the parade."

"Not too long at the High Spot," she answered.

"Don't worry. I'll be there."

He kissed her cheek, got dressed and walked to the back porch. He pulled on his boots and walked to the barn. He had the horses hitched and the plow on its wheels to take it to the north field and was leaving the barn yard as the sun started lighting up the high clouds. With any luck, he would be plowing when the sun crested the mountain top to the east. He talked to the horses quietly as they walked along the outer path to the north field.

He set the plow into the soft, fertile earth and started the horses. He was about halfway down the first row when the sun peeked over the east- ridge and the light became brighter. He was part way through the third row when the sun actually started shining on the field and warming both him and the horses.

"Going to be a sunny day," he said out loud to the horses.

His work went quickly and he was hurrying. He was conscious of the horses and stopped frequently to give them water and let them take a few deep breaths without the weight of the plow pulling on them. He was making good time and knew he was going to finish in plenty of time to make the parade. He felt a little

THE BUTTONS

excitement himself at being able to have a good, cold beer, maybe with a couple of friends and then watching his kids enjoy their day in town. Even in the depression it was a good day to be alive. He guided the horses expertly and made his turns efficiently, and the earth responded as he worked the field.

Charlie was plowing exactly the next to last row and had just made his turn when he saw a rider on a horse gallop--or maybe even running--along the old stone wall at the other end of the field and into the woods. The rider was dressed in a Confederate uniform or at least a Confederate coat. Charlie thought it was probably some veteran or some veteran's relative dressed for the parade showing off on his horse. A small part of him remembered the stories of Confederate soldiers and even some Yankee soldiers appearing along the creek where there had been a big battle and where many were killed. A lot of the locals were pretty sure that area was haunted by the ghosts of those unfortunate soldiers. It was just by the last row of corn in the edge of the woods that the horse reared and made a noise.

Charlie's attention was taken away as a rock hit his plow blade. He stopped the team. When he looked back up, the rider was gone. He yelled into the woods, but got no response and did not hear the horse running or walking away. He moved the rock from beneath his plow, and plowed on to the last row. He set the plow in the ground and started down the last row. The horses knew they were about done, and he had a hard time stopping them when he got to the place by the woods where the horse had reared. He got them stopped a few feet past where the rider had disappeared into the woods.

HALLOWEEN BEDTIME STORIES

He walked over toward the edge of the woods. He looked at the ground and could not see any prints. The leaves were not torn up, and the soft ground near the fence where the horse had run had not one single hoof print.

"Maybe, I 'm seeing ghosts now boys," he said to the horses. "Let's finish this up and get back home. He was just picking up the reigns when he spotted something glinting in the sun. He said, "Whoa, team."

He walked toward the glint and stooped down. There in the dried leaves lay two shining new brass buttons clearly marked C.S.S. Louisiana 3rd. He thought to himself, a ghost wouldn't leave hardware. That rider probably fell off the horse when it reared and was too embarrassed to stay around. I'll take them with me, and, if I spot him at the parade, I'll return his buttons

He finished his plowing and made his stop at the High Spot. He had a wonderful couple of beers with Bill and another friend. He even got to the parade in time to see the first entry which made Mary smile broadly.

The day passed with great fun and celebration, and Charlie mused at how much fun a family with two adults and ten kids could have on about two dollars. He looked carefully at the entries and asked about any officers from Louisiana who had moved to the area or any stories of relatives of anyone from Louisiana.

It would be nearly twenty years later that a school historian would hear Charlie's story and drive up to his lawn gate. The teacher would tell Charlie that what he most likely found was some buttons off an old Confederate coat that had been lost. Sometime in the late 1860's, a horse thief and carpet bagger had taken a horse

THE BUTTONS

in Winchester and was running from the sheriff of Fredrick County when he rode into the woods and disappeared. They searched the woods but never found him, although they did find the horse. It was the following winter when some hunters found a skeleton down in the open area near the creek where I understand you have some crops planted. There was a badly deteriorated old Confederate coat, but nothing else was found. The sheriff's department went and looked all around and hauled the skeleton parts and buried them at Potter's Field in the county cemetery. Maybe that explains the buttons you found.

"Might I see them?"

"Indeed, you can," he said.

He went into his secretary and picked up the buttons. He was still amazed that they looked like brand new and shined like nothing he had ever seen before.

The teacher held them in her hand and marveled at the brightness and lack of wear and said, "These seem to be something special, Mr. Sanders. Take good care of them."

"I will, Charlie answered. "But somehow, I don't think it matters what I do to them. If they can go through a war, lay under a dead, decaying body and be in ground for sixty years and look like this, I don't think I'll hurt them any. Besides, that is a great story, but you don't know how I found them or what I saw that day. I think they are even more special than you may guess."

HALLOWEEN BEDTIME STORIES

Chapter Four
California. About 1990 something......

Bob Allen picked up the phone and dialed Dan Sanders.

"Hey, we finally have a date to talk to these insurance guys, and that will decide if and when we go to court. How does Tuesday after next sound?"

"Sounds like a long time after the fire to me, and sounds like they are going to have to come up with some inconvenience money or rental money and more," Dan replied.

Bob smiled and said, "And don't forget your good ole lawyer. He is gonna get paid too. Don't worry Dan. They will have to do this right. We won't settle for less. Now, don't you forget any pictures, or family members who can swear to having seen your valuable antiques. Well, you get it. Any proof will really help."

"I don't have anything yet, Bob, but we still have some stuff from the house to sift. I have plenty of family who know about the antiques and may have some pictures showing some of them. I'll get on it. Sue and I'll stop by on Monday before we go meet with those bastards so we can review everything."

"Great," Bob responded. "See you soon."

Dan knew the next part of putting together some of the things and pieces of things they found would be very hard on Sue, but he knew it was time to do it. Dan called Sue at work he started, "Hey Sue, do you have any plans tonight with the kids or anything?"

"Not really," she responded. "Why?"

THE BUTTONS

"Well, as much as I hate to do it, it's time for us to sort through the stuff we found at the house and the stuff the cleanup crew found and see which things we use to help prove our claims with those insurance bastards." (He had taken to never saying insurance without following it with the word 'bastards'.)

Sue took a short breath. "Yeah," she said. "I know we need to do it. Let's get a nice bottle of wine. I'll arrange to have a baby sitter watch the kids and get them to bed, and we will just go out into the garage and look through all that stuff. Then we will drink that bottle of wine."

"Good idea," Dan responded. "I think it is important to keep the best attitude we can. After all, it is the best chance we may have to get some of those things replaced."

That evening everything went as planned. Dan and Sue gathered their scraps of metal, book spines, ash covered bits of picture frames, and unknown pieces of twisted metal. While it was a difficult thing to do, it was also somewhat healing in that they found some things that brought back wonderful memories. Granted, the item was incomplete or damaged, but it was still special because of the memories it invoked. He had kept most of the pieces of her jewelry that he had found away from her until this evening. As he showed her the remains of her garnet ring and one end of a melted favorite necklace she had some moments of tearfulness, but she also smiled through the tears at the memories of when he had given her these treasures.

After about three full hours of going through everything Sue said, "Well, it is not much, but on the

HALLOWEEN BEDTIME STORIES

other hand, it goes a long way toward proving what we have been saying and what our witnesses will say if it gets to that."

"I wonder if we have everything" Dan asked himself as much as asking Sue. "Because, we still have very little in the way of the antiques."

They quickly recapped the inventory, and he shrugged. "Guess that is it."

Sue said, "Well, we haven't inventoried our clothes."

"Not much to inventory there," Dan said. "I only got one suit out and a handful of shirts and the jeans I grabbed. In fact, I haven't even seen those jeans for months now. I started wearing some of the clean ones that fit. You know, the ones you got from the shelter. I don't even know when I wore them last, but they were my only clothes other than my suit for the first week or so after the fire."

"I know where they are," Sue said. "They are hanging on the hook at the back of the kids' closet. When we first moved in here, we thought that would be our room then decided the kids would like it better if they could be in a room together after the fire, so we took the smaller one. I think we just forgot to move some of our clothes into the new closet with all the activity. But I saw those jeans just the other day."

"I am going to sneak in and get them." Dan said.

"No!" Sue exclaimed. "You'll wake the kids. Get the jeans tomorrow. You promised to drink this bottle of wine with me. Now Mr., let's get started cause I need the relief."

They shared the wine and a few tears along with

THE BUTTONS

a few laughs. It had been a good evening; the healing process felt like it had begun and they were going to be OK.

It was Saturday, three days before the meeting with Bob and a couple of days after Dan and Sue had completed their inventory when Dan remembered his jeans in the kids' closet. It was Saturday, and he wanted his jeans. He walked into the kids' room and into the closet and saw the jeans on the hook. There were gray ash stains up to the knees. He suddenly remembered when he wore them last; it was the last night he had been to the house alone picking through the ashes. It was the night the battery on the car had died, and he decided it was the end of his efforts at digging through the debris. He grabbed the jeans and carried them triumphantly into the living area where Sue was playing with Billy, their youngest.

"Ta-da," he said. "Looky here what I found. My jeans. I'm gonna wash and dry them and wear them. It will feel great to have my own jeans."

Sue smiled up at him and said, "There is a load of kid's clothes washing now just toss them in." Dan started toward the laundry room. "DON'T FORGET TO CHECK THE POCKETS BEFORE YOU TOSS THEM IN," Sue yelled.

Dan reached into the pocket and felt something. It all came back. It was the last night he had been at the house sifting through debris. It was very dark, and something had glinted in the light. Whatever it was, it felt hinged. He withdrew the object.

"Well, I'll be damned," he said. "SUE, COME HERE. YOU GOTTA SEE THIS!"

HALLOWEEN BEDTIME STORIES

"What is the big deal?" she asked as she walked in.

Dan held out his hand and opened it. There in the palm of his hand lay two buttons. One button's attachment eye had wedged through the other's attachment eye so they seemed to be stuck together.

Dan pulled them apart, and holding one in each hand, said. "Granddaddy's buttons. Look at them; they still look like brand new. Makes the hair stand up on the back of your neck doesn't it? You know these are the famous ones he found when he saw that ghost rider on that horse way back in the 1930's or sometime around there."

Sue nodded. She knew the story well and had heard it hundreds of times whenever a new family member would ask about the buttons or one of Dan's brothers would recall the story when they looked at or held those buttons.

"Yeah," she breathed. "Wow, they really must be special; just look at them. They look brand new."

Dan said, "Know what this means? Means we have proof about some of the antiques that were in that cabinet. Wait till we show Bob these babies on Tuesday."

Sue said, "I have to admit, there were a lot of times that I thought the story about those buttons was a bunch of superstition and story-telling, but I would never question anything about them again."

Tuesday came all too soon. The Sanders were busy at work and were getting pretty fed up with dealing with an insurer who was clearly dragging their feet. Their recent inventory and the event of finding the

330

THE BUTTONS

buttons had given them a sense of confidence in their position, and they came into Bob Allen's office ready to not only start a fight but to carry it through and finish it. Bob immediately noticed that they had regained their composure and their swagger. He started by saying,

"Hi, Dan. Hi Sue. You two look like you are doing much better then when we last talked."

Sue spoke first. "We are doing great now, Bob, and we are ready to get what we deserve from that insurance company." She glanced at Dan and held up her hands like a band director and silently counted one, two, three, and together they all said "those bastards" and laughed.

Bob said, "Well it is good to see you are back to yourselves. I don't know exactly how hard this will be, but what have you got to show me?"

Dan and Sue started with some of the jewelry items. Sue then showed Bob at least twenty pictures taken in and around the house that showed some of the items in question. Dan was next showing some melted tools, melted picture frames and the pictures he had brought from his desk at work.

"This is all good stuff guys. I think with the bits of rings and pictures we will have enough.

"That ain't all," both Dan and Sue said at the same time. Dan reached into his pocket and withdrew two shining buttons.

"Now these have a story with them that everyone will want to hear, and it is a story that is easy to verify. Let me tell you about these pretty little buttons." Dan began his story with his Grandfather Charlie getting ready to plow his north field somewhere

HALLOWEEN BEDTIME STORIES

in the Shenandoah Valley in Virginia in about 1930.

Bob had picked up the buttons and was studying them, "I never really noticed these at your house before Dan."

"Well, they are more of a family story, and I guess I haven't ever told it much to anyone else," Dan said. As he told the story and about how the buttons were found, Bob seemed very interested. A couple of times during the story he said... "Unbelievable!" "No way!" As Dan concluded the story with the fact that he had found these buttons in almost total darkness, Bob was shaking his head slowly back and forth. Dan looked at Bob who seemed to be placed in a trance by the story.

Bob was looking intently at the buttons and mumbling, "C.S.A Louisiana 3rd, No, way." He repeated it again.

"Well, what do ya think?" Dan asked. "Bob, what do ya think?"

"Oh," Bob answered. "I think we have one more story to hear, and it is mine to tell. Then we need to figure out what these are doing here," he said holding the buttons out in front of him.

Bob began, saying, "Dan, I can't be sure these are the buttons in my story, but here goes. My great, great, grandmother was named Elizabeth Johnson, and she was a slave on a plantation owned by some white people named Johnson close to Baton Rouge, Louisiana. She was evidently treated very well by her owners and loved them dearly. When her old master, a Mr. Reid Johnson, was called up to fight with the Louisiana 3rd in the Civil War, she wanted to protect him. So she went to an old slave man named Noah who was said to be a

332

THE BUTTONS

voodoo man. And"………….

About an hour later, Bob finished his story by repeating what Lizzie had wanted…"For those buttons to help Mr. Reid and his family". But since they were lost and your grandfather found them how could you be family?"

Dan said, "Well Bob, you are assuming that they still have some power. Maybe it is like my granddad said, maybe they are just indestructible. You know, because of the spell the old man put on them."

Sue looked at Dan and said, "But wasn't one of those pictures in the cabinet of someone named Johnson?"

"Sure," Dan replied, "but that was my great grandfather on my mother's side. They were not from Louisiana; they are from a small town in southern Illinois. Ellingham, I think."

"No way," Bob boomed. "That is where the Johnsons, who were my great, great, grandma's owners, moved to from the plantation in the late 1870's. How did you get involved with them?"

"Let's see," Dan said excitedly. "My mother's mother was a Johnson from Ellingham. She married my granddad whose last name is Barton; they lived in Indiana. Then, during World War II my father, Patrick Sanders, the second to youngest boy of Charlie Sanders who found the buttons, met her and they married."

Both men smiled and looked at each other. "UNBELIEVABLE!" they both shouted. "No wonder we were such fast and close friends. Those darn buttons were pushing us right along. Guess the magic is still working and those buttons ARE still in the family."

HALLOWEEN BEDTIME STORIES

The meeting with the insurance company the following week was a slam dunk. The company agreed to all the requests and terms requested by Mr. Allen. The Sanders and Allen families were having a celebration dinner with the buttons sitting in the center of the table as they repeated parts of the incredible story that had brought them together.

Meanwhile, at a small store near the Twin Creeks crossroads in Louisiana a young man shook his head and said "mmm, that's the best magic trick I seen in my whole life; is it your best one?"

"Not even close," the old man answered. "Course I ha' been doin' magic a lot longer'n you been alive."

"Yeah, how old are you anyway, Noah? Are you really the one in the Bible like folks says?"

Reaching for the back of his head the old man says, "I can't rightly remember, but based on the condition of a couple of buttons in California and that wish I made, I'm likely to be around for a lot longer."

Happy Halloween…..

There are events that seem to take on their own lives. Events that happen out of the blue.

We can't understand the whys or even the way that things happen but they do. I believe that sometimes there are forces at work around us that we cannot begin to understand. Nor can we have any impact on them. Sometimes the best we can do is face our adversity and our successes with the knowledge that we are partially in control and partially along for the ride. The best we can do is work at the things we control and try to not be too disturbed by the things we do not control. In some lucky

THE BUTTONS

circumstances, we actually figure out the story that is behind an event. Other times we have to make them up....I want to thank Charlie Muller for brain storming the ideas of this story with me years ago. I told him the story of my granddad seeing the vision of a Confederate-clad rider and finding the buttons on the spot. And how, my brother, Steve, collected the buttons as part of his fairly extensive collection of family memorabilia and when his home burned during the 1990's the buttons were found intact. Most of the story is fiction, but my granddad told me about the finding of the buttons as truth. I know he believed it to be true. I also know that in a severe house fire where nearly everything was destroyed, the buttons survived.

I was sharing the story with Charlie Muller one day when he offered that a novel could be written about the buttons. He even proposed a story about a spell being put on the buttons to give them survival power. My mind supplied other details and a story formed. I changed names and created characters who are truly fictitious people. I have no idea about how Steve settled his house situation after the fire but I know it was a long process with a lot of hard work and emotion. So if you heard part of the story before as a family ghost story, you can know that some of it is said to be true, but most of it is fiction. As usual I must thank my beautiful Judi for taking my rambling thoughts and turning them into readable pages. One last thought. I have always had a mind for fiction and wonder if maybe I got some of it from my grandfather????
BOOOOOOOOOOOOOOOOOOOOOOOOOOOOOOOO.
Followed by maniacal laughter.